Sunflower Persona
Valerie Kain

Copyright © 2025 by Valerie Kain

All rights reserved.

No part of this publication may be reproduced, distributed, or transmitted in any form or by any means, including photocopying, recording, or other electronic or mechanical methods, without the prior written permission of the publisher, except as permitted by U.S. copyright law. For permission requests, contact valeriekain.writing@gmail.com.

The story, all names, characters, and incidents portrayed in this production are fictitious. No identification with actual persons (living or deceased), places, buildings, and products is intended or should be inferred.

Cover Design by Andy Payne

Edited by Brooklyn Marie with Brazen Hearts Author Services

1st edition 2025

For anyone with a gloom of their own.
You matter. You are enough. Keep fighting.

Content Warning

Content Warnings: This book is intended for an 18+ audience and contains some heavy themes. Reader discretion advised.

The male lead of this book struggles with depression and passive suicidal ideation. He is not actively suicidal during the events of the story, but past attempts are mentioned on page. His mental health is a central focus of the book and may be triggering to some.

Additional potentially triggering content is as follows: attempted sexual assault (not by the male lead), date rape drugs/roofies, alcohol use, the mention of parental death due to cancer, and some on page violence (not graphic)

A Note From the Auhtor

Classic City Romance is a series of interconnected standalones. You do not need to read the other books in the series in order to read *Sunflower Persona*, but you can meet Gage and the rest of the crew in *Dear Roomie*.

Contents

Chapter 1
Kori

In theory, making friends shouldn't be that hard. You meet someone, find common interests, and then *boom*, friendship. At least that's how it looks from the outside. I've never had the same luck.

This year will be different; it has to be.

Two years slipped between my fingertips because I was too scared to put myself out there. I wasted my free time camped out in my dorm room, gaming on my PC with online strangers. It wasn't a bad experience—my kill/death ratio was unmatched—but I never found a place where I belonged at Georgia State. Not in the way my parents always talk about when they reminisce about their college years.

This transfer to the University of Georgia is my chance to try again—to find my people. I'll manifest it into existence by sheer force of will if I have to. So mote it be.

The only flaw in my plan is I have no idea how I'm going to do it.

Muffled laughter and music bounce down the hallway, spilling into my room. It's a stark contrast to the silence wrapped around me. The only sound in my tiny white cell is the low hum of the AC. I didn't think it through when I selected a single. A roommate would make this whole thing so much easier; safety in numbers and all that. Plus, I would have been guaranteed to know someone. It was a strategic misstep on my part, but I can't change that now, so I have to put my big girl pants on and figure this thing out on my own.

At least I'm not completely alone.

"It's Friday night in Athens. What do you think I should do, Daisy?"

The rubber duck that's tucked away on the built-in shelf behind my desk doesn't answer. I'm not crazy—I don't expect her to. Sometimes it's easier to work through my thoughts when I say them out loud. My dad gave her to me when I told him I wanted to go into computer science like him. "Rubber ducking" is a method programmers use to work through problems in their code, but I've taken the concept to a whole new level. Over the years, Daisy has become my best friend and closest confidant. It's not like she's had much competition.

"Yes, going downtown is probably my best chance of meeting people, but what do people even do there? Is it only drinking? Is that even fun? You know I've never drank before."

Judgment radiates from her beady black eyes.

"I know, I know, you're a duck—you don't drink either. I am twenty-one now, though. It's probably time I saw what the hype is about. If I hate it, I can just come back and play *Monster Hunter* all weekend."

It's not the most thought-out plan in the world, but it's good enough. Athens is known for its bar scene, and UGA is a notorious party school. You know what they say—when in Rome, do as the Romans do. I'm bound to meet at least one person if I go out tonight.

The bees in my stomach buzz around like pinballs inside an arcade machine the entire time I get ready. It's not like it takes me long—I don't have many "going out" clothes. I land on a bright-yellow crop top, low-rise jeans, and chunky white platform sandals. The matching yellow bucket hat calls to me from my dresser, but Y2K is probably the wrong vibe for the night. Instead, I thread golden rings and clasps into the lighter ends of my long box braids, all the way up into the dark strands that match my natural hair. A few coats of mascara and a swipe of lip gloss later, I'm ready to do this thing. At least, that's the lie I tell myself as I walk out the door.

***

This was a mistake.

Neon lights shine from every bar's window, mixing with the foggy night air to create a technicolor haze. That on its own wouldn't be so bad. But combined with the disharmonious sounds of multiple songs fighting for dominance and the stench of urine, spilled beer, and the juice from overripe dumpsters mixing in the gutters, it makes the tiny "downtown" feel like a fever dream—or my waking nightmare.

Bees spring to life below my skin, crawling around with their barbed feet, and it only gets worse every time an unfamiliar body bumps into mine. With how packed the streets are, it happens more than I would like. How can so many people fit in one place?

I can't get a clear thought in over the surrounding cacophony. It takes every ounce of my willpower not to melt down where I stand or cover my ears and flee. This is why I never went out in Atlanta; I wasn't made for this type of overstimulation. Against my better judgment, I keep my attention locked in front of me and breathe through my mouth as I maneuver through the maze of students.

The farther I get from the central hub of E. Broad Street and College Avenue, the thinner the crowds grow. Each bar I pass has a smaller line than the last until, finally, I find one that's dead compared to the others: Cutter's Pub. There's no line, no blaring music, and only a few light-up signs advertising different beers. I hand my ID to the man checking them at the door and breathe a sigh of relief as he motions me inside.

The whole world depressurizes as the door swings shut behind me. All the stimuli that bombarded me are blocked out by the thick wood. Tension melts off my body, and the itching under my skin eases. It's still loud, but the soft rock playing is meant to be a backdrop to the hum of conversation, not overpower it completely. The lights are low, matching the grungy industrial decor, and the bar is busy but not packed.

Now for the making-friends part of this mission.

I scan the room, assessing the other patrons, while I try to figure out where to begin. Everyone seems content with the groups they're with, and those who are alone don't exactly fit the profile I'm looking for. It was too much to hope I would find another twenty-something girl looking for friends who also love to play video games and watch old monster movies. Hell, at this point, I would take looking for friends without any of the other qualifiers.

A pair of women hanging out near the bar seem like my best bet. The light from behind the counter shines off the taller woman's rich brown skin—which is several shades darker than my own—making her seem ethereal. Her natural coils are cropped close to her head, unlike her shorter, curvaceous friend, whose hair is picked into a large afro that seems to defy gravity. I would love to be able to do my hair like that, but thanks to my mom's genes, my curls aren't tight enough to hold that style.

I drift closer to them, careful to make it seem like I'm not approaching directly, until I'm situated beside them at the bar.

Step one: complete. Now what?

I'm really bad at this whole planning thing.

My ears prick up as I tune into their conversation and realize I know exactly what they're talking about.

"...and I almost got disintegrated, but I rolled a natural twenty on the save. Left me with one hit point." The shorter woman takes a sip of her drink with a smug smile.

I've never played D&D, but I have multiple runs in *Baldur's Gate 3*. That's basically the same thing. I can contribute. All I need to do is open my mouth and chime in.

Easier said than done.

"You really should record your sessions. I bet you could make a killing with a podcast or a stream," her friend replies.

Come on, Kori. Say something.

"Nah, no one would want to hear us play. Half of the time is melodrama, and the other half is really childish sex jokes. We aren't Critical Role, and I don't think we have the chops to be."

Any time now. Ask what class she plays.

"Girl, I think you're selling yourself short. But you do you."

Fuck. I can't do this.

The bitter taste of disappointment coats my tongue as I hang my head and walk to the other, less crowded side of the counter. Why did I ever think this was a good idea? There is no universe where I make friends by talking to random strangers at a grimy pub. I can barely approach people I know.

"What can I get you?"

Clipped words snap me from my daze. My focus turns to the man behind the bar, and I do a double take. The bartender is absolutely massive. I'm not a short woman, and even with the added height from my platforms, the bartender still has inches on me. His bearded face matches his surly voice. I wouldn't call him handsome—his nose is too flat and slightly crooked, and his puffy ears stick out at an awkward angle—but I find him striking. The way his black T-shirt stretches against the bulk of his chest and arms adds a whole new level to his appeal.

My mouth goes dry as I stare at him like an awestruck idiot. I can't help it, though. Everything about him screams *dangerous,* and I think I could use a little danger in my life.

"You okay there, miss?" he asks with that same apathetic tone.

"Just peachy." My bright smile isn't returned.

I don't think he's being rude on purpose. I think he's terrible at his job. Customer service isn't for everyone. Lord knows I barely lasted three days when I tried to get a server job freshman year. Turns out you have to talk to people all day and make eye contact with strangers. No, thank you. So I totally get his whole resting bitch face thing.

"Are you going to order something?" the bartender snaps when I don't say anything else.

Well, excuse me for not realizing he was waiting on me.

"Yes," I tell him with a definitive nod of my head, "I'm just not sure what."

"Well, what do you like?"

"Yellow," I answer without a thought.

Danger's lips twitch with the barest hint of a smile, and his eyes flash with something. I'm not sure what, but it's the most life I've seen in those otherwise hollow pools of storm-cloud gray.

"Not exactly what I meant, but good to know. I meant which drinks do you normally go for? Vodka? Tequila? Rum?"

"I'm not sure. I've never had alcohol before."

That leaves him speechless. And the way he cocks his head and pinches his brows together is comical.

"What? Never seen a bar virgin before?" I challenge.

"Give me your ID." The sharp command has me fishing out my wallet without a fight.

He looks it over twice before handing it back with a resigned sigh. "Okay, Yellow, I'm going to need a little bit more to go off of here."

"I like things that are sweet."

Unintelligible grumbling falls from his lips as he turns and starts mixing different liquids into a shaker, giving me a front-row view of his perfectly sculpted ass. Goddamn, this man is a snack and a half. Not being one to waste an opportunity, I take advantage of the chance to give him a good look-over. He is definitely older than me. The lines on his face paint the picture of a man who has seen the harsher sides of life. It's hard to pinpoint an exact age, but if I had to guess, I'd say probably close to thirty. Strangely, that doesn't bother me at all. If anything, it makes that spark of a crush grow a little brighter.

"This one is on me. Happy belated birthday, Kori."

The drink he places on the bar is bright yellow, and the rim is adorned with an array of fruit slices. It even has one of those tiny paper umbrellas stuck in the side of a strawberry.

The unexpected gesture causes a swell of emotion to rise and lodge itself in my throat. Hot pins prickle behind my eyes as tears pool there.

I'm being ridiculous. There is no reason for me to get this worked up over something so small. He probably does things like this all the time, but outside of my parents, Danger is the only person to wish me a happy birthday, even if it's a couple weeks late.

"Thank you…" Not knowing his name is something I need to rectify. I can't keep calling him "Danger" after he went and did something so sweet.

Conflict crosses his features before he finally answers with a curt "Gage."

It suits him. There is no way a man like that could be named something basic like Johnathan or Tim.

"Thank you, Gage. I'm Kori." I reach across the bar to shake his hand.

He watches it for a few seconds like it might bite him before wiping his palm on his jeans and wrapping his massive hand around mine. Rough calluses rub against my fingers, leaving a tingling sensation even after he pulls away.

"I know."

Another customer calls out, stealing his attention before I can say anything else, and I'm left alone once again. At least this time I have a drink to keep me company. A mix of sweet, fruity flavors bursts across my taste buds as I take my first sip of the cold liquid. If this is what all alcohol tastes like, I understand why people drink.

No one else holds my interest after the encounter with the bartender. Everyone is so cheerful, and loud, and *young*. I mean, I'm young too, but they feel more like a species than my peers. The only person I have any desire to chat with is Gage, scowls and all. But he's working, and hanging around would make me a nuisance. There's something about him that resonates deep within me—whatever it is that gives him those empty eyes.

Ice rattles in my empty glass as I push it around with my straw. Sure, I could order another, but I don't think this is my scene. I'll look to see if the university has a gaming club. Maybe my luck will be better there.

"Can I buy you another?" a baritone voice asks as I push away from the bar.

The man it belongs to couldn't be more different from the one occupying my thoughts. He exudes an aura of charismatic self-confidence, garnering looks from other women as he moves closer to me with an easy smile on his lips. If I hadn't met Gage a short while ago, I'd likely be entranced by his charm as well, but the sandy-blond locks and frat-bro aesthetic aren't doing anything for me now.

"No, thank you. I think I'm actually going to head out."

I place my glass on the counter and shove a few dollars in the tip jar before I brave the streets again. They are busier now than they were before I went into the bar, but knowing I only have to bear it for a few minutes lessens the torture.

Rambunctious shouts echo down the hall as I make it back to my room. Looks like whatever trouble my dormmates are getting up to has only intensified in the few hours I was gone. Their noises don't bother me—it's not like they're banging on my walls or anything.

After wiping away the city's grime in the shower, I change into my pajamas and cocoon myself in my favorite lemon-colored fleece blankets. The only light in the room shines from my laptop screen, where an old creature feature from the '80s plays. Normally, my focus would be glued to the screen, but tonight, my mind keeps drifting back to the stoic man at the bar. I should have talked to him again. Knowing I might never get that chance leaves a dull ache in my chest.

It's in the fates' hands now. But I swear, if they give me the opportunity, I won't waste it again.

Chapter 2
Gage

"Man, you should have seen this chick."

My friend's drunken commentary is no more than a buzzing in my ears. Luck would have it that the rest of our crew couldn't come out tonight, leaving Nathan to hit the town on his own. Of course, for him, "hitting the town" means pestering me because I don't charge him for his drinks and I listen when he rambles about women and heartache. We still have a few drinks to go before he hits that second stage.

"She had legs for days and an ass so juicy it makes you want to take a bite out of it. Her rack left something to be desired, tho—"

With my quick slap to the back of his head, his hat goes flying, taking the rest of that thought with it.

Even I have my limits.

"Knock it off. I know you're an asshole, but this is a lot, even for you."

"Sorry, I was only trying to paint an accurate picture for you. You have a field ripe for the picking here. If I were you, I'd be going home with someone new every night."

He fetches his hat off the floor and slips it on with the bill facing back. Paired with the half-buttoned trop top and board shorts, the look screams "I'm a douchebag," but at least I don't have to look at the stupid fish on the front of it anymore.

"Well, I'm not you, and I have no interest in taking undergrads home with me."

Or anyone, for that matter.

It's been years since I've had any desire to take a woman to bed. Pleasure loses its appeal when you spend each day focusing on surviving to the next.

"Your loss, man. It worked out well enough for Morgan."

"Morgan is twenty-five, not almost thirty-five. It would be creepy if I tried it."

"More for me, I guess." He chugs the rest of his beer and drops the empty can back on the counter. "Wish me luck."

A middle finger in the air is the only thing he's getting from me.

A dark cloud of melancholy settles over me as he swaggers off to find his next conquest. As annoying as my friends can be, their presence is a reprieve from the oppressive, gloomy aura that clings to me. It's always worse when I'm alone, and over the years, I've found it's possible to be completely isolated even when surrounded by a bar packed with people.

Not for the first time tonight, the strange woman from earlier floats back to the forefront of my mind. Little Miss Yellow couldn't have looked more out of place if she tried. I doubt most people noticed. They were too drunk to be that observant, but I registered every awkward move she made. It was like she had an aura of her own—a lonely one that kept her stuck on the outside, locked in orbit without a chance at breaking through.

Against my better judgment, I took pity on her. The gnawing in my gut wouldn't let me do anything else. Normally, I have a rule about not making small talk with the customers. It only encourages them, and the last thing I want is to hear some stranger's life story. Yellow wasn't like that, though. Despite the sadness in her eyes, everything about her was bubbly and cheerful, and not in an annoying way either. She didn't feel the need to drag the conversation out any longer than it needed to be. I can appreciate a woman like that.

That doesn't mean I wanted to talk to her again, and even if I had, she was gone by the time I made it back around to where she was sitting. A woman like that wouldn't waste her time with me, anyway. I've seen my face, and I've been called both ugly and intimidating more times than I can count. Beyond my looks, as a thirty-four-year-old high school dropout who works in a bar, I don't exactly bring much to the table. And if that didn't scare someone away, the gloom would.

***

After the last patron leaves and the front door is locked, Cutter's is surprisingly peaceful. Soft rock plays over the digital jukebox in the corner while I try to wipe away at least some of the stickiness from the bar top. Artificial lemon and cleaning chemicals mix in the air, giving the place some semblance of respectability. Not like the illusion won't be ruined once we open tomorrow.

Even in the peace, the gloom is present. It's especially heavy on nights I lock up on my own, made worse by the alien atmosphere outside. Neon lights scatter in the low-hanging fog, casting the deserted streets in an eerie glow. Stepping out the door is like walking into the Twilight Zone. It's been years since I started working here, but my hackles still rise every time I traverse the abandoned streets.

Head up and eyes alert, I walk the few short blocks to my car. The looming dark cloud chases me, gaining ground with each of my hurried steps. Its cold tendrils reach out, creeping into my mind with the caress of a lover and the promise of rest.

Maybe this is the night I finally let it catch me—maybe tonight is the night I can finally get some peace. It would be all too easy to fade away into oblivion. No one would miss me. I'm nothing but a burden to my friends, and they will all go their own way eventually. This isn't a town most lay roots in.

The sight of my lonely old Camero is enough to break away from the gloom's grasp. I jog the last few feet—my aching knee be damned—and as the door slams behind me, the last of those dark wisps fade away, taking the insidious thoughts with them.

Thank fuck.

Three pictures tucked into the dash remind me exactly who it would hurt if I gave into those intrusive desires. I couldn't do that to my ma, or to my brother and Karis either.

With an unsteady breath, I crank the engine. Harsh rattling shakes the car as the old girl sputters to life. She limps along the shadow-soaked roads, flashing a slew of warning lights I've chosen to ignore. One day, I'll have the funds to take her into the shop, but for now, duct tape and foolish hope will have to do.

Yellow's face flashes into my mind again. If there's a woman who understands foolish hope, it's her, with those too-trusting russet eyes. I've never seen anyone look so perfectly cartoonish before. Her wide button nose and full lips are something straight from a princess movie. If woodland creatures flock to her when she sings, I wouldn't be surprised.

I don't know if that level of naivety is a blessing or a curse. Either way, it's not something I've ever known. Even as a kid, I was all too aware of how cruel the world could be. To go this long without realizing that harsh truth—I can't begin to conceptualize it. That type of ignorance is cultivated by privilege I've never come close to tasting.

A loud *pop* and sharp jerk snap me from my thoughts as my car slows to a crawl. *Fan-fucking-tastic.* I maneuver the hunk of junk off to the side of the empty highway and pop the hood. Smoke billows out through the crack before I can even get out to open it fully. There is no way I'm fixing her tonight.

Just my fucking luck.

My fingers dig into my palms as I fight back the surge of violent anger flooding my veins. Roaring blood is the only sound that echoes in my ears as my jaw tightens and my teeth grind. It takes several long moments for me to regain my composure, and when I do, I pull out my phone and call the one person I know will always pick up.

The phone barely rings twice before a blunt yet groggy "Where the fuck are you?" cuts through the air.

Karis has never been one for rude awakenings, but that doesn't stop her from keeping her cell's volume on at night "just in case." That fact has saved my ass more times than I care to admit. This isn't the first time Brandy has failed me.

"I need your help." My shoulders slump as the full weight of my situation sinks in.

No car means I'm going to miss work, and if I miss work, I'm going to get fired. Thus starts another hopeless cycle of needing cash without having the means to get it. Fuck me. I probably have to open another credit card I'll never be able to pay off. Anything to make sure I don't lose it all because of this goddamned piece of shit car.

"No shit, Sherlock. Now what's your location, and do I need to bring my kit?" she snaps.

"I'll send you a pin with my location. As for your kit, I think this might be more than you can handle."

"That bad?"

"I haven't even looked."

"Fuck. Well, send me the link. I'll be there in a few. The least I can do is give you a ride home."

The sound of her bike roaring to life fills the line for a brief second before it goes dead. I guess I'm riding bitch.

Smoke seeps through the AC vents, driving me out into the humid night. Stars litter the sky, brighter and denser than I've seen them in a long time. Or maybe I never take the time to look.

That's how Karis finds me—leaning against my car, staring at the sky, and ignoring the problem literally billowing over less than five feet away. To her credit, she doesn't fire off a snarky quip or give me shit for not even opening the hood.

Silence envelops us as she kills her engine. For a moment, not even the cicadas dare resume their incessant screeching. Loose asphalt crunches under her heavy boots as she bypasses me and heads straight for Brandy, popping the hood open with a hiss of pain.

A plume of thick smoke engulfs my friend, and she lets out a stream of unintelligible curses, but other than that, she doesn't say a word. She drops her helmet to the ground and matches my posture beside me.

"How fucked am I?" I ask after a few tense moments.

"Pretty damned fucked," she replies. "What the hell even happened?"

"I don't know. I was driving home, it made a loud noise, and then smoke."

"With no warning?"

"No. I've had a couple warning lights on for a few weeks." Months, if I'm being honest with myself.

My face twists with a grimace and my chest heaves with a sigh. Everything about this situation could have been avoided if I had swallowed my pride and asked for help weeks ago.

"I can't do anything to fix it tonight. I say we leave it. We can call a tow truck out to get it in the morning."

"Fuck."

That's going to run me at least a hundred dollars. Repairs might be minimal, or they could cost thousands—thousands I don't have. Hell, even the hundred is going to be tough. If I shuffle around some money and only pay the minimum on a few bills, I should be able to pull it off and still be able to pay my rent on time. That's assuming I'm still able to get to work. Even if I can, I'll never be able to afford the repairs, and I sure as hell can't finance a new car.

Nausea turns in my gut as real panic takes hold. I'm so goddamned screwed. One fucking misstep, and I'm going to be dragged back down to the bottom again. No, below the bottom. At least when I took that blow to my knee, I had no control over the outcome. This, though, is all on me.

"Hey. Earth to Gage." Karis snaps in front of my face. "Eyes on me, asshole."

Her sharp words are the lifeline I need to pull myself out of my spiral.

"You good?" she asks. Unusual gentleness softens her impish face.

"I'm fine." I grunt out the lie.

"Sure you are. Come on, let's get you home."

She picks her helmet off the ground and heads back to her bike. I've always hated that thing. Partly because it's a death trap and partly because she never lets me drive. Tonight, I don't have it in me to give her shit about it as I follow her and straddle the seat behind her. She's always tiny, but sitting between my legs, she feels dainty and fragile. If I told her that, she would kick my ass into next Sunday.

Wrapping my arms around her adds another layer to the awkwardness. As much as I love the woman, this isn't a position I want to be in with her. It's far too intimate. She is practically my sister—not that I have a real sister to compare it to—but I wouldn't want to hold my brother like this either.

When people talk about riding a motorcycle, they often talk about the exhilaration and sense of freedom they feel. I think they are full of shit. A deep pool of dread churns in my chest the entire ride back to the apartment. Images of us splayed out on the street, bloody and broken, flash through my head until we finally come to a stop in my run-down complex.

A dog barks from a nearby window as I hop off my ride, and the telltale aroma of weed drifts from somewhere in the back.

Home sweet home.

To my surprise, Karis cuts the engine and follows me up the creaking wooden stairs to my unit. I should have seen this coming—it's in her nature to meddle.

Familiar darkness greets me as I push open the door. Normally, I wouldn't even bother with the lights, but for my friend's sake, I fumble for the switch and flood the room with a dim orange glow.

"So what's the game plan?" She flops onto my ratty old couch and props her booted feet up on the coffee table like she owns the place.

"Don't have one." I pull out two beers from the empty fridge and crack them open.

My grocery budget has been limited over the past few weeks. Money is always tight this time of year. When classes aren't in session, business is as dry as the Sahara. Now that the students are back on campus, things will pick back up.

I hope.

"Don't lie to me. I know you've been running through scenarios since before you called me."

And none of them have shown me a way out of this mess. All I can see is a chain reaction that ends with my life in pieces.

With a sigh, I join her and take a sip from the chilled can, but the contents are tasteless on my tongue. Karis doesn't push me any further—she knows it won't get her anywhere.

"The only solution I see is getting another job. But without a car, that's pretty much off the table. I'm not sure how I'm going to keep up with the ones I already have without reliable transportation," I say, then take the last bitter sip. The alcohol works to take the edge off my desperation, letting me actually think.

"See if you can get a job downtown, then. That way you only have to figure out the commute once. Preferably a morning shift, like a coffee shop or that bagel place on Clayton Street. You can walk to the gym between shifts in the morning and shifts at Cutter's."

"That still leaves getting to work and back home."

"Take the bus? Or a rideshare? I know that's an extra expense, but it's better than not making money at all."

Fuck. She's right.

If things get desperate enough, I can probably stay with Morgan and James, but the last thing I want is to intrude on their honeymoon phase. I don't think I would leave that without mental scars.

"I'll give you a ride downtown in the morning, and you can ask around to see if anyone is hiring urgently. After that, I'll give you a ride over to Double Teep so you can coach the brats. You can start stressing about things on Sunday."

"Fine. You coming back bright and early?"

"Fuck no, I'm crashing here."

Of course she is. It's a good thing I kept her toothbrush from last time.

"Sure. I'll grab something for you to sleep in." Before I step into my room, I add, "Thank you, Kare."

She waves off my thanks with her attention locked on her phone. That doesn't make my gratitude any less real.

After I get her settled on the couch, I slip into my room for a short few hours of fitful sleep. Alone in the dark, my gloom finds me again, relentlessly reminding me that things will only get worse from here.

Chapter 3
Kori

What do normal people do on Saturdays?

Football, I think. But the season doesn't start for a few more weeks, and even then, I don't think watching people throw around balls and knock each other over is for me. Sports weren't exactly something my family was into when I grew up. But maybe I should give it a shot here? I might have more luck making friends there than I did at the bar.

That doesn't help me today, though.

The view from my room overlooks a large quad that sits between several other dorms. It's the perfect vantage point to observe the average college student in their natural habitat. With my best David Attenborough impression, I glance at Daisy and narrate the scene.

"If you look below us, you will find a group of upperclassmen congregating on the green. They often meet in smaller circles known as 'cliques,' and these groups rarely interact. Watch as two cliques sit side by side without ever interacting. Oh. What's this? A rare treat, indeed. It seems as if we will get to witness a courting attempt.

"The male college student approaches a group of females with swagger in his step. It's a bold move, but knowing that females of this species often travel in packs, the lone male won't likely have a chance to catch her on her own. The group of females stops, and judging by their defensive posture, the male will not be successful in his attempt. But let's see how it plays out..."

A fit of laughter overtakes me, cutting my bit short before the poor guy walks away dejected. That right there is why approaching people is so hard. The risk of rejection is so much higher than the potential reward.

"What do you think I should do, Daisy?"

The only thing I am sure of is that I can't waste today sitting around my dorm. I might not make any friends out there, but the odds still beat the zero percent chance I have staying here.

This would be so much easier if I had social hobbies.

"Exploring is a good option. I could go see what downtown is like in the light of day."

Surely it won't be the same hellish experience it was last night.

When I was growing up, my parents would tell me stories about their time at UGA. One complaint they both had was how hilly the campus is. I thought they were exaggerating, but Athens gives credence to the "walked uphill both ways" anecdotes. At least my ass will look great by the time I graduate.

Without the crowds and the constant bombardment of sound, downtown is actually kind of nice. Sweet floral scents drift in from the North Campus gardens, covering most of the foul odors from the night before that still cling to the gutters. In the chaos of the evening, I didn't notice all the shops and restaurants. They take up more window space than the bars by a large margin. Most are basic, but some ooze that weird Athens charm my parents never shut up about. My best chance at meeting someone I vibe with has to be in one of them.

I don't make any friends in the first vintage store I check, but I do find several unique pieces to add to my wardrobe. It's a win, even if it's not what I set out to do.

Sunlight blinds me as I step back outside. It takes several seconds for the dark spots to fade from my vision, and the sight that greets me when they do has my stomach springing into a gymnastics routine worthy of the Olympics.

It's him.

Across the street, Gage stands in front of a crowded coffee shop, looking surlier than he did last night. Hell, the scowl that never left his lips might have actually been his customer service face, because the look there now is downright mean. People are giving him a wide berth as they pass, going as far as crossing the street when they see him.

Of all the people in the city, it had to be him. The cruel fates must be laughing at me now. They heard my promise and tangled our threads.

With a heavy sigh, he drops back against the window and runs a hand over his face. A strange pang of recognition hits me again, resonating all the way to my bones. My feet carry me in his direction before I can think it through. I couldn't fight it if I wanted to. His anguished brooding has a leash on my heartstrings.

He doesn't react as I approach him. I'm not sure if he doesn't notice me or if he's hoping I'll go away if he ignores me. Not much has changed about his appearance since last night. I'm not sure why I expected it to. It's not like bartending requires a specific uniform. The only change is instead of a plain T-shirt, he's wearing one branded with the logo for some place called "Double Teep." I file that bit of information away and build up the courage to speak to the mountain of a man.

"Hey." My voice comes out in a strained squeak.

It gets his attention, though. His lashes open without any haste, and he glares at me with the intensity of a raging storm. That's the only reaction he gives. I guess we aren't doing the whole "hi" thing.

"Gage, right? From Cutter's? We met last night. You probably meet a ton of people every night, though, so it's totally cool if you don't remember me. I'm Kori, in case you forgot."

An abrupt bark of nervous laughter stops my rambling. Never once does his steely expression change. The man doesn't even blink. This was a bad idea. Scratch that, this was the worst idea. I think he would rather swallow glass than talk to me, but that knowledge doesn't stop more words from spilling past my lips.

"I wanted to check and see if you are okay."

That gets a reaction.

His face softens, and for a brief moment, confusion overtakes his features, but the stone mask reappears in an instant. Even so, that glimpse told me more than any words could have. He isn't used to people worrying about him, or at least strangers. When was the last time someone asked how he was? Who does he go to when he needs a shoulder to cry on? It could be me if he's willing to let me in. Everyone needs someone to have their back when things get tough. I know I do.

"I'm fine," he huffs.

"You don't look fine."

"Not your concern." His words leave no room for argument, but there's no malice in the tone.

"What's going on? Maybe I can help."

"Unless you can get me a job, I don't think you'll be much help."

"A new job? What happened to the bar?"

"We can't all be lucky enough to survive off one job. Cutter's isn't cutting it anymore." His mouth snaps shut before his lips twist into a grimace. "What the fuck am I even doing? I don't have time to waste standing here talking to you. Sorry, Kourtney, but I really have to go."

Shaking his head, he pushes off the wall and disappears down the street without a backward glance.

Okay then. Nice talking to you too, asshole.

His rejection lances through me with a twisted barb, but its sting is dulled by my outrage. The audacity of this man. Next time, I won't bother checking in on him. Clearly, he doesn't need my help.

Although...if I *could* help him, rubbing that in his face would feel really good. Mom always says kindness is the best revenge.

Hanging in the window where he stood is a Help Wanted sign with "urgently" scrawled between the words with a thick marker.

That's strange.

Why didn't he go here? If he did, why didn't they hire him? Maybe that's why he was in such a bad mood. I'd be pissed off too if I were in his shoes.

The smell of fresh coffee rams into me with the force of a tidal wave as I walk into the shop. By sheer force of will, I repress the urge to gag and keep pushing forward. Coffee has never been one of my favorite smells; it's too strong—like bleach or, God forbid, leather—completely overwhelming my senses.

How am I supposed to function when all I can do is smell? It's awful. But I'm not doing this for me—I'm doing this to be the bigger person. There's a wait to get up to the counter, and by the time I do, the young guy at the register looks beyond frazzled. On a second glance, it becomes clear he's the only person working behind the bar.

"What can I get started for you?" His smile is strained and, paired with the bags under his eyes, looks more manic than friendly.

"Nothing, actually. I saw the sign that you were hiring. Is that true?"

"Yes"—he breathes out a relieved sigh—"my manager will be here in half an hour. You are more than welcome to wait until she gets here to talk with her."

Ah. That makes more sense. He wasn't rejected, just never got a chance to interview.

"A man came in here before me, yeah? A big guy with a scary-looking face? But he couldn't wait?"

A look of confusion falls across his face. "Yeah...how did you know that?"

"He's a friend. I'm actually out here helping him find work. Did he leave a résumé with you?"

When the guy nods, I put on my best attempt at a flirtatious smile and bat my lashes at him.

"Do you think I could have it?"

If Gage can't interview for himself, I'll have to do it for him.

***

Not to toot my own horn, but I crushed Gage's interview. Mr. Broody Danger should be receiving a call with the news any time now.

The warm glow of satisfaction burns in my chest as I walk back to my room with a spring in my step. *And he thought I couldn't help him.* I've never been happier to prove someone wrong. Maybe this will show him that I'm not some annoying kid wasting his time. Then he might actually give me the time of day.

I can't rub it in his face if I never see him again, though. The fates showed their hand, but I have no guarantee they will intervene again. If I want to pursue this, I need to take the reins from here on out.

The name on his shirt—Double Teep—pops back into my head. That could be the connection I need. Maybe he will be more receptive when work isn't involved.

"What do you think, Daisy? Would it be weird if I looked it up?"

Almost certainly, but that doesn't stop me.

It doesn't take me long to find it. The first search result is for an MMA gym about a mile north of campus. I don't know a ton about him, but fighting fits. His face looks like it's taken enough hits. Knowing they were likely sanctioned makes me like him even more. Everyone thinks they want a tough guy until they try to start something with some random person who looks at them funny on the street. It's different when it's a sport—at least in theory.

The big red Request More Information button beckons me to click it. It would be so easy for me to show up and pretend it was another act of fate. But what would I say if he asked me why I was there? Lying isn't my strong suit, and I've never had any interest in trying martial arts before now.

"This crosses the line from weird into obsessive, right?"

Judgmental plastic eyes stare back at me.

Yup. She's right. Pressing that button would be crazy.

I close the tab before I do something to embarrass myself. There are other ways I can go about making our paths cross. It wouldn't be *that* weird if I showed up at the bar again. That's what people do on Saturday nights. And if he wants nothing to do with me, maybe I'll have some luck making other friends.

Chapter 4
Gage

Saturday nights always bring in the largest crowds, and tonight is the rowdiest it's been since the semester started last week. Rowdy is good—it means there are customers. With any luck, the tips will be enough to cover what I spent on a tow truck this afternoon, with enough left over to stock the fridge. As long as no other unforeseen expenses pop up, I should be on track to make rent next month.

Especially with the new job.

I'll have to make some concessions on sleep, but it wouldn't be the first time.

My body acts on autopilot as I serve drink after drink to the never-ending line. In my head, I'm tallying each tip as it gets added to the jar. The take is good, but nowhere close to what I need.

"Fuck, man, the chick I told you about yesterday is back."

The shaker bottle nearly slips through my fingers as Nathan's voice yanks me out of my head.

"What chick?" Karis's spine stiffens to attention as she scans the room with a predatory smile.

Just great. The last thing I need is these two competing for who is the biggest idiot tonight. Where is Morgan when I need him? At least one of my friends has some sense when he isn't too busy getting his dick wet.

"Her. The one in yellow."

That one word has my head snapping toward the door.

What the fuck is she doing here again? And what the fuck are my friends doing checking her out?

The muscles in my jaw clench as I resist the urge to knock them both upside the head for the way they're leering at her. Nathan takes a step in her direction, but that's as far as he gets before I catch him by the collar and pull him back to the bar.

"Leave her alone." The harsh growl in my voice is a shock even to me.

"All right, spill. Who is she?" Karis asks.

Goddamnit. She's never going to let this go.

"She's no one."

"If she's no one, then you'll have no issues with me going over to talk with her?" From his smirk, I think Nathan is enjoying this a little too much.

My fingers tighten in the rough fabric as my jaw clenches again. I couldn't explain the reaction if I tried. This woman is no one to me—that wasn't a lie—but she sure as hell isn't going to be someone to him either. She deserves better than that. My friend wouldn't care that she's clearly out of her element and desperate for connection. He would treat her like any other woman in here, not thinking twice about how his actions might hurt her. I would hate to see her bubbly optimism fade.

"I don't know her well. We've only talked a few times. What I do know is she is too good for your sorry ass. So you are going to leave her alone."

"But I have a chance, right?" Karis asks.

"No. We are all going to leave her alone."

The last thing she needs is our bullshit in her life.

"Fine. Are we supposed to ignore her if she tries to talk to us?" His smirk only grows wider.

"No," I say with a frustrated growl.

"So what *can* we do?" Karis asks. "I need answers now because she is heading this way."

As if it burned me, I release my grip on my friend's collar and try to smooth away the nonexistent wrinkles on my shirt. Dark patches of spilled liquor stain the fabric, but I can't do anything to fix that. At least the black cloth hides the worst of it. Karis snickers, but I ignore her. My attention is fixed on the woman making her way toward me with as much bravado as a fawn crossing a street.

It's so different from the confident way she approached me this morning. God, I was such an ass to her. I don't blame her for being hesitant. She didn't deserve one ounce of my attitude earlier.

"Hi, Gage." She mumbles the words at the ground while twisting a long braid between her fingers in front of her chest.

What's her name again? Fuck, she's told me it at least twice now, but it didn't stick. It starts with a K...I think. Krista? Kari, maybe? Fuck. I'm an even bigger piece of shit than I thought. My apology won't mean shit if I screw up her name while making it.

"Hey...Yellow." I cringe as soon as the words pass my lips.

The snort of laughter from my friends confirms it sounded just as bad outside of my head.

"How's the job hunt going?" Her eyes never leave her worrying hands.

"Pretty good, actually. I'm starting at the Bean Bar in the morning."

That drags her attention from the floor. As her gaze meets mine, she smiles, and a sharp pang flashes through my chest. For a moment, I'm captivated. Dark ridges add depth to those russet pools, making it look as though her eyes are made up of miniature mountains. The spell breaks as she blinks and diverts her focus to something over my shoulder.

"That's great news. I'm glad everything worked out for you." She bites on her lip and resumes her fidgeting.

It takes everything in me not to grab those nervous fingers and still them with my own. She shouldn't be scared of me—she wasn't before. No, I fucked that one up by treating her like shit.

"I'm sorry I was short with you earlier."

An apology won't fix things. Hell, I don't deserve her forgiveness.

"Don't worry about it. You were busy, and I came up and started bothering you out of nowhere. Kind of like I'm doing now…" Her face twists into a grimace as she bites on her lip again. "I'm sorry. I'll just go."

"Wait." I grab her hand, stopping her before she can flee.

Electric currents dance along my palm where our skin meets, and I yank my hand away in shock. With a quiet gasp, she turns back around, and her chest heaves. The classic rock and din of chatter fade into a buzz in the background. All that exists is me and her.

I really need to learn her name.

"Don't leave us hanging. Why is she waiting?" Karis's snark-filled words shatter the moment.

As Nathan chuckles beside her, Yellow stiffens. Her face falls as she looks between my friends with wide-eyed panic. There's no salvaging this—at least not tonight. Goddamn, they are awful sometimes. She takes a step back, ready to flee, so I blurt out the only thing I can think of to make her stay.

"Let me make you a drink. On the house."

"No, thanks. I'm going to go now," she says with about as much conviction as a field mouse.

Shit.

This time I don't stop her as she beelines out of the bar. All that would do is make her more uncomfortable. Another pang shoots through my chest. When I saw her before, her awkward aura was still cheerful and bubbly—like a sunflower—but today, her bright charm has all but wilted away.

I did that, and now I need to find a way to make it right.

"Yellow?" Nathan questions as soon as the woman is out of earshot.

Unfortunately, he was on his best behavior when she was here. He doubles over as his whole body shakes with laughter.

"You don't know her name, do you?" Karis asks with a shit-eating grin.

"No," I admit with a defeated sigh.

"But you like her?"

"No." The lie comes out far too quickly to be believable.

"Sure. You take the time to talk to all the lost little ducks that waddle their way up to the counter. That's definitely something I've seen you do before."

"Gage? Friendly?" Nathan gasps out before falling into another fit of laughter.

"I don't *not* like her"—I hold my hand up to stop whatever comment my friend is about to make—"but I'm not into her. She's practically a kid. It would be beyond weird if I saw her like that. I don't want to see her get hurt, that's all."

Calling her a kid puts a sour taste in my mouth. It's clear that woman isn't a child, but she's still only twenty-one. A thirteen-year age gap is practically the same thing. I'm already the creepy old guy who hangs out with college students. It's not hard to imagine what people would say if I got involved with one.

"Keep telling yourself that. So what are you going to do about her?" she asks.

"Nothing."

There is nothing to be done. If I see her again, I'll apologize for my friends' shitty behavior and move on with my life. I don't have time to take in another stray. My crew keeps me in enough trouble as it is.

Maybe that's why I'm so drawn to her. At one point or another, all of my friends were outsiders who were struggling to find their place. Yellow reminds me of them. If everything wasn't so fucked right now, I might have been more willing to invite her into the fold. I think she might just fit. But things *are* fucked, so that won't be happening anytime soon.

"Nothing?" Karis asks, raising a brow.

"Yup. I have too much going on to worry about a lost girl."

"Fair enough. Speaking of, do you need me to give you a ride home tonight?"

"Nah, I'll get a rideshare. Can't keep asking you to cart me around."

"Sure you can. You know I don't mind."

I wave off her concern with a grunt. The last thing I want is her charity. Plus, it's not like I intend to go home tonight, anyway.

Our conversation ends there. The next wave of demanding students crashes against the bar, and it doesn't stop coming until it's time to lock up. At some point, Nathan leaves with a random woman, and Karis dips out not too long after.

Herding the last drunken customer out into the streets takes longer than it should. The air is buzzing with more chaotic energy than normal—likely the result of the city coming to life for the first time after lying dormant for several months. No one is ready to go home yet.

As soon as I turn the lock, I spring into my end-of-shift routine with more haste than normal. Every second wasted is sleep I'm losing. My urgent energy is enough to keep the gloom at bay for now, but I can feel its icy tendrils creeping into the corners of my mind.

The only task I take my time on is tallying tips. Each dollar counted is a chip off the mountain on my shoulders.

It's enough.

Not a lot, but enough that I'm able to breathe a little easier.

In an instant, all the adrenaline drains from my bloodstream, replaced with overwhelming fatigue. My energy plummets like a kite without a breeze. It takes more effort than I'd like to admit to finish closing down. At least my head is too foggy to focus on the gloom.

With cement feet, I drag myself out of the bar. Things have calmed down. The air is quiet enough that I'll likely be able to get a few hours of sleep.

I was lying when I told Karis I would get a rideshare. Money or not, I don't see the point in trying to get home, only to have to be back in less than three hours to open at the Bean Bar. There are more than enough places to crash around campus in a pinch. I should go to the learning center and find a couch there, but the walk is farther than my dead feet can carry me.

The empty fields on the edge of North Campus are as far as I get.

Karis would kick my ass if she knew I was doing this, but what she doesn't know won't kill her. This isn't the first time I've had to rough it on the streets. Hell, one night is nothing compared to some stints I've done before.

To my tired body, the grass is as comforting as any bed would be, and within minutes, I start to drift to sleep. My focus should be on my surroundings—there's always the risk someone tries something, regardless of what I look like—but my every thought drifts back to Yellow.

I bet if she saw me like this, she would pretend she never met me. I'm so far below her level, she shouldn't even be talking to me. She is the brightest of blooms, and I'm nothing but dirt beneath her roots. My bullshit is already tainting her bright aura; if I let her in, I might ruin it for good.

Chapter 5
Kori

With every day that passes, the sterile walls of my room inch closer, closing in around me on all sides. Why did they have to be white? It makes the space feel more like a prison than a home. Or an asylum. Maybe that was intentional, because I'm going crazy locked in here.

Outside of meals and classes, I haven't ventured outside again. Not since I fled from Cutter's like a princess fleeing the ball. The difference is I didn't have a magical night with a prince first or a fairy godmother waiting in the wings to make everything better. All I got was an awkward conversation and ridicule from the man I was—am—crushing on and his friends. I seriously doubt he's going to come chasing after me with a glass slipper to declare his feelings. This isn't a fairy tale, and even if it was, I'm not exactly the princess type.

He isn't single, anyway. There was way too much familiarity between him and the goth woman for her to be anything but his girlfriend. They fit together well—their scaries match. Given the choice between me and her, I would have chosen her too. She's everything I'm not: small, edgy, and confident. With her in the picture, why would Gage ever take a second glance at me?

That's right, he didn't.

It was a stark reminder of why I don't go out of my comfort zone—and why I don't have friends. Loneliness sucks, but it's never humiliated me.

When I can't stall any longer, I grab my bag and head for the bus stop. Fuzzy dark fabric clings to my arms within minutes of stepping into the blistering heat.

It's the wrong season to wear a hoodie—I know that—but knots tangled in my gut with every other outfit I tried on this morning. They left too much exposed.

No one spares me a second glance as I squeeze onto the bus like a sardine in a can, or as I make the brisk walk down the street to the right building. A blast of freezing air crashes into me as I step through the door, coating my damp skin with a layer of goose bumps.

Where is everybody?

The rattle of the AC mixes with the buzz of the fluorescent lights overhead, filling the almost empty hallway with an ominous hum. The only other person is a man sprawled out in an alcove desk with his attention locked on his laptop. Each hesitant footstep on the linoleum tile echoes behind me as I approach the classroom. My heart flutters like a hummingbird, beating its wings against the curve of my neck. It's like the opening scene of a slasher flick. This is the moment the creepy monster or masked slasher jumps out and kills an unsuspecting girl, setting the stage for the ordeal the final girl survives.

Despite every instinct telling me not to, I reach for the door. The handle turns a fraction before the lock prevents it from going any farther.

What the fuck?

I try it again, but the result isn't any different. It's not a surprise, but it also doesn't ease any of my confusion. Each door I check to the lecture hall is the same. *Did I miss a memo or something?* I pull out my phone to check, and sure enough, that's exactly what happened. An email with the subject line "CLASS CANCELED" sits unopened at the top of my inbox.

Oh.

An airy chuckle slips past my lips at my stupidity. That leaves the question of what I'm supposed to do now. There are hours before I need to be back for my next class, and as much as I would like to, going back to my room seems like the wrong way to spend that time. Maybe that cute vintage store has new products. The girl who worked there did say they put new stuff out every week. Hell, I can even grab breakfast while I'm out. It might be fun. What are the odds I run into Gage again?

As it turns out, quite high.

After a significantly less compacted bus ride, I step out into the floral-scented air and stroll along the sleepy city streets. The Bean Bar is the one spot brimming with activity as people queue to get their morning dose of caffeine, and behind the counter is the man I can't seem to escape. Once again, the fates have tangled our threads. Okay, so I might have helped him get this job, so him being here shouldn't be a shock, but still, out of all the shifts, he has to be working this one.

The dark-blue apron and matching baseball hat do nothing to lessen the intensity of the scowl on his face as he messes with the large espresso machine. A cloud of steam erupts in front of him, and he jerks away. As it clears, he looks up, and his gaze meets mine through the large pane of glass. Lightning crashes through me—there is no other way to describe the sensation—paralyzing me where I stand. His face softens as he cocks his head to the side, the drink in front of him completely forgotten.

Someone knocks into my shoulder as they pass, severing that electric connection with a hastily mumbled "sorry." *What am I doing?* My face grows impossibly hot, sucking all the heat from my gut and leaving an aching ball of ice in its place. He must think I'm a stalker. Who else stands outside someone's place and stares at them like a complete weirdo? Not normal, sane girls. Whipping around, I flee. Again.

"Yellow, wait." The rich timbre of his voice wraps around me like a lasso, pulling taut and locking me in place.

Something stirs in my stomach. Not butterflies—these beating wings are far too big. Seagulls, maybe. The fluttering is violent enough to come from one of those abrasive creatures.

"Shouldn't you be working?" I muster all the bravado I can while still refusing to face him, but the slight quaver to my words shows my hand.

"I'm on break."

My spine stiffens as his voice comes even closer than before.

"Mid-rush?"

"Yup. Told them it was important."

Yeah, right. That's the last thing I am to this man. With a scowl of my own, I whirl around to give him a piece of my mind.

"That's rich. How am I important? You don't even remember my name." A bitter bite of laughter bubbles past my lips.

His face twists into a grimace, and he runs a hand over his face. Good. He should be a little ashamed of himself.

"You're right, I don't. I'd like to, though."

Oh, he's on a roll. The only response I give is another scoff as I cross my arms in front of my chest.

"I deserved that," he mumbles. "Look, I wanted to tell you that I'm sorry for how my friends acted the other night. It wasn't cool. And I'm sorry for acting like an ass the other day. It's not an excuse, but I've got a lot of shit going on right now, and you caught me at a bad time. I was frustrated at the situation and lashed out at you."

"Okay. Thanks, I guess."

My fingers dance in my palms while I wait for him to make his next move. I have no idea what comes next here. The apology was already out of left field, so I'm flying through this encounter blind.

Those pesky seagulls riot as he sighs and takes another step forward, encroaching on the edges of my personal space. The smell of roasted coffee clings to his uniform, but I don't actually hate it when it's coming from him. Dark bags that definitely weren't there the last time we spoke hang beneath his bloodshot eyes. That's also new—and troubling. If I were a betting gal, I'd say he hasn't slept in days.

"Are you okay?" Without thinking, I reach both hands up and grab his face to get a better look.

Shit.

I jerk them away and take a giant step back before he can snap at me about boundaries. It's not like I haven't heard that one before. Everyone from my parents to my therapists have tried to instill that in me, but every so often, I slip up. Like now, for instance.

"I'm sorry," I blurt out, moving even farther away.

Warmth spreads along my arm when he reaches out and curls his fingers around my wrist. The barest hint of a smile plays at the edge of his lips, dulling some of his sharper edges.

"It's fine. Really. I'm pretty used to having hands all over me."

The seagulls dive into the sea of dread in my gut, raising the tide of the toxic liquid and letting it course through me. It's no surprise that he's used to having hands on him. I'm sure he has endless opportunities to hook up with women looking for a little danger. Not like I care. It's not my business, anyway.

Pinpricks of heat radiate from where his hand is still flush against my skin. *Holy shit*, his hands are big. His palm nearly encircles my wrist on its own. If it wasn't for that grip, I would take off like a bat out of hell. My face tightens as I glare at the shackle—like that will do any good.

"Not like that." That ghost of a smile vanishes as his face twists into a grimace, but he doesn't release me. "Goddamnit. My brain isn't working right today. I coach at an MMA gym down the street. Jiu-jitsu destroyed my personal bubble years ago, especially once I took over the kids' program. Those little hellions love to climb all over me. Who needs a jungle gym when you have Coach Gage, right? I...I'm going to stop talking now."

Pleasant pressure builds in my chest as he rambles. It's adorable, and my teeth bite into my bottom lip to keep the dopey smile off my face.

"Good to know. My bubble is pretty big, but I'm bad about remembering other people's exist."

"Shit, sorry," he hisses and drops his hold on me.

The loss of contact sends a visceral wave of bitter-cold disappointment through me. I didn't mean that he was in my space.

"It's fine." My cheeks heat as I wave off his concern.

There I go, making things awkward again. That's the Kori special. What would a normal person do in this situation? Small talk, probably, but I've never been able to figure that one out. I think we are past the point of talking about the weather.

"So, kids?" I ask. "That doesn't exactly mesh with the whole 'big scary man' vibes you've got going."

He huffs, which I think was supposed to be laughter, and shrugs.

"It's something that was thrust upon me back when the gym opened, and as the years went by, I never stopped."

"So you enjoy it, then?"

"Honestly, yeah. More than I ever thought I would."

I start to ask him more, but he lets out a large yawn, reminding me of the question he conveniently never answered before.

"Seriously, are you okay? You look like shit."

Weariness overtakes his features, his shoulders slumping as he lets out a deep sigh. It only lasts for a moment before his face returns to its neutral mask, but in that split second, he lets me see more than words could ever express. He's not okay.

"I'm fine. Just tired."

If tired means bone-deep exhaustion, then sure, I guess he's just tired.

"Gage—"

"I have to get back inside," he interrupts. "I'm glad I ran into you."

He doesn't wait for my reply before turning and jogging back toward the shop. As his hand finds the door handle, he pauses.

"What's your name, Yellow?" he calls out over his shoulder.

"Kori."

"Kori." For the first time, his lips curl into a genuine grin. "I'll see you around."

Alone again, I'm finally able to breathe—and think—but none of what just happened makes any sort of sense. That might have been my princess moment. Is there a fairy godmother hanging around somewhere too?

I think he wants to see me again. He wouldn't have said what he did otherwise. With our threads tangled, I don't think we have much of a choice either way. That doesn't mean I have to sit around and wait for a higher power to intervene. I'm taking my fate into my own hands.

The tab with his gym, Double Teep, is still open in my phone's browser. I pull it up, click the button to request more information, and fill out the contact form. Now all that's left to do is wait.

Chapter 6
Gage

*B*right sunlight radiates from the cloudless sky, blinding me with its brilliant rays. It should be hot, but the sun's kiss against my skin is nothing more than a faint tickle. I shield my face with my hand and take in my surroundings through squinted eyes. Sunflowers in endless rows over rolling hills paint the landscape all the way to the horizon in every direction, stranding me in the middle of a yellow sea.

Yellow.

The lone word sends sparks of awareness tingling down my spine.

Why? And why is the aroma of sweet citrus drifting off the blooms? Why is that scent familiar?

"Hello?" I shout into the dazzling void, but nothing returns my call.

Idling will get me nowhere, so I step deeper into the field. The stems grow taller as I pass—impossibly so—until they tower over me like a forest of trees. The thick petal canopy blocks out the sun, draping the ground in a blanket of shadows.

Cold fingers of unease claw down my spine, standing the hairs on the back of my neck on end.

Beyond the edge of my vision, something watches. With every step I take, it follows. My pace quickens with the rapid beating of my heart, but even then, the gloom never loses ground. Darkness closes in around me as it stalks closer, but it never comes into view.

I'm going to die.

That thought paralyzes me where I stand. The shadows peel away from the trees, morphing into cursed specters that dance around me in a threatening display.

"Gage," an ethereal voice calls to me on the breeze.

The sound is so familiar, yet entirely unplaceable. I search for its source through the shades, but I'm blinded by the cyclone of night.

Then there is light.

With a golden flash, my demons are banished, and she remains. I understand now why the sun's heat was dulled—sunlight is nothing but a cheap imitation of her aura.

Her gaze finds mine—those large orbs the same golden-brown hue as her skin—and she extends a hand to me with a smile. Buried within the depths of my mind, something churns. Recognition. A name. It flitters through my head like a hummingbird on a breeze, not staying still long enough for me to pin it down.

"Who are you?" The words spill from my lips like molasses from a jar.

"I'm—"

"Asshole, wake up. Your appointment's here." Karis's sharp command yanks me from unconsciousness.

If I wasn't already awake, the two striking pads that slam into my chest a second later would do the job.

"I'm up. Jesus, woman. Has anyone ever told you your bedside manner sucks?"

The pads fall to the floor with a *thud* as I uncurl from the cramped confines of my makeshift bed. A stack of spare mats in the storage closest isn't exactly five-star accommodations, but after a rude wake-up from campus police this morning, I'll take sleep where I can get it. It took over an hour for me to convince them I wasn't crazy or on something, just desperate. By the time they finally decided I wasn't a threat, it was already time for me to go to work, cutting my two hours of planned sleep in half. At least I'm allowed to drink as much coffee as I want at the Bean Bar. I don't think I'd have survived otherwise. The only thing getting me through today is that when I leave here, I get to go back to my apartment and sleep in my own bed.

"There's a reason I didn't go to med school. Now, if you want to keep napping, I'll let Morgan get the commission," she snarks as she walks away.

No fucking way am I about to let that happen. I love the guy, but it's every man for himself out here. He at least has his stipend to hold him over, plus I know his girl will never let him go hungry.

Ignoring the pins and needles in my legs, I follow my friend and try to shake off the remnants of that bizarre dream. What the actual fuck is wrong with me? I have no right to be thinking about Kori like that—fuck, I shouldn't be thinking about her at all. That sunflower comparison was dead on, though. Her roots have embedded themselves deep within my brain, whether I want them there or not.

Bleach mixed with sweat stings at my nostrils. The unpleasant odor does wonders to settle my head. It's a Pavlovian response. Nearly two decades of training will do that.

The calm doesn't last—not when my dream woman is standing in the tiny lobby, chatting away with my most sane friend. Whatever she and Morgan are talking about has her fully animated, swinging her arms around in erratic patterns as she speaks. It's so similar to the way Karis gets sometimes that a smile pulls at my lips. That is the only similarity between the women. My friend is a night alone in the frozen wilds, while Kori is a stroll through a garden on a mild summer's day.

As Karis joins them at the front desk, Kori's movements falter. The infectious smile fades from her face, and her spine stiffens. Karis either doesn't notice or doesn't care as she closes in like a shark circling its prey.

What the hell is that about?

My pace quickens while Kori shrinks in on herself. Best friend or not, I know exactly how much of an asshole Karis can be when she wants to be, and she has that gleam in her eye that means trouble.

"Hey, Kori. What are you doing here?"

Her panicked eyes snap to mine when I call out, and her whole body relaxes. The relieved smile that overtakes her features stirs *something* in my chest—an uncomfortable, pulsing ache. No one but the kids in my classes has ever looked so goddamned happy to see me.

"You remembered."

"Of course. But that doesn't answer my question."

A rosy tint darkens her cheeks as she drops her eyes to the floor. "I-I'm, ah—"

"She's your appointment," Karis supplies.

She's my appointment? There is no fucking way. Running into her a few times downtown is one thing, but for her to end up here without prompting is another altogether. I know I mentioned the gym, but not by name. This is either some cosmic intervention bullshit, or she's stalking me. And she's far too innocent for the second...I think.

"I didn't know you had any interest in martial arts."

More stunted ramblings fall from her plush lips as her gaze darts between my friends. Right. She freaked out the last time they were around too. Thank God Nathan isn't in yet, or she might have run for the hills the second she got inside.

"Come on. Let me give you the tour."

I wrap an arm around her waist and shepherd her away from the others. This close, a whiff of sweet perfume dances in my nose. Citrus—exactly the same as the flowers from my dream.

How the fuck did my sleep-deprived brain summon that one? If you had asked me this morning what she smelled like, I couldn't have told you. I don't exactly go around sniffing pretty women and committing their scents to memory. But that knowledge was there, buried deep down. Like a goddamn creep.

As we walk, the tease of her cleavage glows under the fluorescents, catching light with each shallow breath. Fucking hell, that is the last place I should be looking. I avert my gaze and focus my attention on showing her around. She is silent as I point out each of the mats, show her the tiny locker rooms, and lead her to the weight room in the back. It isn't much, but I never said the tour was grand. In the room by ourselves, her breathing finally slows. Normally, this is when I would dive into my pitch to get her to join, but getting the sale is the last thing on my mind.

"What do you think?" I ask as I sit on the spare mat in the corner and motion for her to join me.

"It's...um...very padded." She plops down without grace and gestures to the foam around us.

A snort of laughter catches in my throat.

This girl has never stepped foot inside a martial arts gym. Hell, she probably doesn't know what we do here. I bet *Karate Kid* is the most exposure she's ever had to something resembling the sport. She doesn't strike me as the type who's into UFC.

"Why are you here? How did you even find this place?" *Why can't I escape you?*

The pitch of her voice rises as she lies, "I've always wanted to learn judo."

"Jiu-jitsu."

"Bless you."

It's a struggle to keep a straight face.

"No. Jiu-jitsu is what we teach, along with Muay Thai. Judo is a different sport altogether."

"Oh." She buries her face in her hands with a heavy sigh.

"Why are you here, Kori?"

"Do you promise you won't think I'm weird?" The words are muffled against her palms.

I grunt in response but make no promises. As cute as she is, if she says she hacked my phone or put a tracker on me, I won't be able to withhold judgment.

She lets out a deep groan and flings herself back on the mat.

"Fine. I saw the name of the gym on your shirt the other day and looked it up. I know nothing about fighting, but I thought it might be fun."

"That isn't that weird. The whole point of those shirts is marketing, anyway."

"Really?" she asks, sitting back up.

"Yup. Coach David will be glad to know it worked."

My chest tightens again at the way her whole face lights up as she relaxes.

"I'll spare you the pitch," I tell her and cough away the weird sensation. "If you aren't sure, don't sign up now. Come back next Tuesday at seven and try out a class. If you like it, then we can talk membership."

"It's a date." Her eyes widen as the words spill out, and she drops her focus back to the ground, sucking her thick bottom lip between her teeth.

A shiver courses through me at the sight. She needs to stop doing that shit, or I'll show her exactly how those lips deserve to be treated.

"Come on, I'll walk you out."

In one smooth motion, I'm on my feet, and I help her off the floor. She stands with as much grace as a newborn foal, stumbling forward and catching herself on my arm. Another wave of her fruity scent washes over me. It's even more mouthwatering mixed with the sharp pinch of her nails digging into my skin.

"Sorry," she hisses as she jerks away.

"No personal bubble, remember?"

"Right. How long have you been doing this, exactly?"

"I've been with the gym since it opened, but I've been training under Coach since I was sixteen. So eighteen years, give or take."

"Holy shit, that's a long time."

Almost as long as you've been alive.

Fuck me, she's young—too young for me to have any business messing around with. Whatever this weird...interest...I have for her is, it can't go any further, or I'll cross the line into creep territory. Despite my growing trepidation, I keep talking. I've been an ass to her enough already.

"It's all I ever wanted to do," I tell her with a shrug. "My dad showed me *Rocky* for the first time when I was six, and I was hooked. I knew I wanted to be a fighter. While the other kids were playing games during recess, I was shadowboxing."

More spills out than I intended. Something about this woman makes it far too easy for me to bare my soul. That might also be the sleep deprivation.

"Why here? I know you said no sales pitches, but this place has to be special if you've stuck around this long. So sell me on it."

"It's a good gym. We are way more family-oriented than some of the others in the area, and it's a lot more welcoming to those who are looking for a hobby, not a career."

"That's great, but it doesn't tell me why you've stayed."

"What do you know about Coach David?"

She cocks her head to the side in question and thinks. "Not much. That's the owner, right?"

"Yes. David Boyd: two-time UFC featherweight champion, and he holds the record for the fastest submission in UFC history."

"That's impressive?" she says, but her inflection sounds as if she isn't quite sure.

"Sure." I shrug.

His credentials are legit. When I was younger, I looked at him with stars in my eyes, but after nearly two decades of knowing someone, the novelty wears off.

"His résumé is why I started, but that's not why I stuck around. He was a beast back in the day, but he's also one of the best people I know. Wouldn't want to train under anyone else."

And I doubt I'd still be alive if it weren't for him.

When I was in the depths of my despair after my injury, he was there, and he never gave up on me. He didn't let me quit—on MMA or on life. Once I was cleared to resume physical activity, he dragged my sorry ass back into the gym and told me I was in charge of the kids. He gave me something to live for, and I'll never be able to repay him for that.

Of course, I'm not telling her all that.

"Do you think I'd like it here?" she asks. "Sports have never been my thing. I'm more of a video game girl, if I'm being honest."

"It's hard to say. I think you'll like the people and the culture, but neither of us will know if you'll like the sport until you try it."

"We'll see on Tuesday, I guess."

Chapter 7
Gage

Across the crowded bar, the door swings open. As if captured by a magnet, my head snaps in its direction. Again. The customers in front of me are drunk enough they don't notice my momentary distraction, but their orders fall on deaf ears as I search for any glimpse of yellow among the sea of neutral tones and Georgia red.

My hopes turn to stone and plummet to the depths of my gut when there's no sign of Kori. Not that there would be. She hasn't come by Cutter's in weeks. Not since that night she ran out when I tried to apologize. That hasn't stopped me from checking every time that goddamn door opens. After our conversation at Double Teep the other day, I thought—fuck, I don't know what I thought.

I shouldn't be thinking about her at all.

With a deeper scowl than usual, I grab a mix of light beers and hard seltzers and dump them in front of the kids I ignored. One girl raises an eyebrow and opens her mouth—no doubt to let me have it about their order being fucked up—but the words die on her lips as her friend elbows her in the side while frantically shaking her head. The brave one looks between me and the drinks for several seconds, contemplating. Whatever she sees on my face is enough for her to make the right decision and grab the cans before scurrying off.

Smart girl.

"Who pissed in your Cheerios?" Nathan asks as he takes her vacated space.

I don't give him the satisfaction of an answer as I grab a can of his favorite beer and set it on the counter. He grabs it and takes a swig before focusing back on me with a mischievous glint in his eye.

Fuck me. His antics are the last thing I want to deal with right now.

"What? No 'Hi, how's it going' for your best friend?" he asks.

"Karis is my best friend," I deadpan.

"Ouch, man. That hurts. But the point still stands."

"What point?" Karis asks, sliding up beside him like some sort of dark fey creature summoned by its name.

"That Gage added extra asshole to his coffee this morning and will barely talk to me."

Here we go.

"How is that any different from normal?"

"Just look at him, Kare Bear. The crossed arms. The scowl. The 'look at me too long and I'll end you' glare. It's like he's trying to drive the customers away."

"Well, looking at your ugly mug would put me in a sour mood too," she quips.

"Jeez. What is this? Gang up on Nathan day?"

"I haven't said shit."

"Sure, but your attitude says enough."

I only shrug, but Karis's gaze narrows in on me.

"What's with the resting murder face, anyway?"

The door opens again, and the rest of my friends' bickering becomes background noise.

Come on, Yellow.

She doesn't show—not that she should. Hell, I don't even want her to. What would I do then? Talk to her? Yeah, right. Girls her age don't come downtown to make small talk with the washed-up bartender. They come out to get fucked or fucked up. The thought of Kori doing either makes me grind my teeth.

Karis is staring at me with raised brows and an all-too-knowing smirk when I turn my focus back to my friends.

"Expecting someone?" she asks.

"No," I grind out.

"Well, it certainly looked like you were."

"We're here, and Morgan said he wasn't coming out, so I don't know who it could be. He doesn't know anyone else," Nathan chimes in, his expression mirroring Karis's.

I cross my arms and wait. If I don't engage, they will get bored and move on.

"It's clearly someone. Maybe a certain lost duckling?" she muses.

"No," I growl with too much vehemence and immediately curse myself for taking her bait.

"Holy shit. She's right." Nathan's smile widens to a full-on shit-eating grin. "She's hot, man. I can see why you're into her."

My hands clench into fists against my biceps.

"I'm not into her. She's practically still a kid."

"You know as well as I do that Yellow isn't a kid."

Despite my hobby, I'm not a violent man, but hearing that word from his mouth has me questioning that.

"Her name is Kori," I spit.

"Fine. Kori isn't a kid." He must sense how close to the edge I am because he concedes without pushing me further.

"She is compared to me."

"By that logic, Morgan and I are kids compared to you."

"That's different," I huff.

"How?"

"Just is."

"I call bullshit, man."

"Seconded," Karis pipes in.

"Whatever. I don't have time for this right now."

I don't wait around for their responses as I stomp over to a group of actual paying customers vying for my attention.

Kid or not, Kori is way too young for me. Sure, she doesn't act like a kid, and she sure as hell doesn't look like one. I can admit that she's attractive, but that's as far as I'm willing to bend. None of it matters because I'll never be good enough for her, anyway. I'll never be good enough for anyone.

With that sullen thought, I throw myself back into work, pushing my body harder than necessary. It makes it easier to ignore the looming dark cloud when I'm on the brink of exhaustion.

My friends' worried gazes drill into my back, but I don't talk to them again. There's enough work to be done that I can stay busy without looking like a complete asshole for ignoring them. I'm not good company like this. Eventually, they give up and head out, leaving me alone to stew in my self-loathing.

I deserve nothing less.

***

On dead feet, I drag myself up the creaking wooden stairs to my apartment, my aching knee protesting every step. Walking all the way from Cutter's was likely a mistake, but it's worth it to avoid paying for a rideshare. I don't have twenty-three fifty to spare.

Inside is pitch black and as quiet as a grave. Once upon a time, I enjoyed coming back to the silence. This apartment was my sanctuary from the constant bombardment of stimuli that comes with a night at the bar. But over the years, something changed. What was once peaceful has become my hell. Now I hate that there's nothing for me to come home to.

The gloom thrives in the isolation. It hides in the darkness, waiting to ambush me as soon as I step through the door. Tonight is no exception. My melancholy has already lowered my defenses, making it easy for the gloom-barbed tendrils to embed themselves in my head.

Bone-deep weariness overtakes me. Day after day, I run myself ragged, and all I have to show for it is more goddamn bills. Paper crumples in my hand before I throw the mail onto the growing pile on the counter. I don't have to see the envelopes to know they're all reminders of what I owe. As if I wasn't aware enough as it is. Those are problems for me to deal with tomorrow. The only thing I can do right now is sleep, and if I'm lucky, maybe I won't wake up.

I stumble through the shadows toward my room, ignoring the rioting pangs of hunger. Making food requires more energy than I have. Rough plaster rubs against my calloused fingers as I search for the light switch. With a *click*, the dingy yellow bulb flickers to life overhead. My room isn't anything special. It's bare bones, except for the plethora of plants overtaking the shelves near the windows.

They are the only thing that brings me any semblance of joy in this place. It wasn't my idea to start collecting them. Karis decided she wanted to give plants a try. That experiment lasted approximately ten days before she realized they were more effort than she was willing to give. She brought the first succulent over half dead and told me it was my problem now. I didn't know anything about keeping plants then, but nursing the poor thing back to health was strangely satisfying. Seeing it get better as the days progressed gave me something to look forward to. One turned into twenty, and before I knew it, I was surrounded by greenery.

Even though I'm exhausted, I grab the mister to tend to my plants. I take my time with them, making sure they each get exactly what they need, even though my body aches and the layers of grime coating me could peel off me like a second skin. For a few blissful moments, I get lost in the routine. Focusing on each of their specific needs provides a brief reprieve from the oppressive cloud.

It doesn't last. I can only ignore reality for so long.

That pile of mail in the kitchen is a constant reminder of how fucked up my life has gotten. It's a never-ending cycle. Every time I start to get ahead, *something* happens that wipes all my progress. The universe must be out to get me. I don't know what I did in a past life to deserve this, but my entire existence is tainted with a karmic level of misfortune. No one is this unlucky; I must be paying penance for something.

I don't actually believe that.

But sometimes it helps to pin everything on something out of my control. It's easier than admitting I fucked everything up on my own.

Chapter 8
Kori

Buildings shouldn't be intimidating. Stone and steel don't have the capacity to be anything beyond inanimate materials, and it takes action and intention to create fear. A static structure doesn't have either of those. It would be like saying a tree is intimidating. Or a boulder. Yet somehow, approaching the tiny warehouse gym feels like walking toward my certain doom.

Okay, so maybe it isn't the gym itself but the uncertainty that waits for me inside. After my last visit, I looked up what jiu-jitsu actually is, and it seems terrible. I get what Gage meant about not having a personal bubble anymore. From what I gathered, the sport boils down to aggressive floor hugging. I don't want to aggressively floor hug anyone, let alone sweaty strangers. No, thank you. Not my idea of a good time.

Daisy and I debated for hours if I should even come. There is no doubt in my mind that I'm going to hate it, but I didn't want to stand Gage up, so here I am, hyping myself up in the parking lot like a fool.

One class, and I never have to do this again. I can do one class.

The bell above the door rings as I step inside, and I'm stunned by a wave of sound punctuated with the high-pitched squeals of children's laughter. More shocking than that is the deeper, bellowing laughter that comes along with it. The sound isn't one I've ever heard, but I immediately recognize its source.

Gage is laughing...with children?

This I've got to see.

A low wall separates the front mat from the doorway, and several parents are gathered around, watching whatever spectacle is happening on the other side. As casually as I can manage, I join them, and the scene taking place on the other side nearly causes my ovaries to explode.

When I heard children, I pictured actual kids, not toddlers, but the tiny people swarming around Gage can't be more than five. He is on his knees, letting the kids climb all over him like little spider monkeys with an actual smile on his face.

It's the smile that does me in.

What I thought was a crush before was mere embers compared to the raging inferno that sparks to life in my chest.

"He's really good with them," one of the moms tells me, without taking her eyes off the mat—no, him.

Jealousy crackles through me like lightning. I recognize the look on her face because it's mirrored on mine. She wants him—who wouldn't after seeing him interact with the kids? Hell, half the parents here have similar looks on their faces.

"Looks like it," I mumble, holding back the urge to glare.

"Which one is yours?" she asks.

"Oh, no. I don't have kids. I'm just early for my class."

"That's my Jack." She points to the blond-headed child with his arms wrapped around Gage's neck. "He absolutely idolizes Gage. I swear all I hear at home is 'Coach Gage this' and 'Coach Gage that.' It is really useful for discipline, though. All I have to do to get him in line is threaten to tell Coach Gage, and he is on his best behavior."

I'd be on my best behavior for Coach Gage too.

"I'm Ashley, by the way."

"Kori," I tell her, but I don't have time to say much else before Gage calls the class to order.

The authoritative command he barks out has me going stiff at attention along with the rest of the kids, which causes Ashley to burst out laughing beside me. Her laughter draws his attention from the class, and for the first time, he notices me among the spectators.

He barely glances at her before his gaze lands on me. His face goes blank for a breath, and then his lips curl into a wry grin and his eyes soften in a way that has my heart melting. I hold my hand up and wiggle my fingers in an awkward wave. His hand twitches at his side like he wants to respond, but he doesn't and directs his focus back to the class.

For the first time, Ashley's attention is fully on me. So is the attention of every mom in this room. Hell, even a few dads are staring in my direction. The looks on their faces range from curiosity to outright hostility. Both make me wish a wormhole would open up and suck me into an alternate dimension where the clouds are made of cotton candy, and everyone is an anthropomorphic bird.

Or I could bolt to the locker room. That is the sane option here.

"Girl, what was that about?" Ashley asks before I can go through with my plan.

"I have no idea," I tell her with a shrug.

"Well, honey, I'm jealous. Gage has never looked at any of us that way, and not for lack of trying on some of our parts." She casts a disapproving look at one of the other moms, whose shirt's neckline plunges so deep that her tits are practically hanging out.

I don't really know what to say to that, so I shrug. Gage and I are more than strangers, but we aren't friends. Not that I haven't hoped for more. Sharing that seems like a bad idea. It's way too personal to get into with someone I met all of five minutes ago. Although that might be how people make friends. I've got the meeting-people part down, and our common interest here is Gage; I don't want to talk about that, though. He is mine, and I want to hide him away like a dragon protecting its hoard.

The rest of the class passes without further conversation. Watching the kids makes me feel a bit better about what I'm about to get myself into. If the kids can do it, so can I. Although most of their time is spent playing games that help them grow comfortable with the different movements without actually drilling. The time they do spend working on technique looks like they are hugging and falling at each other.

It's freaking adorable.

So is how seriously Gage treats it. He never once addresses them as if they're anything but tiny adults.

As he calls the class to an end, he catches my eye and attempts to escape from the mat. Heavy emphasis on *attempts*, because between the kids and their mothers, everyone wants his attention. He doesn't push any of them away and even gets down to the kids' level when speaking to them. It's a complete one-eighty from how he acts at the bar.

"Hey, Kori. Are you ready for your first class?"

Unease crawls down my spine as the familiar low rasp of Gage's goth friend comes from behind me. *Friend.* Ha. That's wishful thinking. The dose of reality pops my swelling heart and sends it flying around my ribcage like a deflating balloon. It doesn't matter how hard I'm crushing when he isn't available.

"I—"

"Perfect. You are going to love it. I'm going to pair you up with one of the other newer girls, but flag me down if you have any questions." She wraps an arm around my waist and guides me to the center mat without waiting for my response.

"You coach too?"

"Nope, I just help out sometimes. Chappy is the woman in charge tonight." She jerks her head toward a tall, slender woman in the center of the room with a clipboard.

"What about Gage?"

"He only coaches the brats."

"Is he not going to train?"

"These classes are below his skill level."

"Oh."

There goes any hope I had of talking to him today. I should have bailed when I had the chance. This was never anything more than business for him, and I built it up to be something more.

"Evelyn, meet Kori. I want you to work with her today."

The woman she introduces me to looks about as comfortable as I feel. She's wearing the same karate costume that everyone else is, but hers is stiffer and whiter than the rest. No one told me I needed a uniform. I'm going to stand out like a freak in my neon spandex.

"Hi," Evelyn says, raising her arm in an awkward wave.

"Hi," I mimic.

"You two are going to get along great. Have fun." The terrifying woman smiles in a way that seems more threatening than friendly and leaves us on our own.

"Sorry about Karis. She can be a lot," Evelyn says with a sigh as she fidgets with the end of her thick chestnut ponytail.

I file away the name for future reference. It beats calling her "the goth girl." Especially since she doesn't have the same edge here. It makes sense. I wouldn't wear a full face of makeup or a dozen rings to work out either.

"Wait, you guys are friends?"

"Yup, and she's been pestering me to join her here for months. I tried to explain to her that my idea of a good time doesn't involve rolling around on the ground with sweaty men. Wait, that makes it sound way dirtier than it actually is—and like I'm shaming people. People can do what they want with their bodies. I just don't want to be touched by strange men all the time. Especially for exercise."

Her full cheeks grow pinker with each sentence she rambles.

"Then why are you here?"

"Karis is nothing if not persistent, and she always gets what she wants. Fighting it is futile."

"She sounds lovely." Sarcasm coats the words.

"She is...a unique person. But a great friend to have."

"So does that mean you know Gage too?"

"Sure. I—"

"Line it up," Karis shouts, cutting our conversation short.

My partner grabs my hand and leads me to the end of the line. We bow in, and then I'm in hell. No one told me there would be running or jumping or rolling. I'm fully ready to quit by the time we finish the warm-up. Fuck this workout thing. I'm out.

The only thing that keeps me on the mat is Gage watching from the fence. My skin prickles with the awareness of his gaze. It's unnerving.

Once we start focusing on the actual technique, the situation gets a little better. There's a lot less moving and a lot more learning. Plus, the only person I have to touch is Evelyn. All things considered, it isn't so bad. She's as clueless as I am, so we spend most of the class laughing at how awful we are instead of drilling anything properly. That part is actually pretty fun. By the time class comes to an end, I'm conflicted about what I want to do.

"Okay, spill. Why has Gage been watching you for the past hour?" Evelyn asks once we're dismissed.

Her question causes me to trip over my feet.

"Are you sure he wasn't watching his girlfriend?"

"Girlfriend? Gage? That's a good one." She wipes away fake tears from her eyes as she laughs.

"Isn't he with Karis?"

That sends her into a fit of giggles so intense she doubles over.

"You're funny," she says once she catches her breath.

"So that's a no?"

"Hard no. Like, not even if they were the last two people on earth levels of no."

"But they seem close."

"Oh, they are, but not like that. Which brings me back to him watching you."

"He wasn't watching me."

"Sure, and I'm not—"

"Hey, Kor," Gage cuts in as we step off the mat. After a second, he adds, "Evelyn," but he doesn't glance in her direction.

Maybe she was on to something, because I could burn alive from the heat in his gaze.

"Have fun, girl. I'll catch you in striking Thursday," my new friend says as she scurries away.

"So what did you think?" he asks once we're alone.

"It was..."

"You hated it, didn't you?" His brow furrows and his lips purse into a scowl.

"No. I didn't hate it," I say in a rush. It's a lie, but I'll say anything to get that unguarded look back on his face.

"But..."

"It wasn't what I was expecting. Warm-up sucked, but the rest wasn't so bad."

"'Wasn't so bad' isn't the same as enjoying it."

"I liked Evelyn."

"But that's the only thing," he concludes.

"Yeah," I say with a defeated sigh.

I wanted to love this place like he does. *So much for finding a common interest.*

"You aren't going to offend me if you decide this isn't for you."

"But—"

"Seriously. No hard feelings. And if you like Evelyn, you should come to Cutter's tonight. I'm working, but the whole crew is coming out for a few drinks."

Nervous energy dances under my skin, begging me to claw at it for some relief. Evelyn, I can deal with. But the whole crew? That means Karis will be there. And the other man from before—the one with the flirty smile that doesn't reach his eyes. And those are only the ones I know. He could have a dozen more friends, and I doubt they want anything to do with me.

"I'm not sure." I run a hand over my other arm, pinching and twisting the flesh with each pass to help ground me.

"Hey," he says and catches my hand in his massive one before it can do any more damage.

The all-encompassing heat soothes the swarming nerves into a dull buzz. His thumb runs along the back of my hands, straightening out my tense fingers one at a time until they relax back into their neutral state.

"No pressure. Think about it, all right? I'm sure Evelyn would be thrilled if you came."

"Okay." I can at least promise to think about it.

The corner of his lips curls in the smallest hint of a smile before he drops my hand.

"Let me walk you out."

All I can do is nod. If I open my mouth, I'll say something stupid and ruin whatever this is. He stays a step behind me as he walks me to the door, too far to touch, but close enough my whole body tingles with awareness.

It turns out that thinking about it doesn't take long.

As soon as I'm free from his intoxicating presence, my choice becomes crystal clear. I can't *not* go. This is the opportunity I've been so desperately looking for to make new friends, Gage and my crush be damned. If something *does* happen there...well, that'll be icing on the cake.

Chapter 9
Kori

*H*ead up. Make eye contact. Smile.

The mantra plays on repeat in my head as I march through the near-empty city streets. It's a completely different vibe than the weekend. Hell, it's practically a ghost town in comparison. I'm sure it not even being ten is also a contributing factor.

I think I like it better like this.

There's no line outside Cutter's, and the crowd isn't any thicker inside the hazy bar. It's certifiably dead. Aside from Gage's friends grouped up by the counter, there are only a few lone strangers tucked away in quiet corners with their liquor.

"Kori, you made it." Evelyn waves with enthusiasm, as if I couldn't have found the group on my own.

Unsurprisingly, Karis and the flirty one are here too. Both locked in an animated conversation with Gage, who's leaning against the other side of the bar with a bored expression. The man who greeted me the first time I went to Double Teep is also here—dressed for an office, not a bar—with a blond woman in his arms who he stares at like she's his entire world. My eyes gloss over the pair. Giving them any more attention would feel like intruding on a private moment.

With a sheepish smile, I wave back and walk closer. At Evelyn's exclamation, Gage's attention shifts from his friends, and his face softens with a half smile. I don't have a chance to process it or respond, because my new friend greets me with a hug and starts introducing me to "the whole crew."

"You already know Gage and Karis, obviously. The love birds are Jamie and Morgan."

"James," the blond woman corrects but doesn't take her focus off her boyfriend.

"And this is Nathan," Evelyn continues, not missing a beat as she gives a name to Gage's other friend.

"We've met," Nathan says with a flirty smile that feels forced, slinging an arm over my shoulder. "Good to see you again, Yellow."

My whole body stiffens under his touch and the skeevy way he purrs the nickname.

"Her name is Kori. Use it," Gage practically growls and pulls his friend's arm off me with a sharp tug.

Nathan's smile only widens, but he puts his hands up in surrender. "My bad. It's good to see you again, *Kori*."

"Don't mind him. He doesn't know how to be anything but an asshole," Karis says as she maneuvers herself between me and her friend. "I think he was dropped on his head as a baby."

"You're one to talk. You love to push people's buttons," Nathan protests.

"But I'm not a creep when I do it."

"I'm not a creep."

"Oh really? Let's ask Kori. Hey new girl, do you think Nathan is a—"

"Enough, both of you," Gage cuts in with a glare.

They both grumble under their breath but turn their attention away from me. The tension in my shoulders eases, and I give my savior a grateful look.

"I would apologize for them, but if I did that every time they acted like idiots, it's all I'd ever do."

"They aren't too bad," I say as I twist one of the gold hoops through the strands of a braid.

"You don't have to lie on their account."

"They're a lot," I admit.

"That's an understatement," he says with a huff. "Do you want a drink?"

"Sure."

"Let me guess. Something yellow?"

My cheeks grow hot as I hide my face in my hands. "You're never going to let me live that one down, are you?"

"Probably not. Did you have something else in mind?"

"No," I admit with a groan, and he chuckles.

"Then sweet and yellow, coming right up."

He doesn't go far as he mixes up my drink, and unlike the last time he did this, he doesn't take his eyes off me as he tosses around the shaker and bottles with unexpected dramatic flair. If it were anybody else, I'd say he was goofing around and putting on a show for me, but it's Gage. He wouldn't do that, would he?

Stormy eyes twinkling, he slides the ice-cold glass over to me and waits for me to take a sip. It's clearly a different drink than before—there's sugar on the rim instead of fruits, and the color is less orange. I don't know if different is good. What if I hate this one? Would I have to drink it anyway? I can't not try it either—not after he spent the time making it for me.

I steel myself and take a tentative pull from the straw. Tart lemon and sweet peach fill my mouth, even more delicious than the drink he made last time. My eyes widen as I take another, larger sip.

"Good?" he asks.

A satisfied grin breaks through his stoic mask as I nod with vigor.

"I've been playing around with different drink options that meet your criteria."

His confession fills my chest with warm honey. Or maybe that's the alcohol. Either way, Gage has been thinking about me. Maybe as much as I've been thinking about him.

"Do you watch movies?" I regret the words as soon as they leave my lips.

I'm not great at this whole small-talk thing, but nine out of ten times, movies are a surefire way of getting people talking. In my experience, everyone has opinions on the matter, and people love talking about their opinions. Even surly bartenders...I hope.

"What?" He cocks his head to the side but doesn't seem put off by my question.

That's a good a start as any.

"Movies. Moving pictures on a screen, typically with sound and color. Good way to spend free time."

"I know what movies are. Who doesn't watch movies?"

"You'd be surprised. My roommate freshman year didn't watch movies at all. She claimed it was a 'waste of valuable time.' Although in this case, it was a dumb question. You already told me about watching *Rocky*, and unless you watched that and decided 'no more movies ever again,' you probably still watch them." The words pour out of me in a blathering stream.

"Yes, I like movies. I used to watch more but haven't had time for things like that these past few years."

"Do you have a favorite? Or at least a favorite genre?" I ask, and he shrugs.

"Sports dramas are my favorite. Preferably about fighting. But anything with fast cars or explosions will hold my attention."

"That's way more normal than I was expecting. I was thinking you were gonna say something wild like you are into period pieces or Hallmark Christmas movies or something."

"I'm a simple guy. What you see is what you get. No bullshit."

"I'm seeing that. Not everyone is so forthcoming about who they are. I hate that. Those types of people are impossible to read, and I already struggle with reading people as is. At first, I thought you were all mysterious because you were quiet and broody, but now I think that's just who you are. It's not a mask you hide behind. I like that."

"Are you saying you like the fact that I'm boring?" His question is tinted with the barest hint of amusement.

"Shut up, you know full well that isn't what I meant."

Gage smiles.

Not that half smirk that sometimes pulls at the corner of his lips, but an honest-to-God smile that even has the corners of his eyes crinkling. It's a miracle. I swear the sky opens up and lights shine down from the heavens while the angels' trumpets sound from the clouds. Coaxing this from him should get me halfway to sainthood.

Call me Saint Kori, the patron saint of amusing broody men.

That smile changes his face completely, softening his bolder features into something beautiful, and my stomach does a somersault worthy of an Olympic athlete.

"What about you? Is your sunflower persona a front, or is it the real Kori?" he asks, and that goddamn seagull comes back with a vengeance.

I have no clue what he means with the whole "sunflower" thing, but he says the word with affection, not malice, so I'm choosing to take it as a compliment.

"I don't have the type of energy to pretend to be anything other than the real me."

"Does that mean your favorite movies are chick flicks or something? I could see you being really into *Legally Blonde*."

"Ouch," I tell him with a laugh. "Is that really the vibe I give off?"

"Well, what do you like?"

"Do you know what kaiju movies are?"

"Like big monsters and *Godzilla*?"

"Exactly that. I love those. Especially the Japanese *Godzilla* franchise."

"I mean, big monsters fighting is cool."

"It's so much more than big monsters fighting. The original *Godzilla* blended the Shinto religion with the fears and trauma of the Japanese people to create an allegory of the devastation that occurred in Hiroshima and Nagasaki. As the franchise expanded, it continued to use current issues regarding humanity's destruction of the planet in order to send a message."

The urge to explain in more detail is overwhelming, but I keep my mouth shut. No one ever wants to hear me ramble about old Japanese movies, and I've been ridiculed enough for my interests over the years to know when to keep it quiet.

Normally by this point, people have either tuned out, or they give me their best please-shut-up look. Gage isn't looking at me like that, though; he is still giving me his full attention, and the remnant of that smile is still on his face.

"I didn't know that," he says in a deep timbre. There's a spark of something in his gaze that has heat rising to my face and my eyes dropping back to my fidgeting hands.

This time it's my turn to shrug.

"Not many people do. It's really cool once you look into it. The newest era has more of a focus on climate activism, but the movies have been really good. They're on Netflix if you're interested."

"I'll have to check them out. Maybe you—" He's cut off by the other bartender shouting his name.

"We're out of Tropicália. Need another keg from the back," she continues.

Gage sighs and pushes away from the bar.

"Duty calls. I'll be right back."

It isn't until he disappears that I remember we aren't alone.

His friends are all watching me with looks ranging from confusion to curiosity. The only one who doesn't seem shocked is Karis. She looks more pleased than anything.

"So, new girl, are you any good at pool?" she asks.

The question breaks the awkward tension in the air, and the rest of them avert their stares. Their judgment is visceral, worming its way into my veins, making me itch from the inside.

I swallow back the need to scratch away the unease and answer in the strongest voice I can muster. "Never played."

"Then you definitely need to see a master at work." Nathan threads his fingers together, cracking his knuckles as he stretches his arms and rolls out his neck.

"As if," James says with a snort and pulls out of her boyfriend's embrace. "You'd have more luck learning from Morgan than this fool."

"Morgan sucks," Karis fills me in with a mock whisper.

"What the fuck? I'm awesome at pool," Nathan protests.

"If flirting with girls at the table is playing, then sure, you're the best," James says with a condescending grin.

"You're one to talk."

"What's that supposed to mean? You know I could kick your ass any day of the week."

"Oh yeah? Prove it, then."

"Fine," she snaps, "but let's make this interesting. Winner gets complete control over the next game night."

"Oh, come on. I don't want to play Pictionary *again*."

"Sounds like you're admitting defeat already," she taunts.

"Fuck it. Fine. I hope you like Risk." He sticks out his hand, and she grabs it in an aggressive handshake before the pair storms off toward the tables in the back.

Morgan sighs as he watches his girlfriend go, but the love-sick smile never leaves his face.

"I should make sure they don't kill each other," he says and follows them.

"Come on, new girl, this is bound to get interesting." Karis doesn't wait for a response as she drags me behind her.

Evelyn falls in step beside me with a sheepish smile.

"I've learned it's best to just go with it."

I figured that one out on my own.

They've got the balls racked in the middle of the table by the time we make it back there, and they are arguing, quite loudly, over who gets to make the break shot. Morgan already looks defeated as he runs a hand through his messy curls.

Karis beelines in the pair's direction. I'm not sure if she's planning on mediating or getting in on the action.

"Is this normal for them?" I ask my only remaining companion.

"Pretty much. You should see them at game night. Half the time, I'm convinced it's going to end with one of those three killing each other. They probably would if Gage didn't keep them in line."

It isn't hard to imagine him wrangling his friends. From what I could tell, he does a great job with the kids' classes, and this trio acts like overgrown toddlers.

I wouldn't mind if he wanted to boss me around either. The thought alone sends a shiver of need to my core.

"That sounds like a lot of fun." The words come out breathier than I intended.

"You should totally come to the next one," she says, thankfully oblivious to the direction my thoughts have taken.

"You don't have to invite me out of pity."

"It's not a pity invite. It will be fun. Plus, I think Gage would like it if you came."

"Pfft. He wouldn't care."

If he wanted me there, he would invite me himself.

"I'm pretty sure that man said more to you in the past twenty minutes than he's said to me in the entire year I've known him."

"He was just being nice."

"Gage doesn't do nice. Trust me on this. At least give me your number so I can send you the details."

Fuck it. What's the worst that could happen?

***

James and Nathan came out the gate swinging, and their intensity hasn't wavered since the game started. I'm not the only one drawn in by their competition. Several other patrons wander over to watch the carnage—because that's what it is. For all his cocky talk, Nathan never had a chance. At some point, Evelyn drifted closer to the table, leaving me alone on the outskirts.

"Some game, huh," an unfamiliar voice rasps from behind me.

Too fucking close.

Hot breath crawls down my neck, thick with the stench of stale tobacco, making my stomach churn and spine tingle with unease. The pit in my gut has every alarm in me screaming.

"Sure." I duck my head as I step away from this stranger, but he follows my movement, staying too close to my back for comfort.

"What's a pretty girl like you doing in a place like this by yourself?"

Nausea threatens to rise as he runs a clammy hand down my bare arm before bringing it to rest on my waist with a bruising grip. Rationally, I know I can pull away and tell him to fuck off. If I make a big enough scene, the others are bound to notice, and they wouldn't let anything happen to me...right? Regardless, my body won't listen to my mind. I'm paralyzed—like a deer locked in place while it watches its impending doom.

"I'm not alone." I don't sound nearly as confident about that as I should.

Gage's friends are less than twenty feet away, but the distance seems like forever with *him* looming behind me. They are all too wrapped up in their spectacle to notice how uncomfortable I am. I risk a glance at the counter, hoping maybe I'll be able to catch Gage's eye, but the bar has gotten busier since I got here, and the growing line of customers occupies his attention.

It looks like I'm on my own—not like that's anything new.

"Sure you aren't, sweetheart. Either way, you aren't alone anymore. How about you let me buy you a drink, and you can tell me a bit about yourself."

"I already have a drink," I manage to squeak.

"Not a problem. We can skip straight to part two, then."

"No, thank you," I protest, but I doubt it will do anything to deter him.

"Come on, sweetheart, I—"

"Hey, Kori, are you all right?"

My whole body sags with relief as Nathan comes into view, with Morgan and Karis flanking him from a distance. I never thought I'd be grateful to see his hollow smile. Although there's nothing but rage in his empty eyes now.

"I am now," I say, and this time when I move away from the creep, he lets me go.

Even with his hands gone, my skin crawls where his hand touched me. I'm going to need an extra-hot shower to get the feel of him off me. Nathan wraps a protective arm around my shoulder, and the friendly facade falls away.

"You can fuck off now," he says with a sneer.

"Hey, the lady and I were just talking." The creep takes a step in my direction, but Nathan angles himself so he can't get any closer.

"And now the conversation is over. So, like I said, fuck off. Or we are going to have problems."

The creep hesitates for a moment before stepping back with a shake of his head.

"Bitch ain't worth the trouble," he spits as he walks away.

Karis crowds my other side as soon as he's gone, and on a cue I miss, Nathan transitions me into her arm and storms off toward the bar.

"Are you okay?" she asks as she guides me back to the group.

"I'm fine," I lie.

I should be fine. He didn't do anything more than invade my space. It's not like he groped me or said anything particularly untoward. Still, the encounter has me more shaken than I'd like to admit. Who knows what would have happened if the others weren't here?

"If you say so," she says but doesn't push the issue further, which I'm thankful for. If they make a big deal out of what happened, I might break.

She drops her arm once I'm back in, safely surrounded by the others. No one says anything for a moment, and a bubble of awkward energy grows in the air.

I take a large sip of my now-warm drink, finishing it off, and ask, "So who won?"

"Jamie," Evelyn says without the cheer I've come to expect.

"Cool," I mumble and let the silence overtake the group again.

Eventually, they fall back into casual conversation, but the vibe is wrong. Everyone is too still and the banter forced. Nathan stays at the bar with Gage. Both men watch over us with stormy expressions. It's not surprising from Gage, but the rage is wrong on Nathan's face. He's too pretty for that.

Fuck.

I did this.

That awkward bubble grows, heating my body with every expansion. Sweat trickles down my back, but it does nothing to stop the burning. Nausea rages in my stomach, drowning all the seagulls and butterflies—and whatever else lives there—in the pools of boiling lava. I ignore the feeling for as long as I can manage, but it overwhelms me completely.

"I'm gonna go to the bathroom," I tell Evelyn.

"Do you want me to go with you?"

"No, it's okay. I'll only be gone a moment."

"Are you sure? You don't look so good."

I wave off her concerns, even as she disappears down the tunnel.

The world spins with each step I take. I'm not sure if it's seconds or hours that pass, but eventually, I make it to my destination. I stumble over the threshold and beeline to the sink. Water is good. Water will cool me down. The first splash of cold liquid on my face is euphoric. The second is orgasmic. I would weep from the sweet relief that simple action provided. But it's not enough. I'm still burning alive.

Darkness creeps into the edges of my spiraling vision, and it's only then that I realize something is very, very wrong with me. I need to find Gage. My danger-man can fix anything.

With that singular thought, I try to stumble to the bar, but the darkness creeps closer and closer the more I fight to move. The world is a million miles away as I push through the door, into the secluded hallway. Just a few more steps, and I'll be okay. Once I get back into the bar, Gage will save me.

I only make it one more step before the world slips away completely. As I float in the dark, the burning finally stops.

"Hello, sweetheart." The cruel rasp cuts through my moment of peace.

Ice floods my veins as panic fills me, and then there's nothing.

Chapter 10
Gage

R age.

A storming, thunderous feeling more intense than I've ever felt billows and builds within me, growing stronger and more violent with every minute that passes.

Someone had the nerve to touch Kori in my bar. The motherfucker had his hands on her, scaring her, and I was fifty feet away completely oblivious to it all. *Nathan*, of all people, had to step in to rescue her from the creep. Not to say I'm not grateful, because I am. He saved my girl while I was too busy serving fucking drinks to realize she was in trouble.

It should have been me. Just like it should be me comforting her and making sure she's okay, but once again, my friends are cleaning up my messes. Karis and Evelyn have her sandwiched between them like a pair of overprotective mother hens.

The dark cloud around me is a tangible entity. Not one customer has approached me since Nathan came over and told me what happened, choosing to wait as long as needed to buy from the other bartender on duty. My friend acting as a sentry at my side definitely isn't making me seem any more approachable. Tips are going to be fucked tonight, but money is the last thing on my mind.

Yellow breaks away from the group and staggers toward the bathroom in the back. Her unsteady gait sets my spine on edge. It's closer to what I would expect from someone after several drinks, not one, and I know for a fact she's only had the drink I gave her. The creep didn't get the opportunity to get more booze in her system.

I track her until she disappears down the secluded hallway, then let out a curse. Have they always been so isolated? Goddamnit, that's a recipe for trouble. How the fuck has no one complained about it before?

A few seconds after she leaves, Evelyn looks at me and beelines for the counter.

"Something's wrong with Kori."

Chills run down my spine at those fear-filled words. My dread is mirrored on Nathan's face.

"What do you mean, something's wrong?" I ask.

The timid woman flinches at my harsh tone, but I can't find it in me to care. I'm sure Karis will give me an earful about it tomorrow.

"I—she—well—" she stammers without ever getting to the point.

My fingers clench at my side in impatience. Nathan catches my eye and gives a subtle shake of his head. *Fuck.* I bite my tongue and let him handle it. All too easily, he slips on that carefree mask he wears like a shield and gives her a charming smile. It's a good show, but there's still tension coiled under his skin like a snake ready to strike.

"Hey, take a breath and try that again," he says as he puts a comforting hand on her arm.

She follows his instruction and, after a moment, tries again, more grounded than before.

"She was acting like she was drunk or high or something. Her words were slurring, and she could barely walk straight. But I know she hasn't had enough to drink for that."

Fear grips my throat in taloned claws, ripping away my ability to breathe. Nightmare scenarios flash through my mind, getting worse with each scene that plays out, but the themes are all the same—my sunflower getting plucked from the soil and torn to pieces by malicious hands.

"Thanks, Evelyn," he says, and starts in that direction.

At least one of us is thinking clearly.

His departure spurs me into action, but I only make it a few feet before the whole world tilts on its axis.

Yellow stumbles—no, she's dragged out of the shadowy alcove by a strange man who has no fucking right to touch her. The edges of my vision fade as the storming cloud of rage rolls in, stronger than before.

I don't know who this fucker is, but he's going to regret the day he decided to mess with my girl.

I vault over the counter, and I'm on them before he even realizes what's happening, ripping her from his slimy hands and pinning him against the wall.

"Gage?" Kori whimpers.

She clings to me, her legs barely stable enough to hold her up.

"What the fuc—" His words are choked off as my forearm digs into his windpipe.

"What did you give her?" I growl in his face.

"I didn't give her shit," he wheezes, and beads of sweat form on his forehead as he swallows deeply.

"Don't fucking lie to me," I snarl.

Thunder bellows in my head, urging me to inflict as much pain as possible on this bastard. Without a hand free, the best I can do is put more pressure on his throat. Sick pleasure fills me as he starts to claw at my arm, his face growing more and more red with each second that passes.

"Hey, man, that's enough."

I whirl around as someone touches the back of my arm. If I had a hand free, he'd be meeting my fist.

"Fuck, Gage." Nathan takes a step back and raises his hands in surrender. "I know you care about her, but you need to let him go."

Let him go? As if. He'll be lucky if he leaves this bar conscious.

"Seriously, man. Don't fuck up your life because of this asshole. Think about the consequences here. You could lose your job or get arrested, and you know you won't be able to work with the kids anymore with a record. Focus on your girl. She needs you right now."

Goddamnit all. When did he become the rational one?

With great effort, I pull my arm away. The creep sags onto his knees and sends my friend a grateful gaze.

"Thanks. I owe you one. This psycho—"

Nathan's fist crashes into his jaw in a nasty uppercut, and the asshole drops to the floor without finishing his sentence.

"Go. I'll take care of things here." He tosses me his keys and flashes me a cheeky smile.

"Thank you," I tell him and sweep Kori into my arms.

She's so weak—so goddamn fragile. It only adds to the storm. I have half a mind to let Karis and Evelyn take care of her so I can teach that fuck a real lesson, consequences be damned. Her tiny whimper as she burrows her head into my chest is the only thing that keeps me from turning around.

The world around me is still a blur as I walk through the door. My entire focus is on the woman cradled against me. I'm sure I'll have a mess to clean up tomorrow—if I even have a job to come back to—but I'd do it again in a heartbeat to keep her safe.

Maybe once things calm down, I'll examine what that means.

A pit forms in my gut as I work to get her situated in Nathan's car. She doesn't react at all to being manhandled and positioned so I can fasten her seat belt. Her head lolls and her body sags against the strap as I pull away.

Fuck.

Whatever he gave her is strong.

"Can you hear me, doll?" I run a knuckle down her clammy cheek, and not even her lashes flutter in response.

Fuck.

Fear churns in my core. She needs to go to the hospital, but a bill like that could ruin someone. It would ruin me. Hell, it did. Can I live with myself if I fuck her over like that? Can I live with myself if I don't take her and she ends up seriously hurt?

Fuck.

Fuck. Fuck. Fuck. Fuck.

I back out of the spot and head toward my apartment. If she gets worse, I'll take her in, but I can't risk screwing her over like that. The drive passes by in a blink. One minute I'm getting on the loop, and the next I'm pulling up to my unit, with no real memory of what happened in between.

As soon as I park the car, I throw open the door and jog around the front to get Kori. She stirs, letting out the softest pained moan as I pull her back into my arms. The sound stabs straight into my chest, but it's an improvement. At least she's responsive.

"We're almost there," I murmur.

She doesn't give me any answer—not that I expect her to. I doubt I'll be hearing anything from those perfect lips for several hours. And I doubt she'll want anything to do with me once I get her home either. It's my fault she's in this state. If I hadn't invited her out, none of this would have happened. She should be safely tucked away in her dorm, painting her nails or watching a monster movie, but I fucked that up by opening my stupid mouth.

Getting her inside is harder than I anticipated. It doesn't help that my knee screams with every step I take. Every ache and pain in my weary body is intensified as the adrenaline fades from my system. Maneuvering her through the door while protecting her unconscious form is another thing entirely, but I manage and take her to my room, placing her on the bed with all the care she deserves.

Bile rises in my throat as I assess her state without danger clouding my perception. A fresh sheen of sweat coats her forehead, soaking the stray hairs around her ashen face. I grab a damp washcloth from the bathroom and wipe away the worst of it. My chest tightens painfully as she whimpers and stirs under my fingers.

I'd give anything to swap places with her.

"I'm so goddamn sorry," I whisper into the void. The thick knot in my throat makes anything more than that impossible.

Never have I felt so helpless. Not even when I was stuck in bed after my surgery; my recovery was at least in my control then. Now all I can do is wait while Kori suffers.

Exhaustion seeps into my limbs, weighing them down like lead, but sleep and I won't be getting acquainted tonight. Watching over her is more important than my own needs. If anything, it's my penance for not keeping a close enough eye on her and letting this happen.

There isn't a good spot in my room for me to post up. The space is too small for more furniture than my bed and dresser, and I'm not about to crawl under the sheets beside her. I would be as bad as the man who drugged her if I did that. The floor isn't an option either. It's too low for me to keep her in my line of sight, and I'll be damned if I take my eyes off her for a moment. Never again will I let my negligence cause her to come to harm.

I lean against the wall, watching for any change in the subtle rise and fall of her chest. Tonight I'll be her sentinel, unwavering even when the gloom finds me in the dark. It swirls around me, spewing vitriol instead of the normal seductive promises of peace. Somehow, this is easier to ignore. The evidence of my failures is here in front of me, and I already hate myself enough for letting it happen. My gloom can't make that any worse.

***

It's nearly sunrise by the time Kori starts to stir. She lets out a soft groan as she rolls over and kicks off the blanket I wrapped around her when violent shivers racked through her body. After several minutes of her tossing and turning, her lashes flutter open. Once...twice...three times before she loses the fight to keep her lids from falling shut again.

I know the feeling. My tired eyes burn from staying awake all night. Every blink feels like I'm grinding them against coarse sandpaper, and they grow heavier with every minute that passes. Her movement wipes the exhaustion away in an instant, and I push away from my post to crouch by the side of the bed.

"You're all right," I croon as I run a knuckle over her cheek.

She's still too cold and clammy to set my worries at ease.

I'm not sure if it's the sound of my voice, the caress, or a mixture of the two that startles her, but her eyes snap open, and she scrambles to sit up with a sharp gasp.

"Hey, it's okay. You're okay." I don't make another move to touch her as I reassure her.

Her chest heaves as she scans the room in quick, frantic passes. After a moment, her gaze focuses on me, and she stiffens before the tension drops from her shoulders like a marionette with its strings cut.

"Gage." She says my name like I'm the best thing she's ever seen.

My chest tightens at the reverent sound. It keeps doing that when she's around. I should probably get that checked out at some point. There is no way this is healthy. Heart palpitations are never a good sign. With my luck, I'm probably dying.

"Yeah, Low, I'm here."

She relaxes back onto my pillow with a hum.

"I don't feel good," she murmurs, her words still slurring from whatever drug is in her system.

It takes everything in me not to reach out to her again.

"I know." Believe me, I know. "What do you need right now? Water? I'll go grab a glass."

"Don't go!" Her eyes widen in panic as she turns toward me and grabs my arm, squeezing it like a vise, stopping me before I can stand.

"All right, no need for that. I'm right here. I'm not going anywhere."

Her grip eases, but not by much. Though it's not like her grip was particularly strong to begin with. Even if it was, I would let her squeeze me until my skin bruised and bones broke if it took away some of her fear.

She doesn't say anything else for several minutes. She doesn't pull her hand away either. Her eyes fall shut, and if it weren't for her rapid breathing, I'd think she passed back out.

A silent tear escapes from behind her lashes, and my restraint snaps. Even I have my limits, and seeing her shaking in my bed pushes me beyond their edge. I brush away the stray droplet with my thumb, hating the way another takes its place.

"Hey, you're okay. You're okay." The knot in my throat makes my voice gruffer than normal. I try to swallow it away, but the thick lump is unmoving. The words are useless anyway. Nothing I can say could ever make this right.

"I'm scared," she admits in a whisper that breaks my heart.

So am I, but I'll never tell her that. The only thing I'm good for is my ability to stay calm in situations like this, and I've already lost my head once. I'll be damned if I do it again.

I move my fingers from her face to her iron claws on my arm, coaxing them loose, and wrap her hand in mine. My thumb caresses the back of her hand in slow circles as I bring it closer to my face. I don't kiss her—I don't deserve that—but rest my lips against her skin.

"Will you lie with me?" she asks.

"Kori—" I start to protest, but she cuts me off.

"Please. I know you'll keep me safe."

Goddamnit all. There is no way I can deny her. Not when she's looking at me with those tear-filled Bambi eyes. Pain shoots through my knee as I stand; it doesn't do well being locked bent for too long. I slip off my shoes and join her on the worn mattress. The lumps never bothered me before, but Yellow deserves better than this—than me.

My body is stiff as I lie beside her, careful not to touch her despite the lack of space on the full-sized mattress. Her hand creeps along the bed until the edge of her pinky brushes against mine. She lets out an annoyed huff when I don't react and grabs my hand, striking like a snake hunting its prey.

"Thank you," she murmurs, and I squeeze her fingers.

After a few minutes, her exhaustion takes over, and she slips back to sleep with soft snores. I try to fight it—I promised myself I'd watch over her—but not long after, I fall unconscious too.

Chapter 11
Kori

Consciousness arrives on the back of a galloping horse. Or at least that's what the steady pounding in my head feels like. My mouth is so dry, my lips sting as I peel them open, and my tongue is about as useless as a sponge. It's a struggle to pry my eyes open; the bright light streaming in from *somewhere* feels like a knife stabbing into my brain with every crack. My dorm doesn't get sunlight like this.

Where the hell am I?

Groaning, I force my eyes open and sit up, pushing down the wave of nausea that threatens to overtake me when I move. As I take in the room, memories of the night before come back to me in flashes, starting crystal clear but becoming hazier and hazier until there's nothing at all. Nothing except Gage.

Why he decided I was his problem is a mystery, but I'm grateful he didn't let that asshole do whatever it is he planned for me. Thinking about those possibilities has bile rising in my throat. Last night could have been really, really bad. I owe him so much for keeping me safe. He didn't have to get involved.

The man in question is notably absent, even if his scent still lingers—clean and fresh with no frills, just like him. Save for the overflowing shelves of plants, his space is exactly what I would have expected. They are a stark contrast to the otherwise utilitarian array of mismatched furniture.

I didn't know he collected plants—but why would I? We aren't friends. Well, we weren't. Yesterday's events have shifted my perspective on the matter. I might not be his friend, but he is the closest thing I have to one in this city.

A neat stack of clothes sits folded on the bedside table next to a glass of water and a bottle of pain pills. It's another thing he didn't have to do but did. I snatch the cup and gulp back the lukewarm water like it's the best thing I've ever tasted. As far as I'm concerned, this water is nectar from the gods.

I swallow a couple of pills with the remaining liquid and climb out of the bed. Damp fabric clings to my skin, constricting my limbs. What I wouldn't give for a shower. Or a toothbrush. Hell, I'd take mouthwash at this point. Anything to stop feeling like death warmed over.

Fresh clothes will have to be enough. The buttery-soft T-shirt hangs on me like a dress. Its design is worn beyond recognition, but the maize color brings a smile to my face. Sure, it could be a coincidence, but I want to believe Gage specifically selected this shirt for me. The sweatpants are also huge. The length isn't awful, but I have to tie the drawstring tight and roll the waistband up to keep them secure.

I creep across his room and crack open the door. The smell of something delicious wafts from down the hall, pulling a growl from my empty stomach. All at once, my hunger hits me like the Kool-Aid Man bursting through a wall. Saliva pools around my tongue, and I practically float down the hall like a cartoon character as I follow the sweet aroma.

His back is to me as he cooks something in a pan on an ancient stove. It has to be from, like, the '90s or something. I'm surprised the thing still functions. He doesn't notice me as I approach, so I take the moment to drink him in.

Somehow, he looks even bigger in less clothing. The black tank top is tight against the muscles in his back, and his thick arms are on full display. His mass hasn't been sculpted for vanity. It's raw and powerful, just like him. The sweats he gave me match the pair he's wearing, but they look a million times better on him. Out of everything, his ass has to be my favorite feature, and it looks edible in the dark-gray fleece.

"Everything all right?" he asks in that low, even way of his without taking his attention off the pan.

Shit. How did he know I was here? He totally saw me checking him out.

"Fine," I squeak, heat rising to my cheeks.

I grit my teeth through my embarrassment and join him by the stove.

"How are you feeling?" He glances in my direction before turning back to flip one of the pancakes frying in the skillet.

"Not great. My head is pounding, and it feels like I got hit by a truck. The water and meds you left have helped mitigate some of that already, though. Thank you for thinking of me."

"It's the least I could do." His shoulders slump as he lets out a weary sigh.

He shuts off the burner and moves the pan off the heat. Silence hangs in the air between us for several seconds before he turns to face me. The tortured twist to his features is so unlike his normal unwavering calm that I nearly recoil.

"I'm really fucking sorry, Kor," he rasps.

Sorry? For what?

"Why are you apologizing? Unless you're the one who put something in my drink."

"Fuck no," he growls.

"Then why on earth are you acting like it?"

"Because I invited you out, and I didn't stop this from happening."

Sparks of annoyance flash, igniting into a smoldering flame. The whole self-flagellation thing really isn't cute, and I'll be damned if he gets to throw himself a pity party when *I'm* the one who actually got hurt.

"Yeah, no. We aren't doing this," I snap, waving my hand in front of him to make it perfectly clear what *this* is. "I don't want to hear apologies for things you had no control over. Especially not when you saved me. I don't remember much of what happened last night after we left Cutter's, but I do remember you watching over me, caring for me, and holding my hand when I was scared. So unless you want to apologize for that too, zip it."

His lips part, but he snaps them shut before he can spew the nonsense that was brewing. It's a good thing, too, because if he keeps going on like this, that tiny spark will grow into a raging inferno, and no one wants that.

He blinks as the torment fades from his face, and after another moment, he says, "Okay."

"Good," I huff, crossing my arms in front of my chest.

Sheepishness replaces the annoyance as the embers turn to ash. After everything he's done for me, I had to go and get snippy.

"I'm going to start a fresh batch." His mere mention of food has my stomach growling again. "If you want to shower or use the restroom, it's the room across from mine. Karis has some things here that you can use. I put them on the counter with a fresh towel."

Breakfast sounds great, but a shower would be even better. I mumble out "Thanks" and head back in the direction I came.

Like everything else in this apartment, the bathroom is cramped and dated, yet clean. The stack of toiletries is exactly where he said it would be, but it's more than some simple soaps and lotions. How often is she staying over to need all of this? Jealousy swarms in my chest. Even though Evelyn said there was nothing going on between Gage and his friend, the evidence here points in the other direction. There are more skincare products piled on the counter than I have back at my dorm, and it isn't the cheap stuff, either. Who keeps a collection like that at "just a friend's" house?

I crack open one of the bottles and take a deep sniff. The scent is nothing short of luxurious—rich and spicy in a way that's meant to seduce. This one bottle probably costs more than my entire self-care collection. A few extra minutes won't hurt. It's not like breakfast is ready yet, and he *did* say to use whatever I want.

Thirty minutes and eight products later, I'm feeling much more like myself. My head still hurts, but the pain has dulled to an ache that's easy to ignore. I slip his oversized clothes back on and head back to the kitchen, feeling like I've walked out of a spa.

Gage is leaning against the counter with his arms crossed, waiting for me to return. Two plates stacked high with pancakes sit next to him on the chipped linoleum. Maybe I could have done that a little faster, but his stoic face lacks condemnation. His eyes meet mine as I cross over the threshold, and the stony mask breaks as the corner of his lips twitches into a smile.

The look falters when I reach him, morphing into a pinched grimace that he quickly schools. But not quick enough I don't notice.

"What was that look?"

"It's nothing."

"Don't 'it's nothing' me."

"You smell like Karis. I don't like it," he says with a grimace.

He doesn't?

I'm not sure if I should be pleased or offended.

Before I can decide, he shakes away the expression and grabs his plate. "Come on. You need to eat."

"Thank you." I follow his lead and grab my plate.

My forehead pinches as I scan the space. There's no table, or even stools to eat at the counter. It's like no one ever eats in here at all. He sees my expression and grimaces before sitting on the dingy plaid couch. Springs fight to free themselves from the worn fabric, prodding my ass as I settle on the feeble cushion beside him.

"Normally, I just eat standing after I make something," he says and takes a bite.

"You cook?"

He shrugs and shovels another forkful into his mouth.

"Not well, but some things are hard to fuck up. Like pancakes from a bottle."

"And eggs," I say as I push the scrambled fluff into the pooling syrup before taking a bite myself.

"Please tell me you did not just dip your eggs in syrup."

"What? It's good."

He raises a disbelieving eyebrow before shaking his head with a huff.

"If you say so."

"Try it," I goad.

"I'm good."

"Please, for me." I flutter my lashes, giving him the most over-the-top pleading look I can muster.

"Fine," he sighs, then dips his eggs into the sugar-filled liquid. He only chews once before his face twists in disgust, but he powers through and swallows.

"That's awful," he says.

"Maybe you just have bad taste," I protest.

"Sure. If that's what you need to tell yourself, Low," he says with a hint of a teasing grin.

"Low?"

"Yeah, like Yellow." His gaze drops to his plate as the tips of his ears grow red.

Butterflies erupt at the unexpected nickname. They twist my tongue into a knot, leaving me completely lost for words. At least it's better than the alternative. I could get so nervous I ramble nonsense like I did during my first assignment in my public speaking class—

"Oh shit, what time is it?" I jerk upright in my seat as the reality of life beyond these walls crashes into me.

"Almost ten," he says without urgency.

"I'm late for class." I start to get up, but he stops me with a firm hand on my thigh.

"No, you're skipping your classes."

The sparks are back, and this time, the kindling is quick to catch fire. He's got some nerve trying to dictate my life.

"What the fuck, Gage. I could miss something important." I shove his hand away and hit him with a scorching glare.

He scoffs, ignoring my ire.

"Nothing is more important than your health. You were drugged last night. Classes can wait."

"I'm sorry, I don't remember putting you in charge."

"You put me in charge the moment you begged me to stay. Now eat."

My jaw twitches as I grind my teeth, but I don't push back further, or I might snap. Following instructions has never been my strong suit. When I was growing up, my parents called it oppositional defiance. They put me in therapy for it and everything. Over the years, I've gotten a better handle on it, and my therapist gave me plenty of coping exercises, but his bossy attitude is hitting all the wrong buttons.

"Yes, sir," I snip with saccharine cheer as I stab into my fluffy stack with the force of all my pent-up frustrations.

He stiffens beside me and breathes in deep through his nose. For several seconds, he sits there tense and unmoving except for his fingers digging into his leg.

"I'm teaching you self-defense," he says, breaking the tension.

"What?" The words make sense individually, but I can't process them together as one statement.

"You heard me. It wouldn't have changed anything about last night, but I don't want you going back out until you can protect yourself."

The nerve of this man is unending.

"I bet you didn't force Karis to do self-defense lessons so she could hang out with you."

"You're right, I didn't. But she has a brown belt in jiu-jitsu, a black belt in judo, and teaches self-defense seminars at the gym once a quarter. She works with Evelyn and James a few times a month too."

"So why isn't she the one who's going to teach me?" The question drips with my defiance.

"Is that what you want, Kori? Because if it is, I'll call her right now and get it scheduled."

His calm, ocean-gray eyes lock with my heated glare as he meets my challenge head-on. Our wills war against each other in a silent battle, but in the end, I'm the one who gives in first.

"No. I'd rather do it with you," I admit. "I have a condition, though."

"Hit me with it."

"I don't want to do it at the gym."

"Why not?" he asks.

"Well, for one, it smells like a locker room and bleach, but I'm also not good at that sort of thing. I don't want people watching me."

"What if we went when I could promise it was just us?"

That wouldn't be too bad...

"Fine," I concede.

"I'll text you to iron out the details. Now finish eating so I can take you home."

Yes, sir.

Chapter 12
Gage

Nathan's gloved fist comes hurtling toward my face. The move is telegraphed—which is a habit we've been trying to break—and I should be able to dodge it easily. "Should" being the operative word because my head isn't in it today. The bell over the front door rings, and for a split second, my attention is pulled from the drill. I'm not sure if I'm too slow in my recovery or if he's too quick to take advantage of it, but his fist catches the side of my ear. It's hardly even a hit, but he lets out an excited whoop as if he won a title fight.

"Butler! Focus!" Coach David calls out from the front of the mat.

"Sorry, Coach," Nathan says, but that self-satisfied grin doesn't fall from his face.

"Lucky hit. You telegraphed that shit from a mile away," I tell him, and we resume our sparing.

"Oh yeah? If it was so telegraphed, then why did you let it hit you?"

I respond by throwing a combo of my own, shifting us both to get him backed against the fence.

"He was too distracted. Probably thinking about Kori," Karis says as she corners her own opponent on the fence beside us and throws a nasty punch into his gut.

"Fuck no," I try to argue, but the mere mention of her name floods my mind with flashes from last night. My attention falters, and Nathan is able to free himself from the fence. "Holy shit." Nathan's smile widens to a full-on shit-eating grin. "She's right."

"Shut up," I growl, and put all my focus back into kicking his ass.

The problem is, Karis is only half right. Yes, Yellow is on my mind, but she's a bright spot in the chaotic sea. The Bean Bar fired me for not showing up this morning, which wasn't surprising. I knew what might happen when I chose to stay by her side. And my employment status at Cutter's is still unknown. My friends didn't give me any updates besides Nathan's ominous text claiming "everything's handled." Coming from him, that could mean literally anything from burning the bar down to paying off the witnesses.

"No one is judging, man. Go for it if you like her. If you don't, I just might. She's hot," he teases.

My teeth clench around my mouth guard, and I catch Nathan with a knee that has a little more force behind it than it should during training. He grunts in pain and is stunned long enough for me to move into his space. In a real fight, this is where I would take him to the ground, but I let him go and reset the drill.

"Leave her alone."

"I was joking. I know she's your girl."

"She isn't my anything."

"Yet."

"Butler! Maher! Less talking, more sparing," Coach yells, killing that cursed conversation.

My focus doesn't improve as our class continues. By the time Coach calls it to an end, I'm sweaty and even more frustrated than I was when I stepped on the mat.

"You still look fucked. Want to hit the weights and burn off some of that angst?" Karis asks as she falls in step at my side.

"Sure." Maybe the soreness will be the distraction I need.

Nathan follows us and steps up to spot me without a word. Neither one of them pushes me to talk while we work through reps, but their unasked questions buzz in the air like angry hornets. They only add to the building tension under my skin, begging to be unleashed. I go harder than I need to, trying to push those feelings away, but it's useless. By the time I call it quits, my muscles are jelly, but the crawling hasn't lessened.

"How's Kori holding up?" he finally asks as we move to pack up our shit.

"She's handling it better than I thought she would." *Better than me.* "She had more to say about my attitude than what happened. But that could be her way of coping."

"It's better than her having a breakdown," he says with a curt nod.

"Thank you for having my back last night, and hers."

"Don't sweat it, man. That's what friends are for."

I've had friends come and go over the years, and very few would have acted the way he did. For all his faults—and he has plenty—he's a good fucking friend. Karis and Morgan too. They are better than I deserve. He would laugh me off and give me shit for going sappy on him if I tried to tell him that, so I squeeze his shoulder once and let it drop.

"What about you? You good?" Karis asks.

"I'm fine," I lie. "Would be better if I knew if I still have a job."

"What kind of question is that? I told you everything was handled," Nathan says.

"That's not a lot to go on."

"Do you see the lack of trust, Kare Bear?" he tuts. "Your job is fine. Evelyn and James helped out behind the bar while Morgan did damage control with customers. Karis and I dealt with our would-be rapist, and he won't be causing any problems for you. In fact, I'd be surprised if you see him at Cutter's again. I took his ID too. So if your girl wants to open an investigation, we have his info."

That's...a lot—more than I was expecting.

Reality hits me all at once: we are okay. Somehow, we dodged every bullet the universe fired in our direction and made it through mostly unscathed. Manic laughter bubbles past my lips. The tension that's held my back stiff since I saw Yellow stumble out of that alcove snaps, and with it goes any will to stay on shaking limbs. I sink down to the mat, laughing like a lunatic as I let myself relax for the first time in weeks. My friends lock eyes, holding a silent argument while glancing at me with worry on their faces.

"You sure you're okay there?" Karis asks, then takes a tentative step toward me, hesitating like I've gone mad.

Who knows, I might have.

I wave off her concern and try to rein in the giddy relief.

"Thank you. Both of you."

"Yeah, yeah. We're the best. I know," she teases and plops down beside me.

"So when are you going to ask her out?" Nathan asks as he joins her.

Looks like we're back on this.

"I'm not," I tell him with a stern glare.

"Come on, man. We know you're into her."

"And?"

Denying it is hopeless. There's something about her I can't get out of my head—my sunflower has me tangled in her roots. But infatuation passes. Soon enough, someone worth her time will catch her attention, and she will forget all about me. She will be nothing more than a bright blip on the dark landscape of my life.

"And you should do something about it," he challenges.

"I'm no good for her."

"Bullshit," Karis interjects.

"I'm serious. She deserves a man who can take care of her."

"What do you call last night, then?" she asks.

She has a point. But my ability to take care of her physically was never in question, even if I failed to keep her safe.

"Financially," I amend.

"Don't do this, man." The sharp anger in Nathan's tone catches me off guard.

In one explosive movement, he stands and paces around the weight room. Each step vibrates with agitated energy.

"Do what?"

"This whole self-sabotage thing."

"I don't know what you're talking about."

My life is shitty enough without me sabotaging it.

He whirls around and pins me to the mat with a heated glare.

"Bullshit, man," he huffs. "You're acting like a fucking pussy, and you know it. For the first time in years, there's something good in your life, and that terrifies you. You have a shot at having some real happiness here, but your woe-is-me attitude can't deal with it. So you're going to let it slip through your fingers like you always do and blame it on karma or fate or whatever fucked-up bullshit you're using this week as a scapegoat to avoid personal responsibility."

A frustrated growl spills out as he kicks a stack of pads, knocking them into a scattered pile on the floor. I chance a glance at Karis, but from the smug look on her face, I'm on my own—and maybe this was a long time coming. Hell, it wouldn't be the first come-to-Jesus meeting we've held on these mats.

"Goddamnit, man. I'd kill to be in your shoes right now. I had my shot and ruined it, and I regret it every fucking day. So I'd be running, not walking, to make that woman mine if it meant I might have the chance at love like that again." My friend pauses, taking a few seconds to center himself with a deep inhale. When he speaks again, his words are more resigned than angry. "I'm sorry for getting snappy, man. It's just—"

"You miss Chelsea."

He swallows deeply and nods. "I don't want you to miss out on an opportunity to find love. They don't come around very often."

"Who said anything about love."

I'm still trying to figure out how to be Kori's friend.

"Call it what you want. A connection, maybe. I've been with enough women to know that spark is rare."

"Oh, we know about the women," Karis quips.

"Between you and Morgan, I've seen what heartbreak does. Do you really think it's worth pursuing something knowing it most likely won't last? I mean, just look at you. You're still hung up on the girl who broke your heart months ago. Wouldn't you be happier if you never took the chance in the first place?"

"Fuck no, man. I wouldn't trade a moment I had with her for anything."

"Cringe," Karis says as she stands and grabs her things. "I've got plans, but you two can sit around and talk about your feelings for as long as you need to."

"Plans with who?" Nathan asks. "We're right here. You don't have any other friends."

"I promised Evelyn I'd go volunteer with her. It's how I got her to join the gym."

"So I take it you won't be coming by Cutter's tonight?" I ask as she walks out of the room.

"Probably not, but that just means you and Nathan can spend more time braiding each other's hair."

In unison, we flip her off, and without looking at us, she responds in kind.

"Lover boy's right," she calls out before disappearing around the corner. "Ask her out."

Great. With my luck, Morgan will start in on this next time I see him too. As annoying as it should be, I know it's because they care far more than they should.

"Come on," I say as I stand, "we have time to get a few miles in before I have to leave."

"Drinks on you tonight?" he asks with a cheeky grin and hops on a treadmill.

"Aren't they always?"

I jump on the machine beside him, set the speed higher than is comfortable, and run until my body is exhausted and quivering. It's a stupid move—my bad knee is going to punish me for it tomorrow—but at least for those few blissful minutes, my mind is at peace.

Chapter 13
Kori

There isn't a single car in Double Teep's parking lot. Gage assured me we would have the place to ourselves since the gym isn't open on Sunday, but I was under the assumption he would still be here. The whole self-defense lesson thing hinges on it.

Hey, I'm here.

Perfect. Be right out.

A few seconds later, the door opens up, and he steps out onto the small stoop. The sun glistens off the sheen of sweat coating his skin. God, he looks absolutely lickable. His posture straightens as his gaze lands on my car, and he heads in my direction, moving with a slight limp that definitely wasn't there a few days ago.

"Hey, Kor—" he starts to say, but I cut him off.

"Are you okay?"

"It's just an old injury acting up. I went a little too hard the other day, and I'm paying for it now. I'll be fine, though. I'm used to it," he says with a grimace.

"Shouldn't you be resting it or icing it or something?"

I'm not pre-med or anything, but I know continuing to push an injury is a recipe for disaster.

"It's not the worst it's ever been," he says with a shrug.

"Are you sure? We can reschedule today if you need to—"

"I'm fine. I promise if I thought I needed to, I would rest it."

"Fine. I guess you know your body better than I do."

"How are you? Still feeling sick?" He scans me over as if he might find the answer to his question there.

"I'm good. No lingering effects at all."

"And you've been sleeping?"

"If that's your way of trying to subtly ask if I'm traumatized, the answer is no. I've been sleeping like a baby. No nightmares. No anxiety."

But plenty of dreams about him—the type that wakes me up hot and desperate with need. And now he's here in front of me, even sexier and more unobtainable than in my fantasies. But thinking about him like that has heat rising in my cheeks.

"Good."

"So exercise..." I can't meet his eyes as I change the topic.

"Sure. If that's what you want to call it," he says with a chuckle and leads me inside.

The gym is less awful when it's empty. There's no cloud of humid sweat to choke on, and the stench of bleach is nothing more than the faintest hint. It's quieter, too, almost eerily so. If the warehouse was any bigger, it would be straight up ominous.

If it bothers Gage, he doesn't show it. He slips off his shoes and steps onto the mat, then waits for me to join him.

"All right, today we are going to focus on the basics," he calls out once I do.

The words are louder than I expect—like a drill sergeant calling their troops to order. My spine stiffens, and a spark of electric tingles cascades through me.

"We're going to start you with a warm-up, and I'm going to use that to assess your current level of fitness. After that, we are going to focus on awareness and assertiveness. We will see how you're feeling after that and go from there. Any questions?"

"No, sir." I don't recognize the breathy tone of my voice.

"It's Coach, not sir," he barks out. "Understood?"

A fresh wave of tingles courses through me. Why is this whole commanding thing so freaking hot? I'm used to him being bossy, but this is on a different level, and I think I like it. Self-assured is a good look on him.

"Yes, Coach," I rasp in that same alien way.

"Start with skips around the mat," he says and turns away from me.

I spring into action, hating myself with each second that goes by. It fucking sucks, and things only get worse with every sharp order he issues. The torture is endless. Finally, an eternity later, he calls for me to stop, and I drop to the mat in a heap of sweat and exhausted limbs.

He doesn't remark on my pathetic display of athleticism. The plodding of his feet against the mat is the only sound other than my ragged breathing. His large frame moves past my peripheral vision toward the lobby. After a few seconds, he returns and sits beside me, then cracks open a bottle of water and hands it to me. I sit up and snatch it from him, guzzling it down like whatever the opposite of a rabid animal is. Stray drops dribble down my chin, dripping onto my shirt. Once the bottle is drained, I set it to the side and wipe away the mess.

I look up and find Gage's attention glued to my lips. His face is locked in a stony mask, but his eyes are intense. My face flushes as my chest cracks and caves in on itself. How I would love to curl up inside of it and hide from his scrutiny. I didn't think he would judge me *this* hard.

He coughs to clear his throat and says, "You should carry a water bottle with you. Hydration is important."

"Yes, Coach," I say with a sarcastic eye roll.

"I'm serious. I don't want you passing out on the mats."

"What? Too much paperwork?" I tease.

"I don't care about paperwork. We make Morgan do all that." The stony mask cracks as a smile plays at the corner of his lips. "You ready to keep going?"

"Keep going? You mean there's more?" I whine.

"That was the warm-up."

With a groan, I sprawl back on the mat, slinging an arm over my face. If I can't see him, he can't see me and can't make me do any more physical activity.

"I quit. I'm going home to play video games. This was the second worst idea I've had all week."

"Come on, now, it's not so bad. The worst of it is over."

"That's easy for you to say when you look like that." I sit back up and wave my hand in front of his body.

He is pure fucking sex.

The worn Double Teep T-shirt pulls tight against his chest, and his arms fight against the restrictive sleeves. By no means is he the bulkiest guy I've ever seen, or the guy with the most defined muscles, but he isn't small either. My mouth waters at the thought of what might be hidden underneath the confines of his clothes. I have a feeling my dreams haven't done him justice.

"I've been training for years," he says with a shrug. "We will get you there eventually. But if it makes you feel any better, today is going to be more educational than physical."

"So no more jumping?"

"No more jumping," he assures me with a smile, and in a blink, the soft look is gone and his "coach face" makes another appearance. "First things first, being aware of your surroundings can help prevent you from needing to defend yourself in the first place..."

He falls into a well-rehearsed lecture, and I listen with rapt attention. Most of it is common sense or things my mom used to tell me when I was growing up, like "don't wear headphones when walking by yourself" and "stay off your phone, especially at night." Regardless, I hang on to his every word. His voice is hypnotic; he could tell me I needed to wear roller skates and sing the alphabet backward in order to stay safe, and I would do it. That has to be why he hardly ever talks—he knows his own power.

"Any questions?" he asks, and I shake my head no. "Good. The next thing I want to cover is being assertive. Being loud and bringing attention to the situation is often enough to get someone to back off and get the attention of people who can help.”

Right, the exact opposite of what happened the other night.

“How do we practice that?”

“Stand up.”

Looks like we are doing the physical thing again.

As much as I don’t want to, I drag myself back to my feet.

“We are going to have to do a bit of role-play here. To demonstrate, I need you to be the attacker. Start to approach me, and I’ll show you what you need to do.”

I do as he says, and as I close in, he puts his hands out in front of him and shouts, “Stop. Don’t come any closer.”

I freeze.

“The important thing to remember is to not give them your back, force distance by keeping your arms between you, and be loud.”

“Sure, that might work for you, but I doubt my shouting is going to scare anyone away.”

“Maybe not. But it might get someone’s attention or make them pause. Now I’m going to approach you, and I want you to do exactly what I did, okay?”

I nod, and he starts his pursuit, slowly circling me as he inches closer. My arms go out in front of me like he instructed, but the shout lodges in my throat.

“Come on, Kori. Yell at me,” he snaps.

“Don’t come any closer...” The words are nothing more than a mousy whisper.

“You can do better than that. Get angry.”

“Stay away from me,” I try again. My voice is steadier but still lacks force.

“Again,” he growls. “It’s like you aren’t even trying.”

The condescension lacing his words causes my hackles to rise and annoyance to bubble and churn. This was his idea. It’s not my fault I’m awful at it.

"I'm trying," I growl right back, but my anger is no more intimidating than a mewling kitten.

"Oh yeah?" he challenges. "That isn't what it looks like to me. From where I'm standing, it looks like you're too scared."

"Fuck you, Gage," I snap.

"That's it, Low. Curse me out if you have to. Be mad."

He starts circling me again, going back to the goddamn game and goddamn so-called training. I'm over it. Done.

"Get the fuck away from me, asshole." This time, the shout falls past my lips with ease.

He stills for a second, and my gut clenches in anticipation of his anger, but it never comes. A larger smile than I've ever seen forms on his lips, and my core clenches for another reason entirely.

"That's my girl," he says with a proud grin.

His girl? That's news to me, but I don't hate the sentiment.

"I want to see that every time. And if someone is stupid enough to try to fuck with you again, you unleash all that rage. Got it?"

"Yes, Coach."

"Good. Let's do it again."

My throat is raw by the time he decides we've done enough for the day, but half an hour of yelling will do that. Surprisingly enough, I actually had fun. Although I think that had more to do with Gage than the activity itself.

"You did good today," he says as we walk out the door.

Even after hearing it repeated all day, my chest still grows warm from the compliment. Every time we finished a rep, he showered me with praise. I think I could have walked in a straight line and he would have told me I was doing amazing.

"We didn't actually do that much defending. I thought you were going to teach me how to kick someone's ass."

"Unless you are willing to commit to practicing it, all that would do is instill you with a false sense of confidence, and that's how you end up getting hurt."

"And if I was willing to commit?"

"I'm more than happy to keep working with you if that is what you're asking. Next time we can start working on some basic escapes."

"Next time being..."

"The bar isn't open on Sunday, so this time works well for me. Is next week good for you?"

"It's perfect."

He's perfect.

What I felt before was barely embers compared to the raging inferno that *Coach Gage* ignites. On the mats, he sheds that broody shell of his and becomes this confident force to be reckoned with. I can't help but imagine where else he might let this version of himself shine. My dreams are going to go in a whole different direction.

"Are you going to the game night thing tonight?" I ask as I try to push away the invasive thoughts.

This isn't the time or place for me to be thirsting after him.

"At Morgan's place?"

"I think so? Evelyn just sent the address." I pull out my phone and show him the text.

"Yeah, that's it," he confirms. "I'll be there. Are you thinking about coming?"

"Maybe, I'm not sure. Should I?"

Is it really an invitation if it only comes from one person? The rest of the group might not even know she offered. What if I show up and ruin their fun...again? She could have only asked to be polite, or maybe out of pity. They all might think I'm a stage-five clinger if I show up there. I shouldn't go. I won't go. Playing *Monster Hunter* by myself will be just as fun.

"I'd like it if you came." The soft words snap me out of the death spiral of thoughts plaguing my mind.

"Really?" I squeak.

"Of course. It will be fun, and the others have been asking about you."

They have...?

Fuck it. Making friends has been my whole mission, and it's staring me in the mouth. I'd be a fool not to take it—or at least a coward.

"Then I guess I'm in."

"Good. I'll see you then."

With an awkward wave, he turns and walks toward the road.

"Where are you going," I call out.

"Home."

"On foot?"

"It's only a few miles."

"There aren't even sidewalks out here. Let me give you a ride. It's the least I can do to pay you back for today."

He hesitates for a moment before he relents.

"You don't need to pay me back, so that isn't what this is, but I'm not too proud to accept the ride."

He doesn't say anything else as he climbs into the passenger seat. The ceiling of my sedan is so low he has to bend his neck to fit, but he doesn't complain. I toss him my phone to plug his address into my GPS and shift the car into drive.

"Do you walk everywhere?" I ask once we get onto the main road.

"Feels like it right now. My car is fucked, and I haven't had a chance to fix it."

"You're good with cars?"

"Nope. Karis is, though. She told me what's wrong with it, but it all sounded like gibberish to me. Once she finds a good deal on the parts she needs, she will try her best to repair it. We just haven't had luck there."

"That sucks."

"Yeah, but I can't do much about it now but wait."

Guilt claws at my throat. How much time did he spend walking here this morning to help me? We didn't even do anything. I just yelled at him for hours.

The lump in my throat makes it too hard to speak. I turn up the radio, letting the cheerful pop hits fill the silence instead.

He doesn't move as I put the car into park outside his unit. The air between us practically vibrates in anticipation—the question is, anticipation of what? His stare locks on my face again, sharpening with that same intensity from earlier. My mouth waters as a flash of heat sparks in my core.

This is when he kisses me, right?

That's what always happens in the movies in situations like this.

My tongue darts out, wetting my lips, and he pinches his eyes shut. He takes a deep breath, and when his lashes open, his gaze is fixed on something on the other side of the windshield.

"Thank you for the ride," he says before climbing out of the car, and he doesn't look back as he limps up the old wooden steps to his door.

Bitter disappointment washes through me, followed by a wave of embarrassment. He isn't into me like that, and he never will be. I need to make peace with the fact all I'll ever get from him is friendship. It's what I wanted to begin with, and it will have to be enough. It's for the best anyway. Relationships kill friend groups. I'm not sure it would be worth the risk to pressure something with Gage, only to lose this new group of friends if it doesn't work out.

Resolve fills me as I pull out of his complex. No matter what happens, things between us will stay platonic, even if my heart is begging for more.

Chapter 14
Kori

Loud shouts and intense banter bleed into the hallway. If I wasn't sure which unit was James and Morgan's, I would be now. The words are muffled, but it's clear things are getting heated. It's probably nonsense anyway; from what I saw the other night, I think bickering is their love language. At least that diverts attention away from me.

I swallow against my growing nerves and knock before I can back out. The bickering inside stops, and after a few seconds of silence, the door opens.

"Kori, glad you could make it." Morgan's face is flushed, and his frazzled eyes dart between me and the scene behind him even as he greets me.

It's a Renaissance painting come to life. Karis and Nathan are frozen in place in a heap on the floor. His head is trapped between her legs, and she's reaching for something he's holding in the air above her. James watches it all from a perch on the back of the couch, and Evelyn is sprawled on the cushions, cuddling with a huge German shepherd.

The only person not actively involved in their chaos is Gage, which isn't surprising, considering he seems to be the referee for their shenanigans. He's a few feet behind our host, leaning against the kitchen island, and unlike his friend, his attention is fully locked on me. A ball of glowing heat forms under the intensity of his gaze. Dragging my eyes away from him takes physical effort, leaving me with the same type of breathlessness I felt after the brutal warm-up he inflicted on me this morning.

"Looks like I missed out on the fun," I say, ignoring the pounding in my chest.

Nathan glances in my direction, and Karis takes advantage of his distraction to roll him to his back and yank whatever he's holding out of his hand.

"New girl, you made it," Karis cheers as she pops up off the floor with the grace of a cat.

With that, the room comes to life again. James shoos the dog off the couch and drops onto one of the plush seats beside her friend, Karis claims the spot on Evelyn's other side, and Morgan moves to join his girlfriend, leaving me standing uncomfortably in the doorway.

Gage gives me a half smile and beckons me inside with a tilt of his head. That look sends my heart into a fluttering tailspin. That bitch is out of control. We *just* decided we weren't going to do this anymore.

"Welcome to the nuthouse," he says as I join him near the kitchen. "If at any point you decide you've had enough, blink twice and I'll get you out of here."

"Stop trying to scare her away. We promised we would be on our best behavior," Nathan says as he pulls himself off the floor and heads in our direction.

"If what I walked in on is your best behavior, I'm scared to see what bad looks like," I tease.

I'm not sure where the boldness came from. It probably has something to do with spending my afternoon being forced out of my comfort zone. Gage snorts, and his playful friend shoots me a mischievous grin and a wink. As he moves closer, those playful features disappear, and his eyes make a quick pass over my body in the same assessing way Gage's did this morning. Whatever he finds must be satisfactory, because he lets out a deep breath and his smile returns, softer than before.

"I'm really glad you could make it," he says as he pulls me into a one-armed hug.

I stiffen under the unexpected contact, but it doesn't last long. His arm is jerked away from me, and Gage is there, glaring at his friend.

"Hands off," he growls.

"Sorry. My bad. Don't need to go all caveman on me, man."

"I'm not super big on touch," I tell him with a grimace.

"Noted. Won't happen again. Sentiment stands, though. It's good to see you again."

I give him an awkward smile and inch closer to Gage. How do you even respond to something like that? Say thank you? You too? Is this one of those drive-thru situations where the cashier says "Enjoy your meal" and then I say "Thanks, you too," and then we both look at each other awkwardly until I drive away? Because that's what it feels like. Thankfully, Evelyn, being the saint she is, cuts in before I make a fool of myself.

"What are we playing tonight?" she asks in a soft voice.

"I won back at Cutter's, so technically, it's my pick, but I think Kori should get to choose," James says.

"Pick Risk," Nathan says with a smirk.

A pillow flies across the room and smacks into his face as he turns back toward the couch. James lets out an excited cackle as the weapon finds its mark. Morgan shakes his head, but there's nothing but pure adoration on his face.

She turns her attention to me and, with a syrupy-sweet southern draw, says, "Pick anything *but* Risk."

"Or Scrabble," Karis adds in.

"Ignore them." Gage's voice rumbles in my ear.

Fuck me, I didn't realize how close he had gotten. It's insane how quietly a man his size can move.

His hand drops to hover against my back, not quite touching but close enough that my skin tingles with awareness, and he guides me over to a bookcase filled with games.

"Pick from this shelf." He points to the one with the least number of boxes.

"What's wrong with those?" I gesture to the shelf below it that's overflowing.

"Those are either broken or banned."

"Banned? Why?"

"Between James, Karis, and Nathan, things can get...intense."

"But Twister?" I ask.

"Morgan pulled a muscle."

"Monopoly?"

"Karis and James held us hostage until well after 2 a.m. while they battled it out."

"That weird Arkham game?"

"Too many rules. We never even played that one."

"Okay, that all makes sense, but what about Hungry Hungry Hippos?"

That one brings a visible cringe to Gage's stony face.

"That's why it became the 'broken and banned' shelf. Karis got too into it and broke the handle off her hippo. That plastic was wicked sharp and cut her hand pretty bad. I spent the rest of that night with her in the ER of St. Mary's while she got it stitched up."

"She's lucky to have a friend like you," I tell him, but that bit of information isn't the least bit surprising. Not after the way he took care of me.

"I'm the lucky one. I don't think I'd be here right now if I didn't have her to talk me off the ledge when things get bad." A dark cloud rolls in, overtaking his features and twisting them with stormy despair. The change is brief. As quickly as it came, the cloud is blown away by a sharp gust of wind, leaving a stoic, empty look in its place.

"She can be a real pain in my ass, though," he says with an awkward chuckle that doesn't lighten the load of his confession.

As much as I want to know more, this isn't the time or place to push the issue.

There are too many options, so I grab our hostess's pick and take Pictionary back to the group.

"Oh, you guys are so going down," James says with glee when she sees the box in my hand.

"If you are so confident, we get Kori, then," Karis says.

"Get Kori for what?" I ask.

"Our team. James, Morgan, and Evelyn vs. me, Gage, Nathan, and now you."

"Oh."

"Does this mean I can bring Sophie next time to even out the teams?" Nathan asks.

"Who?" Morgan asks.

"The girl I've been seeing."

"Fuck no," Karis interjects. "And don't pretend it won't be a different chick by the time we do this again."

"Yes, you can bring a date," James says, glaring at Karis. "It will even out the teams, and I don't want y'all trying to dispute your losses due to 'fairness.'"

Nathan and Karis continue to bicker as James removes herself from Morgan's hold and retrieves a large pad of paper and an easel from somewhere down the hall.

"Dang, they take this seriously," I murmur mostly to myself.

"Yes, they do," Gage says, materializing behind me again—this time with two kitchen chairs in tow. "And James is an artist, so we are almost certainly going to get our asses kicked."

He sets the seats down across from the others, with only a short few inches between them, and settles on a chair, arms crossed in front of his chest in a way that makes the thick bands of muscles in his forearms pop. My mouth goes dry at the sight. Goddamn, this man is on another level.

"Do you need something?" Gage asks, and I jerk my gaze away from him and drop it to the floor.

"Um...No...I'm sorry." If the ground could open and swallow me now, that would be great.

"You sure? Not even a water? James normally offers. I think we threw her off her game."

Oh.

The snare that wrapped itself around my lungs loosens. That was an actual question, not some dig at me checking him out.

"Water would be nice, actually," I tell him with a tentative smile.

He makes a sound of acknowledgment and goes into the kitchen to get me a drink. When he returns, he puts the glass of ice water on a coaster on the coffee table and sprawls out in the chair beside me. His knee brushes against mine, and my body jolts as if I was a marionette whose strings were pulled tight by some unseen puppeteer. Gage's touch is gone in an instant, and his attention tilts in my direction. The smallest hint of a frown playing at the corners of his lips.

I want to say something. Tell him he merely shocked me and that *his* touch was more than welcomed, but I don't get a chance before Karis's voice cuts through the air.

"So who's up first?"

***

"How the fuck is that supposed to be a toothbrush," Karis shouts at Nathan as another round passes without our team scoring any points.

"What do you mean? That part is a tooth, and this is a brush," he shouts back as he gestures to the unintelligible scribbles as if that would give them any sort of shape.

The game descended into chaos the second James flipped the timer and started on her first drawing. I thought Pictionary was played one team at a time, but based on the way Karis, Nathan, and James have hurled trash talk at the others and actively tried to sabotage their drawings, it's clear they aren't playing by the written rules. Gage was right about James being good at this, though. We never stood a chance, even with the "advantage" of having an extra member on our team. James is pretty much the Van Gogh of the game. Nathan, on the other hand, is the Picasso, and I doubt Picasso was good Pictionary.

"It looks like an ass getting spanked by a spiked paddle," Karis snaps.

If I squint, I can see it.

"Why would 'Spank' be in the Pictionary deck? Or 'Ass'? James said no when I offered to buy Pictionary After Dark," Nathan fires back.

"I don't fucking know, but that's what it looks like."

"You come draw if you think you can do better."

"Enough, both of you. Or I'm adding Pictionary to the banned-games shelf," Gage cuts in.

Hello, Coach Gage.

The sudden surge of emotion in his voice—the authority behind it—sends a shiver all the way to my core. He doesn't need to yell. The sharp command carries over their bickering, rendering them both silent.

"Not Pictionary. It's my favorite," James whines.

"Take it up with dumb and dumber," Gage tells her. "But it's going in time out."

"Fine," she sighs. "Y'all want to play something else or call it for the night?"

I check the time and wince. It's not *too* late, but late enough that getting up for class tomorrow is going to suck. I'm not sure what the rest of their schedules look like. Tonight has been fun—way more fun than going out to the bar was—and I don't want to be the one who ends it.

"I've got an early class tomorrow, so I say we call it," Evelyn says, unknowingly saving me from my own internal war.

A couple of the others mumble similar sentiments and begin cleaning up the area around them. I stand to help, but Gage grabs the chair he brought me and puts it away, not leaving me much to do. They all move around each other so seamlessly, like this is something they do all the time, and I don't know what to do. I'm just sort of here, an outsider looking in. I drift over toward one of the walls to get out of their way.

"Did you have fun?" Evelyn asks as she joins me on the edge of the room.

"It was great." They are great. Together, they have found the thing I've been searching for—friendship that feels like family.

"Good. You should come around again, then."

Emotions lodge themselves in my throat, and my hopes fly higher than they have any right to. I know a vague invitation to hang out again doesn't mean much—people hand those out all the time with the messed-up notion that it's somehow polite. But I don't think she means it that way. I wouldn't be here now if that was something she did. Although that could be my naive hope talking. I want her to mean it. I want to belong.

"I'd like that," I tell her and turn my attention to the group. "Thank you for having me. It's been fun."

I give them an awkward wave and start toward the door.

"Wait, let me walk you to your car," Gage says and starts moving.

"Oh, I didn't drive." I stop him before he gets more than a few steps in my direction.

"You're walking?" He spits the question like it personally offended him.

"My dorm isn't too far."

"It's dark."

I can't help but roll my eyes at that. Based on his tone, "it's dark" is Gage for "there's no way in hell you're walking," but I could be wrong. I'm still learning how to speak his language. I guess we're back to this him-making-decisions-for-me bullshit again.

"So? I used to walk around Atlanta later than this. Athens is nothing compared to that," I argue, and the muscles in his jaw tighten.

"At least let me walk with you. Please."

The "please" almost gets to me. I'm about to agree, but Karis interrupts me before I can.

"And how are you getting home, then? Because in case you forgot, I'm your ride. Evelyn walks home alone all the time, and you never say shit about that."

"It's different," Gage growls.

"The fuck it is. Kori is a grown woman. The last thing she needs is your overbearing ass trying to tell her what to do," Karis snaps back.

It's only then I realize how quiet the apartment has gotten. Everyone is staring at Gage and Karis with a wide range of expressions: Evelyn and James with concern, Morgan with confusion, and Nathan looks amused at the whole situation.

"Where do you live?" Evelyn's soft, almost melodic voice cuts through the tension.

"Rutherford."

"I'm next door in Myers. I can walk with you if you want," she offers.

"Is that to your satisfaction?" Karis asks Gage with a mocking sneer.

Gage huffs, which I assume is his way of relenting. I don't get him. He barely said a word once the game started, but then gets all growly when I want to walk home alone. From how Karis is acting, this isn't normal behavior for him either.

"Sure. That sounds good. Ready to go now?" I ask.

Evelyn nods, and I grab my stuff to follow her.

"Thank you again for having me," I tell James before I walk out the door.

Evelyn stays silent as we step out into the humid night air. The tension from inside follows us even as we make it back onto campus.

"Okay, spill," she says when she can't hold back any longer.

"Spill what?"

"What's going on between you and Gage?"

"Nothing?"

It shouldn't be that hard to believe we are friends.

"You can't tell me what happened in there was nothing."

"What do you mean?"

Talking? That's nothing unusual. Hell, I'm talking to her now. Isn't that what people do with their friends?

"How could you not see it? The longing glances, the getting close without touching," she gushes. "I think that's the most I've ever heard him talk. Normally, it's just one-word answers or those annoying grunts."

"Oh. He does grunt a lot," I say with a laugh, "and huff."

"How could I forget the huffs? He's all 'Me too manly for word. Man no need word. Word bad.'" Evelyn does her best caveman impression, which has us both bursting into a fit of laughter.

"Have you known them long?" I ask.

"About a year now. But I've been friends with Jamie longer. I met the rest through Morgan, and our other friend Chelsea dated Nathan for a while, so our groups sort of merged. She graduated last spring, though."

The rest of the walk passes by with comfortable small talk. That should be an oxymoron, but somehow with her, the words flow easily. All thoughts of Gage slip from my mind as we talk. Yes, I might have a crush on him, but crushes are fleeting. Friendship—especially from a group like this one—is far more valuable. In the most convoluted way imaginable, I somehow stumbled upon exactly what I was after.

I manage to stick to my convictions for a whole forty-five minutes before he goes and ruins it.

> Did you get home safe?

My heart ramps up to one hundred miles a minute as I read and reread the text. It *still* hasn't gotten on board with this whole only-friends program.

> I did.

> Good.

The "typing" pop-up appears before I can respond, flashing in and out of existence several times before disappearing altogether. With each repetition, the fluttering in my chest dwindles into disappointment.

Dejected, I toss my phone on my side table and get ready for bed. But the notification waiting for me when I'm done spurs those feelings to life again.

> I'm glad you came tonight.

I fight the urge to kick my legs and squeal like a girl from an early-2000s teen movie. It's a stupid reaction to have because of a text from a friend. A completely platonic, hot-as-sin friend.

I'm glad I could make it.

Get some sleep.

Yes, Coach.

I'll see you next Sunday.

Bring water.

I roll my eyes and put my phone away for the night. No matter how hard I try, I can't keep the giddy smile off my face as I drift to sleep.

Chapter 15
Gage

K ori's late.

Twenty-three minutes late, to be exact—not that I'm counting.

Who am I trying to fool? Of course I'm counting. With every minute that's ticked by, the barbed grip on my lungs has grown tighter. I'm surprised my feet haven't worn a path in the floor from how many times I've paced the perimeter of the mats.

She hasn't even responded to my text checking in. Logically, I know that means she's probably driving or doesn't have her phone on her, but the gloom can smell my worry and is using those seeds to plant worst-case scenarios in my head.

As I turn to restart the path, the bell over the door rings out through the air. My whole body whips around to the source of the sound, and all my tension melts away at the sight of Yellow dressed in her normal vibrant hues. The matching set looks good on her, and the tight spandex doesn't leave much to the imagination.

She gives me a sheepish smile and lets the door fall shut behind her.

"Sorry I'm late," she says as she drops her things on a bench in her rush to the mat.

"Is everything all right?"

"Yeah." She bites on her bottom lip as she grimaces, drawing my gaze straight to her mouth. "I got distracted and lost track of time."

"And you didn't think to text?" The question comes out tinged with annoyance.

She shrugs and drops her eyes to the mat.

"Phone's dead. It's the main reason time got away from me. I didn't have my alarms to remind me, and by the time I noticed, I didn't have time to charge it."

"Aren't kids your age supposed to be glued to their phones," I tease.

"I'm not a kid," she huffs.

Don't I know it. My cock has been half hard from the moment she walked through the door.

"That doesn't mean you aren't attached to your phone."

"I take offense to that," she snaps, placing her hands on her hips for extra emphasis.

Her sass does nothing to help the situation in my pants. If anything, I think I like her feisty *almost* as much as I like it when she calls me coach. The breathy way she says those words goes straight to my dick every time, and it plays on repeat in my head whenever I let my mind wander. Hell, I've heard it in my fucking dreams.

Goddamnit, this is not the time for that. I'm not even into the whole submissive thing, but something about those words coming from *her* lips in *that* voice makes me question that. I should not be questioning that, though. Not here. Not with her.

"Do you really think you can pigeonhole me in with everyone else my age? I'm wired too wrong for that." She continues on, unaware of my internal battle.

"No, you're right. You are something special."

"Are we going to do this self-defense thing or what?" she grumbles, looking anywhere but at me.

"If that's what you want. Go ahead and give me five laps around the mat." The words come out harsher than I mean them too.

She follows my orders without complaint—not even a grumble under her breath—even though I know I sound like an ass. There's a difference between authoritative and angry, and I'm blurring the line. She doesn't deserve that from me; she isn't the one who's done anything wrong. I'm the one I'm frustrated at. I'm the coach, and I should be able to control my reactions to her better. These thoughts and this setting don't mix.

I use the warm-up time to get my body back in control. Thankfully, my dick stops acting like an asshole when I refocus on the task at hand. By the end of the ten-minute warm-up routine we normally run the fundamentals classes through, Kori is panting and drenched in sweat.

"Okay, I take that back. Go back to making fun of me for being a kid. That was way less torturous than this." She braces her hands on her thighs, but this time, she doesn't end up on the floor.

We take improvement where we can get it.

"That was good."

"It didn't feel like it."

"Grab some water, and we can get started for real."

"What's on the agenda today, *Coach*?"

She looks my body over with heat sparkling in her eyes. I get this type of look from both women and men alike when I'm at Cutter's, and normally the brazenly lusty gazes do nothing more than make the skin on the back of my neck crawl. From Yellow, though, the look sets my skin alight in a different way.

My body shouldn't be reacting to her like this; it's wrong. She's trusting me to be her coach, goddamnit, and I'm taking that trust, chewing it up, and spitting it in her face by thinking of her like that. I'm the authority here; it's my responsibility to enforce these lines. This isn't the first time a student has expressed interest in me. But it *is* the first time I feel something in return.

It's the first time I've felt anything in a long time.

As much as I hate to admit it, Kori is a beautiful woman. This goes beyond that, though. There are millions of beautiful women in the world, and they don't all get my cock hard with only a few breathy words. Yellow is different. I want to get to know her beyond that, and that alone is enough for me to know

I need to keep my distance. She doesn't need someone like me in her life—not when she has so much potential ahead of her. All I would do is hold her back.

She bites on the inside of her lip in a way that should be criminal as her eyes continue to climb toward my face. I don't flinch when her gaze meets mine; Kori does, though. Her brows jump almost comically on her forehead, and those wide eyes of hers drop to the mat.

"That's up to you." I cough to clear away the raspy edge clinging to my words. "We can keep practicing assertiveness or move on to something more physical. I know you don't like to be touched, so the choice is yours."

"We can get physical," she says, and starts to sing off-key as she dances around the mat.

"Was that an '80s music reference?" I ask, still caught off guard by her display.

She stills, her face going completely blank.

"I figured it would be easier if I spoke in terms from your era," she says with a solemn nod.

It takes a moment for the teasing to register. Her sincere mask is too good. It's only when a smile turns the corner of her lips, breaking the facade, that it hits me.

"I'm old, but I'm not that old," I say with a bark of laughter. "But that was probably deserved."

"Probably," she scoffs with a playful eye roll.

"Okay, I definitely deserved it."

"That's more like it." Her smile breaks through completely as she sasses me.

Like a fucking sharpshooter, that look pierces straight into my chest, making my heart ache in a way that isn't actually unpleasant. I cough away the feeling and focus on the wall over her head. There is no way I'll be able to get through today otherwise.

"Do you have any experience with self-defense outside of our lesson last week?" I take the topic back to the reason we're here. Maybe, if luck desires to be kind, we can get through this without me making a fool of myself.

She shakes her head no, which is exactly what I assumed. That's good. I won't have to unteach bad habits like I've had to do with others.

"In that case, we are going to focus on two things today. Simple strikes and basic escapes."

Slipping into coach mode is like putting on a leather boot that has been properly broken in; it feels so natural that I sometimes wonder if this is the state I was meant to be in. Kori's demeanor shifts with the change. The spark of mischief leaves her eyes as her spine straightens, and she watches me with rapt attention, clinging to every word.

"The most important thing to remember is that fighting should be your last resort. Prevention is key in keeping yourself safe, and that starts with your awareness, but we went over that last time. If the situation does require you to fight back, I'm going to make sure you have every tool possible at your disposal. Let's start with a jab."

I demonstrate the simple punch and correct her posture as she tries to mirror my motion. A spark of pride shimmers in my chest when she doesn't tuck her thumb like I've seen so many novices do.

"Very good. Now drop your shoulder a little." I run my hand along the tense muscle, easing it into the right form.

Her exposed skin pebbles under my fingers as a small quiver runs through her. Goddamnit. I should have asked her to wear a T-shirt today. The thick straps of her tank top don't cover nearly enough skin. How am I supposed to focus on teaching when she reacts like this every time I get close? Not that I'm any better. Every fucking interaction adds sparks to the already electric air. There has to be a breaking point eventually; static can only build so long before it has to discharge.

After she gets comfortable with the movement, I grab a set of pads so she can practice on the real thing. I hope she never has to use what she's learned, because some of the kids in my toddler class hit harder than her...and have more coordination.

"That was great," I tell her, and she beams. "In the moment, striking with the heel of your hand may be a better option, but we will focus on that next time. If you do have to hit someone, do you know where you should target?"

"Their groin?"

"That's right. Along with their eyes, nose, or throat. Sometimes your hands might be restrained—like if they grab you in a bear hug—and you won't be able to punch your way out of it. Normally, I would demonstrate with a partner, but it's just us. Stand behind me and grab me."

Her hands barely close around the width of my arms and chest.

"Like this?" she breathes against my shoulder blades.

"Perfect. Now watch what I do."

I walk her through the maneuver several times before we swap places. My arms have no difficulty wrapping around her frame, and the scent of soft citrus fills my senses. How can she still smell so sweet after everything I've put her through today? She stiffens for a split second before she relaxes into me. Heat radiates from her body, seeping into mine as her ass brushes against my crotch. That subtle motion—intentional or not—brings back that prickling sense of awareness to every one of my nerves as my cock stirs in my pants again.

It looks like Yellow isn't the only one getting an exercise today. Goddamn, I feel like a high schooler with his first crush.

"You are supposed to try and escape," I rasp into her ear when she doesn't start the rep.

"Oh. Right," she says and starts to wiggle in my arms.

Even without resistance, she struggles to free herself from my grasp without much success. It's like everything I told her to do went in one ear and out the other. The only reason she escapes is her writhing makes my cock harder—painfully so—and I let her go before she notices my body's mutiny.

"Did I do it?" she asks with a smile on her lips.

"Not exactly," I tell her and try to will my dick back into submission. "Let's try that again."

I force thoughts of anything but the woman in my arms through my head to distract myself, and twist my bad leg in a way I know will send pain shooting through my knee.

It works...enough.

This time, Kori is more in control too. She still flails, but she remembers to make space and drop her weight to the floor. Neither of us is expecting it when she slides out of my hold, and her foot catches on mine as she tries to steady herself. The awkward misstep rips her balance from her, sending her tumbling toward the mat—and me.

My instincts from over a decade of training take over as she falls. I clutch her to me and let myself go to the ground with her, twisting us so I take the brunt of the impact. All technique is overshadowed by my need to protect her, and I hit the floor harder than I anticipate. Stars swim in my vision as the air is knocked from my lungs, leaving me stunned while she lands on top of me.

"Oh my God, I'm so sorry."

Her hands run over my face and body, checking me for injury as she scrambles to get off me. Her clumsy movement doesn't help anything. A stabbing pain shoots through my side as her knee somehow connects with my kidney.

I stifle the groan and grab her hips to stop her squirming. "Easy now."

She freezes under my fingers with her knees planted on both sides of me, her face flush and pupils blown.

"That's it," I praise.

Now that she's calmed, I should let her go, but I can't do it. She feels too right here in my hands—like she was made for me to hold her. Her curves mold perfectly in my palms.

Without thinking, I tighten my grip and stroke my thumbs over her waist. Her breath catches, and she starts to abuse her lip with her teeth again. Fucking hell, the woman is trying to torture me.

"Stop that." The words come through clenched teeth.

"Yes, Coach," she says in a sultry whisper as she rubs her ass over the front of my pants.

She gasps when she comes in contact with my rigid erection. This time, the burst of pain wasn't enough to push away my arousal. Her tongue darts out to wet her lips, enticing me even further from the boundaries I tried to keep.

"Fuck. I'm sorry, Kori."

I try to lift her off me, but she squeezes her legs, locking herself in place. That spark of hunger returns to her eyes as her gaze roams over my face. Time freezes as she brushes her lips against mine in the most tentative, barely there kiss imaginable.

For a moment, I'm stunned as my brain and body try to reconcile what's happening, and then I'm all in. Before she loses her nerve and pulls away, I move one of my hands from her hip and bring it to her face. The raging beast of need and desire demands that I ravage her—that I claim her and make her mine—but Kori deserves better than that, so I return her kiss with a tenderness I didn't know I was capable of. My lips match her shy energy, gently caressing and sucking with no move to deepen it. It's the softest kiss I've ever experienced, but it sets my body alight with need in a way the filthiest kiss never has.

She grinds down on me as her tongue slips out, tentatively probing for entrance. That turns my brain back on. Before we take this any further, I pull away, but my hand doesn't leave her face.

"I shouldn't have done that." My eyes fall shut as my thumb strokes her cheek. "I'm—"

"If you apologize one more time, I'm going to...well, I don't actually know what I'll do, but you won't like it. So save us both the trouble of finding out by keeping your mouth shut," she snaps, jerking her face out of my grasp and clambering off my lap.

"I'm serious. That shouldn't have happened."

"You know what, you're right. Lesson learned. I won't be making that mistake again."

"Kor, hold on—"

"For what? You made it pretty clear I misread that situation, which is fine. I get it. It happens. But please let me flee with at least some of my dignity intact." Her voice cracks on those last few words, sending a crushing shockwave of guilt through me.

All I can do is nod and watch as she rushes out the door, knowing full well that I royally fucked up.

Chapter 16
Gage

Scalding water rains down around me, hot enough that my skin aches from the burn. It's only another layer to the pains that plague my body. After Kori fled from the gym, I punished myself on the treadmill, pushing myself until I couldn't physically keep going. I don't deserve a comfortable shower. This is my penance for fucking everything up—for hurting her.

Flashes of this afternoon play on repeat in my head. I try to focus on the broken look that invaded her bright features so I can remind myself exactly what I did wrong, but *other* memories keep slipping in as well: the taste of her lips, her curves under my fingers, the way she felt grinding against my cock, the sultry whisper of "yes, Coach" as she follows my commands without question.

What kind of goddamned monster am I that I'm thinking of her like that when I shouldn't have the right to think about her at all. But God, she looked edible, covered in sunshine that hugged her every curve. No one looks anywhere near as good in that bright hue as Kori does. Just the thought of her spandex-covered ass has my dick twitching to life again.

If I were any worse of a man, I would have let her go further today. I would have ripped that yellow from her skin and found out if she actually tastes as sweet as I've imagined.

With a groan, I drop my head to the plastic shower wall and grip my cock in my hand. I'm going to burn in hell for this, but I'm unable to stop the fantasy from playing out in my head while I work myself to an orgasm.

The pleasure builds inside me as I imagine stripping the sunlight off Kori and tasting every inch of her, licking and sucking on her pert tits before finally moving my attention to her pussy. She's wet for me, practically dripping as she begs, and I drop to my knees in front of her.

"Yes, Gage," she moans in that same breathy tone while I bury my tongue inside her.

She tastes like heaven, the perfect mix of sweet and tangy. My cock twitches in my hand, and I come with a grunt as my fantasy Kori's face twists with her own pleasure.

The euphoric high only lasts long enough for the now icy spray to wash away the mess, and shame rapidly replaces it.

This is a new low.

I don't think I've ever felt more pathetic or like such a creep.

Fuck.

This can't happen again, and those fantasies can never happen at all. I pushed her away for a reason. She deserves more than I can ever give her. I need to distance myself from her, and if that means pulling away from the group, I will. She needs my friends more than I do, and she will be better for them too. Maybe it's for the best. None of them need to be hanging around with the creepy old pervert. After this, I'm not sure I don't deserve to be alone.

Numb, I drag myself out from under the spray, barely taking the time to dry myself off before slipping into an old pair of sweats. Even in the light of day, my gloom is stronger than ever. Its shadows dance at the edges of my vision, casting a dark shroud over the otherwise bright apartment. I don't have the energy to fight it. Not now. Not after today.

It circles in closer, growing more and more oppressive, as I cross the hall and drop into my bed. The smallest hint of Yellow's citrus scent clings to my pillowcase. I should have washed it, but I couldn't bring myself to get rid of that reminder of her. Now I wish I had, because it only adds to my self-loathing.

The gloom descends completely, bombarding me with intrusive thoughts and harsh reminders of why I should finally give in and let it win. I've battled it long enough to know all I can do is lie here and bear it.

Time passes by in a blur in my dissociated state. It might have been minutes or hours, but it's Karis's voice that pulls me out from under the crushing waves of melancholy.

"We've been knocking for fifteen minutes," she shouts from down the hallway. Whatever she was going to say next dies on her lips when she sees my state and mumbles "shit" under her breath.

Shit indeed. But it's not the first time Karis has found me in the midst of a meltdown. Hell, it's the main reason she has a key. I went dark a few years back, and she damn near took my front door off its hinges when I didn't respond to any of her check-ins.

She disappears from the doorway, her voice continuing to carry as she addresses the "we" she mentioned.

"Go ahead and get started without me. We'll be out in a few minutes."

"But Kare Bear, I have no idea what I'm doing," Nathan whines.

"Then grab a beer and wait," she snaps, "but we need a few."

"Fine," he grumbles, and the front door closing echoes from the living room.

A heartbeat later, she's back in my room. The mattress dips beneath me as she sits by my waist.

"How bad this time," she asks.

There isn't a hint of judgment in her voice—there never is.

"Pretty bad," I tell her. Lying now would only cause more problems.

"Bad enough I need to send Nathan and Morgan home?"

Goddamnit, she had to bring the whole cavalry. As much as I'd love to tell her yes and go back to wallowing, I know that isn't what I need.

"No. I'm fine. I'll be fine."

I hope.

The room spins as I sit up and blink away the last of my daze. Sunlight still trickles in through the window, so I couldn't have been out of it for too long. That's good at least.

She hums in acknowledgment as she stands and moves to inspect the plants by the window. I know she has no real interest in my collection; she's giving me space to reorient myself without an audience. It's the same song and dance we go through every time she finds me like this.

I swing my legs off the side of the bed, sitting with my back to her as I try to convince myself to take the final step and stand. Maybe I'm not as fine as I want to be.

"What was the trigger?" The shadow of her fingers fidgeting with the long, thin leaf pinched between them plays on the wall in front of me.

Normally, I have no issues telling her all my sordid secrets, but any mention of Kori gets caught in my throat.

Karis lets me stew for a few minutes, not pushing me further despite the heavy silence in the air.

"Does this have anything to do with your lesson with new girl today?" she finally asks.

"I hurt her, Kare," I rasp.

"Like, physically? Or something else?"

"I kissed her, then pushed her away like trash."

She sighs and sits at my side.

"You're an idiot," she says and drops her head to my shoulder.

"I know."

"Honestly, the guys are much better equipped to handle this than me."

"Why are you all here? Not that I'm not grateful you showed up."

"I just have a sixth sense for these things...and I might have gotten a deal on the parts you need."

My spine straightens with that last bit of news.

"You did?"

"Yup. Brought the boys out to get them installed."

"Why? They don't know shit about cars."

"But the three of y'all will keep me entertained while I work."

"Thank you, Kare. Seriously. For everything."

"It's what friends are for. Now, are you ready to go face idiot one and idiot two?"

"As I ever can be. How much do I owe you?"

She waves me off as she heads for the door. "Don't worry about it. Like I said, I got a deal."

I grumble but don't fight her on it while I follow her through my apartment. She only stops to grab the case of beer from my fridge and carry it outside. My other friends are waiting on the steps in front of my porch, each with a can in their hands. If I was feeling more like myself, I would give them shit about mooching off my alcohol. But in the grand scheme of things, the twenty-dollar case is meaningless. It's a fraction of what I owe them for this.

"About time you showed your face," Nathan says as I step through the door. "I was starting to think you didn't want us around."

"Like that would stop you from showing up," I try to snark back, but my voice sounds hollow.

Morgan's forehead pinches, but he doesn't say anything at my tone.

"I'm surprised to see you, though," I address my more perceptive friend. "How did you get James to let you off your leash?"

He flips me off, but his face melts into a love-sick grin. "She's been in her studio all day, so I figured I'd grace you with my presence."

"God, you are so whipped," Nathan chastises, and Morgan doesn't even argue.

"You're one to talk," I call him out.

"Like you aren't completely hung up on Kori."

The mere mention of her name sucks all the air from my lungs, and the gloom swirls around me with a vengeance. My whole body stiffens while my face morphs into a hollow mask.

"Shit," Nathan mutters. He might be oblivious, but he isn't blind. "What happened."

Karis drops the box next to the stairs and tosses me one of the cold cans.

"Yeah, Gage, tell them what happened, and I'll see if I can bring your piece of shit back to life."

With catlike grace, she maneuvers around our friends and pops the hood of my car parked in front of the staircase. I didn't give her my keys, but that didn't stop her from taking them. Hell, I'm surprised she gave me warning that she was going to fix the damn thing instead of stopping by while I was at work and then delivering my keys like some sort of mechanic fairy.

I crack open the beer, taking a long drink before joining them on the steps.

"I fucked everything up," I tell them and take another sip.

"Oh yeah, that's real specific," Nathan says.

"Things got...out of control at our lesson today."

"You? Out of control?" Morgan asks.

"Yeah. And in the heat of the moment, I let her kiss me."

"And that's a problem...?" Nathan prompts.

"Yes, it's a problem. One, nothing can ever happen between us, and two, I might have pushed her away and told her it was a mistake. She was pretty upset when she left."

Karis snorts and pulls her head out from under the hood. "Why are you boys so fucking bad at this. I swear y'all have more drama than any woman I've ever known."

"Hey, I have no drama," Nathan says.

"Oh yeah? So you aren't still pining after a woman you dated for a few months a year ago?" When he doesn't respond, she crosses her arms and continues, "That's what I thought. Morgan finally has his shit together, but last year was a whole clusterfuck. And now Gage is torturing himself over a woman who is absolutely into him and has no baggage holding her back."

"Her liking me isn't the issue," I growl.

"Then what is?" Nathan asks.

"I'm not good enough for her," I practically shout.

"Goddamnit, are we seriously doing this again," Nathan snaps. "Maybe you're right. Maybe you aren't good enough for her if this is how you are going to treat her."

"I don't know what to do," I admit as my frustration starts to fade. "I've tried being her friend, but I don't think I can do that anymore. There is too much tension between us. It will only lead to a cycle of hurt every time I push her away."

"Then stop pushing her away," Morgan says.

"And then what?"

"You see where this thing goes."

"I don't know how to do that."

"What? Let yourself be happy?" Nathan's voice drips with bitter sarcasm.

"Be with a woman for more than a night. I've never done the whole relationship thing. I have no idea how to treat her right," I admit.

I didn't have time for a relationship when I spent most of my younger years training to make a name for myself, and I never had the desire after my dreams came crashing down.

"Well, not being a self-sabotaging asshole would be a good place to start," he snaps.

"It's easy," Morgan says, ignoring the tension between me and our friend. "Loving James is the easiest thing I've ever done."

"Nothing about that woman is easy," Nathan scoffs, though the bitter edge to his voice softens.

Morgan punches his shoulder, but there's no malice behind it, and just like that, all the aggravated energy dissipates.

"Let's say I did want to see where things went. Where would I even start?"

"Women like to be spoiled, and they like to show off to their friends. You should—" Nathan starts to say, but Karis is quick to interrupt him.

"Ignore all of that."

"What? You can't tell me you don't want to be spoiled from time to time," he asks.

"As a one-off, sure. But every woman I've been with has cared way more about spending time together than monetary things."

"Karis is right," Morgan says. "What women really want is to form deep, emotional connections. You need to be vulnerable with her and show her the parts of you no one else sees. Opening up to James is what drew us together."

"That's stupid." Nathan waves him off. "What you need to do is shower her in gifts and take her on dates she can brag about."

"Fuck, you date shallow women," Karis says.

"And what do you recommend, then?"

"That you should be yourself, spend time with them doing things you both enjoy, and let things play out naturally."

Both Morgan and Nathan scoff.

"Fine. Ignore me, then. What does the gay woman know about women anyway." She shakes her head and turns her attention back to my car.

"The first thing you have to do is apologize for being an ass today," Nathan says.

"That's assuming I decide to pursue her."

"No, you should apologize regardless."

"It's probably better if she hates me."

He throws his hands up with a huff and grabs another beer from the case. "Man, I love you, but you are a lost fucking cause. But you need to get over yourself, or you're going to keep hurting her."

"What do you propose I do, then?"

"Make up your goddamn mind, for one. Figure out what you want and stick to it."

"I want to live in a world where I can be worthy of a woman like her."

"You live in this world. So either find your worth, or you let her go."

He's right. I need to let her go.

I finish off my drink and grab another as dread pools in my gut. The feeling doesn't dissipate as the topic drifts away from relationships or my other problems, or as dusk replaces the daylight. Even once Karis gets the engine to turn over, that black hole remains. Morgan dips out as soon as his girl texts him to summon him home, and Nathan leaves not long after.

When it's only the two of us left, Karis cleans up her tools and lets herself back inside my apartment. She won't leave me alone again after my spiral; she knows how easily the gloom can creep back in once it's gotten a foothold. I give her a few minutes to make herself at home and clean the grease and oil from her hands before I follow her inside. She's parked on my couch when I do, flipping through the channels on my TV like she owns the place.

"You're never going to let yourself be happy, are you?" She doesn't even look in my direction.

"I don't think I know how."

She sighs and pats the cushion beside her, and I don't have it in me to do anything but follow her unspoken command.

"You are going to regret this," she says as I drop beside her.

"I think I already do."

She gives me a sad, knowing nod and switches the topic. "I ordered takeout. Watch the door while I shower."

I nod, but my mind is barely in the room. It's too busy mourning the beautiful fucking sunflower that will never be mine.

Chapter 17
Kori

Evelyn's room is bigger than I expected.

Between the kitchenette and separate bedroom, it's basically an apartment tucked inside the dorm.

More importantly, it is very *pink*.

Not that there's anything wrong with pink—other than yellow is objectively superior—it's just not what I expected her room to look like. The shade is a soft pastel that coordinates well with the accents of gray and cream, giving the space a delicate and feminine feel.

I'm scared if I move, I'll disrupt the peaceful balance she's clearly worked hard to craft. At least the couch is comfortable. It makes a perfect base for me to perch on, unmoving, like a gargoyle. All my muscles are stiff enough to be stone.

Sounds stream from the TV, but they are nothing more than muffled noise to my ears. No matter how hard I try, I can't tune in to the program. At least my host doesn't have the same hang-ups. She's engrossed in the drama on the screen. It's the whole reason I'm here. She invited me over to watch some reality show with her—Love Something-or-Other. They aren't my normal cup of tea, but I wasn't going to pass up the opportunity to get out of my room. Or my head.

Perhaps it wasn't the best choice, considering I'm trying to distract myself from my own romantic failings.

God, what even was that kiss?

I thought I read the signs right—the most obvious being his clear, and large, erection—but I was wrong. I googled it once I stopped wishing the floor would open up and eat me; apparently, men's bodies simply do that sometimes, attraction or not. That would have been really helpful information a few days ago. Would have saved me from some real embarrassment...and maybe our friendship.

Because that is absolutely over now too.

My resolve to keep things platonic dissolved the second I saw an opportunity for something more, and my worst-case scenario came to life. The text from Evelyn this morning was a definite shock, all things considered. I assumed Gage would have me blacklisted from his friends and I'd never hear from any of them again.

Evelyn stirs beside me as the credits roll and the next episode cues.

Shit, has it been that long already?

"How are you settling into Athens?" she asks.

"I'm settling. It definitely feels more like a college town than my last school did, which has been a nice change of pace."

It's all too easy to get caught up in the hustle of downtown Atlanta, and before you know it, two years have passed by with nothing to show for it besides the grades on a transcript. I never would have made friends the way I did here...it's more likely I'd have gotten mugged.

"Why did you transfer? If you don't mind me asking."

"My parents are alumni, and I wanted to get my degree from their alma mater. They actually met here when they were in school. I grew up hearing the stories about how this place shaped their lives for the better."

"That's so sweet."

"Sure," I snort. "Until they start getting into the details of it. They absolutely hated each other at first. They were in the same program, same organizations, and they are both competitive as hell, so I'm sure you can imagine how that played out."

"But they fell in love," she swoons.

"Yeah, they did. Sickeningly so."

"This place has a way of doing that," she says with a knowing smile. "If you need any recommendations for things to do and places to check out, let me know. I did my undergrad here too. There is way more to Athens than Cutter's and Double Teep, no matter what Karis and Gage would have you believe."

"Wait, you're in grad school?"

Why on earth is she wasting her time with me?

"Yup. James and I graduated last spring. Morgan, Nathan, and Karis are all in grad school too, and James and Gage are working, obviously."

"Why are you in the dorm and not in an apartment or graduate housing?"

"I'm a graduate assistant. I was an RA for most of undergrad, so I already had an in with housing."

"That sounds like a lot of work."

"It can be, but it's worth it for the pay. Housing is stupid expensive."

Her words leave me feeling two inches tall. Never once have I had to worry about how much money I'm spending to be here. My parents have always had it covered. I've never had a job, either. They wouldn't let me work in high school, and I never had a need after. It never really occurred to me that my new friends might have had different experiences.

"Speaking of finding love in the Classic City, has there been any movement on the Gage front?"

Her question causes my heart to harden and drop like lead into the pit of my stomach. It looks like Gage hasn't told his friends about what happened between us. That's probably for the best. Everything would be so much easier if we could pretend it never happened. But it did, and talking to Daisy about it has gotten me nowhere.

"Oh yeah, if you consider raising the white flag movement," I say with a bitterness clinging to my words.

The playful expression falls from her face.

136

"What happened?"

"I kissed him, and he pushed me away. He said, 'That shouldn't have happened' and then tried to apologize like I wasn't the one who ambushed him. So yeah, I'm pretty sure anything that might have been brewing between us is officially dead in the water."

I sigh and sink back into the couch, clutching one of her petal-pink pillows to my chest to give my hands something to fidget with.

"That sucks," she says and mirrors my posture. "Karis was so sure he was into you too. But maybe it's for the best."

"What do you mean?"

"Like, do you not find him...I don't know, intimidating?"

"Intimidating? Why would you think that?"

Gage might be a lot of things, but that isn't a word I'd use to describe him. Intense, sure, but he's never made me feel uncomfortable being around him. If anything, his presence is—was—soothing. Even after the kiss, I know nothing will happen to me when he's around. Hell, I even like it when he touches me. Those calloused hands make my skin crawl in a good way.

"He doesn't talk much," Evelyn says with a shrug, "and he's always scowling at something. I'm not even sure if he *wants* to be our friend, or if he only comes because Karis drags him along. And after what happened at the beach last year..."

"Wait, what happened at the beach?"

"Jamie's ex attacked Morgan, or at least tried to. He got one punch in before Gage stepped in and had him restrained without throwing a punch himself. I didn't actually see it myself, but I've heard the stories enough."

"Why is that intimidating? It sounds like Gage de-escalated the situation without violence. Isn't that a good thing?"

"No, you are right. I think it's more the fact that he could have caused some serious damage if he wanted to. I'm probably making assumptions here, but you've seen him. The man is a giant."

Yes, I have, and before the disaster that was our lesson, I wanted to see more of him. Clothing optional.

"He also wasn't nearly as restrained when you...got hurt...at Cutter's. I don't think I've ever seen him that enraged or out of control. It was terrifying, and it wasn't even directed at me. If Nathan hadn't intervened, I think he might have done real damage—not that that asshole wouldn't have deserved it—but I'm talking irreversible, life-altering shit. Like 'Gage ends up in prison' levels of anger. Even Karis and Morgan looked scared—not of him, I don't think, but of the consequences."

Okay, that's a lot.

After a certain point, my memories of that night disappear aside from a few scattered, hazy flashes, and in every one of them, Gage is nothing but a steady and safe figure. The rage she describes doesn't mesh with that at all.

A knot forms in my throat as I comb through this bit of information, letting it reframe every interaction I've had with the infuriating man. Still, it doesn't reconcile, and I can't decide if it paints him in a new light.

"I thought you were his friend?"

"Fuck. I am. Well, sort of. It's a whole story. After Chelsea graduated, it was only Jamie and me left in Athens. I'm sure you can tell Jamie and Morgan are a bit...clingy. So I got closer to Morgan's friends, but even then, I'm closest with Karis. Nathan is cool, too, but Gage has always been more of a presence than a persona.

"Goddamnit, I'm rambling. Yes, I'm his friend, and I'm not trying to paint him as a villain or anything. He is a good man. The others wouldn't be as unwaveringly loyal as they are otherwise. I guess all I'm trying to say is maybe it's a good thing nothing romantic is happening between you guys. He has demons."

"It would be nice if my heart got that memo."

"Oh, Kori, I'm sorry."

I try not to flinch as she wraps an arm around me and pulls me in for a hug. This group seems keen on the whole touchy-feely thing. I'm not sure how I feel about that. Thankfully, it doesn't last too long, and when she pulls away, she has a devious smile on her face.

"Oh, I've got a great idea."

"You do?" I ask, swallowing back the nerves that look inspires.

"Yes," she says with a firm nod. "We're going to go to Cutter's and show Gage exactly what he's missing out on."

"I don't know…"

"It will be perfect. We can get dressed up, flirt with cute guys, and not look in that jerk's direction."

"I—"

"And if the guys are awful, we can dance like Jamie, Chelsea, and I used to. That always turned heads. Plus, I miss dancing. It feels too awkward to do it on my own."

She looks so excited about the prospect, I can't bring myself to say no.

"Fine. No to the flirting, but I'll go dancing with you."

"Perfect," she says with a happy squeal. "Let me text Karis and find out if he's working tonight. Oh, I'll invite Jamie too. This is going to be so much fun."

Call me crazy, but I have a sinking suspicion it will be anything but.

Chapter 18
Gage

"**C**razy weather, am I right?" Nathan asks as he watches the rain pelt the front window.

The weather? Really?

I don't even justify his comment with a response.

I'm sure he has better things to do at eight thirty on a Wednesday night—like work on his thesis or literally any of the half a dozen women in this bar—but he's wasting it keeping me company. The same way he has every night this week, and he ran out of actual things to talk about halfway through yesterday's shift.

He hasn't said it, but I know he's waiting for me to melt down again over the whole Kori thing.

I'm fine.

Nothing in my life is different than it's ever been.

I'm still just as alone as I was before she embedded herself in my life like a fucking thorn. It turns out roses aren't the only flowers you need to watch out for. Who cares if the world feels even bleaker now without her petals in it? I'm sure I'll adjust.

I drag a damp cloth over the bar top to give my hands something to do. The damn thing is probably the cleanest it's ever been with how many times I've wiped it down tonight, and it's not like we've had enough customers to make a mess of it in between each pass. But it's something to do—and an excuse to ignore Nathan's mother henning.

Soft, dreary rock drifts from the speakers, mixing with the steady battering of rain against the glass to echo my mood. The lack of patrons makes it even more depressing, but we have the weather to thank for that.

No customers. No tips. No joy.

It's nothing less than I deserve.

Thunder crashes overhead as the door swings open and Karis steps inside, soaked to the bone and glowering like that fact personally offends her. She looks around the bar and shakes her head, spraying droplets of water into the air.

"Damn, this place is dead."

I hand her a clean rag as she joins Nathan, but she ignores it, reaching over the counter and grabbing a glass to pour herself something from the tap like a goddamn heathen instead.

"Then why the fuck are you here?" I growl and drop the cloth beside her.

The last thing I need is both of them watching over me like I'm some sort of fragile child.

"Do I need an excuse to visit my best friend at work?"

The devilish grin on her face is evidence enough that she's full of shit. Her eyes sparkle with mischief—a look I know and dread.

"Okay, what am I missing here?"

"Nothing," she lies. "Like I said—"

Before she can finish her thought, I'm distracted by a flash of yellow by the door. Hope dares to raise its useless head, but I sever it before it has a chance to grow. There is no way Kori would be here; this place holds too many bad memories. There's no way she'd ever come back here—even before I ensured she was done with me.

Or so I thought. Because it *is* my sunflower who walks through the door, huddled underneath a splayed raincoat with Evelyn, dressed like sin, and giggling like she doesn't have a care in the world.

I've never been simultaneously so relieved and so mad about being wrong.

What the hell is she doing here looking like all of my sweetest fantasies come to life?

A pathetic ache pulses through my center. Knowing she didn't have nearly as much stake in whatever was brewing between us hurts. Not that I want to see her hurting—that's the last thing I'd ever want—but her smiling face is a sharp reminder of my worth.

"You knew about this, didn't you?" I ask Karis.

"Maybe," she says, and that shit-eating grin only grows.

God-fucking-damn her and her meddling.

"And you didn't think to warn me?"

"Warn you about what? I don't think what Kori does in her free time is any of your business."

But her being in my bar is.

I grumble and swipe the rag along the slick wood with more force than needed.

"Karis," Evelyn shouts and waves as she approaches us. "Can you put on something we can dance to? The vibe is wrong."

"You heard the lady, put on some music they can dance to," my friend tells me with a smirk.

I bite my tongue as I follow the command—I don't have the energy to argue. Evelyn always gets her way anyway, no matter how many times I tell her Cutter's isn't a dancing bar. She gives me those big sad eyes, and I can't help but bend to her wishes—especially if Karis gets involved. If she wants to dance by herself in a shitty college bar, who am I to stop her?

Although I'm not sure how Yellow fits into all of this.

With Evelyn gone, she looks like she's about to crawl out of her skin. What was Evelyn thinking bringing her here so soon? Add in the pressure of standing out against the crowd, and I know my girl is going to shut down. But I'm proud of her for trying. Even if she won't look in my direction.

"Hold on," I tell Evelyn before she can slip away. "Take a bit of liquid courage."

I mix together a quick vodka and lemonade and pour it into two glasses for the girls. It's not as complex or sweet as the other drinks I've made her, but hopefully, Kori will like it nonetheless.

She scowls at me but accepts the drinks before sauntering away with a rhythmic sway to her hips, moving back to where she left Kori on her makeshift dance floor. Once she is no longer alone, Yellow's antsy energy fades.

Maybe I didn't give her enough credit.

Based on the downright dirty looks I'm getting from the normally shy woman, Evelyn heard about what went down. We might as well call James and tell her, too, so the whole group knows how much of a fuckup I am.

The door swings open again, and I let out a string of curses.

Speak of the she-devil...

She walks through the door with Morgan in tow. She beelines for the girls, leaving her boyfriend on his own by the door.

He gives me a sheepish smile as he approaches and sits on one of the ratty stools.

"Let me guess, Evelyn was involved," I say while I grab a bottle of his favorite beer and place it in front of him.

"Yup. James said something about showing a certain bartender what he's missing out on."

I groan and drop my head back to look at the ceiling. Like I need any reminders. Bubbling laughter draws my focus back toward the women. The sight is nothing new to me. After a few drinks, Evelyn begs anyone who will listen to dance with her. But seeing Kori added to the mix, laughing with a smile on her face, builds uncomfortable pressure in my chest. Don't get me wrong, she's awful at it. Her limbs move awkwardly off beat, which is even more pronounced when contrasted with Evelyn's natural grace. But that smile—carefree and unfiltered—I don't think I've seen anything more beautiful.

I'm not the only awestruck idiot ensnared by the trio's bold display. Karis and Morgan watch the girls move with intense heat in their eyes, and that hungry expression is mirrored on the face of every hot-blooded man in this bar. Which isn't saying much given the current occupancy, but the point still stands. Nathan is the only one not affected. It's not that he doesn't look at them. But his gaze is more watchful than lustful; he's a sentry, not a suitor.

Because of that, he notices the pair of men approach them before I do. They are young, almost certainly still in undergrad, and carry themselves with more confidence than is warranted. At that age, they all act like the world can't touch them. I know I did.

Nathan's spine stiffens as the cocky kids orbit the girls, keeping their distance but making their attention known. He leans forward with a scowl, his eyes narrowing on the pair.

It hits me hard that, once again, my best friend is paying closer attention to my girl than I am.

Dread pools in my gut as the two fuckers hype each other up, building up the courage to make an introduction. After several seconds, one takes the plunge, and my dread turns to ice when he approaches Kori.

The only thing that keeps me behind the bar is he doesn't touch her. Fuck me if he isn't actually respectful in the way he catches her attention. This is worse than if he had been a dick about it. Then I'd have a reason to intervene. Instead, I'm forced to watch as this bashful idiot tries to flirt with my woman and, worse yet, as she doesn't push him away.

Come on, Yellow. You know you're too good for him.

Or she doesn't, because she laughs at something he says, and twists a long braid between her fingers.

"Are you seriously going to sit here and watch this?" Nathan snaps at me.

"What would you have me do?"

"Step in there and make it known that she's yours."

"She isn't mine."

144

"Whatever, man."

He goes back to scowling at the kid flirting with Kori, and I'm sure my facial expression isn't much better. Every smile he pulls from her lips is another nail in my already ravaged heart, but I welcome the pain. It's what I'm owed.

The kid says something that makes Kori's face pinch for a brief second before her expression hardens into resolve and she nods.

And then the motherfucker touches her.

He places a hand on her waist and steps in closer. She fumbles with her hands for a second before placing them on his chest, and then they start to sway together without any regard for the beat.

I'm sure they would have figured it out eventually, but I don't give them the chance.

The second he touches her, rational Gage gets shoved into the passenger seat while the need to stake my claim takes over. Nathan scoffs and mumbles a quiet "of course" under his breath when I dart out from behind the bar, but he falls in step beside me as I stalk across the room toward the girls.

I resist the urge to rip his slimy hands from her, tapping him on the shoulder instead, and when he turns, I growl out two simple words. "Hands off."

His arms are in the air in an instant as he takes a large step away from my girl.

"Sorry, man. I didn't realize she was taken. My bad." He doesn't wait for my response before scampering off with his friend.

Smart kid.

Kori, on the other hand, isn't the least bit frightened by my possessive posturing.

"Yeah. I didn't realize I was taken either," she snarls at me, dropping her hands to her hips.

Her defiance stirs something in me that it definitely shouldn't be now. It's almost as tempting as the way she melts under my coaching and the breathy way "yes, Coach" falls from her perfect lips. The same lips that are pressed thin with her barely contained anger.

"You know that isn't what I meant."

"Then what the absolute fuck was that display of alphahole douchebaggery?" she shouts.

If the bar was any more crowded, I would be concerned about making a scene, but my friends make up a quarter of the patrons, and I really couldn't give a fuck what anyone else thinks. They can go next door if they want an undisturbed drink.

"He was touching you." It's a miracle the words come out as calm as they do when the thought sends a fresh wave of mindless violence through me.

"And? He asked me first, and I said yes."

"Why the fuck would you do that?"

"Because I wanted to, and because despite you acting like you own me, we aren't together, and you made it pretty clear we never would be."

"That doesn't mean you should let men touch you whenever they want."

Nathan winces beside me and whispers, "You fucking idiot."

"Do you even hear yourself right now?" She takes a step forward, standing straighter as she gives me a piece of her mind. Her face thunders with rage that rivals the storm outside. If her joy was beautiful, then fuck me if her rage isn't awe-striking.

"I didn't *let* anyone do anything. He asked if I wanted to dance, and I said yes. Because *I* wanted to. He was cute and nice, and if he had asked to kiss me, I probably would have said yes too."

"The fuck you would have," I snap.

"I'm not yours, Gage, so stop acting like you own me. Unless you are going to man the fuck up and make me yours for real."

I open my mouth to meet her challenge, but rational me gains control long enough to stop me from making a promise I can't keep. She isn't mine, and she never will be. It doesn't matter how badly I want to kiss that scowl off her lips.

"That's what I thought. Now, if you'll excuse me, I was having fun with my friends before you ruined my night, and I'd like to go back to that."

"Come on, Kori, I'll dance with you," Nathan says, drilling me with a glare as he wraps an arm around her shoulder.

It takes every bit of my willpower not to throttle my friend.

I take a deep breath and put the group behind me. It's the only way I can bear it. Karis and Morgan are still watching from the bar with pity and disappointment clear on their faces.

"I fucked that one up, didn't I?" I ask as I make it back behind the counter.

"Yup," Karis says.

"And what would you have done differently?"

"Kissed the shit out of her, for one."

"She isn't mine to kiss."

"And if you let her walk out of here, she never will be. You know that, right?" she challenges.

"What do you mean?"

"She isn't going to wait around for you to figure it out. And if tonight is any indicator, she won't have much trouble finding someone who realizes what they have in front of them."

I grumble and grab a wineglass from the shelf, dirtying it with the grimy cloth to give my hands something to do.

"She and Nathan seem to get along well, and they would make a cute couple. He deserves to find happiness with someone as sweet as her," she adds.

Sharp pain flares in my palm as the stem snaps in my clenched fist.

"Shit," I curse as blood pools from a shallow cut.

"Go take care of that." Concern overtakes her features, pushing away the antagonistic teasing. "I'll watch the bar until you get back."

Pain doesn't register as I walk into the back office and fish out the old first aid kit that has been here as long as I have. My heartbeat pulses in the wound, but the sting was brief. It isn't until I pour rubbing alcohol on it that the feeling returns with vengeance. A string of curses spills out as I bandage it and slip on a plastic glove to prevent any biohazard incidents.

When I return, the girls are gone...and so is Nathan.

He wouldn't have—fuck.

No. No. No. Not him. Not anyone. Yellow is *my* fucking woman, god-damnit.

My gut hollows with a black hole of devastation as my heart picks up speed in my chest. If he—if they—

There would be no coming back from that. Not only would I lose my girl, but one of my best friends too, and even Karis couldn't pull me out of that tailspin.

Fear holds me hostage in the doorframe. Stepping back out there means accepting that reality, and that's more than I can deal with right now. My lungs lock in my chest, constricting tighter with every second that passes.

I start to breathe again when my friend steps out of the bathroom al-cove—alone.

"Thank fuck."

His face falls as he sees my wrecked state. It doesn't take him long to put two and two together. He shakes his head as he approaches me and drags me back into the office.

"Man, did you really think I was going to fuck your girl? I thought after all these years, you would trust me more than that."

"I know. I do. I just..."

"Panicked?"

"Yeah." My shoulders slump with the confession.

"Are you ready to get your head out of your ass now?" he asks, and I give him a defeated nod.

There is no way I can fight this thing. Not while she's around, and I don't think my friends will let her go anywhere anytime soon.

"So what are you going to do?"

"Do you think there's a chance I can still beg her for forgiveness?"

"Only one way to find out."

***

I don't give myself time to talk myself out of it as I drive toward her dorm. Never mind the fact that it's 2 a.m. on a school night and the storm has only gotten worse as the night went on. Or that she's probably going to tell me to fuck off and that she never wants to see me again.

It's not until I'm standing in the abandoned lobby of her building that I realize I have no fucking plan here. My entire shift passed by, and all I could think about was getting to her—not what I was going to do once I got here. I don't even know what room she's in or how I'm supposed to get past the locked security doors. At least my only obstacle is a half-asleep kid at the front desk.

Calling her is an option, but that risks her turning me away before I can get inside, and I'm not willing to lose this fight before it's even begun.

I'm done making mistakes where she's involved.

"Hey," I bark at the sleepy kid.

He jerks to attention, and his eyes widen as I approach. On a good day, I would try to make myself seem less intimidating, but today is not a good day, and he is the only thing standing between me and my girl.

"How old are you?" I snap.

"Uh...twenty-two," he says, but it sounds more like a question than a reply.

"Do you like to go downtown?"

He nods, but his eyes are still nervous.

"If you let me through those doors, you and your friends can drink for free at Cutter's until the end of the year."

"I'm—what?"

"You heard me. All you have to do is let me inside."

A bead of sweat forms on his forehead as he looks around, and his throat bobs as he swallows back his nerves.

"Are you a cop?"

I don't justify his stupidity with an answer.

"Shit. Fine. But if anyone asks, I didn't let you in. My boss would fire me for this without question."

A loud *click* sounds from the door as he hits a button under the desk and the magnetic lock disengages. I give the kid a two-fingered salute and don't waste any time jogging over to the door. Truth be told, the kid deserves to be fired. It should not be this easy for a strange man to barge his way into the dorms. Part of me wants to report him for his negligence—how dare he put Kori at risk—but I would feel like the worst kind of asshole if I cost him his job.

That doesn't mean I won't worry about her every time I think of her here alone now.

I pull out my phone and dial Yellow's number once I get inside. She doesn't pick up on the first ring. Or the second.

Fuck.

The hope in my chest crumbles, but my resolve only hardens. I'm fixing things with my woman tonight, goddamnit. Karis was right—if I don't fix this now, I'll never be able to.

One more call, and if she doesn't pick up, I'll wake Karis up to coerce the information out of Evelyn. I'll wake the whole building up if I have to, but I'm not leaving here until I see my girl. The only thing that will get me out of this building is the words "fuck off" coming from her lips.

I dial one more time, holding my breath as the line rings in my ear. My heart swells as her groggy voice finally comes through on the other end.

"Hello? Gage? Is everything okay?"

"What room are you in?" I rasp.

Chapter 19
Kori

"What room are you in?"

The deep, desperate rasp in Gage's voice sends a shiver racing down my spine, straight into my core, knocking away my sleepy haze with a lightning bolt of need.

My stupid vagina hasn't gotten the memo that we are done with him. She really needs to get with the program—we aren't about to melt into a submissive puddle because he calls sounding all hot and demanding.

"What the hell are you talking about?" I snap.

"What. Room," he growls.

"Gage. It's the middle of the night. Can we please not do this now?"

I don't think I can handle any more of his hot and cold attitude today—hell, I think I've had enough of it to last me a lifetime.

"Three seconds, Low, or I'm pulling the fire alarm and bringing you to me."

There isn't a hint of teasing in his tone. Not that he's normally the most expressive, but there is no doubt in my mind he is being serious right now. He's willing to risk a misdemeanor to get what he wants, and right now, what he wants is me. I'm not sure if that's romantic or a red flag. Either way, the threat works.

"I'm in 324, asshole," I say through clenched teeth.

"See you in a few," he says, and the line goes dead.

It takes several seconds for my sleepy brain to register what exactly is happening. Gage is coming. No, Gage is here.

Why is he here?

"Daisy, help. What do I do?"

I've got minutes, no, seconds until he'll be at my door. I don't have time to do anything to prepare. My fuzzy Big Bird pajamas are the exact opposite of sexy. If I try to change, I'll risk him showing up when I'm half dressed, and that will only make things worse.

Or maybe then he'll realize what he's missing out on.

No—I refuse to pine after him. He made his position crystal clear in front of everyone at Cutter's.

"Do you think he'll go away if I play dead?" I ask my duck.

"No," Gage's muffled voice answers from the other side of my door.

Shit.

I pull the silk bonnet off my head and toss it away. I'll deal with it later. My room is a disaster reaching post–kaiju attack levels of destruction. God, he can't see it like this. Without a real plan, I kick the pile of clothes I meant to fold last week under my bed so there's at least some semblance of order. My desk is a mess too. Maybe I can shove that in my closet—

"Open the door, Kori." He interrupts my *Big Comfy Couch* cleanup extravaganza with a gentle knock, but the command in his voice is clear.

"Yes, coming," I squeak.

My hands shake as I answer the door. Despite the buzzing of nerves, I glare as I take in his hulking form leaning against the doorframe with a causal posture that doesn't match the storm raging in his eyes. With agonizing slowness, his gaze roams over my body, and he makes no effort to hide the hunger there. A wave of molten heat floods my traitorous pussy, and my nipples harden into stiff peaks. The asshole fucking smirks as I cross my arms to hide the evidence of my body's betrayal.

I should have left him waiting, misdemeanor be damned.

"What are you doing here?" I snap at the infuriating man.

"What I should have done the first time you kissed me," he rasps.

His lips are on mine before the words have time to process, and the whole world is lost in an explosion of white-hot fireworks. There's no trace of the gentle way he kissed me before. No, it is pure passion as the man devours me. His hand cups my face as his tongue and teeth work in tandem to tease my lips, coaxing them open, and I moan when his tongue brushes against mine. I'm vaguely aware of the door closing as his arm snakes around my waist before he pulls me closer to him, slotting his thick thigh between mine. The added friction pulls another needy sound from my throat.

"Fuck, Kor," he groans, then deepens the kiss even further.

Both of his hands fall to my ass, and then I'm in the air. On instinct, I grip his shoulders and wrap my legs around his waist so I don't fall. He chuckles and drops his lips to my neck while he carries me to my bed.

Panic grips my lungs. Kissing is okay—it's more than okay—but anything beyond is moving way faster than I want to. My fears ease as he turns to sit on the edge with me straddling his lap instead of laying me out like I expect, and they disappear as his lips find mine again.

The thick denim of his jeans does nothing to hide his arousal. It burns against my aching core through the many layers of fabric between us. I grind down against him, desperate for some relief from the pulsing need. He groans against my mouth and nips my lip as his hands travel up along my sides to my clothed breasts. His fingers twist and pull my covered nipples, sending a sharp wave of ecstasy through me. I arch my back, dying to get closer, and he takes advantage of the new position to trail kisses across my jaw to my neck.

Without his intoxicating taste on my tongue clouding my mind, I remember that I'm pissed at him. With a pathetic shove, I push him back, but he reacts as if it had the force of a man twice his size behind it, recoiling and taking both his hands and lips with him.

"Fuck. I'm sorry, Kori. I shouldn't have—"

I slap my palm over his mouth, shutting him up before he puts his foot in his mouth again and says something stupid that makes me even madder.

"If you say this was a mistake, I'm going to smother you with a pillow. Got it?"

His eyes dance with a playful light as he nods under my hand.

"Good. Now what the absolute fuck was this."

I release him and cover myself with my arms. My pajamas feel as revealing as lingerie after what we just did.

"This was me claiming my woman."

"Your woman?" I challenge.

"Yes. Mine." For the first time, doubt flickers over his bullish features. "If you'll still have me..."

Exhaustion overtakes me. This constant push and pull is too much for me to handle right now, especially with his impressive bulge still pressing against my aching center. I climb off his lap and crawl farther into my bed, wrapping myself up in my favorite soft blanket like a Russian babushka. The thick fleece is a shield against the onslaught of emotions I'm too tired to process.

Part of the reason I liked him in the first place was he didn't bullshit me, but now it feels like he's playing games like everyone else. He promised me no bullshit, and here he is, doing the epitome of bullshit.

"I...I'm really confused," I admit in a small voice, gazing up at him from under my bright hood.

I can't focus on anything while I'm trying to decode his intentions and untangle my own feelings. Before today, I would have trusted him at his word, but now I'm not sure, and that makes everything harder.

This is the part where people realize I'm not exactly normal. Normal girls don't shut down when they get overstimulated. Normal girls don't have to actively think to see beyond the surface of the words they're being told.

I'm expecting Gage to realize that too and take off, but he doesn't. He only watches me without a trace of judgment.

"What's got you confused?"

The tenderness in his voice melts some of my icy armor.

"It's barely been six hours since you made it clear at Cutter's that you would never be with me, and it felt like you meant it. Now you're here kissing me and telling me I'm yours, and you sound like you mean that too. So I'm not sure what to believe, or if I can even trust my read on you at all. What happened to no bullshit?"

His face twists as his whole body slumps in defeat.

"I fucked up. At the gym. At Cutter's. Hell, probably even now. When you kissed me, all I could think about was how perfect you are, and how I'd ruin that if I let you get close to me. So I pushed you away, and I kept pushing. But then I saw that piece of shit flirting with you today and damn near lost my mind."

I scoff and roll my eyes. "You did more than 'nearly' lose it."

"Fair enough. I saw you with him and lost any rational sense. But even then, I wasn't man enough to claim you. But that isn't because I don't have feelings for you. I like you, Kori. I've liked you for a while. It just took me a while to get my head out of my ass about it, and this is me trying to fix my mistakes before they become permanent. I don't want to miss out on the chance to get to know you for real. If I'm already too late, I'll go."

My stomach drops as he starts to stand. I scramble out from under my protective cocoon and grab his hand before he can go anywhere.

"No. It's not too late," I tell him.

His lashes fall shut for a moment, and he takes a deep breath before threading his fingers through mine. Silence settles between us. It's not necessarily uncomfortable, but awkward energy taints the air.

"So what happens now?" I ask.

"Now I ask you out." The look in his eye is no less intense than it was when I opened my door. "Would you like to get dinner with me this Sunday?"

"I'd love to," I tell him, and he gives me a glimpse of one of his rare full smiles.

"Good." He runs his thumb over the back of my hand while he speaks. "As much as I would love to stay, you need sleep."

A surge of panic washes through me. What if he leaves and decides this was a mistake too?

"Hey, what's that face for?" He catches my chin in his hand and stares into my eyes.

"I'm scared," I admit.

"Me too. I've never actually done this whole girlfriend thing before."

Girlfriend?

That one word eases some of the anxiety, and I relax into his touch.

He kisses me again, more languid than before—quicker too. It's over before things get a chance to heat back up again.

"You need sleep." He runs his thumb over my petulant pout before he stands for real. "I'll text you in the morning. Lock the door behind me."

He strides out of the room as if he didn't blow in here like a tornado and destroy everything I thought I knew about us. I'm in a daze as I get up and follow his command, and the high doesn't lessen after I climb back into bed with my heart no more than a pile of love-sick goo in my chest.

Gage's woman.

Yeah, I think I like the sound of that.

Chapter 20
Gage

The second I walk into Double Teep, I'm ambushed.

My friends are crowded around the front desk, trying their best to look casual. Morgan is sitting in the chair behind it "working," Karis is sitting *on* it, and Nathan is half leaning against it while the three of them bicker. It's obvious to anyone with eyes they are up to something—and that something is waiting to pester me.

Their attention locks on me as I step inside, and they fall silent. For a brief moment, none of us do anything but stare at each other, unmoving.

"So…" Nathan starts while the others watch on.

"So…" I parrot back.

They're lucky I'm still riding the high from last night. If it were any other day, I wouldn't entertain their antics, but I'm feeling uncharacteristically patient. And I might be itching to fill them in on what went down.

I'm an asshole, but I'm also human. Gossip is in our DNA.

A buzzing energy has been flowing through my veins since I left Yellow's dorm. I barely slept with it vibrating right below the skin. Maybe a verbal purge will get it out of my system.

"Don't play games with us," Karis snaps. "How did last night go? Did she tell you to fuck off? I bet she told him to fuck off."

"She didn't tell me to fuck off."

"Ha. You owe me ten dollars," Nathan tells Karis.

"Shut up. You can't blame me for thinking the girl might have more of a backbone."

"So you and Kori are together now?" Morgan asks, completely ignoring our friends' antics.

"We are going out on Sunday, but yeah. I think we're together."

I mean, I told her we were. But saying yes to one date isn't a commitment. It doesn't matter; she's my girl...unless I fuck up this date like I've fucked up everything else so far.

"What's the game plan for that?" Nathan asks.

Oh, so now he's paying attention. Good to know my love life is more interesting than whatever bet he and Karis have going.

"Fuck if I know. I'm still trying to figure that part out. I'll be honest, I would have been on Karis's side with this. I had no hope she would say yes."

"What does she like?" Morgan asks.

It's such a simple question, but my brain completely freezes. In that second, every conversation I've ever had with my girl is wiped from my memory.

"She likes...yellow..."

"Jesus Christ, you're a lost cause," Karis says, hopping off the desk. "Have fun with your girl talk."

"Man, she might be right if that's all you've got," Nathan says.

"Fuck."

My gloom makes an appearance. Its tendrils of dread creep along my mind, slowly obscuring my bright mood with shadows of doubt. I swipe my hand across my face and start to pace in the small lobby.

I've never planned a date before—at least one that matters. In the past, taking a woman out was a precursor to taking her home. There was no meaning behind it. Every time was the same: overpriced drinks at a mid-range bar that was just swanky enough to be impressive, followed by no-strings-attached sex. It was a simple formula that worked, but I'm not looking for no strings with Yellow. Fuck, I want her to wrap me in all her strings. What's been brewing between us isn't some fling, and it sure as hell isn't a one-night stand. I don't know what the future looks like, but I want her to be in it.

"Stop freaking out. We will help you figure it out," Morgan promises, interrupting my impending spiral.

"What he said," Nathan adds. "This isn't a normal awkward first date either. You and Kori already know each other, so this will be a piece of cake."

"But don't treat it like you're hanging out with a friend. Knowing her isn't an excuse to skimp out on making her feel special. You need to show her you are serious about taking this to the next level, and that this is more than a friends thing."

"How do I do that?"

"Spoil her. Touch her often and casually. Brush up against her, hold her hand, put an arm around her." Nathan answers first, but Morgan is quick to offer his two cents as soon as he stops speaking.

Goddamn, it's like the two of them share the same brain cell sometimes.

"Give her your undivided attention, and use the time to get to know her."

"Bring her something—probably flowers—and take her out to eat somewhere nice. Show her you are putting effort in."

"All right, that seems easy enough," I cut in before Morgan can add to the growing list.

As helpful as they're trying to be, every addition makes my head spin a little more. Dinner and flowers are something I can handle—touching too—but if I let myself get bogged down in the rest, I won't be able to give her the attention she deserves. My nerves are going to be fried enough as is.

"Thank you for the input," I tell my friends, "but I've got to get ready for my class. The kids are going to start trickling in any minute."

"I'll send you a list of some of my favorite date spots," Nathan says as I start to walk away.

My phone starts buzzing before I make it to the locker room. My friend works fast. The list is more than a few suggestions, and I don't recognize half the restaurants on it. Why would I? Eating out isn't a luxury I can often afford. I click on one of the links he sent and damn near have a heart attack when I see the prices.

Forty-eight dollars for an entrée? It's highway robbery. Kori is worth it, though. Fuck, she'd be worth something four times this amount.

Fuck it. I'll put it on my credit card. What's another hundred dollars of debt when the existing total is more than I'll ever be able to pay off. Later tonight, I'll call and make a reservation, and then all I can do is wait impatiently for Sunday to come. With any luck, my nerves won't eat me alive before then.

Chapter 21
Kori

Gage cleans up good.

Not that he doesn't look good normally, or that "cleaned up" is much different from his normal "not gym" vibe. His dark-wash jeans are missing the wear and tear I'm used to and hug his toned thighs like a glove. I can appreciate a man who doesn't skip leg day. He's exchanged his black T-shirt for a button-up that strains against the barrel of his chest. The only thing that's the same is the well-worn black leather combat boots. I like them—they add a hint of suitable edginess to the otherwise plain look.

I'm not sure he would be Gage without that glimmer of danger that drew me to him in the first place.

Although he doesn't look dangerous now, standing stiff in the dorm's lobby with a bouquet of bright sunflowers in his hand. He tugs at the collar of his shirt like it's a snake constricting his neck and looks around the room in darting sweeps. His eyes freeze when they see me standing by the desk, watching him like a creep, and the tension that twists his face dissipates, relaxing back into the stony expression I've come to realize is his neutral state. He doesn't smile, not fully, but the corner of his lips twitches as he takes me in. His eyes, on the other hand, shine. I don't know *what* they are trying to convey, but the heat in them sends a shiver down my spine regardless.

My skirt brushes against my thighs as I bound over to him in a few bouncy steps. He tracks my every movement, and the desire to kiss him is almost unbearable, but I restrain myself. I don't know how he feels about PDA.

"I got you these." He shoves the flowers into my hand in lieu of a greeting and tucks his hands into his pockets.

"Thanks. Should I go put them upstairs or..."

"You can leave them in my car if you want. Or go upstairs. Fuck, I didn't think this through. They probably need water or something." He rubs the back of his neck as he rambles.

"I love them. Now hold on, I'll be right back."

I practically run up the stairs to my room and put the flowers in the first vase-like object I can find. No one has ever bought me flowers before, so I've never had a reason to buy an actual vase. Who needs a vase, anyway? They are a conspiracy by Big Glass to boost their profits. Any container that holds water should work just fine to keep some flowers alive. Right?

With the bouquet tucked in the reusable water bottle my mom bought for me that I never actually remember to take to class, I head back down to Gage. He would get a kick out of my choice in container, and probably tell me I need to drink more water—again.

My date hasn't moved from where I left him and looks even more out of place than before, which is a feat. His awkwardness is endearing. I love that he is willing to put himself in an uncomfortable position for me.

"You ready to go?" I ask as I rejoin him.

He nods and grabs my hand, giving it a soft squeeze before leading us toward the parking lot. It doesn't register until we get outside that he said "his car."

"You got it fixed?" I ask.

"Yeah. Karis and the guys came by last week and got her running again."

"Her?"

"Yup. Kori, meet Brandy—with a *Y*."

I'm not sure what I expected, but an old muscle car somehow both fits and seems wrong. The poor thing is covered in rust and cracks. It's the furthest thing from a shining example of a vehicle well cared for. Gage has to fold himself like a pretzel to even fit inside, and he doesn't look comfortable crammed into the front seat.

"She's..."

"A piece of shit. But she's mine."

The engine rattles over roaring exhaust as he pulls out of the lot and onto the street, but that is the only sound in the car. He doesn't even turn the radio on. The silence gnaws at me; I can't tell if it's the good type or the bad type. Probably bad, since I'm wondering about it, but my date doesn't seem perturbed.

Conversation shouldn't be this hard. It's not like I haven't talked to him since he showed up at my dorm—we've texted. Well, mostly I've texted, but he's always given me a response. Maybe I misread the situation and spent the past few days bombarding him with an endless, unwanted stream of my inner thoughts. Maybe he's merely trying to get through tonight to be polite, and then he'll tell me he never wants to see me again.

My leg starts to bounce, shaking the whole car with it. I don't move for long. His hand crosses the center console and finds a place to rest on my thigh, halting the motion. The touch is unexpected but not unwelcome. Those calloused fingers rub against my bare skin, leaving trails of tingling sparks in their wake.

"You good?" he asks.

"Yeah. Just nervous," I tell him and force my leg still.

"Me too," he says with a chuckle that matches his words. "It's been a while since I've done this."

"Done what? Made small talk in a car?"

"Well, yeah. But I meant the whole date thing."

"Oh."

His confession settles some of the buzzing energy in me. I never got the impression that Gage is the type who sleeps around—not that there's anything wrong with that. He just gives off major leave-me-alone vibes—but I figured he'd have way more experience with this whole thing than me. Knowing he's equally as lost makes it easier somehow—like I'm not alone in this.

"I've never actually been on a real date," I say, and his hand tightens on my thigh. Not in a painful way, but hard enough that I notice the change.

"Fuck," he mumbles under his breath. "Kori, this feels weird even asking, but am I the first man you've ever been with? Was that your first kiss the other day at the gym?"

The serious switch in his tone causes laughter to bubble up in my chest. There is nothing funny about the situation, but my choices are either laugh or shrink under the uncomfortable weight of his questions.

"No. You aren't my first." His shoulders relax at my words, so I keep talking. "I had a boyfriend back in high school, but we didn't do the whole date thing. He said it was a waste of time when we could skip that and go back to his place."

His spine snaps back to rigid attention, and the muscles in his jaw flex from how hard he clenches his teeth. For several seconds, he doesn't say a word while he calms himself with a series of deep breaths.

"Spoiling you could never be a waste of time." The words are said with so much confidence, I almost believe him.

The parking lot in front of the large craftsmen-style house-turned-restaurant is packed. Gage finds a spot, and before I can even get myself unbuckled, he is out of the car and walking around to open my door. He offers me a hand, helping me climb out, and keeps his fingers locked with mine as he leads me toward the entrance.

Inside, he gives our reservation details to a well-dressed host, who leads us to a clothed, candle-lit table in the back. My date rubs his hand over the back of his neck and sits in the too-small chair. The host hands us tiny half sheets of paper that she dubs our "menu" and leaves us to our own devices.

I read over the selection, and then do it again because I'm clearly missing something. *Radicchio? Gastrique?* I don't even know what half the words on the menu mean. Is it too much to ask for chicken nuggets? Hell, I'd take a simple steak. And six options? What kind of restaurant only has six options? Nothing comes close to resembling any of my safe foods. If each entrée wasn't fifty dollars,

I'd be more willing to try something, but not when it's on Gage's dime—he made it explicitly clear that I wouldn't be paying a cent despite my protests.

"Is everything all right?"

A lie bubbles up, but I stop myself before I tell him everything is fine. How can I expect no bullshit if I bullshit him?

"Can we go somewhere else?" My eyes fall shut as I chew on my lip.

"Hey, none of that."

Sparks rain through me as his thumb runs across my mouth, coaxing the abused lower lip out from between my teeth. When my lashes open, he's staring at me with the same intense heat that was there before he kissed me in my room. His hand doesn't fall away as his fingers ghost over the sensitive skin. Each pass sends another wave of sparks through me, setting all my nerves alight with electric energy.

"Hi, I'm Andrea, and I'll be your server toni—"

"Give us a minute," Gage says without taking his gaze from me. There's no mistaking the command behind the softly spoken words.

Our waitress nods and scurries away from the table without protest.

"Now tell me what's wrong."

My whole body shudders when he finally pulls his hand away.

"Nothing's wrong, exactly. This place is very nice, and I really, really appreciate the effort you went through planning this. Like, it's totally great—"

"Kori." He says my name with a soft growl.

"It's just...I don't know what any of this food is, or if I'll like it, and I don't want to ruin our date by hating the food. Especially after you went through the effort of planning it all."

He reaches across the table and covers my hand with his.

"Thank you for telling me, but let's get one thing straight: you could never ruin anything."

My face flushes as his intense stare bores into me.

"So what sounds good?" he asks.

"Promise you won't judge?"

"I promise."

"Can we get Mexican?"

"Mexican it is."

His lips twitch with a smile as he stands and pulls me to my feet. Our fingers stay entwined as we walk back through the restaurant, ignoring the confused looks from the staff. He doesn't let me go until we're back in the car, and even then, the separation only lasts long enough for him to turn on the radio and set it to a pop station before he grabs my hand again and rests them twined together on the center console.

It doesn't take us long to make it to the new restaurant. The scent of peppers and other spices hits me like a delicious wall as we step inside. I feel like a cartoon character being carried into the brightly decorated space on that tantalizing tendril. There's nothing unique about the Mexican restaurant, which makes it perfect. Sure, it's loud and bright, but it's a familiar loud and bright, which makes it safe.

"This better?" he asks.

"This is perfect," I tell him with a smile. "Now let's go get some queso."

A hostess seats us and hands us our menus. We order our drinks, and once the server leaves, we fall back into silence while we look over our options. I don't need to—I always get the same thing—but flipping through the oversized book gives me something to do with my hands and an excuse to keep my eyes off the man in front of me.

So what happens now?

Talking to him was so much easier through text, but I think that's true for most people. Everything is easier with that barrier of tech. People become data, nothing more than names on screens, and you don't have to worry about things like micro-expressions or body language when you can't see someone's face. All you have are the words someone says, and everyone has the same inputs to go off. It evens the playing field a bit. I've always had an easier time connecting online than in person, but I also know those relationships only go so deep. People can hide a lot of who they are behind a keyboard.

"So, how are classes?" Gage asks once we place our orders and the server takes the menus away.

"They are classes," I say with a shrug. "Things are starting to pick up now that the semester is getting into full swing."

"Is that a good thing? I'm a little out of touch. I haven't stepped foot in a classroom in almost two decades."

"It gives me something to do besides playing video games and watching movies all night. Although it seems like all of my professors conspired to have their due dates aligned."

"Right."

An uncomfortable awkwardness surrounds us as we lapse into silence.

Rather than focus on it, I turn my attention to the basket of chips on the table, breaking them into tiny pieces. A sheen of sweat forms on my date's forehead as he watches my fingers work. He swallows hard and wipes away the perspiration with the back of his hand.

"It's hot today, huh," he mutters, and I damn near lose it.

No.

Just no.

There is no way we are going to be so awkward that we resort to talking about the weather.

"Freeze," I tell him, and he listens, but his heavy brow furrows.

"What did I do?"

"The weather? Really? We can do better than that."

"I didn't think small talk would be this hard. I guess I'm more out of practice than I thought."

"Who wants to make small talk? Small talk is terrible. Small talk is for strangers and coworkers you secretly hate. We aren't strangers, and I don't hate you, so let's skip the awkward get-to-know-you bit, okay?"

"Okay." He lets out a deep breath and folds his hands on the table in front of him. "So what do you propose instead?"

"I don't know. I'll look up some date questions. That has to be better than this."

I pull out my phone and google first-date questions. My face twists as I read through the list. I don't know how they managed it, but whoever wrote this somehow created questions that are both incredibly personal and superficial at the same time.

How do you unwind at the end of the day?

Who are you closest to in your family?

What's your favorite season?

Do people seriously ask each other things like that?

"What's wrong?" he asks.

"These are terrible."

"Let me see." He reaches across the table, and I hand him my phone.

He scrolls through it, his brow furrowing deeper with each passing moment. "Yeah, you're right, these suck."

"If you had to eat a crayon, what color would you choose?" I ask the first thing that pops into my head.

"What?" He chokes on a chip as he tries not to laugh.

"You heard me. What color crayon are you eating?"

"Is this a normal pack, or are we splurging for the big one with the sharpener on the back?"

"Sharpener, obviously." *As if we'd waste our time with anything else.*

"That's a lot of options. I'm gonna say one of the oranges."

He can be wrong.

"Why orange?"

"It at least has a food in the name," he says with a shrug. "You'd choose yellow, right?"

"The brightest one in the box," I confirm.

"Nothing is as bright as you, Low," Gage says, and my jaw drops.

That smooth motherfucker.

"Gagriel Maher, did you just use a line on me," I admonish with a laugh.

"Gagriel?" he asks, his lips twitching into the start of a smile.

"Don't change the subject. You were totally hitting on me."

"Of course I was," he says in that gruff monotone of his. "I've got to woo my girl."

His girl.

The certainty in his voice leaves no room for questions, and my heart melts into a pile of goo. I really like the sound of that.

"I don't know if I'm sufficiently wooed yet. Maybe you need to keep trying."

"Is that a challenge?" he asks.

The heated look that darkens his eyes makes my thighs clench together and my mouth water. He doesn't wait for me to respond, which is a good thing, because I'm pretty sure he stole my voice with his gaze. Shadows fall over the table as he leans forward, encroaching on my space, and I lean into him, drawn in by some unseen magnetic force until our faces are only a few inches apart. Our breath mingles in the space between us, and for one long, tortuous second, he says nothing at all.

Then he stands.

That abrupt motion rips through the tension like a porcupine in a bounce house. My whole body straightens as my eyes follow him, and from my seated position, he towers over me. Before I can question him, he moves again. This time, his movements are fluid as he slides into the booth next to me and puts one arm over the back of it so it rests behind me. He isn't quite touching me, but the intention is perfectly clear. It's a claim.

"I didn't like how far away you were." His gravelly whisper kisses my ear, and a shudder runs through me straight to my aching core. "Next time we go out, I want you to sit next to me. I don't want to have to reach across the table to touch you. Is that good with you?"

I didn't know someone could turn me on with their words alone, but when he goes all in-charge on me, I turn into Niagara Falls.

"Yes, Gage," I rasp in a breathy whisper, and the man beside me groans.

"You are so perfect," he tells me.

His arm drops to my shoulders, and he pulls me against him. I don't hesitate to cuddle into his side.

"I haven't told you how beautiful you look yet. That was my mistake. I just got so tongue-tied when I saw you standing there looking like all my sweetest fantasies come to life." He continues to whisper the words loud enough that only I can hear them as his fingers start to trail down my arm. The touch sends delicious tingles through my whole body.

He opens his mouth to say more but is interrupted by the server bringing our meals. I expect him to jerk away from me, but he doesn't even glance in their direction as they put our plates on the table. I, on the other hand, feel like a kid who got caught with their hand in a very muscular cookie jar. My whole face feels hot, and I can't bring myself to look at the server either, but for an entirely different reason.

"How was that for wooing?" Gage asks with a soft chuckle.

"Consider me wooed."

He presses a gentle kiss to my temple, and only then does he pull his arm back so we can eat. My mind is too riled to focus on the food in front of me. For now, I'll count down the minutes until we can leave and go somewhere with a little more privacy. I don't know how far I want to go tonight, but I wouldn't mind a repeat of what happened in my dorm room. We just have to get through dinner first.

Chapter 22
Gage

Kori snorts and chokes on a bite of food as she tries to contain the abrupt fit of laughter. Nothing I said was anywhere near funny enough to get that sort of response, but her joy makes my gut twist and bubble in an unfamiliar way that isn't actually uncomfortable.

I like that I make her laugh. I love how she does it with her whole heart, snorting and choking included.

She is joy personified.

I've never been so enamored with anyone in my whole life. It's got me tongue-tied and acting like an awkward idiot; thank whatever god is listening that she seems to find it all amusing. After the rocky start to our evening, I thought for sure she was going to end things and ask me to take her home, but she surprised me by being blunt about what she wanted. I would be a liar if I said it didn't make me like her even more. I'm too damn old for games.

Everything seemed to fall into place after the awkward small-talk bit. She's kept the conversation flowing with insane questions between bites of food. Things like "if you were a potato product, what would you be" and "if you had to choose, would you go to pirate school or knight school."

I cleared my plate a while ago, but she's been too caught up in her questions to remember to eat. I'm not about to complain. The longer she takes, the more time I get to have her by my side. It's not like the restaurant is busy or they need this table. I'll stay here until this place closes if it's what she wants. Having her next to me, touching her, feeling her lean closer into me as she laughs—well, that's been the highlight of my week. Hell, maybe my year.

"I think I'm done," she says and places her utensils on her half-filled plate.

"You sure? Do you want a box to take that home with you?"

"I'm good. I don't actually have a way to reheat it."

The amount of food left on her plate makes my skin itch with the sense of *wrong*, but I tune out the voice in my head screaming at me about the waste. I drape my arm back over her shoulders with a grunt of acknowledgment. Our waiter doesn't take more than a few moments to notice the change and make their way to our table.

"How was everything?"

"Really good," Kori answers before I can, so I nod along in agreement.

"Are you ready for your check?"

"Yes," I tell them.

"Perfect. I'll be right back with that."

"You don't have to pay for me," Kori says with a huff.

"I know. I want to. I asked you out, I'm paying. Simple as that." Pulling her into my side, I plant a kiss on her temple. "Plus, I've got to take care of my girl."

At those words, she melts into me with a dopey smile on her face. It takes all my restraint not to bend down and taste that smile for myself.

The waiter comes back, and I give him my credit card without looking at the bill. I know it won't be crazy expensive, but I don't want to ruin this moment by thinking about money. I was prepared to spend triple this to spoil her like she deserves. And it's not like I hadn't already done the math in my head while we ordered. Two entrées, two soft drinks, and an appetizer. I've spent enough time serving that I added tip and tax on too. I can afford it—I can afford more—but dread flares in my gut as I take the folio from the waiter anyway.

With a small grimace, I sign the receipt and climb out of the booth. Kori crawls out behind me in the most awkward, uncoordinated way she could have managed. I don't know why she thought that was easier than sliding, but she

172

never moves in the ways I expect. Training for as long as I have has given me a good idea of how a body *should* move, and that isn't it. Once she finds her footing, I offer her my hand and don't let go, pulling her close so I can wrap my arm around her waist instead.

"I don't want tonight to be over," she says with a sigh as we walk out into the humid night.

"We can go back to my place," I suggest and instantly regret it as she tenses in my arm.

"I don't mean for sex," I blurt out, which only causes her to stumble over her feet. "I just meant I didn't want this to be over either. We can go walk around campus instead."

"No, your place sounds nice," she says as her eyes drop to the cracked asphalt.

"Are you sure?"

"Yes, I'm sure."

On the drive back, my hand rests on that spot on her thigh—right below the hem of her bright-yellow skirt—and I rub the skin there while she continues to ramble on with whatever random thoughts pop into her head. She doesn't ask a lot of questions, which is a relief because I don't think I could focus on the road while giving her the full attention she deserves. Having her next to me is distracting enough.

There's no game plan for when we arrive. I wasn't lying when I told her I haven't been on a date in a while, and I certainly haven't brought a woman back to my place—it's been years since I've had any desire to be with a woman at all. Yellow is an anomaly in every sense of the word, and I couldn't begin to explain why.

As we pull up, I expect her to stiffen or at least show some hesitancy, but she smiles at me as I put the car in park. Before I can get her door for her, she is out of the car and climbing the stairs, giving me a perfect view of her thick thighs and the round cheeks of her ass peeking out from under her skirt. A growl builds in my chest as I scramble out of the car after her. No one else is around, which is good, because that view belongs to me now.

I bound up the stairs behind her, crowding her, but leaving space between that ass and my growing erection. I don't want to scare her; I meant it when I told her this wasn't about sex, and I have no plans to go back on that. That doesn't change how every single one of my nerve endings is in tune with her every movement. She was made at a frequency my body can't ignore. I can only imagine what it will be like when she is finally ready to touch me. There's no doubt in my mind it won't be as perfect as the rest of her. I'll probably make a fool out of myself—I'm out of practice, and my stamina isn't what it used to be—but I'll make sure it's good for her.

Her sweet, fruity scent floods my senses as I reach around her to unlock the door. It takes every ounce of willpower not to spin her and kiss her senseless against the peeling wood. My apartment is dark, like always, but for the first time in a long time, I don't dread stepping inside. How could I when I brought my own bit of sunshine home with me?

She waits near the doorway while I move through the darkness to turn on the overhead light. The sudden bright flash is jarring, and we both flinch. Most nights, I don't even bother with it; the bulb under the microwave is enough for me to move around without knocking into things. I wish I would have turned that on instead. Under the orange-tinted glow from the ceiling fan, my apartment feels dingy and small.

It *is* dingy and small, but the lighting doesn't help.

"Do you want a water or coffee?" I ask as uncertainty floods me.

"I'm good," she says, wandering over to the shelves of pictures near the TV.

My fingers twitch with the urge to stop her. I don't like people inspecting my stuff and invading my privacy. Every moment that has ever felt important is memorialized in those cheap particle board bookcases: my family, my friends, remnants of a dream that never got to be. I'm a sentimental fool. The only reason I let her explore is Morgan said I needed to do the whole emotional vulnerability thing, and this is a good start. It might be easier for me to tell her about myself and my past if she has specific questions. Maybe this will be more successful than the whole fancy date advice I got from Nathan, because that was a load of shit.

I give her a few minutes to take it all in and head to the kitchen to grab myself a glass of water. I'm not thirsty, but it's something to do besides stare at her like a creep. When I come back to the living room, she's still poring over the shelves.

"Find anything interesting?" I ask as I step up behind her to look over her shoulder.

"Is this your mom?" She points at a photo of Ma, my brother, and me in front of a Christmas tree in her apartment.

"Yeah, and my brother Layne."

"Does she live close?"

"Nah. They're both back in Boston, but I make a point to visit a few times a year to see them."

Ma would wring my neck otherwise. She hated when I left, even if she understood why I needed to do it. The least I can do is make sure I stop by for the major holidays.

"That's really sweet," she says.

"Layne and I are all she has. My dad passed away when I was in high school."

Kori gasps and reaches behind her to grab my forearm.

"I had no idea. I'm so sorry, I didn't mean to dig up old wounds."

"It was years ago, and I'd rather talk about him than pretend he never existed. He had cancer, but it all happened so quickly. One day he was complaining about a pain in his chest, and a few months later, he was gone. Ma took it hard, understandably. They were high school sweethearts, and he was her whole world. She didn't even have time to grieve properly—not with two kids to support and a job that would've fired her at the drop of a hat for missing her shifts. I think she should have let them fire her. It's not like it was enough anyway. Money got tight, so I dropped out and got a job washing dishes that paid under the table and didn't mind breaking a few labor laws."

"Gage..." she starts, but I don't want her sympathy.

"None of that. Tell me about your family. Are you close?"

"Yeah, we're close. It's just my mom, my dad, and me. I don't have any siblings, and my grandma passed a few years back. They live a little over an hour from here, but we video chat at least once a week."

Her attention shifts to another frame. This one has a picture of Karis and me at the belt ceremony where she got her purple belt a few months after she joined Double Teep. The photo beside it is almost identical except instead of purple, her belt is brown, and the one on the end is the two of us after I got my black belt.

"How long have you known Karis?"

"Damn, it's been close to six years now, I think."

"Six years? How old is she?"

Kare would kill me if I spilled that she was rapidly approaching thirty, so I just shrug and wrap my arms around my woman. She melts against me, resting all her weight against the front of my body.

"Do you remember the other night?" she asks and looks back at me with a shy smile.

As if the memories of her lips against mine and the way she rubbed her pussy against my aching cock haven't been the center of every dirty thought I've had over the past few days. I think I've jerked off more in the past seventy-two hours than I did in the six months before I met her.

"Which night?" I ask, bending to kiss the curve of her neck.

"You know exactly which night I'm talking about," she says with an adorable, annoyed huff, even as she tilts her head to give me more access.

"What about it?" I ask with my lips against her skin. I don't trail them along the column of her neck like I want to—not yet, at least. The last thing I want is for her to feel any sort of pressure to do anything physical with me. I promised her tonight wasn't about sex.

"I want to do that again."

"Do what again? I need you to use your words so I know exactly what you want me to do to you," I whisper in her ear.

She stiffens, and for a second, I think I've pushed her too far, but then she lets out the sweetest fucking mewl I've ever heard.

"I want you to kiss me again. Like you did before."

That's the only permission I need.

I spin her around and crash my lips against hers. This kiss is filled with every ounce of desire that's been burning under the surface of my skin from the moment I saw her standing in her dorm looking like sin and sunlight. Her energy matches mine as she throws her arms around my neck and pulls me even closer.

"Is it still all right if I touch you?" I ask, my chest heaving as I gasp for air.

She nods, and I close the gap again, teasing the seam of her lips with my tongue. I grab her ass, squeezing the soft flesh as I lift her up to a more comfortable level. She wraps her legs around me, and the heat of her pussy presses against my abs. My cock throbs behind the restrictive denim of my jeans.

"Couch," she gasps, and I move my lips to her neck as I carry her there, ignoring the sharp twinge of pain that shoots through my leg when I twist in the wrong direction. This is way more pressing than that.

She straddles my lap, and in this skirt, the thin cotton of her panties is the only thing separating me from the sweetest part of her. Even through the layers covering me, I can feel how damp that fabric is as she grinds down on my bulge.

Fucking hell, she feels good.

I let out a hiss and bite down on her shoulder to keep myself from taking this further than I intended. *This isn't about sex,* I repeat in my head, but I barely believe myself when she's grinding against me with such abandon. My hands slide up her body to cup her small tits. If I didn't, I was going to start guiding her hips, and that isn't what this is about. She is the one in control here.

My lips find hers again, capturing her tiny moans as she finds pleasure against my weeping cock. I haven't come in my pants since I was a teenager, but if she keeps this up, I just might. That thought is enough to snap me out of the lusty haze. Not because there's anything wrong with the act, but because I promised her no sex, and I don't want to cross that line without her explicit permission.

"Kor, baby, hold on." I grab her hips to put some space between us, and the disappointed groan that falls from her swollen lips is almost enough to break my resolve.

"Why? What's wrong?" she pants.

Her eyes seem almost black from how large her pupils have blown. I'm sure mine are just as bad. This woman is a living aphrodisiac.

"Nothing is wrong, but if you keep doing that, you're going to make me come."

Her head cocks to the side as she thinks, and then her lips curl into a devious smile. I don't think I like that look.

"Kori—" I start as she deliberately rubs her pussy along the length of me. "I'm serious, you don't have to do this."

"Gage, shut up," she says and steals any further protest with a kiss.

She grinds on me with more deliberate thrusts. I can't pry my hands from her hips, not now, not when she's taking the lead on pushing things further. Tentatively, I move her, pulling her against me in a way that has me seeing stars, and from the way she moans, I think the friction is good for her too.

My orgasm sneaks up on me and hits me with the force of a freight train. I smother my groan against her lips and slow the motion of her hips as my cock twitches and spurts in the confines of the cloth.

"Why did you stop," she asks with a pout.

"'Cause you milked me dry."

"Oh." Her eyes widen as she looks between my face and my crotch, and then she smiles with impish glee.

"Did you like making me come like a teenager with no self-control? Do you like knowing how hot you get me?"

She sucks in a breath and bites her lower lip as she nods.

"You are trouble," I tell her with a playful growl.

Me. Playful. I didn't see that one coming, but Yellow brings out a side of me I thought died years ago.

She laughs and buries her face in the crook of my neck, peppering the skin there with soft kisses. I hug her closer, more content than I can ever remember feeling. The question of what to do next is the only thing that keeps me from fully losing myself in the moment.

I'll be damned if I leave my woman wanting.

"Hey, Low?" I mumble against her hair.

"Hm."

"Do you want me to get you off too?"

Her reaction is immediate. Those gentle kisses stop as she turns to stone in my arms.

"Hey, what just happened?" I urge her head back so she can see my face and how serious I am about there being no pressure here. "You are in control here. We do whatever you want to do."

"I-I just...I-I don't know if I'll like that. I've never done *that* before." Her eyes drop to look at her hands.

She's never done what? Been fingered? Had an orgasm?

I want to ask her more, but this isn't the time. Selfishly, I don't want her thinking about some other asshole when she's with me. When the day comes that she's comfortable enough to try these things with me, I'm going to make sure she feels so good she won't remember that it could be any other way. I want to ruin her for anyone else the same way she's ruining me.

"Okay. We don't have to find out today. Want to cuddle and watch a movie, or do you want me to take you home now?"

"Movie, please," she says and relaxes back into my chest.

"Mind if I go change first?" I ask as heat rises in my face.

I can't believe I seriously let her dry hump me to completion.

Kori pushes me away with a giggle, and I rush to change. I don't want to waste a second of the time I have with her, because at some point, she's going to realize she can do so much better than me.

Chapter 23
Kori

Lines of code blur together on my screen, turning the already hard-to-read characters into a sea of hieroglyphics. I blink to refocus my eyes, but it doesn't do much to help. What I thought made sense hours ago reads like nonsense now, which is only confirmed when I get *another* error when I try to run it.

"Daisy, I give up," I say with a frustrated huff as I click out of my assignment.

It's clear I'm not making any more progress on it tonight. I'll try again with fresh eyes in the morning and inevitably get annoyed when the fix is something obvious like a missing semicolon. It's always a fucking semicolon.

A clear head would help as well. It's impossible to focus when everything reminds me of Gage. All it takes is one glance at the flowers on my desk, and my mind wanders back to our date. I could lie and say my thoughts are innocent, but the memories of how he made me laugh and the fun we had together are what occupy my daydreams. His touch, his taste, the power I wielded over him as I coaxed his body into submission: those are the things I keep coming back to.

God, that look on his face when he came. I don't think I've ever been more turned on in my whole life. It's a heady feeling to have a man like that at your mercy. It's not something I'd ever experienced before last night, but I'm already craving it again—craving him again—and the constant horny brain is making getting anything else done an impossible feat.

Exhibit A: my incomplete assignment.

Exhibit B through Z: the list of assignments due this week I haven't even started.

If that wasn't bad enough, I haven't heard a word from him beyond a generic "good morning" text this morning. I replied in kind, and then there was nothing. No check-ins about my day. No random memes. Sure, I didn't initiate anything either, but the proverbial ball is in his court. Everything I've read online says not to double text, or I'll come across as clingy and scare him away.

It's stupid; I feel like we are playing games now, and we never did that before he asked me out. Things were easy between us—texts were sporadic but never with any pressure. Now the whole dynamic has shifted, and I don't know what to do. I really want to talk to him, but I don't want to scare him away by being too much.

I tend to ruin things by coming on too strong. At least that's what I've been told by friends in the past when they decided they were done with me. What if Gage sees how weird I am and decides he's done with me too?

"What would you do in my shoes?" I ask the duck.

Of course she tells me to text the man. She's always had more confidence in her little plastic shell than I've ever dreamed of having.

"But what do I say?"

Telling him I miss him already would be coming on too strong, but if I don't say anything, he might think I'm not interested. Why can't there be step-by-step instructions on how to do this whole girlfriend thing? That would make this one thousand times easier.

"I could ask him about his day," I muse.

That is the sane option here. It's an open-ended question—the forums I read said those are good for getting conversations flowing.

What's the worst that could happen from one text? Gage could decide he made a mistake asking me out in the first place, tell me he never wants to see me again, and all of his friends block me on everything, leaving me completely alone again, but the odds of that happening are slim.

I think.

Realistically, he leaves me on read. I can deal with being left on read.

Fuck it.

I grab my phone, but my fingers freeze before I can craft a message. What do I say? Should I use emoji? Exclamation points? Those might make me seem too enthusiastic.

Why is this so hard?

I take a deep breath and type the first thing that comes to my mind and hit send before I can chicken out.

Hi.

"Hi." Really. That's the best I could do?

I throw myself onto my bed with a dramatic groan and prepare to wait, but the message is read before I can lock my phone, and three little dots pop up on the screen.

Hi.

The teasing is clear even through text. It would help if I had a game plan going into this. I start to type, then delete the message, and then I do it again in an endless cycle of uncertainty.

What's up?

My boyfriend's text stops the worrying.

I can hear you overthinking through the screen.

Anxiety's hold on my heart loosens as the next message comes through less than a second later. He double texted. That has to mean something, right? Maybe the games really are all in my head.

There's only one way to find out.

I take a deep breath and let my fingers fly, blocking out the voice in my head telling me I'm being too much and spilling my truth.

I don't know. I wanted to talk to you, but I couldn't think of anything to say.

I find that hard to believe.

Nothing interesting, at least.

Again, hard to believe. Everything you say is interesting. You keep me on my toes. I like that.

I like you.

Shit. That was too much. His response comes through before I can backtrack on my admission.

I've got thirty before I need to leave for my shift at Cutter's. Can I call you?

He doesn't wait for my response before an incoming call pops up on my screen.

"Hi," I squeak as I answer it, and a low chuckle comes through the line.

"Hey, Low."

His rich timbre washes over me, sending a warm tingle down my spine and lighting me up from the inside. It's been less than a day since I've heard his voice—which is no time in the grand scheme of things—but the sound is a drug, soothing the growing itch of withdrawal.

"Is everything okay? Why are you calling?"

"Do I need a reason to call my girl besides wanting to hear her voice?"

"No, but you saw me yesterday."

"That was yesterday. I miss you."

"It's too soon for you to miss me," I protest despite the butterflies swarming in my stomach.

"Says who?"

"I don't know, the internet? We've only been on one date, that's way too early to be missing each other like this."

"One: we've known each other for weeks. Yesterday might have been our first date, but by no stretch was it our start. Two: fuck what anyone else thinks. The only people whose opinions matter when it comes to our relationship are us. Three: are you saying you miss me too?"

"Maybe..."

"When can I see you again?" he asks with a desperate rasp.

"Why are you asking me? You are the one with a million jobs."

"It's only two now. But I work every night this week. You could come by Cutter's. I'm sure the crew would keep you company."

The "yes" is on my tongue, but Daisy's beady glare keeps it from slipping past my lips. She knows how many hours the pile of unfinished assignments with looming due dates is going to take for me to finish, and it's too many for me to spare a night going out with friends—even if I really want to.

"As great as that sounds..."

"You can't," he finishes for me, sounding dejected.

"I have too much schoolwork to get done this week. It's like my professors conspired to set all their due dates at the same time."

"Are you busy this Saturday? I've got most of the afternoon free."

"No, I'm available."

"Perfect. Then I'm taking you out."

"That sounds like a statement, not a question."

"Because it wasn't," he says in the no-nonsense way that makes me want to do very dirty things to him.

"Yes, Coach," I rasp, and based on the low growl he gives in response, he knows exactly where my head is at.

"Go to bed, or work on your assignments. I'll call you again tomorrow, okay?"

"Okay."

"Goodnight, Kori."

"Goodnight, Gage," I say, and the line goes dead.

My body isn't enough to contain the overwhelming swell of emotion in my chest and flurry of butterflies in my stomach. Until this moment, I never understood the whole "kicking your legs" thing that is always in rom-coms, but the urge is there. Maybe it would release some of this all-consuming giddiness. There's no way I'll be able to focus on my assignments like this, so I put on a movie and try to relax enough to get some sleep. It doesn't come easy. My thoughts are full of Gage and my anticipation of tomorrow. I hope it's always like this—I can't imagine being with him and not spending each day looking forward to the next.

Chapter 24
Gage

Air rushes through the open windows as I drive toward Kori's dorm. The sun is out, birds are singing, and I'm...giddy?

The fluttery emotion feels foreign in my chest. But things have been good. No—more than good. My car is fixed, I've got my woman, and business has picked up at Cutter's, so bills won't be a concern again until December.

Minimum payments are still on-time payments.

The relief is like a thousand-pound barbell has been removed from each of my shoulders.

All week, we've texted back and forth, but I haven't had a chance to see her since I drove her home from my apartment. Between her schoolwork and my jobs, it was impossible to find a few hours where we both could slip away. That changes now—I owe my girl a date.

As I pull into the lot outside her dorm, I fire off a text and climb out of my car to meet her. I only make it a couple dozen feet in her direction before a bright-yellow blur flings herself at me. Her arms wrap around my neck, and I instinctively catch her. Those sweet glossy lips of hers find mine with unexpected zeal, and I'm powerless to do anything more than bend to her will and kiss her back.

"Hi," she says, breaking the kiss far too soon.

"Hi," I breathe back, and the bands of my arms tighten around her. I'm not letting her go anytime soon.

"I missed you," she sighs as she melts into my hold.

The ache those words bring to my chest is hard to ignore.

"I missed you too. I don't have to go into Cutter's until ten, so I'm yours for the next few hours."

I don't put her down as I walk back to the car. Several students stare at us with disapproval on their faces, but as soon as they meet my hardened glare, their eyes fall away. They can look at me however they want to, but they don't get to judge my woman like that.

"What did you have in mind?" she asks.

"I wanted to show you one of my favorite places. If that's okay with you?"

"That sounds perfect."

My lips find hers again for a quick kiss before I put her feet on the ground. By the time I drop into the driver's seat, she's buckled in and practically vibrating with her uncontained excitement. It's infectious; her joy coaxes a smile to my lips. I've never smiled as frequently as I do around her.

I turn up the radio and switch through the stations until I find something that matches the mood. The upbeat pop anthem is new to me, but based on the way she starts to nod along to the beat, I know it's the right choice. I prefer to ride without music, but I noticed how antsy she got in the silence, so I'll learn to love the noise.

"I don't have Bluetooth, but feel free to change to whatever station you want," I tell her as I pull out of the parking lot.

This time her leg doesn't shake, but my hand falls to her thigh anyway. I'm not going to waste any opportunity to touch her. She lets out a content sigh and wraps her hand around mine. The small gesture has my chest tightening as my heart twists itself into knots.

Comfort this quickly has to mean something, right? Sure, there are still awkward moments, but in the few weeks I've known her, she's slotted herself into my life so seamlessly it's like she's always belonged. I don't know what to make of it, but I'm not about to squander it either. A man like me doesn't deserve something as perfect as her. Until the day she realizes that, I am going to do everything in my power to make sure she knows how grateful I am that she's mine.

A wave of unease washes through me as we approach our destination. The palms of my hands grow damp, so I move them both to the peeling steering wheel. Flakes of loose vinyl cling to my sweaty skin.

Oblivious to my growing nerves, Kori continues to sing along to the music under her breath. I *shouldn't* be this nervous, but it's only the second date I've been able to take my girl on, and I want her to love it here as much as I do.

This is my favorite place, and she is quickly becoming my favorite person, which makes it far too easy to build up some romanticized fantasy in my head. I don't want to ruin today because I had some preconceived ideas that were never a possibility.

It's so stupid—I don't do fantasies.

I didn't do girlfriends either, yet here I am completely enamored.

Fisting a handful of loose change from my cup holder, I jump out of the car to get Yellow's door for her, and I'm gifted a brilliant smile as I open it and offer her my hand.

"Ever the gentleman," she says with a chuckle and allows me to help her out.

The hairs on my neck tingle as her eyes bore into me while I grab the bag I stowed away in the back seat. Good, let her be curious. She will learn about my surprise for her soon enough.

"Ready?" I ask and entwine my hand with her tiny one.

"Yup. I can't wait for you to show me all your favorite plants."

"I don't think I have a favorite plant. They are just plants," I tell her as I lead her toward the visitors center.

"We can pick out a favorite together, then. I don't know much about plants, if I'm being honest. My mom tried to start a garden once, but that experiment only lasted for a few weeks before she got bored and moved on to something else. Scrapbooking, I think, or it might have been macramé. You are going to have to teach me everything you know."

"I'm no expert—" I start to tell her, but I'm interrupted by a familiar voice calling my name.

"I haven't seen you since the summer. I thought you had moved without telling me," Miss Dorthey, my favorite of the staff here, chastises as she hobbles over from her spot behind the small podium that serves as a front desk.

"Never," I tell her, and I don't fight it as she pulls me into a hug. "Things have been crazy these past few weeks. My car was out of commission, and I've been busy."

Her eyes move to Kori as I mention being busy, and her face softens with a knowing smile. "I can see that. Are you going to introduce me to your friend, or are you going to leave an old woman to make assumptions? You know I can come up with some quite creative ideas."

"No assumptions needed. Miss Dorthey, this is my girlfriend, Kori." I wrap my arm around Kori's waist and tuck her into my side. "Kor, this is Miss Dorthey. She helps take care of the visitors center."

"It's a pleasure to meet you," Kori says in a shy tone and ducks her head toward the ground.

"Oh no. The pleasure is all mine. You know Gage has never brought a woman here before, except for that wild hellion friend of his. What's her name again..." She snaps her fingers as she tries to remember.

"Karis?" Kori supplies.

"Yes, that's the one. At first, I thought they were together, but she about bit my head off when I suggested it. I'm glad he brought you by. I've been worried about him being alone for so long. Loneliness is nothing but trouble for the soul. There are times I can see the dark cloud follow him in here. He needs a good woman to help chase that darkness away and bring a smile back to his face."

I swallow back a groan. This is the exact sort of thing that doesn't fit in the whole romantic fantasy date.

"I'll do everything I can to make him happy," Kori declares. The conviction in her voice surprises me and makes my heart ache in my chest.

Miss Dorthey nods along with the same seriousness before turning her attention back to me.

"What are you kids up to today?"

I don't comment on the fact I stopped being a kid a decade ago.

"We're on a date," I tell her.

"That much is obvious," she says, rolling her eyes, "but don't let me hold you up. You go have fun, but bring her back one day when you have time to chat."

"Yes, Miss Dorthey. It was nice seeing you."

She gives me another quick hug and does the same to Kori before shooing us both into the conservatory. I drop the change into the donations box before we get too far. It's not a lot, but I like to contribute where I can.

"She was so..." Kori says as we get out of earshot.

"Pushy?"

"I was going to say sweet. It's clear she cares about you."

I shrug, but her words make my gut turn uncomfortably.

"Do you want to explore the garden first or get your surprise?" I ask to change the subject. I want to focus on us, not on people who care about me when they shouldn't.

"Surprise?" Her whole face lights up with the question.

"Mhm, or we could go walk around for a bit—"

"I want the surprise."

I can't help but smile at her enthusiasm, but the curl of my lips brings Miss Dorthey's words back to the forefront of my mind, and my face hardens into stone. She might make me smile more than I have in years, but I won't place the burden of my happiness on her.

"Gage? Are you okay?" Her voice cuts through the looming storm like a beam of sunlight.

"I'm fine. Let's go."

I grab her hand, leading her through the garden until we reach the large grassy field in the back, and find a quiet spot to claim. Most families with energetic children stick to the play area near the front. We aren't alone, but the air here is tranquil. The mild breeze carries the first hints of fall, cutting through the humid heat of summer, and both students and locals had similar ideas on how to take advantage of the weather.

Several other groups have set up blankets to lounge on around the edge of the field, and I pull one out of my bag to do the same. I was going to bring the hole-filled throw I keep on the back of my couch, but James offered to let me take one of hers. Morgan must have talked to her about my plans after we caught up at the gym during the week, but even then, the gesture was unexpected. James and I have never been friends like that. My pride almost made me turn it down, but the blanket is way nicer than anything I had to offer, and Kori deserves the best things.

Once that's done, I pull out the containers of snacks from the bottom. There's nothing fancy about the food, but Kori's face lights up when she sees the array of snacks as if I've just pulled a gourmet five-star meal out of my bag. She grabs a pack of the gummies I saw stashed in her room and plops down on the blanket before I finish unpacking.

"You made me a picnic?" she asks with wide eyes.

"Um...yeah. If you don't like it, we can do something else."

"Shut your mouth before you say more stupid things. I love it. You got all my favorite snacks. How did you even know I liked these?"

I shrug and sit next to her on the blanket. She grabs a handful of gummy packs and a few cookies from another container before moving closer to lean against me. I wrap an arm around her and pull her even closer, and for the first time in years, I feel completely at peace.

"Thank you for doing this, Gage. No one has ever done something like this for me before."

"You deserve the world, Kori."

I'm sorry I can only offer you this.

Things would be so much better if money wasn't a concern. Simple snacks could have been a full meal, and I could have gotten her a gift like I wanted to. I looked, but nothing felt right. I thought about getting her flowers again, but that felt redundant in a garden, and anything else I found I thought she would actually like was out of my budget. Who knew vintage Godzilla paraphernalia cost so much?

"But I've never done this for anyone before either," I add on. I don't want to ruin this by sulking.

"Never? I figured you treated all your girlfriends this good."

"That would require me to have had a girlfriend before."

"Wait, what?" She sits up straighter and pulls back to look me in the face.

"I told you before, I've never been in an actual relationship."

"How? Why? I'm sure you've had more than enough opportunity. I mean, look at you."

My throat tightens as the urge to shut down this whole line of conversation nearly chokes me. This is the exact type of thing I wanted to avoid today. I don't want to ruin our date by talking about me, but I also don't want her to think I'm hiding anything from her. Goddamnit. Morgan said to be vulnerable, and there isn't getting any more vulnerable than this.

With a sigh, I lie back on the blanket and wrap my arm around my girl so I can pull her down with me. She comes readily, resting her head on my chest, and I'm sure she can hear my heart beating wildly in my chest.

"Fighting in the UFC was always my dream. It's the only thing I can ever remember wanting, and I wanted it with everything in me. I lived and breathed to train, and that didn't leave any time for me to devote to being in a relationship, so I didn't. And after..."

Just thinking about that night makes my leg ache.

"After what?"

"I had been fighting in the local circuits, making a name for myself, while Coach tried to use his connections to get me a fight in the big leagues. Things were going well. My record was favorable, and I was riding a win streak that was getting the right type of attention. Then it all ended with one bad kick to my knee.

"I completely ruptured both my ACL and MCL, and there was significant damage to my meniscus as well. Everything I had ever worked for was ripped away from me with one kick. I wasn't in a good place after that. Getting in a relationship was the last thing on my mind."

I take a breath and brace for her reaction. People tend to fall into one of two camps: pity or judgment for how much I let it all affect me. I don't want either from Kori. She is quiet for a few moments as she rubs her hand up and down my arm.

"They couldn't fix it?" she asks in an oddly even tone.

"I had the reconstruction surgery, but I don't have insurance, so I came out of it with more debt than I knew what to do with. Recovery time with rehab is supposed to be a year, but there were issues with the first surgery, so I had to go through it all again, which only added to the mountain of debt and my recovery time.

"It was almost two years before I was able to get back on the mats, but by that point, it was like starting all over. I didn't have the same time to commit to training because I had bills to pay, and even if I did, the surgeon's warning about reinjury rates made it clear that I would only be setting myself up for more pain if I continued to push myself the same way I had been. I had to make a choice, and the risks involved with continuing competitively seemed too great."

"Gage, I'm so sorry."

"Wasn't your fault. Wasn't anybody's. Just an accident that could happen to any fighter when they step into the cage."

"Are you in a good place now?"

"Yeah, I am," I lie.

Having her around these past few weeks has gotten me the closest I've been in years, but I don't think "good" is ever in the cards for me.

"Coach David helped me through the worst of it, and he wouldn't let me quit the sport completely when I tried. I've had my ups and downs over the years, but I made peace with what happened a long time ago. It's nothing for you to worry about."

She goes quiet again, and I am more than content to lie here with her in my arms.

"What is your dream now?" she asks after a few moments.

"I don't have one. I'm just trying to survive."

"That's no way to live. What do you want? Right now, in the moment."

You.

"Right now, I want to finish our snacks and show you around the garden."

"I think that can be arranged."

She grabs a few more cookies and shovels them into her mouth like they're the last thing she'll ever eat.

"No need to rush. We have all afternoon, and I'd like to lay with you for a little while. Only if you want to, though. We can go explore."

I start to get up, but she pushes me back down, giving me the cutest attempt at a mean mug as she does.

"I want. Now lie down so we can cuddle."

"Yes, ma'am," I tell her, and she lets out a content hum as she snuggles up against me.

I have to fight the urge to pull her tighter to me and relax with her in basking under the sunrays.

"That cloud looks like a chipmunk doing ballet." Kori breaks the peaceful moment by pointing at a cloud.

It looks nothing like a chipmunk or any mammal, but I nod along anyway. She smiles and continues to point out the shapes she sees in the clouds. I'm not sure if she actually sees these things or if she's just spitting out the first things that come to her mind. Either way, she finds joy in it, so I point to a cloud and ask for her input. From the look she gives me, you would think I gave her everything she's ever wished for and more with that one question. Fuck me if my pride doesn't grow; I put that look there, and I never want it to go away. I don't care what it takes, I will give this woman the world because she deserves nothing less.

An idea strikes me like a bolt of lightning. I can't give her a lot, but that doesn't mean I can't spoil her in my own way. There's no way I can pull this off on my own, but this is what friends are for, right?

With Yellow thoroughly distracted by the clouds, I send a quick message to Morgan, laying out my idea and asking if he can help. His response is quick, and with that, my plans start to solidify. It's not the world, but it's a start.

Chapter 25
Kori

My phone buzzes as the bus comes to a jerking halt at the stop in front of the arch. I don't need to check it to know that it's Gage and that he's probably wondering where I am. Still, I pull it out and shoot off a quick response, letting him know I'll be there in a few minutes, and book it off the bus and down the street toward Cutter's.

His gaze is on me the second I walk through the door, and like Medusa, that burning look turns me to stone. I swallow back nothing as my mouth goes completely dry from the intensity. In a few large steps, he's out from behind the bar and closes the gap between us, looming over me as he crowds my space. Without a word, he cups my face and captures my lips in an earth-shattering kiss.

The move catches me completely off guard and turns my legs to jelly. This is not what I expected from him today. Yes, we've gone on a few dates over the past couple of weeks, and he calls me his girl, but that doesn't necessarily mean he wants people to know we're together. Things between us are so new, so it makes sense that he might want to be cautious. Although I'm pretty sure that's a non-issue now.

Cheering and whistling from the drunken patrons bring us back to reality. He pulls away enough to look at my face but stays in my bubble. If it were anyone else, I would hate it, but I'm coming to realize I am more than okay with having Gage nearby—which is a good thing because he wasn't lying when he said he has no concept of personal space. Although he's never this touchy with any of his friends. Maybe it's only my space he likes to invade. He has stuck to me like glue at any given chance since we started going out.

"Is everything okay?" he asks in a hushed voice, loud enough for only me to hear.

"Yeah, I'm good. I couldn't decide on what to wear and then had a bit of an eyeliner mishap."

"You're gorgeous with or without that shit."

Warm fuzzies stir in my chest even as he turns and walks back to his post. Strangers weren't the only people privy to our show. All of his—*our?*—friends are gathered around the counter with varying degrees of amusement on their features.

"So I take it things between you two are going well?" Evelyn ambushes me as I join them.

"Yes, things are going quite well." My face flushes thinking about how *good* things are.

"Come on now, you gotta give us more than that," Karis pipes in.

"Like you haven't heard it all from Gage."

"Actually, I haven't," she says with a huff and glares at the smug man. "Gage is being annoyingly tight-lipped about your relationship. I need some details, woman."

I glance at my boyfriend for guidance, and he gives me a small nod as his lips curl into a grin.

"Okay, fine. But I'm not doing this here. I don't want to inflate his ego by gushing about him in earshot."

Karis gags, but Evelyn is already on her feet and dragging me toward an empty high-top near the front.

"Don't worry, lover boy, we'll bring her right back," Karis says as she follows. Nathan is two steps behind her, but she turns and pins him with a sharp stare. "Girls only."

He sighs but sits back down beside Morgan and James.

"Spill," Karis demands once we're on our own.

"What do you want to know?"

"Everything!" Evelyn says with glee. "What is he like once you get past the porcupine exterior?"

"I don't know, he was never exactly Mr. Prickly with me before all of this. He's always been incredibly attentive and patient with me, so that hasn't changed."

Evelyn gives me a "go on" look, and I sigh. She isn't going to relent on this.

"The main difference is how much more touchy he is. Like, I'm talking a hand on me at all times, touchy. He smiles more often, and he is more playful."

"Gage smiles?" Evelyn asks in disbelief.

"Shut up. Everyone smiles."

"Not Gage, at least not often," Karis adds as she goes to take a sip of her drink.

Pride blossoms in my chest. There's something satisfying in knowing all his smiles are only for me.

"How is he in bed? A man like that has to know what he's doing," Evelyn asks, and Karis chokes, sputtering liquid down her chin.

"Don't answer that, Kori," she says with a deadly glare.

"Oh, come on, don't be a stick-in-the-mud."

"I'm sorry I don't want to hear about my best friend's penis." Karis's words are far too loud, drawing odd looks from the strangers around us.

"We haven't actually done that yet," I admit and cast my eyes toward the table.

I don't know why admitting that feels so shameful. It's not that I don't want that— because I do—it's just that every time things start to get hot and heavy, he stops them. Hell, he hasn't even let me take his shirt off, let alone get him off again. It's torturous. If I didn't feel the evidence of his arousal, I'd think he wasn't into me at all.

"Oh, thank God." Karis breathes a sigh of relief as Evelyn sits up to her full height.

"I'm sorry, what? How have you not climbed that man like a tree?"

"I—I'm—" I stammer, and a look of understanding flashes across her features.

Only I'm not sure what she thinks she's understanding here.

"Ah. I see. Well, whenever you are ready, I'm sure he will make your first time great."

Sweet baby Jesus, kill me now. Why does everyone keep thinking I have no experience?

My head falls into my hands as I let out a groan, and Karis snickers. If I knew this was where today was going to go, I would have stayed back with Nathan.

"I'm not a virgin," I mumble through my hands.

"Wait? Is he?" she asks, and Karis snorts.

"Definitely not," Karis says, and jealousy crackles through me, followed quickly by rolling unease.

Maybe I'm not enough for him.

Who knows what kind of women he was with before me? They may not have been relationships, but he had no issues jumping into bed with them. Why won't he do that with me? He says I'm his woman but won't fuck me like it.

"Then why aren't you two going at it like rabbits?" Evelyn asks.

"When I find out, I'll let you know," I say with a sigh.

Because believe me, I crave him. I want to take those next steps with him. I want to know what his cock feels like inside me. My dreams are filled with fantasies of him "taking care of me," but the second I try to make those dreams a reality, he pulls away.

"Oof," Karis says with a chuckle. "I could go talk some sense into him if you—"

"No!" I practically shout and drop my face into my hands. "Please, anything but that."

I would die from the embarrassment.

"Fine, but the offer stands. Now let's get you back to your man before he loses his patience, comes over here, and throws you over his shoulder like a caveman."

"Okay, but that might be kind of hot..." Evelyn muses.

I shake my head, but she isn't wrong. It would be hot as hell if he fireman carried me into the back office and made his claim on me in front of everyone here.

"So what is everybody planning for fall break?" she asks once we make it back to the bar. "I take it we aren't going back to the beach?"

"Hard pass on that one. I think last year ruined beaches for me," James says with a grimace. Everyone but Evelyn nods along in agreement.

I zone out as everyone talks about their plans. Gage and Evelyn are the only two not planning to use the long weekend to get out of Athens for a few days. The conversation continues from there, but my attention is solely on my boyfriend. I'm unable to focus on them with how close he is, how good he smells, and how badly I want to touch him in ways that are wholly inappropriate in front of others.

"Come back to my place tonight." His murmured words break through my lust-addled daze.

"Don't you close?"

"Is that a problem?"

Only for my sleep schedule. But for him, I think it's worth wrecking my circadian rhythm.

"No. I don't think it is."

***

Cutter's is eerie when empty. If it wasn't for the low hum of old rock ballads playing over the speakers, I'd be thoroughly spooked. Well, that and the hot-as-fuck man wiping down the high-tops.

"Anything I can do to help?" I ask from my seat on top of the bar's long wooden counter.

"You being here is help enough."

"Are you sure?"

"I'm sure. All that's left to do is mop, then I get to take you home with me."

He goes back to his tasks, but every few seconds, he looks my way and smiles. I'm sure he would be done much faster if I wasn't here distracting him. Or if he would let me freaking help. At least I'm getting a show out of it. Watching his muscles strain and flex against the tight fabric of his flimsy shirt, and those veins...

A shiver runs through me.

The only thing better than watching would be touching, and I can't do that until he's done closing up, and he would be done by now if he wasn't being a stubborn ass.

"I feel useless," I moan and lie back to sprawl on the freshly cleaned counter.

My boyfriend chuckles, and a few seconds later, his form blocks out the light, casting me in his shadow.

"You could never be useless."

He offers me a hand and pulls me back up to sit, positioning himself between my dangling legs. God, he is massive. No one has ever made me feel so tiny. No one has made me feel so safe either. If he wanted to, he could wrap himself around me completely, shielding me away from the world and all of its sensory overload.

"Dance with me." He doesn't ask. No, those words are filled with Coach Gage's commanding edge.

"What?"

"You heard me. You've danced with Nathan, all of the girls, and that punk-ass kid. I think it's time I get a turn."

"By that logic, I should dance with Morgan too."

"Kori," he growls.

"Okay."

He grabs my hips and hoists me off the countertop, and he doesn't put me down until he finds an empty spot to his liking.

"You know I'm really bad at this, right? I stepped on Nathan's foot, like, eight times."

"Oh, I know. But I'll let you in on a little secret—so am I."

He guides my hands to his neck and wraps his own around my waist, pulling me flush against his chest. Then he starts to sway. He was right that he is just as bad at this as I am. For someone who is so graceful on the mat, it's like his body refuses to listen to his brain once a beat is involved. Our limbs move awkwardly, and every step is off beat, but I don't think I've ever experienced a more perfect moment.

A thick ball lodges itself in my throat, and my eyes prickle. I rest my head against his chest to hide the overwhelming swell of emotion. It's too early to feel this way, right? He's only been in my life for a few months and only been mine for a fraction of that time. I can't love him yet.

The tight, warm pressure in my chest says otherwise.

He starts to sing along to the music—horribly off-key—but the words of epic loves and happy ever afters break whatever remaining hold I had on my emotions. A tear trickles down my cheek, and I bury my face further into his shirt. Once that dam breaks, my chest heaves with a sob.

And with that, the precious moment shatters. He pulls me from the comforting warmth of his body, and his hands cup both sides of my face. Fear dances across his features as he looks me over with a frantic gaze.

Way to go, Kori. My stupid emotions had to get in the way and ruin everything.

"Hey, baby, what's wrong? Talk to me." His voice cracks with the desperate plea.

"I'm just happy," I tell him, feeling like the biggest idiot who's ever lived. "You make me happy."

Those stormy eyes grow glassy, and then his lips are on mine.

One hand slides around the back of my neck in a firm but gentle grip, and he deepens the kiss, plunging his tongue into my mouth. My tongue flicks out to meet his, pulling a groan from deep in his chest. That sound sends a shiver of need through my whole body. I throw my arms around his neck and pull him even closer to me.

"Goddamnit, Kor, you are so goddamned tempting," he growls as he pulls himself away from me with a pained scowl.

Me? Tempting?

This man clearly needs to look in a mirror. He is the most tempting thing I've ever seen. I need him closer to me, not pulling away. I let out a soft whimper, which pulls a raspy chuckle from his throat.

"Fuck mopping. The floors will just get dirty again tomorrow. Let's get out of here."

He grabs me for one more steaming kiss, before dragging me toward the door, leaving the cleaning supplies scattered where he left them. Whoever opens tomorrow is going to be pissed, but I can't find it in me to care. I need him, and tonight, I'm not going to let him push me away when things get hot and heavy—I'm going to be enough for him.

Chapter 26
Kori

Gage's apartment is a comfortable place for me. It's a bit antiquated—Gage would say it's fucking old—but it's far homier than the sterile white fluorescence of my dorm room. It could use a splash of color, maybe some bright blankets to break up the dingy browns and beiges, but his overflowing racks of plant life do a decent enough job. It's charming in a way that no amount of plushies or posters or extra-fuzzy blankets can bring to my dorm room.

I like it, or maybe I merely like it because it's his. Either way, I think this place is turning into my second home, a place where I can let my walls down fully. But for the first time, the apartment feels daunting, and that has everything to do with the nervous ball of anxiety beside me.

He fumbles his keys to the ground as he goes to unlock the front door, and he bends down to get them with curses on his lips.

"Sorry, Low," he says with a sheepish smile as he picks up the keys.

Okay, so nervous Gage is kind of adorable. He's been fidgety since we closed down Cutter's. Hell, he even rambled on the way over, telling me all about the kids in the classes he coached this morning, and he never rambles.

He tries to unlock the door again, and this time, it swings open with ease. He moves to the side and falls in step behind me as I walk through the door, into the dark. I'm only able to make out the outlines of furniture from the glow of the porch light creeping in from the doorway, but Gage's large frame blocks most of that from getting through. The room grows pitch black when he shuts the door behind us, and my heart thunders in my ears.

"Gage..." My voice is shaky as I choke out his name.

"Shit. Hold on. I'm fucking this all up."

His movements are lost in the shadow, but I can hear every scrape and rustle as he stumbles around behind me. The noises sound louder than they likely are with all of my senses on high alert. After a few long seconds, he lets out a satisfied grunt, and the room floods with dim warm light from hundreds of fairy lights strung up in crisscrossed patterns between the walls.

I blink as my eyes adjust, and when they focus, I realize that isn't the only change. The couch has been pushed to the far wall, and Gage's mattress has been dragged out in its place. More blankets and pillows than I thought he owned are piled on it, making a bright, eclectic nest of mismatched colors and fabrics in the center. Yellow flower petals decorate the floor around the bed, and at the foot is a large flower arrangement with matching blooms.

Tears burn behind my eyes, but I blink them away before they can fall. There is no way I'm letting him make me cry twice in one night. I can't believe he did this for me—nobody has ever cared about me enough to go to these lengths.

"Surprise," Gage says as he steps forward to wrap his arms around me from behind. His low voice is thick and raspy as if this is affecting him the same as me.

I relax back into his hold, and I swear nothing has ever felt more right. He holds me tighter and tucks his face into my hair. I think he's saying something, but I can't make out the words over the roar of blood in my ears.

"When did you have time to set this up?"

His arms squeeze me tighter as he shrugs. "I was pretty confident in my ability to get you home with me."

"You didn't need to do this," I say once my voice feels steady enough not to break.

"You're right. I didn't need to do anything, but I wanted to. I know I can't give you everything you deserve, but I wanted to do something to show you how much you mean to me."

His words cause a flurry of unfamiliar sensations to ripple through me. The feeling is an all-consuming, almost painful ache in my chest, although it's not necessarily unpleasant, just more than I can handle. It's a deep-seated need that only Gage can satisfy. Even being in his arms, there is too much distance between us; I need him closer like I need the air I breathe.

I twist in his embrace and seek his lips with my own in a sloppy, desperate kiss. He doesn't protest; instead, he groans and devours me with the same burning intensity. My hands find the hem of his T-shirt and slip underneath. His skin is hot and smooth under my fingers, and I can only imagine what it will feel like pressed against me without these layers of clothes between us.

It's time I find out.

I tug at his shirt, trying to pull it over his head without breaking our kiss. Unfortunately, I don't think that's possible, and I let out a frustrated huff against his lips.

"Fuck me, Low," he groans as he pulls away.

"I'm trying," I huff.

He smooths his shirt back down, and I damn near growl. I want more of him, not less, goddamnit. I reach out again, this time going for his belt, and I can feel he's just as aroused as I am. My hands drift south to cup his bulge, but he stops me, catching both my wrists together in his giant hands.

"Hold on a second. I didn't set this up in an attempt to get into your pants. Movies and cuddling are the only things on the agenda. This is still your rodeo. There is no pressure for anything more."

"And if I want more?" I challenge. I don't know where the boldness comes from, but it has a strong effect on Gage. He swallows heavily as his tongue darts out to wet his lips.

"If you want more, you are going to have to tell me what that looks like. You are in control here."

"Take off your clothes," I command.

The speed at which he pulls his shirt off and struggles with his pants would be comical if the situation were any different, but the air is far too charged with electric need for me to laugh. He stands before me in nothing but his boxers. His hand hovers by the waistband, and he gives me a challenging look, daring me to go further.

We will, but first I want to get my fill of him. This is the most he's ever let me see of his body. His torso is a solid mass of muscle, but it isn't perfectly sculpted like some Hollywood actor on the big screen. That doesn't make him any less impressive. If anything, I think I like this more. Gage is real.

His chest is covered in a large, faded tattoo of a bear's head surrounded by vintage-style roses. I reach out and run my fingertips over the thick lines. His eyes flutter shut as a shiver runs through his body. That reaction only fuels me further; I replace my fingers with my lips, teasing the skin with my tongue as I alternate between soft kisses and exploration.

My lips trail down his body, going so low I have to drop to my knees in order to reach. Gage groans as I do, but he doesn't move. His hands clench into fists as his body tightens with his restraint. I stop at his waistband, licking and sucking around the sensitive flesh at his hips.

After a few more moments of teasing, my need to see all of him wins out, and I pull his boxers down. His cock springs free, no less impressive than it looked behind the confines of his clothes. I only have one other to compare it to, but Gage is easily an inch longer, and thicker by an even more impressive margin. Precum leaks from its head, and I can't resist the urge to taste it. I dart my tongue out and lick away the salty liquid, which only makes Gage groan again.

I look up at him, and he's staring at me like I'm the most wonderful thing he's ever seen. The absolute unguarded adoration in his eyes flips my stomach.

"You can touch me too," I tell him, and then I take him into my mouth.

His girth stretches my jaw, but I don't mind it. One of his hands comes to my head the moment I give him permission. He doesn't pull my hair or push my head down farther, he just holds me, like I'm the only thing that can ground him. I lick and suck on the top half of his cock, careful not to take him too far and make myself gag. The salty taste of his precum explodes across my taste buds as I work him with my mouth, and saliva spills past my lips in messy pools. It's not like I have a ton of preexisting blow job skills, but I try to make up for my lack of technique with enthusiasm.

"I'm going to come if you keep going like that," Gage says with a groan as his face pinches.

I pull away and wipe the drool from my chin. There will be a time for him to come in my mouth, but tonight I want more than that.

"Go lie down," I tell him, and he follows my command without complaint.

I follow behind him, peeling off my clothes as I go. He watches my every movement with hungry eyes, stroking himself lazily with one hand.

All of that bold, self-assured attitude flees as I stand naked in front of him. At least he's naked too. This would be so much more awkward if he wasn't.

What happens now?

I know Gage said I'm in control, but does he expect me to climb on top of him and sit on his dick? Or does he want something else? Yes, I have some experience, but I never said it was *good* experience, and I've never tried to be the one in control. What if I fuck it up?

"What's running through that head of yours, doll?" Gage stops his stroking and props himself up to get a better look at me.

"I don't know what to do next."

"What do you want to do?"

"Everything." My cheeks heat with the confession.

"Do you want to have sex tonight?" he asks bluntly, and I nod.

"Words, Kor," he growls in warning.

"Yes, Gage, I want you to fuck me."

He closes his eyes and takes in a deep breath, before looking at me again.

"I meant it when I said I didn't invite you over tonight for this. If you change your mind at any point, you say stop and we stop. Got it?"

"Yes, Coach," I grumble, and the heat in his gaze only grows more intense.

"I'll be right back," he tells me as he gets out of the makeshift bed.

He places a quick kiss on my lips and dashes off toward his bedroom, leaving me naked and alone in the living room.

I should probably do something, like lie down and look sexy and enticing, but I can't make myself move from the spot. Gage returns a few seconds later and tosses a condom packet onto the bed. He walks around it to stand behind me and wraps me in his arms.

"Are you still okay?" he asks and starts to pepper my neck with kisses.

"Yes," I say, fighting the urge to roll my eyes at his constant need for reassurance.

He holds me even tighter, his hot erection pressing into my ass, and his hands start to roam over my body before coming to rest on my breasts. His fingers twist and pull at my nipples while he sucks on a sensitive spot under my ear. The sensation sends an explosion of electricity cascading down my body into my core. Heat pools between my legs, and my pussy aches for his touch.

Thankfully, he seems to read my mind. One of his hands travels along my body, dropping lower until it finds my center. His fingers slide between my folds, gathering the wetness and spreading it to my clit.

"Tell me what you need, Low," Gage rasps in my ear as his fingers tease the area around my clit without actually touching it.

"I need your cock inside me."

He spins me around and devours my lips again. His hands grab my hips, squeezing them as if he can't get enough of me.

"Bed," he gets out between labored breaths and moves me in that direction. Right, bed.

I scramble backward and fall onto the mattress, spreading my legs wide for him.

"Come fuck me, Gage," I command.

He is on me in an instant. His body blankets mine, and I'm lost in the sensation of tangled limbs and sloppy kisses. He only pauses to grab the condom and slip it on before he's right back on me, kissing and licking and petting me in ways that make every nerve ending in my body come to life and my pussy clench with need.

I don't think I've ever been this turned on in my whole life. Sex before was never pleasant. It never felt like my skin was made up of living sparks or like I might actually die if something doesn't fill me and take away that need.

Gage lines himself up at my opening and stops one last time, looking at me for reassurance. I nod, and he slips inside me. He moves slowly, but his size still stretches me more than I'm used to. The sensation isn't exactly painful, but it's new. It's nothing like the sharp, stinging friction I've always associated with the act.

His eyes never leave mine as he works himself to the hilt—he never stops looking out for my comfort. Even in the throes of passion, my needs are his first thought. The burn of tears prickles behind my eyes as a flood of emotion washes over me.

Fuck, I am one hundred percent, without a doubt in love with him.

I reach up and wrap my hands behind his neck, pulling him down for a searing kiss before he sees the fresh wave of tears and assumes the worst again. The last thing I want is for him to stop now.

He doesn't move at first. Instead, he keeps kissing me while buried deep in my center. It feels good, but I need more; I need friction. I whine as I writhe against him, desperate for more. Thankfully, my boyfriend has mercy on me and pulls back to thrust into me. He doesn't hold back as his hips rock forward, and, inside me, his cock hits something that makes the sparks of need explode into full-body fireworks.

I moan, and that sound shreds the last remaining threads of his willpower. He thrusts into me again and again with abandon as he kisses me like he might steal my soul from my lips.

"I'm sorry, Kor. I'm not going to last like this," he says with an agonized tone. I don't get it. Isn't that the whole point?

As soon as the words leave his lips, his body tenses, and his thrusting stutters to a stop. He buries his face in the crook of my neck and lets out a groan. A still beat passes with us locked in a sweaty embrace. He kisses my neck and pulls his body off mine. I whimper again when he pulls out; I still feel that all-consuming need for him. I'm not empty for long. He discards the condom, and before I can move, he has a finger inside me and another on my clit.

"Wh-what are you doing?" I ask.

"Getting you off too."

"You don't need to do that. I can't come." Halfway through my sentence, he hits a spot that makes my whole body shudder, and my words come out all kinds of shaky.

"You can't, or you haven't? Those are two very different things." He doesn't stop moving his fingers as he speaks. With each brush of those sensitive spots, a pleasurable feeling builds in my center.

"Haven't," I admit, and thrust my hip to meet his hands. He hums and focuses on the task at hand.

They feel good—no, they feel more than good. It's nothing like the sharp poking and prodding I've experienced before. Slickness coats me as the desire blooms inside me. That feeling grows and grows, and I writhe on the mattress, seeking more. I don't know what more looks like, only that I need it, or this feeling will eat me alive. The noises that come out of me are desperate and needy and so unlike any I've made before.

"That's it, Low. Let it happen. You can let go. I've got you," Gage swears.

He leans over to kiss me again, and that's the trigger to make that hot, tight feeling detonate inside me. Ecstasy washes over me in waves so intense that darkness creeps along the edges of my vision. All the while, he holds me and whispers reassuring words. He pulls his fingers out as my body stops seizing, and lies down beside me, pulling me onto his chest.

So that's why there's so much hype around orgasms. I get it now.

We lie like that for several minutes as our breathing and hearts even out. I trace my finger over his tattoo and listen to his heartbeat, still riding the high from that release.

"Does this have meaning?" I ask as my finger passes over one of the roses.

"I got it after I won my first fight. I spent the entirety of my winnings on this thing and didn't even take care of it right, but that's beside the point. I heard someone call me a bear in the ring at one point, and I liked that, so I got the bear. The flowers are for my family, though. There's one for each of them on there. Mom, Dad, Layne." He points to each of the roses that form a triangle around the beast's head, with the point right below his sternum.

"Do you think I'll ever get to meet them? Your mom and Layne, I mean."

He stiffens underneath me, and the hand that was rubbing circles along my back freezes with it.

"I don't know, Kor," he starts. His words are too controlled, like he's actively thinking to say the right thing. "Maybe one day, but this distance makes it hard. Who knows if you will still want to be with me the next time I visit."

My bliss is sucked away by the gaping void his answer summoned. He doesn't know if we will still be together then. Doesn't see this lasting long term. My heart crumbles into a pile of dust in my chest. Here I was thinking about love, but clearly, Gage isn't on the same page.

I nod and try to keep my face neutral despite my inner turmoil. The last thing I want to do is ruin tonight. Everything has been so perfect up until now. I must do a piss-poor job of hiding my reaction, though, because he sits up and rolls over so he can look me in the face.

"You're freaking out on me. What's going on? Did I hurt you? Are you having regrets?"

I shake my head but don't give him anything else. If I open my mouth now, I think I'll lose it and start crying all over him again, but this time in a bad way.

"Don't ice me out. I can't fix it if I don't know what's wrong." The hurt look on his face pulls at something in my chest.

"I didn't realize you didn't see things between us going long term." I'm proud of how steady my voice sounds, despite everything.

"What? Where did you get that impression?" He looks so confused that I think maybe I'm the one who is misunderstanding things.

"You literally just said I might not ever meet your family because I might not be around. How else am I supposed to take that?"

"Kori, you are everything I never let myself dream of having. I don't know why you are wasting your time with me when you could do so much better, but I thank whatever forces brought you into my life every day that you are choosing me. The only reason I said you might not be around is because, at some point, you are going to realize I can't offer you everything you deserve."

As quickly as it was broken, my heart mends, but anger floods in where the void stood.

"Gage, I mean this with all of the possible affection, but you are the biggest fucking idiot I've ever met. I am with you because I like *you*. I don't want anyone else. There is no one out there who is better for me than you. I don't want to hear shit like that out of your mouth again, you hear me?"

He opens his mouth to protest, but I glare at him, and he closes it again.

"I hear you, Low," he says with a sigh.

"Good. Would you be open to meeting my parents since they live closer?"

He thinks for a second before reaching out and grabbing my hand. His thumb runs circles over the skin there for a moment, and then he brings our hands to his mouth to place a kiss on my knuckles.

"Of course. I'd do anything for you. When are you thinking?"

"How about fall break? We could do a long weekend at their house. I haven't been back home since the semester started."

"Yeah. Okay. I'll talk to my boss at Cutter's and Coach David to organize the time off."

"Really?"

"Of course."

"Thank you," I tell him with a smile and tackle him on the mattress while I pepper his face with light kisses.

"There's no need to thank me. If you want me to meet them, I will. Now let's get cleaned up and head to bed. Just because I'm used to being up this late doesn't mean you are."

"Okay," I say with a yawn, but I don't get off him.

I want to soak in this moment for a little while longer.

Chapter 27
Gage

Sparring passes by in a blur. Coach David barks orders, and my body follows on instinct, but the words don't stick in my mind. How could they when Yellow occupies every one of my thoughts? I'm so distracted that *Nathan* manages to kick my ass during a few rounds, but I take those losses with a smile on my face—a smile that has gotten more than a few odd looks from other students in the class.

I'm still fucking smiling when Coach calls the class to an end and dismisses us.

"What's got you in such a good mood?" Karis probes as we step off the mat.

"Isn't it obvious, Kare Bear? Our boy got laid," Nathan says with a grin.

"Shut up," I growl, but he isn't wrong.

"James is dying to know how the surprise went," Morgan adds.

"Things went really good," I say, and my face grows hot as the memories of everything we did together at my apartment resurface.

Once wasn't enough. We fucked again after breakfast and again before I took her home that evening. After that first orgasm, she was insatiable. I can't believe I was the first-ever person to get her there, but that knowledge fills me with pride. Her orgasms are all mine. I'm the only man who will ever see the way her nose scrunches up as her release rocks through her. The men she's been with before are asses for depriving her of that, but in a weird way, I'm glad they were selfish pricks. I'm glad this is something that's special between the two of us.

As the night progressed, she grew more comfortable with the idea of me doing things for her pleasure, but to my disappointment, she didn't let me eat her out. I didn't want to pressure her, so I dropped it after she said no, but one of these days, I'll sink my tongue into that delicious cunt of hers and show her what she's been missing.

"She loved it. Thank her again for me," I say in a rush, stumbling over my words.

"Just make sure to wash the blankets before you return them," Morgan says with a knowing smirk.

"Wait, what surprise?" Nathan asks.

"Nothing," I grunt.

He rolls his eyes and looks at Morgan expectantly.

"Gage did a special sleepover date night for Kori and asked James and me for a little assistance getting it set up."

"And you didn't include me?" Genuine disappointment flashes over Nathan's features.

Goddamn, my friends are way too invested in my love life. They need hobbies—or girlfriends—although having James around hasn't made Morgan any less meddlesome. She's nosier than he is. At least they care. I'll take their overbearing involvement over superficial bullshit any day of the week.

"Sorry, man, you lost opinion privileges after you screwed me over with that whole fancy date suggestion."

"That suggestion was fucking great."

"Yeah, well, Kor hated it. I'm lucky she was willing to give me a second shot, or things between us would have fizzled out then and there."

Before he can snap back with some undoubtedly stupid retort, Coach David approaches our group. His presence alone is enough to have my friends biting their tongues and falling into line, showing more respect to him than they've ever given each other. Hell, my spine straightens, too, as I wait for him to speak—it doesn't matter that I've known him longer than anyone else in this gym.

"Maher, can I see you in my office?" he asks.

Fuck.

I'm about to get fired. I can feel it in my bones.

If only I knew why.

Memories of the past week flash through my head in rapid succession, and nothing stands out as fireworthy, but that doesn't mean it isn't coming. Maybe Coach finally realized I'm the wrong fucking man to run a whole program. I've been saying it since day one. There are others here far more deserving of the role than me.

Swallowing back my unease, I follow him to his office. My friends reanimate once we are out of earshot, whispering to each other with what is surely childish glee. If Coach wasn't two steps in front of me, I'd flip them off for their troubles.

The small office is tucked away in the weight room. Unlike the one I share with the other coaches, David's space is kept in perfect order. I can count on one hand the number of times I've been in this office over the past decade. This is his space, and being in it is reminiscent of being called to the principal's office.

He sits behind the pristine desk—there isn't so much as a paperclip out of place—but I don't take the seat across from him, instead choosing to lean against the door as if my heart isn't going wild in my chest.

"What's up?" I ask with a casualness I don't feel.

"Sit down, Gage. This feels like a disciplinary meeting with you hovering there."

"Is it not?"

"Should it be?" he asks, the challenge clear in his tone.

"No. Sorry, I'm just on edge." I push down my nerves and follow his instructions.

"You've been on edge since the day I met you." He lets out a fond chuckle and shakes his head. "What you've never been before is distracted. But these past few weeks, it's like your head has been in the clouds. Want to tell me what that's about?"

Goddamnit. The last thing I need is another motherfucker poking around in my love life. My thoughts drift back to my woman, and my lips curl into a grin.

"See. That dopey-ass smile right there. That's what I'm talking about. I've known you for almost twenty years, and I've never seen you smile like that."

"I'm seeing someone." My face grows hot with the admission.

"Someone I know?"

It takes a second for the true meaning of his words to set in.

"No. She's got no affiliation to the gym. I know damn well you'd tear me a new asshole if I started something with a member."

There is no official rule forbidding coaches from dating members here as long as everyone involved is a consenting adult, but Coach isn't afraid to voice his opinions on the matter. I've heard it a million times over the years. He thinks it's a bad idea, and I agree. The risk of there being a power imbalance is too high, and that means things could end badly for all involved or paint Double Teep in a bad light. Even without the potential for power imbalance, it could still create a bad environment. Gym relationships normally end with someone leaving. Normally, it's the party least committed, and in cases with coaches, it's always the student who sees the door.

I don't think I *could* start something with someone affiliated with the gym, even if I wanted to. That rule has been drilled into my head since I was a teenager. It's almost offensive that Coach thinks I'd go against him now, but I get his need to do his due diligence. I would, too, if I were in his shoes.

He starts to relax when I realize it isn't the entire truth. Kori might not be related to the gym now, but she has been by.

"Well, actually..." I start, and his back goes rigid.

"Which is it? Is she affiliated or not?"

"She did a trial lesson and hated every second of it, but we knew each other before that. Honestly, I think she showed up as an excuse to see me, not because she had any real interest in the sport."

"You know damn well that isn't what I mean," he says as he sinks back in his seat. "I'm happy for you. She must be something special to put up with your stubborn ass."

"Yeah, she is one hell of a woman."

"When can I meet her?"

"You want to meet her?"

"Of course I do. Alison will too. She's been asking about you, and the girls would love to see you. I swear all they talk about these days is 'Coach Gage.' Come over for dinner and bring your woman."

After all these years, you'd think I'd be more comfortable with David and his wife's attempts at building a more personal relationship outside the walls of the gym, but the idea has never sat right with me. He's been my mentor for nearly two decades. To take that clear-cut relationship and try to change the dynamic now is a recipe for disaster. Even then, I indulge him on occasion. They've done too much for me over the years for me to blow them off completely.

"Sure, but it will have to be after the school break."

"Got plans with Karis and the others again?"

"No. I'm going to meet Kori's parents."

"It's that serious already?"

"Yeah, I think it is."

"Damn, then I definitely need to meet this girl. I'll make sure your classes are covered that weekend. Focus on making a good first impression. I'm happy for you, kid," he says as he stands, clapping a hand on my shoulder before leaving me alone in his office.

Kid.

I snort at the thought. Coach is only a few years older than me, but I swear sometimes he still sees me as the scrawny seventeen-year-old who begged him to take me under his wing.

He's right that I need to worry about making a good impression, though. I have no illusions that my relationship with Kori won't come with a healthy heaping of criticism from people who don't know us, but I'm hoping her parents can accept us—me—without too much disdain. I know I'm not the man they dreamed she would bring home, but I will do everything in my power to keep her safe, happy, and loved for as long as she'll have me. All I can do is hope that's enough.

Chapter 28
Kori

Excitement fills me as we pull up the long paved driveway that leads to my childhood home. My parents must hear the rattling roar of Gage's car, or maybe they still keep tabs on my location, either way, they step out onto the front porch before he has a chance to put the parking brake on or kill the engine.

My boyfriend, on the other hand, is frozen in the seat beside me. His spine grew stiffer as we drove through my neighborhood's streets, and that mask of stone-cold indifference covered the relaxed smile I adore. After a few seconds of sitting in silence, he squeezes his hand on my thigh and takes in a deep breath.

"You ready for this?" he asks with a rasp to his words.

"They are going to love you. I promise," I reassure him.

What isn't there to love?

He nods, climbs out of the car, and comes around to open my door for me. I've told him time and time again he doesn't need to do that, but he insists it's something he wants to do, so I let him have it. I'm sure my parents will appreciate the gesture; my dad has always made a point to "show his girls exactly how women should be treated."

His grip on my hand borders on painful as we walk to the door. I squeeze back, trying to calm him, but it does nothing to alleviate the tension holding his body rigid beside me.

"There she is," my mom says as she pulls me in for a hug.

My fingers slip from my boyfriend's grasp during the exchange, and the distance is only made worse when my dad swoops in to hug me the second my mom lets go.

"How have you been? How are classes? Nothing giving you too much trouble, I hope," he says as he pulls back.

"No. I—" I start, but I'm interrupted as my mom sets her sights on my guest.

"Oh, and you must be the boyfriend," she gushes.

I don't even have to look at my man to know his ears are likely growing flush from the attention.

"Yes, ma'am. I'm Gage Maher. Thank you for inviting me to your home."

It's so strange seeing him so formal. My Gage commands rooms with a few words, not whatever this is.

My dad greets him with a firm handshake, and once the initial introductions are done, my mom ushers us inside with the promise of dinner. The stench of burnt garlic slams into us as we walk through the door. I lock eyes with Dad and stifle a groan. It looks like Mom is on a cooking kick again. I guess it was too much to hope they would order in tonight.

"There are pizza rolls in the freezer if you are still hungry later," my dad says with a wink as he throws his arm over my shoulder. We both know my mom's cooking is hardly ever edible. She knows it, too, but that hasn't stopped her from trying.

Gage trails behind us without grabbing my hand again. Even though it's only a few feet, that distance between us aches. His touch has become a constant for me—a lifeline when the world gets to be a little too much. I hate how empty my hand feels without it.

As we approach the table, my parents bombard me with their endless stream of questions. He sits without a word, content to let my parents get it all out. I take the seat next to him as my mom brings out whatever ungodly concoction she created in that casserole dish. My hand finds his under the table, and I squeeze his fingers tight in mine.

Nothing is said for several minutes as we all make our plates. Thank God for premade sides. I can survive off rolls and bagged salad if I need to. It wouldn't be the first time. I grab some mac and cheese, too, even though I know it will be runny. Mom insists on rinsing the noodles once they're done cooking, even though the instructions explicitly say otherwise, so the cheese sauce never sets right. It's a real tragedy.

Once everyone is settled, my dad turns his attention to Gage.

"So, Gabe—"

"Gage," I correct.

"Right. Gage. How old are you, exactly? When Kori said she was bringing home a boyfriend, I was expecting a classmate, not a grown man."

"I'm thirty-four," Gage answers, falling into the curt deadpan he uses around strangers.

"I take it you didn't meet in class, then?" my dad asks.

My head falls back as I stifle a groan. I put my hand on his leg and give it a reassuring squeeze.

"No, sir. I'm not a student."

"What is it you do, then?"

"I'm a bartender," Gage tells him, and his shoulders rise as he sinks in his seat.

"And he works at an MMA gym. He's the head of their kids' program," I cut in. I'm not going to let him sell himself short.

"Oh, that's neat," Mom says. "So you like children? Do you want some of your own?"

Now it's my turn to sink in my seat. It's barely been two months. The topic of kids hasn't even loomed on the horizon, and now it never will because my mom is going to scare him away by bringing up things that she shouldn't.

"I love kids. When I was younger, I had dreams of having a large family, but having children isn't something I want to rush into. As I've gotten older, I've accepted that it might not be in the cards for me. I'm not going to pin my hopes

224

on something that might never happen." He glances at me, and the look in his eye isn't something I can place.

He wants kids? Why didn't I know he wanted kids?

A wave of panic washes over me. Do I want kids? Fuck, I'm practically still a child myself. If I decide I do want kids, it won't be for several more years. Will he resent waiting? Am I holding him back?

Gage grabs my hand and gives it a soft squeeze, tearing me from the thought spiral.

A revelation strikes me like a bolt of lightning, clearing away all my fears. I do want to have his kids. Not now, but in a few years, I would love to give him the family he's always dreamed of. For a moment, the mental image of our future is so clear I'm sure it's a premonition.

"That's a wise outlook to have," my mom says with a thoughtful nod. "And how do you feel about crafts?"

Gage pauses for a moment before a smile tugs at the corner of his lips.

"Depends on the type of crafts."

"I've got a large paint by numbers I could use some help with, but I've got a few coloring books floating around here somewhere if that's more up your alley."

The rest of dinner passes in the same way—my mom asks Gage a million questions, each unrelated to the last, and Gage indulges her curiosities. My dad doesn't contribute; he watches with a tight-lipped look on his face. It's strange; Mom is the more vocal of the two, but Dad isn't normally one not to engage. I don't think I like it very much.

"This was great, Mom," I lie. No one other than Gage took more than a bite from the cursed casserole, and he didn't merely eat it—he cleaned his plate and got seconds. "We've had a long day. I think it's time I show Gage to his room."

"Of course. Tomorrow we can give him the tour. I'll dig out the scrapbooks. Oh, you'll just love them." She turns her attention to him. "Kori was the cutest baby with those chubby cheeks and little pigtail puffs on the top of her head."

I jump out of my chair and try to pull him up with me. This mission is headed toward catastrophic failure; it's time to abort. He lets me drag him to his feet but doesn't divert his attention from my mom.

"I'm looking forward to it. Do you need any help cleaning up before we head to bed?"

Ugh.

Curse him and his manners. Why can't he be, like, thirteen percent more asshole sometimes? I tug at his arm, but he doesn't budge until Mom shoos him away, ensuring him she can handle it on her own.

I huff as I drag him up to my room. He isn't allowed to stay in here with me, but I'm not ready to say goodnight yet.

The door swings open, and I'm hit with the comforting scent of *home*. My parents haven't changed anything. The bed is unmade, covered in a bright pile of blankets and an embarrassing number of plushies, and the walls are still adorned with all my favorite things. They didn't let me paint them yellow, no matter how much I begged, so I covered every square inch with posters and art. You could spend five minutes in here and know everything there is to know about me. The only things missing are the clothes I took with me, my PC, and Daisy.

With overdramatic flair, I fling myself into the bed, letting the avalanche of covers consume me. The mattress dips with my boyfriend's weight a few seconds later.

"You good, Low?" he asks, and his hand burrows through the blankets and finds my shoulder.

"I'm sorry. Mom can be a lot sometimes."

"I think your mom is great. She reminds me a lot of you."

"What? Really? People normally say I'm more like my dad. I don't always know how to interact with people, especially strangers, so I tend to fade into the background and observe. Like him. Mom is so sociable. She can talk to anyone without even trying. I don't have that skill."

"You could never fade into the background, and those people clearly don't see you the way I do."

"And how do you see me?"

"Joy incarnate. My sunflower. The brightest thing in any room."

"Yeah, right."

"I'm serious. The first time I ever saw you, I was captivated. You were you: wholly, happily, and unapologetically, even if you were out of your element. I wanted to bottle it up and store it away for a rainy day. I guess in a way, I did. I found a way to keep you by my side."

Tears prickle behind my eyes as my heart swells.

I love him.

I love him so much that it's a physical pain in my chest.

The words fight against my lips, begging to be let out, but I can't. Saying them and hearing nothing in return is far worse than never saying them at all. If he feels the same, he will say it, and then I'll let him know how I feel. I push the words away by sitting up and capturing his lips in a kiss, putting every unspoken feeling into it. That's all I can give him now.

After a moment of searing heat, Gage pulls away with a groan.

"As much as I love where this is going, it's best we don't get carried away. Your dad already hates me. Let's not give him even more of a reason to."

"Dad doesn't hate you," I protest, but I do put some space between us. He is right that we probably shouldn't get too physical under my parents' roof.

"Did you not see the glare he was giving me all throughout dinner?"

"That's just his face."

"It's not the face he was giving you or your mom. I think he about had an aneurysm when he realized how old I am. Honestly, if I were in his shoes, I'd hate me too. You're his kid, and I'm some older man with no real ambition who's come to try to take you away."

"Gage...you know that isn't how things are between us, right?"

"I know that, but I also know how we look to the outside world. Fuck, I'm probably closer to their age than I am yours. People are going to talk, and they are going to judge. I've accepted that. You mean far too much to me to let the opinions of others hold any water, but I'm aware of them. Your dad is too. He might be misguided, but he has your best interests at heart, so I can't blame him. Hopefully, by the end of this weekend, he will warm up to me, and if he hasn't...well, if he hasn't, I'll just have to keep trying. I'm not the most patient of men, but for you, my reserves are endless."

"No bullshit?" My whispered voice cracks from the emotion welling in my throat.

"No bullshit." The look in his eye is so sincere, so sure, that I can't help but believe him.

It takes everything in me not to throw myself at him and rip his clothes off. That feeling of all-consuming love courses through me again, begging for an outlet.

"I think I should show you to your room now, or I'm going to do something that would definitely get you on my dad's bad side."

"That's a good idea." His hoarse voice sends a shiver of need through me.

The air between us is charged, and that feeling doesn't dissipate as I lead him down the hall to the guest room.

"I'm sorry if it's a mess. Mom uses it as a workshop sometimes, and the level of chaos depends on her current project."

I push the door open and breathe a sigh of relief that things are actually organized—at least by Mom's standards. It looks like she has come back around to the quilt she's been working on for the past eight years, but she has the scraps of fabric neatly folded out of the way. I hover in the doorway, wanting to follow him inside but knowing that defeats the whole purpose.

"I guess this is goodnight, then," I say, making no actual move to leave.

"Goodnight, Kori." He cups my face and gives me one last smoldering kiss before he steps away.

"Goodnight," I mumble, my mind still reeling with need.

The door latches with a soft *click*, and only then do I let the whispered "I love you" slip out.

Chapter 29
Gage

After twenty-four hours with the Wrights, three things have become painfully clear.

One: Mrs. Wright—*Jen*—is the worst cook I've ever encountered. That hasn't stopped me from eating everything she's put in front of me. I know better than to let perfectly good food go to waste.

Two: If you looked up "loving family" in the dictionary, a picture of the Wrights would be there.

Three: I am so far out of my league here, it isn't even funny.

I'm not sure what I was expecting, but it wasn't the cookie-cutter manifestation of the American dream—all that's missing is the white picket fence. Just being in a house like this has had me on edge since we pulled up. I keep expecting her parents to kick me out or accuse me of stealing shit, but her mom has been nothing but welcoming. Her dad, on the other hand...

Well, I wouldn't want my daughter dating me either.

The easy chatter around the table comes to a lull as dinner ends. Not that I had much to contribute to the conversation to begin with, but I'm more than content to watch my woman light up with the bubbly exchange. Under the table, her fingers are woven between mine. All night, she's kept them there, giving me a gentle squeeze every so often while still engaging with her parents. Eating the leathery steak with my left hand was hard but worth it. She'll always be worth it.

Marcus gets up from the table first and starts to clear away the mess of mostly full dishes.

"Dad, do you need help?"

"No, I need your help finding those scrapbooks," her mom replies.

"Do we have to? I'd rather do the dishes."

"I'm sure Gage would really like to see them. Isn't that right?" she asks as she gets up too.

"Yes, ma'am."

Kori's face pinches into an adorable scowl. I mimic the look and place a kiss on her temple before untangling my hand from hers. She tries to keep the stern look, but a smile pulls at her lips and her eyes dance with mirth.

"Go help your mom," I command, keeping my voice low enough that only she can hear it.

"Yes, Coach," she rasps, giving me a sultry smirk, and follows her mom out of the room, swaying her hips with every step. It takes every ounce of willpower for me not to give in to the impulse to smack those perfect cheeks.

Wordlessly, I follow her dad into the kitchen and help with the cleaning. We work in tandem without a sound, and it's not until the last of the mess is cleared away that he speaks.

"Do you drink?"

"Yes."

"Whisky?"

"I'm not picky."

He gestures for me to follow him and leads me down the hall into his office. The cluttered space is a mirror of the chaos that is Kori's room. His desk is the only semblance of order, with its many monitors and meticulously wrangled cables. The rest is filled with mementos of the years that have passed. Mrs. Wright doesn't need to find the photo albums, because there are more than enough pictures in here for me to piece together every stage of Kori's life. Various DC Comics memorabilia—from framed comics to collectible figures—are sprinkled in throughout the personal effects.

He opens up a cabinet and pours a generous two fingers from a glass decanter that's etched with the bat symbol.

"Sit. Let's talk," he says as he hands over the similarly etched glass—this one Superman.

"Is this the part where you ask my intentions and try to warn me off your daughter? Because I already know she's too good for me," I tell him as I take a sip. The liquor is smooth—and expensive. I don't claim to be a connoisseur, by any means, but I know how much I would charge for this shot.

"I've been on the receiving end of enough 'fatherly concern' to do that. Jen's dad didn't approve of us and made both our lives hell for her choices until we finally cut them off. When I had a daughter of my own, I vowed I would never be him. You might not be what I expected, but you make Kori smile, and that's all that matters."

"So this is…"

"Getting to know you."

"Okay."

An awkward silence fills the room as we both fidget with our tumblers without taking a sip. At least I'm not the only one completely out of my element. A picture of Kori on his desk catches my attention. She can't be more than eight, and she's dressed as Starfire, smiling at the camera with a gap-toothed grin.

"Don't tell me you named your daughter after a comic book character."

He shrugs with a wry grin. "Jen didn't realize until she was one. She was pissed at me for weeks."

"My dad did the same to my mom—twice. I was named after the kid from *Pet Sematary,* and my brother was named after the singer of Alice in Chains."

He snorts, and his body relaxes as he takes a sip of his drink. I follow suit.

"So bartender, huh? Any place I'd know?"

"I work at Cutter's."

"Do they still do quarter beer nights?"

"It's a dollar now."

"That's highway robbery," he says with a shake of his head. "How long have you worked there?"

"I've been at Cutter's for a few years, but I've been bouncing around Athens for the past decade and a half."

"As a bartender?"

"As whatever paid and didn't require a high school diploma."

My shoulders clench in anticipation of the inevitable judgment, but it never comes.

"Jen didn't finish high school either. Her family was...well, let's just say the racism was the least of the reasons we went no contact. She moved out once she turned eighteen, got her GED as soon as she could, and worked her ass off to get into UGA in spite of her family's constant attempts to drag her back down. High school diploma or not, she is still the most brilliant and driven person I know."

I know the story is meant to show he relates, but all it does is make me feel ten times smaller. She kept going despite the obstacles presented, and all I've done is shut down and wallow in my own misfortunes. I couldn't even be bothered to take that stupid exam.

The gloom makes its presence known, creeping into the corners of the office as I sink deeper into my seat. So many years have been wasted with nothing but debt to show for them. If I had the same grit as Kori's mom, I could be living like this—in a nice house with a family of my own. My UFC dreams died, but I didn't have to let all the others die with it. I down the rest of my drink and try to keep the self-loathing off my face.

"Can I ask a question I have no business asking?" he asks after a few seconds pass without a reply.

"Sure."

Might as well get it all on the table now.

"Where do you see this going after she graduates? It's unlikely she'll stay in Athens forever."

"I know."

"Don't get me wrong, I know things between you two are new, but I also saw your face when you talked about wanting kids and a family. You can't tell me at your age, you aren't already thinking about the future."

He's wrong. The future isn't something I've ever allowed myself to consider. Why would I when I've never seen myself having one? Before Kori, I spent most nights wishing it would be the one I never woke up from. Now I have something to want to wake up for, and that means it's time to start looking ahead.

"I am now."

"Good." He gives me an all-too-knowing look and finishes off his drink as well. "Now, let's not keep the ladies waiting. Jen gushed all night about showing you these baby pictures."

When I follow him back out into the living room, I leave the gloom behind me. It tries to give chase, but its shadowy tendrils melt into harmless vapor as they try to wrap themselves around me. I'm done letting it control me. For the first time in a long time, I can look toward my future and see a life worth living. The road won't be easy, but I'm going to give Yellow the life she deserves.

***

Peace like I've never known seeps into my very bones as I slowly return to consciousness. Sunlight streams into the room from the cracks in the blinds, catching on the glittering particles of dust dancing in the air. Bird songs are the only sound, and they add to the peace. It's a much better wake-up call than car alarms or screaming neighbors. Familiar sweet citrus invades my senses—a scent that most definitely shouldn't be here. Neither should the bundle of heat tucked against me in the too-small bed.

"What are you doing in here?" I ask my sleepy girlfriend.

"I missed you," she says as she snuggles closer to my side.

"You're going to get us in trouble," I chastise, even as I wrap my arms around her and pull her to fully lie on my chest.

"We aren't doing anything trouble worthy. I just wanted to cuddle."

"Then cuddle away, baby girl."

She wraps herself around me like a koala and lets out a content sigh as I trace patterns on her back.

"I wish we didn't have to go back," she says after a few minutes.

"Why?"

"Because I want to stay like this forever. Once we leave, you get busy with work again and I'll be thrown back into the middle of the semester, and I won't get to see you as much. I really liked having you to myself these past few days."

I did too, and after talking with her dad, I can see a future where I wake up with her by my side every day. I'm just going to have to work for it. Starting with getting my GED.

"The sooner we get back to Athens, the more time we will have together at my place."

I tuck my face into the crook of her neck and pepper languid kisses along her throat. In an instant, she melts into me, arching to give me more access.

"We can do more as soon as we are home."

She will be lucky if I ever let her leave once we get there. There's no reason she needs to stay in the dorms if she doesn't want to. She spends half her time at my place anyway.

"Fine. But breakfast first. My dad is making waffles."

"Please tell me he is a better cook than your mom."

"You will just have to see," she taunts as she climbs off me and slips out of the room.

Thankfully, he is.

Breakfast with her family is an affair filled with sugar and joy, and somehow, after a few short days, I fit. I hope when she meets my ma, Kori will feel this way too. With winter break on the horizon, I need to find out if she wants to make the trip up to Boston with me. It's a big step, but I'm ready for it all.

Her mom tears up while we say our goodbyes, reminding us to come see them more often than once a semester, and then we are off. It might be nothing more than another drive for Yellow, but for me, I'm driving toward our future.

Chapter 30
Gage

Halfway back to Athens, things go to shit.

Brandy shakes around us as the engine's rattling intensifies. She rallies for a few moments longer before a loud *bang* rocks the whole vehicle. The steering wheel jerks in my grasp, and I yank my hand away from Kori's thigh to regain control before we veer off the road completely. My girl lets out a startled shriek, but I can't comfort her—not now.

As the engine sputters its final breaths, smoke pours out from under the hood.

No. No. No.

I thought I could see the light at the end of the tunnel, but it was the train, and reality crashes into me at full fucking speed. There's nothing more for me than this—an endless cycle of patching new holes while the others still leak.

Fuck.

The gloom makes a full resurgence, my earlier convictions be damned. Its dark shadows entomb me, eclipsing even my sunflower's golden light. All-consuming pressure grows in my chest as I guide us to the shoulder. It's like I'm watching myself move from a third-person perspective—I'm aware of my actions but not in control.

As we come to a stop, Kori reaches over to shift the gearstick into park. She's lucky that, in my autopilot state, I remembered to move my foot to the brake. I'm too paralyzed to do anything more than sit here and watch any plans I had for the future drift away with the smoke.

This is what I get for having hope—the universe had to remind me of my place.

She climbs out of the car, but I can't unlock my muscles to follow her. Maybe if I'm lucky, this piece of shit will actually catch on fire this time and take me out with it.

No.

I can't be thinking like this while she's out there waiting on me—relying on me—to get her home safely. Still wrapped in the suffocating tendrils of my despair, I force myself to get out of the car. Kori watches me with worried eyes as she talks to someone on the phone. She doesn't take her eyes off me as she wraps up the call and circles her arms around me, resting her head against my chest. Normally, I'd cherish the gesture, but right now, her embrace is another thing constricting me.

No matter how hard I try, I'm never going to be good enough for her.

"Who was that?" The question comes out sounding hollow.

"AAA," she says. "Tow truck is on its way."

In a flash, the empty pit fills with white-hot anger—undirected, but raging nonetheless.

"Why the fuck would you do that?" I snap.

She flinches back, dropping her arms, and looks at me like I'm a stranger.

Goddamned fucking fuck.

"Because we are stuck on the highway without a working car. What would you have me do?" she snaps right back.

"Call Karis. Nathan. Hell, your dad. Anything but that. Jesus Christ, do you ever stop and think?" I pause and take a deep breath. The last thing she deserves is my anger. "That was uncalled for. I'm sorry, Kori."

The wariness in her eyes breaks my fucking heart. I swallow against the thick knot in my throat and try again without acting like a complete fucking ass.

"Do you think you could call them back and cancel it?"

"Why? We're stuck here," she challenges, and she isn't wrong.

238

"Because there is no way I'll be able to afford the tow all the way back to Athens." Self-loathing rocks through me with the confession. I've tried so fucking hard not to let her feel the strain of my failures, but they are on full display now. "Karis will come get us if I call her, and I can come back with James's truck later and tow it myself."

"Is this really about money? I can pay for the tow truck," she says with a sigh.

"You will not," I growl, and she shrinks back again.

Goddamnit, I'm fucking everything up. For once, can I not pretend like I'm the type of man she deserves?

"I'm supposed to be the one taking care of you, not the other way around."

"Bullshit. Relationships are supposed to be a partnership."

"Kori"—I choke on the emotions clinging in my throat—"please just let me handle this my way, okay?"

"Fine," she says with a resigned sigh and hands me her phone.

Without another word, she wanders away, putting distance between us before she sits on the grassy patch bordering the street and wraps her arms around herself in a tight embrace.

The device is a fucking bomb in my hand. Calling should be a no-brainer, but I can't bring myself to dial. Deep in my gut, I know that if I hit that button, things will be over between us for good. And maybe they should be. My shoulders sag as I trudge over to her and hand the phone back to her, unused. She doesn't even look at me as she grabs it from me or as I sit beside her.

Half a dozen things I want to say run through my head but never make it to my lips. I want to beg for her forgiveness, prostrate myself until she smiles at me again with all that unfiltered joy, and tell her how much she means to me, but the gloom binds my tongue. It's better this way. I was foolish to think I might get to keep her. There's no version of her future with me in it—not where she also reaches her full potential.

Two and a half torturous hours pass before the tow truck finally arrives. Not once during the wait does she even glance in my direction. But it's not like I tried to initiate anything either, no matter how badly I wanted to. Instead, I let the gloom fully invade my mind. It turns out I see things clearer with it around.

This is the first and last time I drag her down with me.

She greets the driver with a smile that doesn't reach her eyes and hands over her—*her parents'*—card without hesitation. Fuck. I'll find a way to pay back the Wrights. It might be a drop in the bucket for them, but I'd never be able to live with their charity. Especially not after the shit I'm about to do.

We squish onto the bench seat, and another forty-five minutes pass in strained silence before we pull in front of my complex. It's scary how the place I longed for a few hours ago feels like a death sentence now. Against my better judgment, I keep my fingers on her thigh, drinking in the feel of her one last time.

"Are you sure you don't want me to take this to a shop?" the driver asks.

"I'm sure. Thank you."

He mumbles something under his breath and gets out to unhook my car. Once we get the shell of a vehicle settled in my spot, I take my keys back and head inside, not looking to see if Kori follows.

She does with barely restrained anger radiating off her in visceral waves.

"So are we just not going to talk about that?" she asks as the door latches behind her.

"What is there to talk about?"

A bark of bitter laughter falls from her lips. "So you didn't have a complete meltdown over a couple hundred bucks?"

My jaw clenches as I resist the urge to snap back at her. No matter how hard I try or what good I can give her, she can't understand what it took for me to get there. Or how hard it is for me to give her what she needs. Fuck, this was never going to last. I'm not the type of man who gets forevers. I'm only dragging her down—she just doesn't realize it yet. But she will. And it's best for both of us if she doesn't waste time figuring it out.

"This isn't working for me," I tell her. My voice is void of any emotion despite the storm destroying me from the inside out.

"What isn't?"

"You. Us. I can't do this anymore."

I can't keep pretending like I'm not slowly stealing your light.

"Oh."

That one word sucks all the air from the room.

"Okay," she says in a hollow tone that sends a shiver of ice down my spine. "I'll just get out of your hair, then."

Panic thrashes in me as she heads for the door, screaming at me that I'm making a mistake. Without thinking, I call out to her before she can leave.

"Kori, wait." My voice cracks with desperation.

She freezes but doesn't say a word.

"Don't think you did anything wrong. You're more perfect than I ever dreamed was possible. I'm the one who's not good enough for you."

Silence hangs in the air, so taut that the smallest shuffle could shatter it. It only lasts a second before she whirls around, glaring at me with unrefined rage.

"Who do you think you are telling me who is and isn't good enough for me?"

The venom behind those words is so concentrated I'm stunned speechless.

"You can end things—I'm not going to fight you on that—but don't put words in my mouth, and don't you dare try to spin this as some sort of noble sacrifice. You're a coward, plain and simple."

"Kori..."

"Tell me I'm wrong."

When I don't say anything, she scoffs and storms out the front door. The sound of her engine roaring to life cuts through the air, and as it fades into the distance, it takes my heart with it.

She might not realize it yet, but this is for her own good. I'm letting her go because I love her too damned much to have her clip her wings by binding herself to me. That knowledge doesn't stop the gaping hole in my chest from pulsing in agony.

I never thought heartbreak would be a physical pain.

A scream works its way out of my throat. It's a mix of all the emotions warring inside me: rage, despair, anguish, frustration, regret. In one swift motion, I swipe everything from the counter onto the floor. The crashing cacophony soothes some of the chaos. Or maybe I find peace in making my environment match my mental state. Either way, once I start, I can't stop, and in no time at all, my apartment is in shambles.

Broken glass litters the floor, crunching under every heavy step, and anything not bolted to the ground has been upturned. With nothing left to destroy and the pain as intense as it was the second she walked out the door, I turn to the only tried-and-true method I know for numbing all my feelings. I grab the unopened "rainy day" bottle of vodka tucked into my freezer, and I drink.

Chapter 31
Kori

A loud *bang* echoes around my room as I slam the door shut with more force than necessary. But damn if it doesn't feel good to get some of this churning, angry energy out somewhere. It hasn't stopped vibrating under my skin—begging for retribution—since I stormed out of Gage's apartment.

Outside of the initial shock, I've felt nothing but all-consuming rage. I'm sure the heartbreak will come later, but I haven't had time to process those feelings when I'm still reeling from the audacity.

Ending things is one thing, but trying to play the martyr while doing it...just no.

He doesn't get to pretend he's saving me. He doesn't get to rip my heart out and act like he's doing me a favor.

I pace around my room with fury driving each step as I play back our last conversation in my head. There are so many things I wanted to say—should have said—that burn on my tongue. The vitriol brewing is so caustic, I'm surprised it hasn't burned through my lips to force its way out.

"Goddamnit, Daisy, why didn't you warn me men were cowardice pigs."

For once in her life, the duck is silent. I roll my eyes and continue stomping around in my tight circle.

"He said he isn't good enough for me. Can you believe him? If he wanted out, that's all he had to say. He didn't have to try to lessen the blow by making excuses for himself."

A frustrated shriek pours out of my lips when I don't get any kind of response. Maybe I've become too reliant on talking with my real friends. Or maybe this is one problem I can't work through on my own.

I need to call Evelyn, but if I do it now, I'm going to snap—I can feel it. She was one of the ones who pushed me at him in the first place. Hell, they all did. I wouldn't be in this position if I had let my crush live on unrequited until it eventually faded away. So as much as my fingers twitch to pick up the phone, I don't. At least not until the last of the irritation bleeds away hours later.

But nothing takes its place, leaving me a hollow husk of the joyful girl who woke up this morning. I keep waiting for something to fill the void—the agonizing pain of heartbreak—but nothing comes.

It's with that emptiness I finally call my friend. She picks up after the first ring.

"Kori? Is everything okay?" Her voice is filled with concern.

Mine would be too if the situation was reversed. We've only ever exchanged text messages before this. Calls are reserved for emergencies and death—breakups definitely qualify.

"Gage dumped me." I hate how calm the words come out.

She doesn't say anything for several seconds. The silence hangs for so long that I check to make sure the line is connected, but it is.

"Evelyn...are you there?" I ask.

"Shit, sorry. Yes. Holy fuck. I'm so sorry. I'm coming over now. What's your favorite ice cream? Scratch that, I'll bring them all. And wine."

"You really don't have to—"

"I'll be there in ten," she says as the line goes dead.

It's more than I was hoping for, but maybe a good old-fashioned girls' night is what I need to stop feeling so hollow. That's what they always do in the movies. Eight minutes later, a knock raps on my door. She's on me before I have it fully open, hugging me tightly with forgotten plastic bags still in each hand. An icy chill sinks through plastic into my clothes—that one must have the ice cream.

"How are you holding up?" she asks once she lets me go.

"I'm surprisingly okay." Scarily okay, actually.

Her lips purse with sympathetic understanding as she ushers me to sit on my bed.

"Chocolate or vanilla?"

I shrug.

"Chocolate it is." She pulls out a spoon and sticks it directly into the half-eaten tub before handing it over to me. "Now tell me what hap—"

A forceful knock cuts her words short.

"Are you expecting someone?" Her brows pinch in confusion.

I shrug again. Talking feels like more energy than I have to give. When I don't make any move to acknowledge whoever's on the other side, my friend gets up. The door is barely cracked before Karis barrels in like a bat out of hell.

"What the fuck happened," she asks as soon as she's inside.

"Oh, hi, Karis. It's nice to see you too. Me? I'm great, so kind of you to ask. Sure, come on in," Evelyn says in an exasperated tone.

"Hi, Evelyn. Hi, Kori. Now what the fuck happened?" Karis asks our friend.

"I'm not sure. We were getting into that before you barged in here."

"Gage dumped me," I supply before they can continue.

Saying it again doesn't make it feel any more real.

"I know, hon." Karis sits next to me on the bed and puts a ring-covered hand on my shoulder. "But start from the beginning."

"I really don't know what happened. Things were really, really good this morning. He was talking about getting me back to Athens so we could spend tonight together and was as affectionate as always. But then his car broke down, and it was like a switch flipped. He shut down completely and acted like an asshole. When I tried to talk to him about it once we got back to his place, he said we were done."

We're done.

Why doesn't that thought stir anything inside me?

"Fuck," Karis mutters as Evelyn swoops in to take the spot on my other side.

"I really hate to be this person, but it's important. How long ago was this, and where did it happen?" Karis asks.

"A few hours ago at his place," I deadpan.

"Fuck," she says again, and without another word, she exits with the same abruptness with which she arrived.

Evelyn shakes her head and ignores our edgy friend's departure, turning her attention back to the forgotten ice cream.

"I'm so sorry, Kori. Gage is an absolute fool if he doesn't see how big of a mistake he's making."

"Can we skip the ex talk and jump straight into the junk food and movies?" I ask.

She gives me a strange look but acquiesces to my request and turns on my TV.

"What are you feeling?" she asks.

"Something that screams feminine rage."

"I've got just the thing."

***

Movies, ice cream, and half a bottle of wine don't actually make me feel any better. But they don't make me feel any worse either. That would require me to feel something other than the aching emptiness inside me. I'm not numb—every thought of him arrives on the edge of a dull blade—but there's nowhere for that pain to stick. I'm hollow; as sharp as those memories are, the ache falls into an abyss after a few agonizing breaths. Maybe after enough time, I'll be filled up by heartbreak, and maybe then I'll finally mourn the way I'm supposed to.

After a lot of convincing, I manage to get Evelyn to leave. She wanted to spend the night "so I wouldn't be alone," but after both volumes of *Kill Bill* and *Pacific Rim,* I decided enough was enough. I couldn't stand the constant look of pity on her face or the way she watched me like I might break down at any moment.

I'm not sure being alone is any better. At least when she was here, I had someone to distract me from my thoughts. Now, in the dark of my room, they keep drifting back to him. How could they not when his presence has tainted everything in here.

The plush fuzz of my favorite blanket is the same one I wrapped myself in when he showed up at my door and claimed me once and for all. The *Godzilla* posters remind me of the nights spent on his sofa, filled with tentative touches as he listened to my endless commentary while we watched the films. Even my favorite color has been ruined. I can't look at the bright hue without hearing the way his voice softened when he called me *Low* or seeing how the corners of his lips curved with a smile that was reserved for me.

Fuck him for embedding himself so deeply into my life in only a few short months.

And fuck him for making it so easy for me to love him.

The surge of emotions I've been waiting for finally makes an appearance, crashing through my body in a destructive wave. A thick lump lodges itself in my throat as hot tears burn behind my eyes.

He is never going to kiss me again, or hold me, or listen to me ramble about whatever nonsense comes to my head. I'm never going to feel that same sense of safety that his presence brought. I'll never hear the rasp of his stern commands when he thinks he knows what's best for me, and I'll never see the spark in his eyes when I fight back. No more late-night movie dates or goodnight texts. We are back to being strangers—worse now, because I doubt I'll be able to escape seeing him. Not if his friends still want me around.

My chest constricts at the thought.

Losing him is hard, but losing all of them...that's what I feared most from the start.

A sob tears through me like an earthquake, letting loose the tsunami of tears. I clutch my pillow to my chest and cry even harder at the faintest whiff of his clean scent that clings to the cotton.

My weeping is endless. Those tears flow until my throat is raw and my eyes swell shut, and even once the well runs dry, my body heaves with silent gasps. I'm exhausted by the time I pull myself together—mind, body, and soul. But as I lie in my pitch-black room, I steel myself against my heartbreak. This will not happen again. Gage Maher will never get another one of my tears.

Chapter 32
Gage

"What the fuck?" Nathan's voice carries down the hallway, followed by a series of loud scrapes and bangs.

A moment of silence follows, but it's broken by Karis's frantic shout of my name. Glass crunches under their feet as they move throughout my apartment.

"Come on, you asshole. Fucking talk to me," she calls out as her shadowy form passes in front of the doorway.

I'm a spineless cunt for not answering her, especially when I know exactly what moment is replaying in her head. I can't, though. Not because I don't want to, but because I don't think I'm physically capable. My body is a lead weight, so heavy I can't even lift my head.

"Fuck. Morgan, go check Cutter's, and Nathan can hit Double Teep. I'll head out to the botanical gardens, but if he isn't there—" Her voice catches in a way that's unlike her. "Fuck, we won't cross that bridge until we get there, yeah?"

More shadows dance over the threshold. So close, but too far to notice me tucked away behind the shower curtain. I'm too exhausted to question how I ended up in the bathtub in the first place. At least I'm still clothed and not completely soaked through.

The flurry of motion outside continues, but the world is spinning too much for me to keep track of it all. The door opens and closes more times than I can count, and I let out a sigh of relief as I'm alone once again.

Loneliness is the only thing I deserve.

My body sags, and my fingers loosen their grip on the bottle.

Huh, I don't remember having that two minutes ago.

The empty glass falls to the linoleum tile with a crash but doesn't shatter as it hits the ground and rolls away.

"Gage?" Karis calls out.

Looks like I'm not so alone after all.

The shadow makes a reappearance in the doorframe and freezes. My friend sucks in a deep breath and mutters "Please don't be dead" as she flips on the light.

Its brightness shoots through my head like an ice pick, and I flinch away with a groan.

"Thank God," she breathes, and rushes over to my side, pulling the curtain open more than the small crack that let me see out.

Towering over me, she assesses my state with worried eyes. From the stinging on my arms and feet, I'm probably cut to shit, but nothing feels particularly deep or intentional.

I'm counting that as a win.

"What the hell happened?" she asks as she sits on the edge of the tub.

I try to answer her, but my tongue won't work. All that comes out is a slurred, incoherent mess. She sighs and grabs a rag from the rack and wipes the layer of sweat and drool from my face before picking a piece of debris off my shirt.

"Stay here," she commands, as if I have any other option.

That cursed light stays on in her absence, but darkness pulses at the edge of my vision as unconsciousness creeps back in. My friend's tired voice telling the others to come back is the last thing that registers before I'm dragged under again.

When the next moment of lucidity comes, all three of them are crowded into my tiny bathroom. Karis is on the floor with her back against the tub, while Nathan leans against the wall and Morgan perches on the small countertop.

"Why didn't he tell us?" Morgan asks.

"Why didn't *you* tell us?" Nathan asks with much more heat.

"It wasn't my place," Karis says. "He still has the occasional depressive episodes, but they are mostly managed, and they have been since before either of you knew him. There was no point in digging up bodies that have been buried for years if he didn't want to. Plus, how exactly would I go about telling you something like that? I can't just say 'Oh, by the way, Gage used to be suicidal.'"

"Fine," Nathan relents, "but knowing could have prepared us better for today."

"I don't think anything could have prepared us for today," she whispers.

"Didn't try to kill myself. Just drunk," I slur.

All three heads snap in my direction.

"Well, you scared the crap out of us either way," Morgan says.

I grumble something unintelligible as my eyes struggle to focus on their faces. There are too many eyes between them, or maybe it's too many thems.

"Okay, he's still useless. So what do we do now?" he asks.

"Clean up his mess and keep him from choking on his own vomit," Karis supplies.

I want to protest that, but the mere mention of throwing up has nausea churning in my gut.

"And once he's sobered up, I can beat the shit out of him for being a fucking idiot, right?" Nathan asks.

"Once he's sober, you'll have to get in line," Karis replies.

"I'll take care of Gage," Morgan says. "It's the least I can do after what he did for me last year."

They grumble their agreement, leaving me with my sanest friend. He hops off the counter and comes to stand at the edge of the tub.

"You really screwed this one up," he says with more pity than condemnation.

When I don't respond, he shakes his head and sighs.

"Sorry about this, but you are covered in questionable liquids and smell worse than Cutter's after a home game."

His words make no sense until the spray of icy water pelts into me.

Payback is a fucking bitch.

***

Stabbing pain lances through my head, pulsating in time to the beat of my heart, and a wave of nausea rips through me. I crack one lid, but the bright glow from the overhead light is too much for me to bear. It sends another flash of pain into my skull, so intense my vision goes white.

What the fuck happened?

It's been years since I've been this hungover.

With a groan, I grab the nearest pillow and use it to cover my head, smothering myself with Kori's scent. For a moment, I find peace, but it shatters as everything comes back to me.

Meeting her parents.

Driving us back.

Brandy breaking down.

Spiraling.

Ending things.

Fuck.

I spring out of bed and sprint for the bathroom, as vomit that has nothing to do with my hangover rises in my throat. The soles of my feet sting with every step as the skin around the shallow cuts tightens and tears them back open. I don't even know where they came from. With seconds to spare, I make it to kneel in front of the toilet bowl as all the contents of my stomach spill out.

"Welcome back to the land of the living," Nathan says from the doorway.

His mouth is curled in a friendly smile, but his eyes burn with the anger he keeps locked under the surface. It's an ire I deserve every smoldering second of. I grunt in acknowledgment and stand, wiping away the remaining mess from my lips.

"How are you feeling?" he asks.

"Like death."

He nods, looks me over, and pulls his arm back before launching his fist at my face. The move is telegraphed. I could easily dodge it, but I lean into it instead, letting the full force of the blow land on my jaw. Whatever his reason, it's probably deserved.

"That was for breaking Kori's heart," he says.

Scratch that. It was definitely deserved. I would let him beat me bloody if he wanted to, and it wouldn't begin to make up for what I've done.

The mere mention of her name sends a pang of emotions through me so intense my knees nearly buckle. I didn't expect letting her go to hurt this much. Her absence is a gaping, bleeding hole in my chest—a physical pain that steals my breath from my fucking lungs.

She's gone.

No, I fucking threw her away. I ruined the only good thing in my fucked-up life like I always knew I would.

"What the hell happened, man?" he asks.

"I fucked up." My voice cracks before I can finish the sentence.

Grimacing, he pulls me in for a hug, but my arms hang limply at my sides. He shouldn't be giving me sympathy. He should be leaving me to wallow in the misery of my own making.

"Yeah, I figured that much out on my own," he says as he pulls away.

"Where are Karis and Morgan?"

"Morgan had class, and Karis is covering your 'brats.'"

"Shit." I've lost a full day to my drunken stupor, and I'd be lying if I said it wasn't preferable to this. Nathan was right; I'm a self-sabotaging bastard.

"Yup. And don't think I'm letting you off the hook with an 'I fucked up.' Seriously, man, you scared the shit out of us. I don't think I've ever seen Karis that freaked out."

My chest tightens as my head hangs even lower with shame.

"Think you could give me a few minutes to freshen up before giving me the first degree?"

"Sure, man." He claps me on the back before leaving me alone with my guilt.

Without my friend to distract me, my mind drifts back to Yellow. My perfect sunflower woman. Is she handling this as poorly as I am? I'm falling apart at the seams, and I'm not the one who got plucked from the soil and discarded like a weed. She must be devastated. The thought of her going through that alone sends another wave of nausea washing over me, but this one I'm able to push back down.

I should be there with her.

I never should have hurt her in the first place.

What the fuck was I thinking yesterday? That's right, I wasn't, and I destroyed the only good thing in my life in the process. As if I didn't hate myself enough already, now I have to live with this.

I can't stand to look at myself in the mirror as I splash icy water over my face and brush the layers of grime off my teeth. The clothes I woke up in are surprisingly clean, and not what I was wearing yesterday, so I throw them back on. Someone must have forced me to change in the night, but I have no memory of it. The last thing I remember fully is sitting on the floor in my kitchen, surrounded by chaos, with a fourth of the bottle of vodka left. After that, it's only flashes.

The smell of coffee and cooking grease greets me as I open the door, and my stomach lets out an angry growl. The last time I ate anything was breakfast with the Wrights, and if Karis is covering my classes at the gym, that was over a day and a half ago.

Shit.

I follow my stomach out into the kitchen and find Nathan has made himself at home at my stove. The room is cleaner than it should be—I was sober when I trashed it—even though some of my stuff is missing and nothing is in the exact right place. I'll add fixing my place up to the list of things I need to thank my friends for.

"You ready to talk?" Nathan asks as he sets a coffee mug on the too-empty counter and turns back to cooking.

I nod as I take a sip of the liquid gold in front of me.

"Okay. So talk. What the fuck were you thinking?"

"Which part? Making the worst decision of my life and ending things with the woman I love, or going on a bender?"

I choke on my next breath as the truth of those words weighs on me.

"Fuck, I love her." The confession spilled out without conscious thought, but that doesn't make it any less true. I'm in love with her...and I broke her heart.

A sharp pang radiates from that void in my chest.

Fuck.

"Both. But start with the first part," my friend says.

"I was thinking that she deserves more than being saddled with me for the rest of her life. I was thinking that I was only going to hold her back."

"So you were being an idiot," he says.

"And a coward," I agree.

"Glad you recognize that. So what are you going to do about it?"

"What can I do about it?"

I broke up with her. There's no coming back from that.

"Fight for her, goddamnit," Nathan growls. "Go to her and beg on your knees for forgiveness."

"What if I don't deserve her forgiveness?"

"If that's your attitude about it, maybe you don't." He sighs and shakes his head. "But if you want to fix this, your window is closing."

"What do I do?"

"You eat, drink some fucking water, and then I'll drive you over to her place so you can beg for her to take you back."

"What if she doesn't want me anymore?"

"Then you learn to live with it."

Chapter 33
Kori

The world doesn't stop spinning just because my heart is broken. The sun still rises, birds still sing, and classes are still on schedule. Despite the hollow ache in my chest, I get up and drag myself to my lectures. Because that's what I have to do. There's no chance in hell I'm letting myself get behind because some asshole hurt my feelings.

The normalcy of the routine is a welcome distraction from the urge to wallow. I push any thoughts of my ex to the back of my mind and listen to my professors with more attention than I've ever mustered before. Maybe breakups are the key to academic success. Thinking about differential equations is way more enjoyable than dwelling on a broken heart.

I stay on campus longer than I need to. My room is lonely, and there are too many reminders of him around for it to be comfortable. It isn't until the sun dips below the trees that I make my way back to Rutherford Hall. An ominous chill clings to the breeze, teasing the first real taste of fall.

It's alarming how quickly the seasons can change, and the seasons of life are no different. One day you can be basking in the sun, filled with joy and life, only for dusk to come, and the next to be filled with cold loneliness and despair. One sunset—one blink—and nothing is what it was before.

I'm not who I was before.

I walk into my dorm and freeze at the mountain of a man hunched over in a chair two sizes too small near the maglock entrance to the dormitory, with a bouquet of equally wilted sunflowers clutched in his white-knuckled fist.

As if he can sense my presence, his head snaps up, and his gaze finds mine across the room. His face is pale, his eyes are shadowed by dark circles, and there's a deep bruise forming on his cheek. A sick sort of pleasure fills me knowing he looks as awful as I feel, but that doesn't explain what he's doing here.

He has no reason to be here.

Everything was made crystal clear yesterday. He doesn't get to come here and try to take it back. Fuck that—no, fuck him and his bullshit games. He can't rip my heart out and then try to shove it back in and pretend like nothing happened.

My heart picks up speed, beating wildly under the intensity of his stare. His eyes run over my body, and I freeze like prey caught in the sights of a predator. An unwelcome shiver runs to my core. My body hasn't gotten on the same program as my head and heart. A lifetime passes in those brief seconds, and then I move, taking a slow step back as if that will somehow stop him from pouncing.

"Low, wait," he calls out, springing from the chair as I start to flee.

"You lost the right to call me that," I snap.

"Kori," he amends, "please just hear me out."

It only takes him half a dozen steps before he's right in front of me, and I curse my traitorous body for relaxing for the first time since I left his place yesterday.

"What do you want, Gage?" I try to keep my voice down despite the venom coating the words.

There are too many eyes on us already, watching this train crash play out in slow motion. I don't want to draw any more attention.

"You," he rasps. There's more emotion in that one word than he normally displays in a full conversation. "I fucked up yesterday, and I'm so sorry. Breaking up with you was the biggest mistake of my life. I freaked out and reacted without thinking. So this is me, begging for your forgiveness."

He holds out the sad flower arrangement, but I don't take the withering blooms. I cross my arms over my chest and keep my chin held high.

"Are you actually ready to talk about what caused you to freak out?" I ask.

"Yeah, I am."

"Come on, let's take a walk."

He nods as he follows me out of the lobby and into the quad. This isn't a conversation I want to have with an audience, but I'm also not about to take him up to my room. My resolve has its limits.

A bitter chill nips at my skin when I step outside, painting it with a layer of goose bumps as a shiver racks through me. I should have grabbed a hoodie, but that would mean going up to my room, and I don't trust him not to follow me up and try to force his way back into my good graces. My grandma always told me never to trust a desperate man, and the desperation is clear on my ex's face.

"Here." Gage shrugs off his jacket and hands it to me. I'm not stubborn enough to freeze in order to make a point.

Tears well as the rough canvas envelops me, but I refuse to let them fall. It's still warm with his body heat and the closest I'll get to one of his protective embraces ever again. I wrap it around me and breathe him in, basking in the sense of security no matter how false it might be.

I find a bench isolated enough from the others and take a seat, urging him to do the same. He sits beside me and fidgets with the sad bouquet, twisting it in his hands without looking up from the bright petals.

"About yesterday," he starts, but cuts himself off with a shake of his head. "Shit. None of this will make sense without context."

"So give me context."

His eyes fall shut as his face contorts. Bits of yellow float to the ground at his feet as he rips and tears at the delicate blooms.

He can't help but destroy beautiful things.

"You remember how I told you I wasn't in a good place after my injury, right?" he asks after several long seconds of silence.

"Yes."

"The thing is, I haven't ever gotten back to a good place. There is this...gloom...that's always lurking in the shadows. Sometimes I barely notice it, but other times its presence is all-consuming, and yesterday was one of those moments. The car broke down, and the gloom descended, reminding me that I'm nothing—that I'll never be worthy of a woman like you."

"And this 'gloom' made you break up with me?" I can't keep the incredulous tone from the question.

"You deserve a better man than me—I don't need any gloom to tell me that."

My face pinches as I fight the urge to roll my eyes. I take a calming breath, and then another, before I ask, "Why are you here?"

"Because I'm selfish enough to want to keep you, even if I know I'll never be good enough. I'm here because I made the biggest fucking mistake of my life yesterday, and I'm hoping it's not too late to fix it."

The raw pain in his voice is a dagger to my already aching heart, but the frantic desperation does nothing but lend credence to my doubts.

"Gage—"

"Hear me out, Low. Please." He reaches over and squeezes my thigh as he fully faces me. "I love you, and I'm a selfish bastard who never wants to let you go."

He loves me? Like hell he does. If he loves me, he wouldn't have pushed me away. If he loves me like I love him, he wouldn't be wielding it like some sort of weapon to cut through my walls and win me back. Hearing it now feels wrong and stirs the pot of heartbreak, bringing it all to the surface. I can't look at him. If I do, the semblance of control I have will snap.

"What happens when the gloom comes again?" The words come out steadier than I feel.

"What do you mean?"

"What happens the next time your insecurities get in the way and you decide you know what's best for me?"

"That won't happen—"

"Bullshit. It happened before we got together, and it will keep happening if I take you back."

He recoils as if I slapped him, pulling his hand away, and utters a defeated "If?"

"Yes, Gage, if. I don't want to do this again—I won't. I'm not a yo-yo. You can't just throw me away and drag me back with the flick of your wrist. My heart isn't a toy to be played with."

"You know that isn't what this is," he growls, anger growing from the seeds of despair.

"Really? Because that's what it feels like."

"Goddamnit, I love you, Kori. Why the fuck would you even think I would do something like that," he snaps.

Good. His anguish is my kryptonite, but his anger reminds me exactly where we stand. It stokes the flames of my own frustrations.

I meet his stormy gaze for the first time since this conversation began. "Look me in the eye and tell me if this gloom comes back and makes you feel unworthy, you will be able to block it out. Tell me with one hundred percent certainty that you will never spiral and break my heart again."

He holds my eyes for a second before they drop back to the shredded petals. His shoulders slump with a deep sigh, and his head hangs as the fight abandons him.

"That's what I thought. I love you, Gage, but I can't love you enough for the both of us."

"Kor—"

"I'm sorry. I really am. But I won't do this. I really hope you make peace with yourself."

"So that's it?" he asks.

"That's it."

Devastation flashes in his eyes before he slams them closed. His jaw ticks and his throat bobs as he fights to regain control over his emotions. After several agonizing seconds, he takes a breath and slips on his stoic mask.

"All right." He stands, brushing away the yellow shreds, and I mirror the motion.

For a heartbeat, we stand there on the edge of the darkened field, our eyes locked together while the air buzzes with electricity between us, and I wish with every fiber of my being that things could be different. He breaks the moment first, taking a deep breath, then turning to walk away. I stop him before he can go too far.

"Wait, your jacket," I call out as I pull off the heavy layer.

His knuckles blanch as they grip the dark canvas.

"Take care of yourself," he commands.

Without thinking, I spring to the tips of my toes and press my lips against his in one last kiss. It's meant to be a quick goodbye, but his free hand cups the side of my face, and he pours every last bit of love into the way his lips dance with mine. That kiss captures all the air from my lungs—no, it pulls my very soul from me—leaving me empty and hollow. This time, he doesn't linger. With a final breath and nod, he turns and walks out of my life for good.

Chapter 34
Gage

I love you, Gage, but I can't love you enough for the both of us.

Those words hurt more than any hate-filled rejection could. They prove what I already knew—I'll never be able to give her what she needs.

The day is well and truly gone now, and with it, all my hopes of fixing what I broke. The window is closed, if it was ever truly open to begin with. For a moment, I held love in my hand, only to let it slip through my fingers like sand. Shrouded in the shadows of dusk, I roam through campus without a destination in mind. It's not like I have anywhere else to be. I told Nathan to leave after he dropped me off because if things went well, I wouldn't need a ride, and I didn't want him around if they didn't.

Sometimes a man needs a moment alone to work through his emotions.

Students avoid me as I sulk along the streets. On a good day, they would likely do the same, but my sullen demeanor isn't doing anything to make me more approachable. Despite the chill, I can't bring myself to put my jacket back on. It's stupid, but if I do, I might erase Kori's presence from it completely, and I'm not ready to let her go.

I don't stop moving until I reach the border between campus and downtown, the busy main street acting as the harsh divide. It's there, where the sidewalk splits, that I have to think for the first time since I walked away from her. Goddamn, I don't want to think. I still don't have a way home, and while that is easily fixed, I'm too much of a coward to face those lonely walls—especially when her presence has permeated every fucking inch of the space that used to be mine. The obvious path forward is to head to one of the dozens of bars and drink away these feelings, but the thought of alcohol after last night is sickening.

Morgan's place isn't too far, and if anyone understands what I'm going through, it's him. It helps that out of all my friends, he's the least invested. Nathan is protective of Kori, and Karis would tear her to shreds if she thought it would make me feel better. Morgan is less biased.

Plus, he owes me.

It doesn't take me long to walk the few blocks over to his building and knock on the door. The confusion on James's face as she opens it would be comical if the situation wasn't what it is.

"Gage?" she asks, as if she can't believe she's asking at all.

"Hey, James. Is Morgan home?"

"Yeah, fuck, where are my manners. Come in." She steps out of the doorway and ushers me inside.

Every time I'm here, I'm struck by how different it feels from my place. The age is the same, and behind the decor, it has the same "landlord special" base. But together, they have made it into a place that feels like a home. A pang of jealousy ripples through me at the happy pictures lining the walls. I should have taken more pictures with Low when I had the chance.

"Can I get you something? You look like you could use a beer."

"No beer." My stomach churns at the thought of consuming more poison so soon.

Part of me craves the blissful indifference a few drinks would bring, but I'm not doing that again. I'm not about to disrespect everything I had with my woman by numbing myself to the memories of it. I want to feel it all, good and bad.

"Water would be great, though," I tack on.

Morgan appears in the hallway as his girlfriend slips into the kitchen, and his face morphs into the same look of confusion, but he schools it much quicker.

"Hey, how are you?" he asks.

"I talked to Kori today," I deadpan. There's no point in dancing around the issue with pleasantries.

"And?" he prompts.

"And it's over. She wants nothing to do with me."

He runs a hand through his hair with a grimace and lets out a very un-Morgan-like curse. "That sucks. I'm sorry."

"She was right to turn me away. Fuck. I don't even know why I'm here. I'll get out of your hair."

"Sit down," Morgan says with an exasperated sigh, "and tell me what happened."

The words lodge themselves in my throat in a thick mass. I swallow against it as I sit on the couch with my back stiff. My friend follows suit and gives me the time I need to get my thoughts straight. It wasn't too long ago our situations were reversed and he was the one nursing a broken heart.

James reappears with a cup of water and places it on the coffee table in front of me. She gives my shoulder a sympathetic squeeze before kissing the crown of her boyfriend's head and disappearing down the hallway with a flimsy excuse about needing to work on something in her studio.

Damn these thin walls. I'm sure the rest of the group will know that I'm here and that it's really over before I leave, but that's easier than me having to do this all again.

"I went to apologize for being an idiot and beg for her to take me back. She heard me out, but in the end, it wasn't enough. She said that she loves me, but she can't love me enough for the both of us. That she can't be with me knowing I will likely spiral and hurt her all over again in the future."

He hums in acknowledgment and nods with rapt attention, but he doesn't say anything else.

So I continue.

"And I get it. Because as much as I love her too, I can't promise her that it won't happen. I'm not good enough for her, I never will be, and that is never going to change."

"Do you want sympathy or honesty?" he asks after contemplating for a moment.

"Honesty." I didn't come here to be coddled.

"Being good enough for her was never the problem. Only she can judge that, and it was crappy of you to make that assertion for her. But that is another issue altogether. The real problem is you aren't good enough for you. That is always going to be the dark cloud over any relationship you are in. And unless you figure out how to be enough for yourself, you are always going to end up back here. Kori was smart to recognize that."

"How do I become good enough for myself?"

"Only you can figure that out. Only you can say what will make you finally see yourself as someone worthy. But if you do make the choice to figure it out, it has to be for you and you alone. Trying to change yourself to earn someone's love is toxic, for you and them."

"I have no intentions of pursuing Kori any further. That chapter is closed."

"Good. What does the next one look like, then?"

That is the question. I don't think I've ever thought about what happens next. I've been too fixated on the past. My conversation with Kori's dad returns to the forefront of my mind.

"I'd like to get my GED," I tell him.

The idea has been rattling around in my head since we talked in his office. I was going to talk to her about it when we got back to my place yesterday, but...

Yeah, that didn't happen.

"That's good." He sits up straighter and leans forward, resting his elbows on his knees. "You know we will help you study as much as you need. And after that?"

"I'm not sure. I don't think the college thing is for me. Maybe a trade. Something where the pay is steady, and I don't have to stress about paying my bills."

"Okay. That's something we can work with. Let me grab my computer, and we can start getting a game plan together."

"Seriously?"

"Of course." The dumbfounded look on his face says I couldn't be a bigger idiot if I tried. "I know the circumstances are different, but you are welcome to crash on my couch as long as you need to."

"I think I'll pass on that one, but I appreciate the offer."

Morgan claps me on the shoulder before going to get the device, and despite my initial refusal, I do end up on his couch for the night. We spend far too many hours poring over my options and building out the pros and cons list of each. James rejoins us after a while and gives her own opinions on the matter. By the time I've made a decision, it's too late to ask either of them to drive me home.

I'm going to be an electrician.

It will take years for me to get fully certified, but it's the first real goal I've had since my MMA dreams died. All I've done for the past decade is survive, but now it's time for a new dream. It might not be as glamorous as a world-famous fighter, but it's better than the rotting state of stagnation I've been in for the past decade. Too much of my life has passed by without me living it. I've been asleep at the wheel, and it's time for me to wake the fuck up.

***

Karis's bike sits outside my apartment like an ill omen as Morgan pulls up to the curb to drop me off. I'm so fucking dead. My phone died sometime yesterday, and I didn't feel the need to charge it. Kori isn't trying to reach me, so why did it matter? But I didn't take into account my best friend wanting to check up on me, especially with how she found me the other night. Fuck. I'm the worst goddamned friend who's ever existed.

"You are so screwed," my friend says with a snort of laughter. "Good luck."

I flip him off as I climb the steps to the ass-chewing that awaits me inside. The light is on when I walk in, and Karis sits waiting for me on my sofa with her back facing me. She doesn't turn as the door falls shut with a resounding *click*, and for the first time in years, I feel like a kid coming home to face my ma's wrath.

"Hey, Kare. Want a beer?"

"It's eight o'clock in the fucking morning. Why would I want a beer?"

"I don't know. I always offer you guys beer when you show up here. I wasn't aware there was a time frame on when it was and wasn't considered polite."

"Oh, fuck off, you know damn well you are trying to deflect. Where the fuck were you last night? You're home earlier than I expected, and you don't smell like a distillery, so I doubt you spent the night drinking your sorrows away." She stands and whirls around in her anger. Her haggard expression sends my stomach spiraling to the floor.

Every ounce of worry is etched on her face. Her eyes are swollen and red, with dark circles hanging underneath, but that doesn't stop her from crossing her arms and pinning me with a cutting stare. The attitude is all posturing. I've known her long enough to tell when she's trying to mask how vulnerable she feels.

"I was at Morgan's," I say in a rasping whisper as my guilt eats me alive.

Her face scrunches and she takes a steadying breath. "What happened? Nathan said he was taking you to talk to Kori, and then you went dark."

"I'm sorry. Fuck. Things didn't go the way I hoped. We're done—for good—and I needed some time to process it all."

"You could have at least checked in. I-I thought we lost you." Her voice cracks on the admission. "Fuck, Gage, for two nights in a row, I've been terrified that I was going to get a call that you were dead."

Tears pool in her eyes, and she wipes them away with angry swipes. With a few large strides, I'm across the room, and I wrap her in a tight hug.

"I'm here, Kare. I'm not going anywhere. I'm okay, I promise."

She collapses into my chest as a sob shakes her tiny frame.

"I was so fucking scared," she chokes out.

"I know," I tell her and guide us back to the couch.

All I can do is hold her and whisper reassurances while she gets it all out. Living with the gloom means I live with a constant bombardment of intrusive thoughts sprinkled with fleeting suicidal ideation. Only once have I ever been low enough to give in to it. It's easy to forget that once is all it takes to scar someone for life, and no matter how much she argues, Karis is scarred. I still struggle with believing my existence is worth her tears and worry, but I won't ever put her through that again. The gloom can do what it wants to me—nothing will be as agonizing as watching my best friend fall apart because of my actions.

I didn't realize how deep the wound went. Goddamnit, it never even occurred to me that Kare might be riddled with anxiety, waiting for something to push me past my breaking point again. Fucking offing myself never even crossed my mind in the past forty-eight hours. My heart is in a million jagged pieces, but I'm not about to end my life over a woman—even if she was perfect.

"I promised you never again. I meant that shit," I tell her once her sobs slow to soft sniffles.

"You're a fucking asshole," she says as she squirms out of my hold to sit beside me on the sofa.

"I know. I'm so fucking sorry."

"Well, don't do it again."

"I don't plan to. I didn't mean to freak you out."

"Maybe you will think before you go AWOL," she says with a half-heart-ed slap to my chest.

"I'm sorry. I got so caught up doing research with Morgan that I lost track of time. By the time we finished, my phone was dead, and we were all exhausted, so I crashed on his couch."

"Research? For what?" Curiosity pushes away the last remnants of her vulnerability.

"The future. I'm getting my life together, starting with a GED."

"Oh shit, you're serious about this."

"Yeah, I am."

I can't keep living the way I've been—if you could even call what I've been doing living.

"Good. You know I'll help out any way I can."

"I know. Morgan and James said the same thing."

She hums and falls silent. After a moment, she speaks again.

"You need to start talking to someone. Professionally. You can't keep doing this shit on your own."

"I will. If I pass the GED test, I'm going to apply for an apprenticeship, and if I get the one Morgan helped me find last night, I'll get benefits. Once I can afford it, I'll find a therapist. I promise."

"Good." The word comes out choked. "I love you. You know that, right?"

"I love you too."

Maybe the universe doesn't hate me completely, because if it did, I know I wouldn't have people like Karis, Nathan, and Morgan in my life—people who love me, flaws and all. People worth living for.

Chapter 35
Kori

My phone rings seconds after I hit send, with Evelyn's name on the screen. She doesn't wait for me to say "hello" before she starts hounding me.

"What do you mean, you aren't going?"

"I didn't think the invite still stood after…well, you know."

"Of course it still stands. The others miss you. Nathan has been bugging me nonstop for weeks about when you are coming out with us again. I figured it was too soon for Cutter's, but you can't skip on Friendsgivmas. The whole point is to spend the day with friends. All of them. Chelsea is even going to call in for a little while."

"I don't know if spending an afternoon with my ex is a great idea."

"Don't worry about Gage. You and I both know he won't bother you."

That's what I'm scared of. Being ignored by him will hurt worse than any rude words or spiteful glances ever could. I've never been on the receiving end of his cold indifference, and even if it's selfish, I don't want to be strangers.

"Evelyn..."

"Please. I promise it will be fun. If it's awful, I will do a *Godzilla* movie marathon with you as penance."

The promise of a kaiju marathon is too great to turn away. Especially when I'm sure this will end up as one of the top ten most awkward days of my life. Mark my words, our next movie night is going to be amazing.

"Fine," I relent, and she squeals.

"Yay, I'll see you in a few."

The line goes dead, and I fall back on my bed with an exasperated sigh. This is a terrible fucking idea. Knowing that, I still start to get ready, grabbing a new oversized sweater dress and slipping it on.

It's black. Yellow doesn't bring the same joy it did before.

***

The furious pounding of my heart echoes in my ears, making it impossible to hear Evelyn's peppy chatter. I smile, nod, and pretend like the nerves aren't trying to burst out of my chest like the creature from *Alien*.

This was a bad idea, made worse by how I don't feel like me. When I went home for actual Thanksgiving last week, Mom insisted that I do a post-breakup makeover with her. She claimed it was a quintessential heartbreak experience.

I'm not sold on its effectiveness.

The nails and bags full of clothes and makeup were excessive, but I'll own up to it being well past due to take my braids out and give my natural hair some room to breathe. In all the movies, the heartbroken girl wears her new look like a coat of armor, but I don't find the same strength. Not only do I have to face my ex today, I'm doing it while cosplaying as something I'm not. The girl dressed in black with dark lips and a thick cloud of tight curls framing her face doesn't feel like me—even if she is hot.

Cold sweat gathers on the back of my neck as we approach James and Morgan's apartment, and I swallow back the icy shard of fear clinging to my throat. In the depths of my heart, I know I'm not ready to see Gage again. Remnants of love still cling in hard-to-reach places, waiting to be knocked loose and cause another cycle of pain. This would be so much easier if I hated him—or if he hated me. Our mutual heartache is a recipe for a bad time for all involved. I should leave now, *Godzilla* be damned. Evelyn knocks before I get the chance to act on the impulse.

James opens the door and greets us both with a warm smile, pulling Evelyn in for a tight hug and then doing the same for me. As if she's as happy to see me as she is her friend. As if I'm not a tagalong they felt too uncomfortable to uninvite.

"Kori," Nathan shouts as I step inside.

The blond man hops off the bar chair, raising a glass bottle in the air as he pulls me in for a sloppy hug.

Why are they all so touchy?

Although I don't hate it as much as I used to.

It's safe to assume this isn't his first drink of the evening—or the second. But beyond that, his excitement seems genuine, at least to me. There's life in his glassy eyes, making them feel more like a shimmering pool than something glacial.

"How have you been?" he asks with an arm still wrapped around my shoulder.

"I've been good," I tell him.

It's not a lie, either. Yes, getting dumped sucked, but I'm not the type to dwell on things I can't change. And I'm sure as hell not going to let one man and his inability to cope consume me. I vented my frustrations to anyone who would listen—and there were lots of them—but over the weeks, my frustration lost its steam, and while my heart is still sad at the outcome of all this, it isn't broken.

Broken implies there is something that has to be fixed.

"Well, you look good. I wasn't expecting you to show up and go all Princess Diana's divorce dress on us."

"Thank you?" I'm not entirely sure that's a compliment, but I don't push back.

Before he can say anything else, another knock raps on the door. This time Morgan is the one who pulls away from the prep happening in the kitchen, stopping only to wrap his arms around his chatting girlfriend and place a quick kiss on the top of her head.

My gaze drops away from the casual display of affection as a dull ache fills my chest. When I look back up, Gage is there—Karis too, but I barely notice her beside the giant of a man. That ache morphs into an uncomfortable throbbing that reaches from my hollow chest all the way to my toes. He's wearing the same outfit he wore to our first date—black button-up, dark-wash jeans, and those well-worn combat boots he loves so much—and he looks about as uncomfortable as he did in my dorm's lobby.

Karis pushes past him into the room, but he doesn't move from the doorway as he stares at me, drinking me in with unbridled desire. I don't move either. I don't think I could if I tried. His gaze is a tractor beam locking me in place while he looks his fill.

Well, I can look my fill too.

That lust in his eyes turns into another sort of heat when he notices Nathan's arm wrapped around me. His nostrils flare as he stomps forward, but the tension shatters as Karis steps between us.

"New girl, you made it," she says without any attempt at faking enthusiasm.

So maybe everyone isn't happy to see me. Not that I blame her. At the end of the day, I was the one who made the final call on ending things—I'm the bad guy here.

"Sorry we're late. Is it time to eat?" she asks our hosts.

"Ask Nathan. He was in charge of the important shit," James says.

274

"Yeah, we can eat," he responds, and his arm falls away as he strolls back into the kitchen.

The group comes alive in a flurry then, bickering and laughing while they fill their plates. Gage and I are the only ones left on the outside. After a few tense minutes, he finally moves from the spot in front of the doorway, but he doesn't join his friends in the kitchen.

"Hey, L—Kori," he says but doesn't look at me again.

Good. It's easier to breathe without the weight of his eyes on me.

"Hey," I respond, fidgeting with one of my thick coils.

"You look...different. Nice, but different."

"Thanks."

He doesn't say anything else before grabbing a plate of his own. With a sigh, I follow him into the crowded kitchen.

I'm definitely getting my movie marathon.

By the time I fix my plate, there's only one seat left, sandwiched between Nathan and Gage at the counter. Fucking perfect. I glare at the back of Evelyn's head before I squeeze into that cursed spot, leaving as much space as possible between me and my ex. Unfortunately, that means getting real up close and personal with his best friend.

"Saved you a seat," Nathan says as he slings his arm over the back of my chair.

"Thanks," I mumble and poke around at the food on my plate with disinterest.

"Listen..." His voice drops as he brings his head in closer like he's telling me a secret. "I have a favor to ask, and you are going to say no, but at least hear me out before telling me to fuck off."

"Uh...okay."

This already sounds like a terrible idea.

"The girls are planning on FaceTiming with Chelsea before we start the 'Christmas' portion of the night, and I'm scared shitless. It's the first time I'll have talked to her or seen her since she left."

"Okay?"

"She doesn't know you. Sure, Evelyn has probably told her all the drama, but that just makes this work even better."

"Makes *what* work even better?"

"You pretending to be into me."

"I'm sorry, what?"

Maybe he's had more to drink tonight than I thought.

"Just for, like, thirty minutes max. All I'm asking is for you to sit next to me and smile in my direction a few times. Maybe a little bit of light touching." He brushes his fingers over my shoulder to show exactly what he means.

"What is the point of this convoluted plan?"

"To make Chelsea think I'm not still hung up on her."

"But you are?" I clarify.

"Oh, without a doubt. But I don't want her to know that," he says with a sly grin.

"Fine," I tell him with a grin of my own.

"Now, hear me out—wait, really?"

"What's the worst that can happen?"

It will certainly be more fun than trying to ignore the brooding man next to me. At least with this scheme, I'll be doing *something* other than wallowing in the awkward energy.

"You are an angel," he says, and I giggle as he places a wet kiss on my cheek.

The plastic fork snaps in Gage's hand with a loud *crack*, drawing my attention away from Nathan and his awful plan.

In the next breath, my ex pushes away from the counter. The legs of his chair cry out against the floor with an ear-splitting screech, cutting off all the conversation in the room. Every eye in the room is glued to him as he grabs his plate, dumps it in the trash, and walks toward the exit without any sense of urgency.

"Thanks for having me," he grumbles and disappears through the door.

The room is completely silent for a beat before Karis and I jump to our feet at the same time. We both freeze, and she catches my gaze with a challenging glare, but I don't wither under the pressure. After a moment, she looks away and nods toward the door. That's the only signal I need to unlock my muscles and chase after him.

"Where the hell do you think you're going," I call out as I follow him into the hallway.

He stumbles over his feet as he stops his retreat. His shoulders stiffen, heaving with each controlled breath he takes, but he doesn't turn to look at me.

"I can't do this, Low." He turns toward the wall and places his forearm in front of his face, and his whole body seems to collapse into it.

There's so much raw anguish in his voice, I don't correct the use of the nickname.

"Do what?" I ask.

"Act like it isn't tearing me up inside to be near you but not be able to reach out and hold you like I want. Pretend that I'm not jealous of every one of your smiles that I didn't put there. See you happy and thriving with my friends, and know that it's in spite of me not because of me."

"Gage—" I creep closer, standing only a few feet behind him, but he's too caught up in his own torment to notice me.

"No, Kori, I don't need you to comfort me. I'm the one who's clearly not coping here. You aren't doing anything wrong by being okay or by having fun with your friends. I just can't be around while you do. Now go back inside and forget about me."

"No."

"No?"

"You heard me. Those are your friends in there. They have known you and loved you way longer than they've known me. So if one of us has to go, it's me."

It's not like I'm not used to being alone anyway. Gage, though—he needs them more than I do. I'm okay with starting over again. They are all he has.

"Fuck that—"

He whirls around but falters when he sees me only a step away. His eyes widen, and for the briefest of seconds, everything he's tried so hard to hide away is written clearly on his features. He's so lost. I can't help but reach out and cup his face to anchor him, and his hand covers mine without hesitation.

"I'm not stealing the people you love from you," I tell him with no room for argument. I still love him too much to be that cruel.

His lids fall closed as he melts into my palm.

"Okay," he says after a beat. "I'm sorry, Kori."

"Don't be sorry. Go have fun. I'll see you around, yeah?" My voice chokes on the lie.

Sparks shoot through my body as he turns his head and places a soft kiss in the center of my palm. My heart flutters with all that stupid love that refuses to go away completely.

"Yeah. I'll see you around," he says as he pulls away and walks back to his friends without a backward glance.

I ignore the stream of incoming calls and texts from Evelyn and Nathan while I take the long way back to my dorm. They won't understand why I had to do this. That I'm not giving up on them, but giving Gage the space he needs to heal. It's not like I'm going to block them out completely, either, but I need to find a place here on campus that isn't so interwoven with him. I need my own space to heal too. And maybe in a few months, we can try the whole friends thing again. Maybe there will be a day when I see his face and my heart doesn't swell with the love that used to be there.

But that isn't today.

Chapter 36
Kori

Making friends isn't hard; keeping them is.

This year was different. I met people, found common interests, and now I'm ignoring every call and text they've sent me since I walked out on Friendsgivmas. That was over a month ago, but Evelyn and Nathan haven't given up. It was easy to leave them on read while I was back home for the break, but I know I won't be able to avoid them forever now that I'm back on campus.

I'm surprised Evelyn hasn't shown up at my dorm yet.

But with those friendships falling apart, I'm back in the exact same position I was in this time last semester—completely and utterly alone. Only this time, I know what I'm missing, and I refuse to let it be gone for long. I'm going to make friends who aren't attached to Gage; I need people who are mine and mine alone.

Unlike last semester, I have a game plan for how I'm going to do this—one that doesn't involve getting drunk and hoping for the best. Which is why I'm making the trek up to the student center on a Wednesday evening when my last class finished hours ago.

I'm joining a club.

The retro movie club, to be specific, and tonight is their first screening of the semester. I'm not exactly sure what that entails, but I do know I'll at least find people with common interests, and that's as good of a starting point as any. Plus, the flyer said it's a creature feature. It couldn't get more perfect than that. Hell, it feels like fate. But so did Gage, and that turned out to be a whole lot of wishful thinking on my part.

Fuck. Maybe this was a bad idea too. It isn't too late to turn back. A semester alone to reorient myself and get over my ex might be exactly what I need. I could—

"Hey, Kori, wait up," Nathan calls out from behind me, interrupting my spiral of self-doubt.

I freeze at his unexpected appearance, and he uses the pause to his advantage and catches up with me, slinging an arm around my shoulders. The easygoing wide smile plastered on his face sends a shiver of unease through me. It doesn't match the glacial anger in his eyes.

"Hi, Nathan," I squeak out.

"How was your break?" he asks, keeping that same cheerful facade.

"Good."

I start to move away, but he moves with me and falls in step at my side, his arm still wrapped around me, anchoring me to his side.

"That's good. How was my break? Good question, Kor. I spent my break trying to get in contact with a friend of mine, but it was like she fell off the face of the earth." His words grow more pointed as the mask falls away, and I grimace.

There's the judgment I deserve.

I don't have a leg to stand on to argue against it. Like a coward, I *did* ignore him over the past several weeks. My gaze falls to my feet as my shoulders climb. This would be a great time for a sinkhole to open up so I can disappear for real.

"Nathan—" I start, but he cuts me off before I can give him a bullshit excuse.

"She wouldn't ghost us now, would she? That would be cruel. Her phone must have broken or something. Because she wouldn't just abandon her friends like that."

"I'm sorry."

"Apologize to Evelyn. She's been worried fucking sick."

"I didn't mean to worry you."

"Then why did you do it?"

"I—"

"Thought it would be easier than talking about the hard things?"

"I didn't think you all would care," I admit.

"Of course we care. You are our friend, and you went completely AWOL. Evelyn was convinced you had died. She almost went to Gage to have him check on you since he knows where your parents live."

"No, don't get him involved."

"That's what I told her. But you should text her."

"I will."

"Good. You should also come to game night this weekend."

"No," I say, putting my foot down. "That's not a good idea."

"Why not? You can't hang out with your friends because your ex will be there?"

"Yes."

"Bullshit. You both are acting like fucking children."

"Says the man who wanted to use me to make his ex jealous."

For a moment, the infuriating man is rendered speechless. I should get a prize for that one. It's a feat I doubt I'll be able to pull off again.

"Okay. That's fair," he concedes.

"I don't want to avoid any of you, but I'm staying away for Gage's sake. You saw what happened at Friendsgivmas. We aren't ready to be friends again. Maybe one day, but right now, he needs you all more than I do, so I'm walking away."

"Giving him space doesn't mean you have to abandon us completely. We can be friends independent of him, and if you had responded to any of our messages, you would know that."

"You're right. I'm sorry."

God, I'm an awful friend.

"So you'll stop this ignoring-us shit?"

"Yes. I promise I'll respond."

"Good. Because you're stuck with me, Kor."

"Like an incurable disease."

"Exactly," he says with a cheeky grin.

With his arm still slung over my shoulder, we walk toward the student center. He fills the air with mindless chatter, and with each step, it becomes more and more apparent that I missed this idiot. I didn't realize how attached I got to Gage's friends. How could I when he monopolized all my attention?

I definitely need to apologize to the others. Not only for trying to ghost them, but also for being so wrapped up in my romantic relationship that I neglected all the other budding friendships.

But that's a future Kori problem. Because even if I do want to keep them, I still need to branch off on my own. I need to know I have people who are strictly on my side.

"This is me," I say as we come to the front of the student center.

Nathan nods and drops his arm from my shoulders but doesn't walk away. Students move around us as we stand in front of the entrance, giving us dirty looks as they pass. Even then, we linger. The question I've been dying to ask bubbles up, dancing along my tongue until I can't hold it back anymore.

"How is he?" I ask and cringe.

"He's doing good. Honestly better than I've seen him in a long time," he says.

Oh.

"That's...good," I say, but the words lack conviction.

I mean it—I think—even if the thought sends a jolt of pain to my battered heart. He deserves happiness. But I hate that he couldn't find it with me.

"You'd be proud of him. The circumstances suck, but you were the kick in the ass he's been waiting for. So he's trying to get better. Not to win you back or anything, but because you were right, and you got through to him when none of us could."

The love that refuses to wither and die swells in my chest. I've always known he was capable of doing anything he put his mind to.

"That is good," I tell him with more certainty, "but I really should get going..."

"Of course. But text Evelyn, and don't be a stranger."

I nod as I turn and walk into the building. A cold blast of air washes over me as I step through the sliding doors, and a low din of chatter fills the air. Not as loud as it can be during the school day, but still loud enough that my nerves are set on edge. With a steadying breath, I push farther inside, heading down the large staircase and into the depths of the building's basement.

This floor is older and more dated than the rest of the building. I follow the signs to a meeting room tucked into a narrow hallway. It's all but empty except for a scrawny guy wearing glasses working on hooking up the projector to his laptop. He doesn't even acknowledge me as I walk inside and take a chair near the back wall. More people trickle in, finding seats spread among the rows and creating clearly defined groups.

And then there's me.

Alone.

I hadn't planned for preexisting groups. Approaching them is way harder than someone individually. I don't think I can slide into a group like that. Getting up the nerve to talk to one stranger is hard enough.

My heart hammers in my chest while I watch my not so carefully constructed plan crumble around me. Then *she* walks in. The same girl I saw at Cutter's the night I met Gage—the beautiful dark-skinned woman whose friend played D&D. The one I was too scared to talk to then.

And she's alone.

If this isn't a sign, I don't know what is.

She scans the room, takes a seat a few down from me in the back, and sprawls out with more confidence than I think I have in my right pinky. Even from the back, it's like she owns the room, and her being here alone is a feature, not a bug.

I try to mirror her posture, uncurling from the tight ball I shoved myself into. Taking up this much space feels unnatural. My limbs are too long and gangly. I'm not sure my poor imitation has the same effect, but I force myself to keep the awkward pose.

I steal glances at her from the corner of my eye, trying to plan my way in. Jumping in with "Hey, I remember you from a bar a few months ago" is a surefire way to make myself seem crazy. My gaze lands on her shirt, and a plan formulates. I recognize the reference as something from *Big Bang Theory*. I've never watched the show myself, but I've been on the internet long enough I get the context and can probably fake enough knowledge to start a conversation.

"Hey, I like your shirt," I say with a smile. I really hope it looks normal because the grin feels feral on my lips.

She looks down and grimaces. "Thanks."

"Are you a fan?" I ask, unwilling to let her short answer be the end.

"Not really," she says, her lips still curled.

"Oh, thank God. I've never seen an episode but couldn't think of a better way to start a conversation," I ramble.

She visibly relaxes and sinks back into her chair with a smile.

"I was worried you were about to ambush me with that cursed show. The shirt was a gag gift from a friend, and it's laundry day."

"No ambush here. I'm Kori, by the way."

"Shaunee," she says and shakes my hand. "You new around here? I haven't seen you at a screening before."

"Transferred in last semester, but this is my first time coming to one of these. I saw it was a creature feature and knew it was time for me to crawl out of my lair and try to make some connections on campus."

I leave out everything that happened last semester. That's not a small-talk story—or one I'd want to share even if we were friends. There's too much baggage there.

"Well, you came to the right place if you like campy monster movies. If Jeremy had his way, we'd watch them every month, but Hannah makes sure that some other classics get thrown into the mix." She nods toward the scrawny guy with the laptop and a girl who joined him in his fidgeting.

"Kaiju movies are my favorite, but I'm down for pretty much anything involving monsters and practical effects."

"I'm a slasher girl, myself. But hard agree on anything involving practical effects. They just don't make them like they used to. Good CGI is great—I'm not stupid enough to try to deny that, but the amount of bad CGI out there almost makes it not worth it."

I open my mouth to respond, but before I can, the pair at the front finishes their setup and turns off the overhead lights. All of the soft chatter in the room falls silent as the title card for *Night of the Living Dead* appears on the screen. Next to me, Shaunee mutters a quiet "fuck yeah" under her breath. The next ninety-six minutes pass by in a blur. As the credits start to roll, someone flips the lights back on, and we let out a collective groan as our eyes adjust to the bright lights.

No one sticks around for long after that.

"Are you hungry?" Shaunee asks as she stands and stretches. "I'm meeting my friend Jayla for dinner at Bolton. You should join us."

A huge grin threatens to overtake my features, but I school it. I've got to play this cool. I can't let her know how her offer has made my whole week.

"That sounds great," I tell her, trying to keep my excitement in check.

She nods and heads toward the door without a word. I scramble out of my seat and fall into step beside her.

"So, Kori, what's your story."

We fall into easy conversation after that, and once we meet Jayla at the dining hall, she joins in as well. I leave out all the drama of last semester and my ex. The whole point of this was to get a fresh start, and I'm not about to taint what could be a new friendship with memories of the man I'm trying to forget.

After we finish eating and phone numbers are exchanged, I head back to my dorm feeling optimistic about my future for the first time since I walked out of Gage's apartment. I don't need him to have a social life—I'm capable of finding my people all on my own.

Chapter 37
Gage

"For fuck's sake, Gage, I can't do this again," Nathan complains as he drops his head on the coffee table.

It's a miracle he found a clear spot among the scattered papers and flashcards that have overrun the small surface. Beside him, Morgan looks equally as over this study session, but I'm not ready to call it quits. Not when it's the last one I'll get.

Karis gave up on actually helping hours ago and is sprawled out on the back of my couch like a fucking cat. Apparently, it's more comfortable than the worn cushions. I think she's just trying to push my buttons so I kick them all out and give them the peace they've been begging for.

"Just one more rep through the deck and we can call it a night," I insist.

"Seriously, man, it's 1 a.m., and we've already been through it six times. You have these questions memorized by now. You've passed the practice test twice. You are going to do fine."

But what if I don't? What if after weeks of studying and spending hundreds of dollars I didn't have to pay for the materials and exams, I fuck it up when it really matters. Sure, I did fine on the first three sections, but those were the easy ones. Tomorrow is math.

It's the test that proves I'm not nearly as big of a fuckup as I thought I was. But only if I pass, and with my history, I'm going to blow it when it counts.

Like the self-sabotaging bastard I am.

Morgan must see the determination on my face because his shoulders slump and he groans.

"James was expecting me home hours ago. She's never going to let me hear the end of it," he says, reaching for another card.

Nathan's arm snaps out like a whip and stops him before he can read the words.

"No. We are done. Gage is more than prepared enough."

"I'm going to say something controversial here, but I agree with Nathan," Karis chimes in as she turns her focus toward me. "You are going to crush it."

The absolute certainty in her gaze calms the whirlwind of nerves raging in my chest. Nathan and Morgan may try to placate me for the sake of sparing my feelings, but not her. Karis wouldn't lie to me. I am more sure of that than I am that the sun will rise in the morning.

"Fine," I sigh as the tension eases from my stiff back. "Thank you all for your help."

"Anytime," Morgan says and gathers his things without a word of protest. He claps a hand on my shoulder, uttering a few final words of confidence before he slips out the door.

The other two are slower to move. Hell, knowing Karis, she might end up crashing here. She's been doing it more and more frequently since things ended with Kori. At first, I think it was because she was worried I would do something stupid again, but lately, our study sessions have gone so late, it's more convenient to stay here than drive all the way back across town.

If I'm being completely honest with myself, her fears weren't unfounded. I'm not sure what I might have done if she hadn't been a thorn in my side for weeks on end. The gloom struck with more vehemence than normal in those days following the breakup. It hasn't been an ever-present force like it was after I fucked up my knee—I've been too focused on my new goals to wallow—but it comes in short, violent bursts.

I'm not sure if that's better or worse.

"I would stay for a drink, but I've got to teach tomorrow morning, and you need to get some sleep in before you take your exam," Nathan says as he follows our friend out.

"I'm not driving home this late," Karis says.

"I figured as much."

"But, *somehow*, Nathan is right again. You need sleep."

"The world must be ending, because there is no way you agreed with him twice in one day."

"One hour," she says with horror.

"Exactly."

"I don't know. He's been different lately, and not in a bad way. It feels like we are getting our pre-Chelsea friend back."

"Don't pretend that you would have agreed with him so easily pre-Chelsea."

"Fine, you have a point. We are getting a more mature version of our friend."

I grunt in acknowledgment, ignoring the unease rippling through my gut as I head to my room. Only one thing has changed over the past couple of months, and that is the woman who still rules my thoughts. I try to block them out, but merely thinking about her comes with a flood. Memories that have so much joy and so much pain interwoven with the type of once-in-a-lifetime love I know I'll never feel again.

My friend has still been in contact with her. He hasn't rubbed it in my face, but I've seen her name pop up on his phone enough to know they talk—often—and every time, bitter jealousy rises in my throat.

But she isn't mine to covet or claim anymore.

I'm glad Nathan is keeping an eye on her when I can't. She needs someone like him in her corner, and I'm pretty sure he needs her just as much. Maybe I'm projecting. It's a good thing either way; I know he'll keep her safe.

I strip and crawl into my bed without turning on the lights. The pillow beside me has long since lost her scent, but that hasn't stopped me from clutching it to my chest every fucking night while staring at the photo of Yellow I keep on my bedside table like some sort of simp. Morgan looks like a man with a healthy concept of attachment compared to my level of pathetic. She isn't even looking at the camera. I snapped the shot while she was filling me in on the differences between two of the most recent eras in the *Godzilla* franchise. Her words went in one ear and out the other. I was too captivated by her pure excitement for the subject to pay attention to anything but her, and I felt the need to capture it forever. And I'm glad I did.

I should have taken thousands of photos of our time together. Eventually, the memories will fade. But now, like clockwork, those thoughts haunt my mind as I try to drift to sleep. It's a blessing and a curse. For as much as thinking about my past mistakes hurts, I'll always be grateful for that short time I had with her.

Even as a fragment of my tortured imagination, her bright light is enough to keep the gloom at bay, and it's with thoughts of my sunflower woman that I finally drift to sleep knowing that if all goes as planned in the morning, I'll be one step closer to being the man she already thought I was.

***

"Anything yet?" Nathan asks for the sixth time in as many minutes.

"Results can take one to three business days," I explain. Again.

"But you got the other results within an hour," he protests.

"And it hasn't even been thirty goddamn minutes yet," I half shout.

His impatience isn't doing anything to help calm my nerves, and I'm going to kick him out of my fucking apartment if he doesn't chill out. Hell, I didn't even invite him over here. The motherfucker showed up and let himself in while I was taking the exam, then started pestering me the minute I walked out.

I really need to get those keys back.

He starts to open his mouth again, and I have half a mind to throttle him, but we are both cut off by my phone chiming. Our eyes lock on the device sitting on the counter. I put it there twenty minutes ago to stop refreshing my email every five seconds.

"Is that it?" my friend asks.

"I don't fucking know. The notifications don't get beamed directly into my head."

"Check, you idiot."

I start to reach for it but hesitate before my fingers brush against the cool plastic. What if I failed? I think I'd rather have a few more minutes of blissful ignorance than deal with the crushing disappointment that might wait for me. I'm not sure I'd find my way out of that spiral.

Seeing my cowardice, Nathan grabs my phone and shakes his head while muttering something I can't make out.

"What's your password." He doesn't try to mask the exasperation in his tone.

"5-6-7-4," I reply automatically.

He types the numbers in, freezes, and lets out an amused huff.

"Seriously, your password is 'Kori,'" he says with a chuckle.

"Shut up. Like yours wouldn't be 'Chelsea' if there were the right number of letters," I shoot back, but the tips of my ears grow hot under his scrutiny.

He shrugs but doesn't deny my claim as he scans over whatever the notification says. Fuck, we are being stupid. That alert could have been nothing but spam. Although with each second that passes without him saying a word, I doubt that theory more and more.

"Is it my results?" I snap once the nerves get to be too much.

A sly smirk twists the corner of his lips. "Now you are anxious to know."

"Nathan," I bark and lunge for my device, but he jumps back before I can grasp it.

"You passed with a 180. College Ready Plus Credit. You fucking did it, man."

I'm stunned as he pulls me in for an enthusiastic hug.

"I passed...?" I ask, completely stiff in his arms.

The information doesn't compute with the disappointment I braced for.

"You did." He shoves my phone in my face so I can see the proof myself, and low and behold, I fucking did.

I snatch it from his hand and start to type a message to my woman, but reality crashes back over me like a bucket of ice water before I can hit send.

She's not mine anymore. But that doesn't mean she still isn't the first person I want to share my good news with, even if she doesn't want to hear it. This isn't the first time I've started to text her, only to remember that isn't an option anymore.

My friend is so lost in his own enthusiasm, he doesn't notice mine wane.

"We need to go celebrate. I'll call Karis and Morgan," he says, already pulling out his phone to send the news to the group chat.

"Yeah, sure," I say, not really listening. A celebration isn't at the forefront of my mind. The GED is great, but it's only a stepping stone to my final goal, and I need to remember that so I don't wander off my path.

"Anywhere but Cutter's, right man?" Nathan jokes.

Of course, that's where we end up. Like Karis, Nathan, and James could all agree on something else. Even suggesting other bars devolved into a screaming match in the middle of College Avenue. I'm not complaining, though. There's been so much change in my life these past few months that the familiarity is nice—even if we are paying for the drinks tonight since it's my day off.

"To Gage finally getting his shit together," Karis says, holding a shot in the air.

The rest of my friends mirror her, and begrudgingly, I do the same before we all slam it back. The moment would be perfect if there wasn't a gaping hole where a certain sunflower should be. Nothing feels the same without her, not even my friends, because they are her friends too. Her roots grew well beyond me. But I ruined it for everyone because I'm too much of a pussy to handle my own feelings.

I'm pathetic.

"So what are the next steps," Morgan asks, pulling my focus away from my self-loathing.

Even in the middle of a celebration of my accomplishments, it finds a way to surface and remind me exactly of my place.

"The application window for the apprenticeship program I want to get closes next week. Now that the GED is taken care of, I can apply to that, and if I get it, I'll spend the next couple of years working and getting training through them."

"You've got this," he says with a gentle smile.

"I fucking hope so. I don't actually have a backup plan here. This is the only program I found that sets you up with full-time work and offers benefits from the start. If this doesn't pan out, I'll have to start looking at becoming something other than an electrician, because I can't wait another six months to apply again. I'm not getting any younger, and it will take several years before I get fully certified."

"Fuck them if they don't want you," Karis sneers. "You would be the best damn apprentice they've ever had."

"Thanks, Kare," I say, brushing her alcohol-fueled praise aside.

"And what about Kori? Are you going to try to win her back now that you've got a solid plan for your future?" Evelyn asks with idealistic hope in her voice.

"No," I bark out sharper than I mean to. "Winning Kori back has never been part of the plan. I'm doing this for me and me alone."

Her face falls, and I can't help but feel guilty. I know she and Nathan are hoping that we will reconnect, but that can't happen, no matter how much I would love to be hers again. Going to her now would spit in the face of everything I've accomplished over the past couple of months. If I make this about her instead of me, I never changed at all, and that would mean I don't deserve her. It's a fucked-up Catch-22. As much as it kills me, Kori is my past now, and that's all she'll ever be.

Chapter 38
Kori

Done up like a life-sized Barbie—courtesy of Shaunee's killer fashion sense and Jayla's goddess-tier hair and makeup skills—and already a little tipsy from the pregame shots, I stroll downtown with a smile on my face. Things fell into place after that first screening back at the start of the semester, and without much effort, I had two new friends without any baggage.

I didn't realize how much I needed that.

I still hang out with Nathan and Evelyn, but their friendship hasn't felt the same. It's too tainted with my memories of Gage, even if they never bring him up without my prompting.

The real problem is that the urge to ask about him hasn't gone away. Five months later, and he still lives rent-free in my head. Or maybe he's a ghost haunting the halls. Evelyn says I need to get laid to get him out of my system—exorcise the demon, so to speak—but the thought of anyone else touching me in the ways he did is repulsing. Gage is the only man who has made my skin tingle with need instead of crawl in disgust.

I'd rather be alone than go through endless trial and error on the off chance I find someone who affects me the same. No, thank you. I'll stick to movie nights with my girls.

Not tonight, though. Tonight they convinced me to go out with them against my better judgment.

The late-April air is warm against my skin—a welcome change from the cooler nights that have dragged on over the past several months. We aren't the only students with the idea of spending their reading day doing anything but what the name intended. The streets are crowded but not packed, which is perfect for me. It means I can actually breathe and enjoy my time out with my friends.

"Where are we hitting first?" Shaunee asks.

"Anywhere but Cutter's." The thought spills past my alcohol-loosened lips before I think it through. The last thing I want to do tonight is face my phantom.

I never did tell them about my history with Gage, or anything about my drama-filled first semester. Hell, I don't think I've even mentioned my other friends to the girls. It's not that I'm keeping them secret on purpose, but I like that divide. The last thing I want is reminders of my ex tainting the only place I've carved out for myself without his influence. I did a damned good job of keeping that separation too. Until now.

Both of my friends stop and give me questioning looks, and I know the gig is up. They will tag team bombard me with questions until I give in for my own sanity. My past is coming back to haunt me tonight.

"That sounds like a story. What secrets have you been keeping from us?" Shaunee asks.

"I might have dated the big bartender for a few months last semester. Things didn't end great between us, and I'd rather not risk running into him."

"You mean the ugly motherfucker who looked like he took a few too many hits over the years?" Jayla asks.

Pain lances through my palms as my nails dig into the flesh. My protective instincts flare for a man who isn't mine to care about anymore, but that doesn't stop me from jumping to his defense.

"He isn't ugly," I snap, and her eyes widen at the tone. My lashes fall shut as I take a centering breath. "But yes, him."

"Well, you have nothing to worry about. He hasn't been around in months," she says with a shrug.

Ice fills my veins.

Where the fuck is he?

"Hey, Kori, you good?" Shaunee asks.

"What do you mean he's not there?" I ask.

My friend shrugs. "He's just gone. Got some fresh blood in there now who is way less brooding."

Is he okay? He has to be okay. Nathan would have told me if he wasn't. Right? Those thoughts do nothing to ease my panic.

He could have lied when he said Gage was doing good. Or maybe the gloom became too much for him over time. Gage could be suffering, and I'm out here living my life without a care in the world. He might need me.

"I—I need to go," I stammer out as my heart jackhammers in my chest.

"Go? Where? It's 11 p.m.," she calls after me, but I ignore her as I try my best to hurry along the sidewalk in my borrowed heels.

I'm not even sure where I'm going. My dorm is in the other direction, and I'm in no state to drive, but I have to see him. I have to know he's okay. After moving away from my friends and the scattered crowd, I stop, pull out my phone, and call Nathan.

"Kori, what's wrong?" he answers after the first ring. His voice alert and sharpened with concern.

"You tell me," I snap. "Where is Gage? Why hasn't he been at Cutter's? Is he okay?"

A deep sigh is the only sound that comes down the line. I can practically hear him shaking his head.

"That's his business," he says in a gentle tone.

The condescending jerk.

"Like hell it is."

"You can't block him out for months and then demand to know about his life on a whim. If you really want to know, ask him yourself. He still has a phone. You still have his number. We both know he'll pick up if you call."

"Fine."

"Kori—" Nathan starts, but I hang up before he can finish the thought.

I *will* ask Gage himself, then.

Fuck it, I'll do one better. Why call when I can go check on him myself?

With the alcohol fueling my confidence, I call for a rideshare, plugging in my ex's address as the final destination. My resolve doesn't start to waver until I'm in the car and halfway to his place. A few shots are enough for some liquid courage, but not enough to make me drunk or stupid. And this idea is the definition of stupid.

My driver doesn't look in my direction as they pull in front of the dark apartment and wait for me to get out. I hesitate for a moment before steeling my spine and climbing out of the back seat. Dim light flickers from the dying streetlamp a few units down, casting his front door in a dark shadow, making the approach even more ominous.

I'm not sure he's even home. A strange truck sits in Brandy's usual spot out front—either the car is fucked, or someone else lives here now. Five months is plenty of time for someone to make major life changes—he could have moved halfway across the country, and I'd have no idea. It's not like his friends were giving me a play-by-play. This was a mistake, but I've made it too far to give up without at least knocking on his door.

With false bravado, I march up the stairs and pound my fist on the peeling wood. The wait stretches on forever without anything happening. No lights flick on inside and no sounds travel through the too-thin door.

And then he's there—a shadowy figure looming in the doorway, wearing nothing but a pair of low-slung sweats that leave nothing to the imagination. Sparks of heat that have lain dormant for months shoot straight into my core. God, he looks every bit as edible as I remember. My mouth dries at the sight, and my tongue darts out to rewet my lips.

"What?" Gage barks as he looks outside.

The harsh annoyance falls away when his gaze lands on me, and something softer takes its place.

"Low?" He says my name on a reverent breath and looks at me like I'm all of his hopes and fears wrapped up in a shiny bow. His hand runs over his face, and then he blinks like I'm a mirage he's trying to clear away. The second it clicks, the softness in his features hardens again. "What are you doing here? What's wrong? Are you okay?"

This isn't a conversation to have on his front porch in the middle of the night. The air between us is alive, crackling like dry kindling in the sun. All it will take is one spark to ignite it into a raging inferno, but I'm not sure if it will be a passionate blaze or a catastrophic explosion of every emotion I've tried to repress. Either option ends with the cops showing up if we give in to it out here, so I ignore his brusque questions and push my way inside.

Static erupts across my bare shoulder as it brushes against his exposed chest. I'm going to lose the plot real quick if he doesn't put a shirt on soon. He closes the door and flips on the overhead light without a word. So much has changed in the dated space that it knocks me off-kilter. It's somehow emptier than it was before—the television is gone, as well as several of the photos that decorated the shelves around it—and I'm almost positive the coffee table is different too.

"Why are you here, Kori? It's late."

In the light of his apartment, I can see the weariness written on his face that the shadows outside hid.

"Why aren't you at work?" I ask, resisting the urge to run my fingers over his tired features.

"Because it's eleven o'clock at night."

No shit, Sherlock.

"I mean in general. You haven't been at Cutter's."

"Been looking for me?" he asks with a hint of a smile, and my heart flips in my chest.

I've missed that elusive expression—I've missed him.

"What? No," I stammer as my cheeks heat. "My friends said they hadn't seen you around in a few months, and I got worried."

"I quit," he says with as much tact as I'd expect from him.

"You *what*?" I screech.

"Goddamn, woman, inside voice. I didn't just walk out or anything. Jesus. I figured Nathan was keeping you up to date with how much you two talk." His hand runs down his face again, but this time it's an agitated motion. When he pulls it away, his cheeks are tinged with a faint pink. "I'm doing an apprenticeship."

"Apprenticeship?"

"Electrical work. Started back in March."

"Gage! That's awesome! I didn't even know that was something you wanted to do. Why didn't you tell me?"

What else have I missed in the months we've been apart?

I throw myself at him, and he turns to marble in my embrace. It's inappropriate, but I can't find it in me to care. I'm too proud of him.

"It's not like we've been on speaking terms," he grumbles as he extracts himself from my clinging grasp, setting me on the ground a few inches away from him, still close enough I can feel the heat radiating from his naked chest.

Tension crackles between us again. The air is ripped from my lungs as I meet his stormy gaze and see the hunger there, and for a moment, it's as if nothing between us ever changed. Unable to resist the magnetic pull any longer, I reach out and cup his cheek in my hand. He tracks my movements with dilated pupils, and he lets out a growl as my fingers make contact.

Why did I ever push him away?

This right here is where I'm supposed to be. That truth resonates to the very bones of me.

"Gage," I all but whimper.

That's all it takes for the kindling to finally catch, and every bit of burning passion I've tried so hard to repress reignites.

I'm not sure who starts it, me or him, but our lips crash together in a sloppy, desperate kiss. There's nothing careful about the clash of tongue and teeth, or gentle in the way he nips at my lips with sharp bites.

Fuck, that's new, and from the wave of molten heat that floods my pussy, I don't hate this rougher side of him. He traces a hand along my side, not stopping until his fingers are at my throat. His thumb presses in, not enough to restrict my breathing, but in an act of pure possession that pulls a soft moan from my lips.

That small sound yanks him from his lust-filled haze. He pulls his lips from mine, but that's as far as he goes. Our breaths mingle between us, and his fingers don't uncurl from around the column of my neck.

"Fuck, that shouldn't have happened," he says, still unmoving.

"Like hell, it shouldn't have. Don't pretend like we both didn't need that."

"I didn't do this shit with the GED and apprenticeship so I could win you back. I did it because you were right."

"I know that—"

"Please, just listen to me for a few minutes. It's important that you know I didn't do this for you. I did it for me. I'm becoming a man I can be proud of. Losing you was my wake-up call, and it was a long time coming, but I can't handle having a taste, only to lose you again. I won't survive it a second time."

"Who said anything about losing me?"

This man is making me eat every word I said when he came to beg for my forgiveness. He's made changes and is learning to be happy with himself—for him. It's all I ever wanted and everything I didn't know I needed to trust him again. My heart is his wholly and completely. All he has to do is accept it.

Chapter 39
Gage

"Who said anything about losing me?"

The whole fucking world freezes around me as those words pass her beautiful, swollen lips.

She is a vision pulled from my sweetest dreams and my dirtiest fantasies. I didn't believe my eyes when I opened the door and saw her standing at the threshold, but it's her. No figment of my imagination could ever taste as sweet.

Her heavy panting as she tries to catch her breath is the only sound that fills the space between us, but the pounding of my heart in my ears nearly drowns it out. My own lungs are locked in iron, the air trapped as the implication of her words bowls through me.

Not lose her...

She can't mean that. She was the one who said we were done for good. But that doesn't stop the fucking spark of hope from igniting as she looks at me with so much burning need. It's the fragile flame that has me petrified. One wrong move and it might go out, taking all the progress I've made with it.

Several seconds pass in tense silence before her impatience takes over, and she lunges for me with an adorable growl. Against all of my baser instincts, I use my perch on her throat to stop her before her lips find mine again.

Fuck. My hand shouldn't be there at all.

Cursing under my breath, I rip my fingers from her flesh. I don't know what came over me, but goddamn if having her melt into my hold didn't feel right.

"Kori, wait," I tell her, stepping away to put much-needed distance between us.

Her face twists into the cutest fucking pout as she crosses her arms in front of her. If the stakes weren't so high, it might coax a smile from me.

"What are we doing?" I ask.

"What do you mean?"

"Nothing has changed."

"Of course it has." She throws her arms up with an exasperated shout.

"Why? Because I'm finally getting my shit together? I meant it. I didn't do it so you would get back with me."

"I know. And that makes all the difference."

"How does that change a goddamn thing?" I growl.

"Because it means you listened to me. You heard the words coming out of my mouth and did something about it. You made the change for you, and because of that, I know it's real. And now I can give you my heart and know I can trust you with it."

My heart lodges itself in my throat. The implication of her words is clear, but I can't wrap my head around them. I can't let myself hope.

"Low—"

"Shut up and kiss me, Gage. I've missed you, and we've wasted too much time apart already."

Fuck. I've missed her too.

"If we do this, there is no going back. This isn't a one-time thing. We start this again, I'm never letting you go," I tell her.

"I don't want you to."

Fuck.

I'm on her in an instant, threading my fingers in her tight curls and holding her so tight she'll never be able to slip through my fingers again. She moans against my lips as her own hands claw at my bare chest with a wildness I've never seen from her, cutting into my skin with a sharp sting. The pain goes straight to my cock.

"Mine," I growl into her mouth as my other hand drops to the curve of her ass, pulling her flush against me.

"Yours," she agrees, digging her nails into my shoulder.

The lance of pain pulls another groan from my throat, which only spurs her on. Her nails dig into me as our tongues clash, and she squirms, searching for something to give relief to her aching pussy.

Her desperation is the hottest fucking thing I've ever experienced, but I'm not cruel enough to deny her what she needs. I move my leg, slotting it between her thighs, and can't hold back a chuckle as she grinds against me with a whine.

"Tell me what you need," I command and move my lips to trail along her neck.

"I need you to take me to your room and fuck me like you love me."

A growl builds in my throat, and I catch her lips in a quick kiss before sweeping her up in my arms and following her command.

She lets out a joyful squeal when I toss her onto my bed, then bites her lip while she waits for my next move. The little black skirt that clung to her thighs rides up, giving me a clear view of the lacy panties underneath. That, paired with her thigh-high boots with dagger-sharp heels, is the sexiest thing I've ever seen. More blood flows to my cock, making me harder than I thought possible, and precum drops from its swollen head. Fuck if this picture won't be seared into my head forever.

Like a predator circling its prey, I approach, crawling over her and caging her against the mattress. Her throat bobs, her pupils dilate, and her tongue pokes out to wet her lips. As tempting as it is to chase it and claim her mouth again, it's another, sweeter set of lips that's calling to me.

"Do you trust me, Kori?"

"Yes," she says without hesitation.

Goddamnit, this woman is everything—her trust after what I put her through is everything.

"Okay. Then I'm going to eat that sweet cunt of yours, and you are going to lie there like the fucking queen you are and love every second of it."

A tremor racks through her body like a violent little earthquake.

"Yes, Coach," she says in a breathy rasp.

I don't give her a second to reconsider. My body shifts to the foot of the bed, and I push her skirt up above her waist. The delicate lace would be so easy to tear, but I don't give in to the urge. The panties are expensive, and I'm fond of this pair now. It would be a shame to never get to see her in them again. I hook my fingers around the elastic band, pulling them down over the faux-leather boots, and toss them to the side. The boots can stay on; I want to feel those wicked heels digging into my back as she comes.

Laid bare before me, she squirms and tries to close her legs, but my grip on her thighs keeps them open for me.

"If you want me to stop, you say so. You hear me?"

"Yes, Coach."

And I dive in.

She jolts as my tongue plunges into her wet heat. If it wasn't for my hand on her, keeping her spread, her legs would have slammed shut, but I won't let her take my prize from me so soon. Her taste is even better than I imagined—and I dreamed about this plenty. Pure fucking woman. God, I'm already addicted.

I turn my attention to her clit, alternating between licking and sucking. It doesn't take long for her to shed her self-conscious reservations and melt into the feeling. She grabs my head—as if I'd ever pull away—and writhes against my face, smothering me with her perfect cunt. Fuck, I could die right here and be a happy man.

Precum drips from my weeping cock with every one of her gasps and moans. I'm sure there's a wet patch growing on my gray sweats, but I don't fucking care.

There's no shame in being turned on by giving my woman pleasure—and she is definitely getting pleasure.

"Gage," she moans and grips me even tighter.

Those sharp heels cut into my back, and I almost fucking lose it. It's by sheer force of will I don't come in my pants, but it's been months since I've had any sort of release, and my body is ready to make up for the missed time.

Her breathing turns into ragged pants, and her grinding gets even more desperate. Fuck, she's close. I know better than to change anything when she's this on the edge. After a few more seconds of riding my face, she comes apart, shuddering and shaking as her arousal soaks into my beard. I don't relent as she slows, drinking in every heady drop of her.

"Too sensitive," she says as she gently pushes my head, and only then do I come up for air with a grin on my cum-covered face.

"One day you are going to sit on my face and let me do that for hours," I tell her. My fingers dance at her entrance, teasing her. She is so fucking beautiful as she squirms beneath me. "Are you too sensitive for my cock? We don't have to do anything else tonight."

"No," she protests, sitting up to reach for me.

As if I'd ever leave her side when she's half naked and wanting.

"No? No, what?"

"No, I'm not too sensitive," she whines.

"So you do still want me to fill that needy cunt with my cock? I want to hear you say it."

"I want you to make love to me, Gage."

Something in my chest snaps, but the sensation doesn't hurt. I feel whole—like she was the missing piece of my soul that's finally come home.

"Okay, darling." The soft tone of my voice is alien, but I don't question it.

I crawl back up the bed to cup her face, rubbing my thumb along her cheek as she melts into the touch. It's hard to pull away from her, but I'm not making love to my woman with her skirt hiked up and her shoes still on. With gentle fingers, I strip her of her clothes while she watches my every move from under heavy lids. Once we are both naked, I put on a condom and position myself between her legs.

"You ready for me?" I ask and stroke her cheek again.

She nods, and I push inside her without any resistance—everything is still slick with a mixture of her cum and my saliva. My heart aches with the force of my feelings as my cock sinks to its hilt. Yes, her tight heat feels amazing, but it's more than that. Being inside her feels like coming home.

Uncomfortable pinpricks burn behind my eyes as my throat tightens. Fuck. I hide my face in the crook of her neck before I do something embarrassing—like start crying while fucking my woman—and start to move. Her gasp of pleasure drives away the worst of the emotional wave, but it doesn't leave completely. I'm still overwhelmed as I thrust into her, driven by the need to be closer to her—even if I'm already buried as deep as I can physically go.

"I love you, Kori. I love you so fucking much. I never stopped," I rasp against the skin of her neck.

"I love you too," she moans as she comes, clenching hard around my cock.

"Please don't leave me again. Don't give up on me. Please fucking stay," I beg as my orgasm rips through me. I cling to her as my cock pulses, filling the latex with my seed.

Fuck, I'd love to fill her for real and watch her grow with my kid. I shake away the unwelcome thought. Now is not the time to be dreaming of the future. We've never talked about kids or marriage or what happens once she graduates. That was my plan before I fucked everything up. I was going to sit her down and have a real talk about what our future looked like—my plans for my GED, timelines for marriage and kids, all of it. I was in it for the long haul, but now I'm not sure where exactly we stand. She said I wouldn't lose her, but promises made while caught up in the heat of the moment mean nothing. There's still a chance she could get up and walk out the door, claiming this was all a mistake.

"I can hear you thinking," she says, running her fingers in a soothing pattern along my back. Tension I wasn't even aware of melts from my shoulders. "What's got you freaking out?"

I pull out of her and settle next to her on the mattress. "What happens now?"

"Well, as comfortable as this is, I would like a shower," she says with a grin.

"A shower?"

"Yeah. Water from a pipe in the wall so you can get clean."

"I know what a shower is."

"I thought so. It would be real awkward if you didn't. Can I crash here? I'd rather not get a rideshare back this late."

Her attempt at deflecting is obvious as hell, but I'm not letting this go.

"I meant what happens with us. What are we doing, Low?"

"I told you earlier that you aren't losing me. So unless you have any objections, I'd like us to try again."

"Really?"

"Yes, really. I know we have way more to talk about, but nothing so important that it will change my mind on that. I want to hear all about your apprenticeship and whatever else you've been up to these past couple of months, but I think it's best if we wait and do the whole catching-up thing tomorrow. If we start now, I don't think we will get any sleep."

"I work in the morning."

"Okay. Then we can talk when you get done. I'm not going anywhere, Gage."

Her words are so fucking sure I can't do anything but believe her. Sensing my acceptance, she turns to snuggle into my chest, and I trace my fingers along her spine the same way she did mine.

"Can I ask you a question?" As much as I hate to pop the bubble of peaceful bliss, this question has been squirming around in the back of my mind since she showed up.

"You don't have to ask."

"Where is the yellow?"

She looked hot as sin standing on my doorstep, but there wasn't a hint of her favorite color on her. I almost didn't recognize her.

"I—it—" She squirms as she stammers and won't meet my curious gaze. After a few seconds, she groans and throws an arm over her face as she looks up at the ceiling. "It reminded me too much of you. Plus, it's a happy color, and I wasn't feeling particularly happy."

"Low, shit. I'm sorry. For all of it. I've never regretted anything more."

"I'm not. As much as it hurt, we both needed something to kick our asses into gear. If it never happened, I would have always used you as a security blanket, and you would have been a bartender your whole life. We are going to be stronger than we were before because we took the time to better ourselves on our own."

"You think so?"

"I know so. But seriously, can we go take that shower now? I feel gross."

"Of course, love," I tell her, and scoop her back into my arms.

I'd carry her through the pits of hell if she asked me to. As I cross over the threshold of my room with her in my arms, I'm struck with a sense of permanence. This is it—the start of our forever.

Epilogue – Gage

You would think after thirteen months of bi-weekly appointments, I'd be used to the constant ticking from the large decorative clock behind my therapist's desk, but the monotonous sound never ceases to worm its way into my head. Maybe that's the intention; for all I know, it could be some advanced technique the doc is using. I should ask Nathan. He's the one who likes all the brain science shit.

My sessions with Dr. Shaw aren't at all what I expected. In the movies, it's always some guy lying on a sofa in a dark room while they talk about their childhood with a box of tissues. This is nothing like that. For one, my childhood was great—it's being an adult that sucks—and two, there aren't any couches involved. These forty-five minutes are spent in a cozy armchair in a well-lit office while the doc helps me work through my thoughts and offers coping mechanisms for when the gloom comes—which has been a less common occurrence since I started coming, so something is working.

"Kori graduated last week, right?" my doctor asks.

"Magna cum laude." I couldn't keep the proud grin from forming if I tried.

My woman is amazing. She's smarter than me—there's no doubt about it—and I'm not the only one who sees it. She had three job offers before her last semester even started, but she turned them all down, waiting until she found the perfect opportunity. One close to home—close to me.

She starts next month.

"That's a big change. How is that?"

I huff and give a half-hearted shrug. Dr. Shaw narrows her eyes and gives me *the look*—the one that means she isn't going to let nonanswers slide. I've gotten it more times than I can count over the course of our time together.

"It seems like a big change, but it's not really. She'll spend her days at work instead of classes, and her name's getting added to the lease, but it's not like we haven't been living together already. What's really different?"

"I suppose you're right. I trust you would tell me if this was triggering anything for you."

The idea is laughable. The gloom feeds on my insecurities, and there is nothing I'm more secure in than where I stand with my woman. It's always been me I didn't trust to do right by her, never the other way around. That's not about to change.

"I'm good. Things are good."

"You've come a long way since we started. I think it might be time we cut back on your sessions. There's no reason for you to keep coming every other week. Let's move to once a month and see how it feels."

"Sounds good."

"You should be proud of the progress you've made."

"Thanks, Doc." My face heats as I direct my gaze to the floor.

It's hard to accept the praise, but she isn't wrong. It's been months since the gloom has gotten the best of me. Hell, I barely notice its presence anymore. The process hasn't been easy, but there was too much on the line for me to give up when shit got hard. I had already had a few sessions with Dr. Shaw before Kori came back into my life, but she has been my motivation to keep going. I promised both of us I'd never let my demons come between us again, and I meant that shit.

"That's all the time we have for today. Like always, you can call me if anything comes up between sessions, but if not, I'll get you scheduled for June."

We say our goodbyes, and I head back to my truck. I don't have a lot of time before I'm due back at the jobsite. There's nothing glamorous about the apprenticeship or electrical work as a whole, but I'm decent enough at it, and it pays the bills far better than bartending ever did.

And as lame as it sounds, it gives me a sense of purpose—like I'm actually doing something that contributes to society. That, mixed with the therapy and my friends' support, has helped me get to a place I haven't been in for a long time. For the first time since my injury, I'm happy. Not just moments, but genuinely in a good place the majority of the time. Life is finally looking up for me, and I'm grateful every day I've got Kori by my side to live it with.

***

The smell of smoke greets me as I open the front door of my apartment. It should be alarming, but at this point, it's almost expected. I learned pretty quick that Kori takes after her mom in the cooking department. That hasn't stopped her from giving it her all despite my protests. She's like her mom in that way too—stubborn.

"Everything good, Low?" I call out as I step inside.

Over the past year, the space I used to dread coming back to has become the place I want to be more than anywhere else. With my woman here, I don't ever have to worry about coming home to nothing but grim darkness and silence. She fills our apartment with so much joy and life. Even when she isn't here, her presence is palpable, and I never want to live without it again.

"Yeah. We might want to order pizza, though," she says with an annoyed huff as she turns away from the stove.

Her face lights up when her gaze lands on me, and before I can blink, she's throwing her arms around my neck. On instinct, my arms wrap around her as I pull her to my chest, and her sweet citrusy scent washes over me.

Even after a year, her affection still leaves me awestruck. It will never make sense to me why a woman like her would love a man like me, but I've stopped questioning it, and I'm never going to let her go.

"How was work?" she asks once she's gotten her fill of me.

"Pretty standard."

"And therapy?"

"Dr. Shaw thinks we should move to monthly sessions."

"Gage, that's huge."

I shrug off her praise and turn my attention to the culinary disaster still smoking on the counter. Accepting compliments is something me and the doc are still working on. It doesn't matter if it's from a stranger or my woman, I clam up.

"What were the casualties of your cooking efforts today." I walk over to inspect it but can't make out what the burnt mush in the casserole dish is supposed to be.

"It was *supposed* to be shepherd's pie. I called your mom for the recipe since you said it was your favorite, and she assured me it was 'foolproof.' I don't think she realized what she was up against."

That is supposed to be shepherd's pie? May those poor potatoes rest in peace.

"What's got you cooking today?"

"It's our anniversary. I wanted to do something special."

It's our anniversary? By what standard? We started dating in September, and if you take out the six months we weren't together, that puts 365 cumulative days of being together somewhere in early March. Hell, we celebrated in March, so I don't know what this is.

"Anniversary of what, love?" I ask, trying to keep the rising panic out of my voice.

"A year ago today, I unofficially moved in. I wanted to do something to commemorate that. Well, to be honest, I wanted to celebrate the day we got back together, but finals made that one impossible, so this is close enough." She glares at the failed meal like it personally offended her.

Unable to resist, I pull her in for another hug, tucking her head under my chin.

"Pizza is perfect. We can do a movie night too. I'll even drag the mattress out here so we can make a date of it."

"Really?"

"Of course, Low. Anything for you."

She springs into action, pulling up the website to order on her phone while directing me around like the little tyrant she is. I bend to her will with a smile and head to our room. Unlike the first time we did this, there's no need for me to rely on my friends to supply me with extra pillows and blankets. Kor brought so many with her that they take up half the space in our closet—her closet, really. My clothes have been banished to my half of the dresser. It's a good thing my wardrobe is limited, or I'd have to start storing things in the living room.

By the time I maneuver the mattress through the cramped hallway, Kori has already pushed the rest of the furniture out of the way, and she's having a quiet argument with that duck of hers. She doesn't even notice me standing at the threshold; whatever "conversation" she's in has all of her focus. It must be heated because her hands are waving around without a care for her surroundings. The sight has every ounce of love I have for her swelling in my chest to the point I think it might burst.

It hits me like a bolt of lightning—I'm gonna marry this woman.

I've always known she is my forever, but it felt like part of a distant future. Now it feels imminent. Like something that should have happened yesterday. This woman is my everything.

Mattress forgotten, I bound across the room and place a gentle hand on her shoulder. She starts to say something as she turns, but I steal the words from her lips with a rough kiss and pull her tight against me.

"Marry me," I rasp once she breaks away for a breath.

"What?" She blinks away the lust-filled daze as what I said catches up to her.

The words weren't planned, but I don't regret them at all. Yellow is meant to be my wife. However, I probably should've bit my tongue until I had time for a proper proposal. She deserves better than this.

"Fuck, I'm doing this all wrong. I shouldn't have said anything. I haven't talked to your dad yet, and I don't even have a ring. Forget I said anything—"

"Yes," she says, cutting me off.

"What?" This time I'm the one reeling.

"Yes, I'll marry you, Gage."

"Fuck. Really?" A dopey grin finds a home on my face.

"Yes, you idiot. We should do it tomorrow."

"That's not a lot of time to plan a wedding."

"Who said anything about a wedding? I want to be your wife. Tomorrow. We can go by the courthouse during your lunch break and get the license, although I doubt they can get us in for an actual wedding on such short notice. I'll call around to find an officiant, and we can do it here."

"We aren't getting married *here*." This place is still old and dingy, even with the added splash of Kori's vibrance.

"Then where do you want to get married?"

The perfect idea springs to mind in an instant.

"I have an idea. Do you trust me?"

"More than anything."

"Then I'll handle everything. All you need to do is show up."

"Will I need a white dress?"

"If you want to. Wear whatever makes you feel beautiful. If that's white, wear that, and if it's a clown costume, you can wear that too."

"I love you, Gage," she says and presses a quick kiss against my lips.

"I love you too, Low. Now help me move this mattress so we can get date night going."

"Yes, Coach," she all but whispers.

Goddamnit, we aren't going to watch anything if she keeps that up.

We move in tandem to set up our bed on the floor, and then she scrolls through the never-ending options to find the movie she wants to watch tonight. It doesn't matter to me what she decides on, I'm not going to watch a second of it. While she's searching, I make a new group chat with all of our friends and send out the SOS. If I'm going to pull this off, I'm going to need all their help.

Epilogue - Kori

hy did I think letting Gage handle everything was a good idea?

That's right, he asked me if I trusted him, which I do, but knowing my man, he's out there planning some grand gesture of a wedding when all I need is *him*. He's a romantic at heart but would balk if I ever called him on it.

He was practically vibrating when we met at the courthouse earlier. After we signed the paperwork, he slipped a ring on my finger, kissed me in a way that set my whole body on fire, and said he would see me tonight.

The ring is a foreign weight on my hand and a gesture I wasn't expecting. Not that I'm complaining—it's gorgeous with its bright-yellow stone set in a golden band. I have no idea where he got it, or how he managed to find something so perfect on such short notice...or how he knows my ring size, because that's something we've never talked about before.

Maybe it's best I don't ask too many questions.

It's been crickets since then—not only from him, but all our friends. I invited Evelyn over so we could freak out together about the fact I'm getting married today, but she said she was busy and would try to stop by later. Shaunee and Jayla were busy too. I didn't even try with Nathan. He'd be the first in line to help Gage with whatever plans he has them wrapped up in today. It wouldn't be the first time my boyfriend—no, fiancé—got them all involved.

Fiancé.

I'm not going to have time to get used to the idea before it transitions to husband. Move over, *90 Day Fiancé*, you've got nothing on us.

316

Now all I can do is wait. It's beyond agonizing. I wish he would have given me some details. Like a timeline...or overall vibes. Hell, I'd take skywriting with cryptic clues at this point. Anything but being left in the dark.

A soft knock on the front door breaks through the endless monotony, and butterflies spring to life, fluttering around with a mix of excitement and nerves. *It's time.* I open the door and find Evelyn waiting, already dolled up in a baby-pink dress with her makeup artfully done.

The sight of my friend brings the sharp sting of her earlier refusal to the surface with an edge of resentment. I didn't realize how much it affected me until now. It would have been nice to have at least one friend with me through this, even though I know they are all working on something *for* me.

"I thought you were busy," I accuse.

She ignores my attitude and pulls me in for a hug with an excited squeal.

"I'm so sorry, I had to finish my other task first, but now I'm all yours." She pushes her way inside without an invitation. "Bridesmaid duty officially starts now. I can't believe you're getting married."

My friend lets out another high-pitched noise and hugs me again.

"It barely feels real," I tell her, smiling as the negative emotions are washed away by her glee.

"Gage was vague on the details. I need to know everything. Was it romantic?"

I choke on a laugh remembering exactly how romantic last night wasn't. It was perfect, though. It was us—no bullshit.

"I think it just sort of slipped out, if I'm being honest. He nearly panicked after he asked, but as soon as he said it, I knew it was right. There was no question. Although this whole twenty-hour wedding thing wasn't part of my plan when I said we should get married today. I'm ready to be his wife—I don't need all the frills—but it's not surprising he's trying to make it something special."

"Of course he's trying to make it special. It's your wedding, it should be. Not to mention that man worships the ground you walk on. He'd do anything for you."

"I know. So what exactly does bridesmaid duty entail?"

"Mainly making sure you are ready and arrive on time without cold feet."

"Don't worry about my feet. They are extra toasty."

"Good. Now let's get you ready to go. We need to leave in an hour."

"An hour?"

That's no time at all. How am I supposed to get ready for a wedding I know nothing about in an hour? This was a terrible idea. I should have insisted Gage do it my way, just the two of us and some legal documents. All of this is too much.

"Don't panic," Evelyn says, pulling me out of my tailspin. "We've totally got this. An hour is plenty of time. Just call me your fairy godmother."

***

The botanical gardens are the last place I expected Evelyn to bring us, but the familiar parking lot is where we end up. True to her word, Evelyn helped me get ready in record time. I ended up in a yellow dress—I don't own any white, and even if I did, it wouldn't feel right—and at her suggestion, we went light on the makeup. She might be magic because, somehow, I feel both beautiful but comfortable and wholly me in a way I never could have pulled off on my own.

Anxiety grips me as we climb out of the car and head toward the entrance.

"All right, be real with me. What's waiting for me in there? Do I need to brace for an onslaught of good-intentioned well-wishers and a crowd whose sole attention is on me?" I ask as she tries to usher me further into the property.

That would be my nightmare.

"Do you think Gage would put you through that?"

"No."

"Then deep breaths. He loves you, and he knows you. He would never plan something you wouldn't also love."

She's right. He's always put my needs above everything else. I take a deep breath to steady my nerves and start down the path. This is Gage, the man I love, the man I'm marrying. Nothing else matters.

The garden isn't as busy as it is on the weekends, but there are still other groups basking in its beauty. They don't pay us any mind as we make our way to the field in the back—the same field Gage brought me to the first time we came here.

He is waiting for me in that same spot, dressed in a nice button-down and a pair of slacks I know he didn't own this morning. There isn't a trace of nerves in his posture as he watches the entrance, and when he sees me, his face lights up with a soul-stealing smile.

No large crowd or huge celebration greets me—just a small group of the people we love the most. My eyes prickle as I notice my parents for the first time. I didn't even think about getting them involved, but now that they are here, I can't imagine doing this without them.

Gage doesn't wait for me to make it to them. With heat in his eyes, he strides across the manicured lawn and greets me with an all-consuming kiss. He doesn't hold back as he claims me with the clash of tongue and teeth. Fuck the ceremony. If our friends weren't here, I'd beg him to drag me somewhere secluded and call us good and married.

"We get it, you like each other. That's why we are all here. But I don't think I need to remind you that this isn't a sanctioned event, and time is of the essence." Karis's sarcasm-laced words break us apart.

Gage pulls back, still wearing that dopey smile, and grabs my hand. "You ready for this, Low?"

"I've never been more ready."

With a gentle squeeze, he leads me toward our friends. Toward our future. Toward our forever.

Afterword

Thank you for reading *Sunflower Persona*. Please take a moment to rate it and leave a review. And if you enjoyed it, tell your friends, shout if from the rooftops, hire a skywriter. But seriously, word of mouth goes a long way.

Book 3 of the series is in the works. Any guesses on whose story it will be? Follow me @valerie.kain.writes or go to www.valeriekain.com to join my newsletter to stay up to date on upcoming releases.

Also by Valerie Kain

Classic City Romance

Dear Roomie

Sunflower Persona

Book 3 (TBA)

Book 4 (TBA)

About the author

Valerie Kain has a lifelong love for telling stories filled with drama and angst. Some of the earliest home videos from her childhood are of her blabbering her tales at whoever would listen. It was only a matter of time before she took that passion to the page. As a Georgia native and UGA alumna, the city of Athens holds a special place in her heart which is what inspired her debut series.

She is currently in her contemporary romance era but has projects in the pipeline that span multiple sub-genres, including dark romance, paranormal romance, and romantasy. Stay in the know by following her @valerie.kain.w rites on Instagram and Tiktok or by joining her newsletter at valeriekain.com.